Twin Stars

By H. Kelvin Jensen

PublishAmerica
Baltimore

PublishAmerica has allowed this work to remain exactly as the author intended, verbatim, without editorial input.

ISBN: 1-60703-052-7
PUBLISHED BY PUBLISHAMERICA, LLLP
www.publishamerica.com
Baltimore

Printed in the United States of America

A special thanks to my good wife Avon, and our kids Doug and Wendy for keeping my computer tuned up. And Michael and Lisa, for proof reading the manuscript of LARIAT CROSS, showing me the way when I was in a heap of trouble. I couldn't have done it without you guys!!

Twin Stars
* A Continuing Saga *

* * * Chapter One * * *

Brush infested coulees are common on the western prairie, a safe haven for mule deer, prairie chickens and cottontail rabbits. The Indian and outlaw made use of them as well, a place to hide in relative safety from the prying eyes of those who might be hot on their trail.

At home in most coulees was an abundance of wild berries, choke cherries, Saskatoon berries and wild strawberries too. The native Indian, wise in the ways of survival, made use of the nutritious fruit in preparing pemmican for their winter food supply.

The seasoned traveler of the wind-swept prairie sought out the coulee, knowing that in most cases they sheltered a cool spring of water.

* * *

Situated in just such a coulee was a simple trail camp, a ring of rocks surrounding a willow twig fire. A prairie chicken was roasting on a spit and a coffee pot was simmering in the glowing embers.

Nearby, having been aroused from her blankets by the arrival of the sun, sat a young girl dressed in the manner of a cowboy. She was leaning against her upturned saddle, meticulously brushing her long auburn hair

Her hair was a hallmark of the Brannon women; starting with her Grandma Brannon. The genes of her grandparents were strong and true, passed down to her Mom, and now to herself, Lynn Brannon Duval.

Not only was the women's hair a legacy, their shooting ability was equaled by no other, including the gunslingers; who had found out the hard way that this was true. Shooting a rifle from the hip was an ace in the hole to the sharp shooting Brannons, a God-given talent responsible for many fresh mounds of clay dotting the boot hills of this border country.

Lynn's mouth was watering from the delicious scent of the roasting prairie hen. She was sure enough hungry and knew that her morning meal would soon be ready to eat.

She wondered what had happened to Little Crow, her self-acclaimed guardian, who she hadn't seen since leaving her river ranch. But he never strayed far, the prairie hen lying beside the fire ring when she roused from her blankets, was evidence of that. It was true that when on a journey such as this, she seldom saw him, but was comforted knowing that he was always close by.

Lynn Duval, the same little Lynn of her Grandpa Bonner's time, glanced down the coulee at her pinto mare, Boots. She loved the little horse who was a faithful companion when out on the trail, or back at her river ranch, it did not matter which.

But she was lonely, worried sick over the big cowboy who had won her heart, and who had ridden to her ranch to see her, finding her not at home. Tears were flowing as she remembered Will Bonner, the cowboy whose life she had saved at her big rock camp on the Chief Mountain trail.

It had been a long, lonely year since she had last seen him, thinking he didn't care. But now she knew that he did care, and was riding into the eastern prairie to find him, to tell him that she loved him and desired nothing more than to be his wife.

Lynn turned to her breakfast and stuffed herself to the brim with the delicious meat of this native bird, and drank her coffee too. She loved coffee, an addiction handed down from her Grandpa Brannon. She as well liked the delicious meat of this wild chicken of the prairie, there was nothing to match it; the larger sage hen was her second choice.

The reason Lynn camped over here, was a modest spring of water pooling near the bottom of the coulee. The horses were always the first to satisfy their thirst, after which the girl cleansed herself as best she could, washing the trail dust from her hair and filling her saddle canteen.

The sun was peeping above the eastern horizon before the girl left the camp in the coulee. She was singing as she rode, her Boots mare and the pack horse were listening with much interest. They knew the girl was happy, her singing made them happy as well. Perhaps? Just perhaps she might catch up to Will Bonner today.

Strangers to the prairie found it to be a lonely place, a vast unbroken sea of waving grass, in reality the country is broken by unseen coulees and rolling dips in the land. To Lynn Brannon it appeared as flat as a table.

She hadn't ridden far until she stopped and gazed in amazement. There before her was the skeleton of a buffalo, complete with a naked rib cage and a massive horned skull. On second glance she could see dozens and dozens more of the same, scattered at random in all directions from where she sat her pony.

What has happened here she wondered? Why have these majestic beasts all perished in this place? Then she remembered Grandpa Brannon telling her of the hide hunters, of the terrible slaughter that had been inflicted on the once vast herds, of the thoughtless, greedy genocide of a species.

Lynn continued on, the sun high overhead before she entered yet another coulee. She was hungry, hot and tired. Time for a noonday break she reckoned. She unsaddled the two horses, who promptly rolled in the grass, then arose shaking themselves with much vigor. Luck was with her as she discovered another water freshet, a spring of cool water pooling at the bottom of the coulee.

After eating her lunch, which consisted of the leavings from the prairie chicken of her morning meal, She found a can of peaches in the pack saddle, a delicacy of the old West. She was smitten with the delicious fruit, and ate it all with much pleasure.

As the day advanced, the girl became uneasy. She found herself scanning the horizons of this vast emptiness, many times this happened. What has happened to Little Crow? Where was her Jenni mule? Jenni should have caught up to me by now, she reasoned, she always has!

Most of all, where was her cowboy Will Bonner?

Much later her vigilance was rewarded. Uttering a squeal of delight, Lynn spotted a faint speck on the distant horizon. She knew that it was a horse and rider heading her way, and it was coming on fast.

"Sure hope it is my cowboy coming to find me," she said, excitement rippling through her tiny frame like an aspen leaf in a night time breeze.

"It is Will Bonner—I just know it is!"

With a touch of her spurs, the pinto bounded into action, the packhorse behind struggling to keep up.

Lynn Brannon Duval, the girl from Lariat Cross, headed across the distant prairie to meet the cowboy who would become her husband. The meeting of the two riders was a day to be remembered, the horses sliding to a stop, the riders leaping from the saddles to wind up in each other's arms. Smiles and giggles were exchanged, tears and kisses too. Lynn had known it would be a happy reunion for them both, the start of a new life together along the river.

* * *

Following a path of least resistance, a river flowed eastward from the Rocky Mountains. The restless waters could not be stopped, following a time-worn trace across the prairie. Onward it flowed, to carve a path through the sandstone outcroppings of a wilderness valley.

A warm, humid day was drawing to a close in the valley, a mysterious region inhabited by antelope, coyote and wolves. Not uncommon to the area were rattle snakes and unfriendly Indians.

High in a sandstone cliff a whippoorwill cried into the advancing darkness. It was a lonely sound, echoing across the stream and onward into the prairie, there to be lost by the howl of a lobo wolf.

An ominous silence returned to the valley, only to be broken by the chatter of a happy girl and the talk of a cowboy, who come riding in from the west. Much to the delight of them both, they had found each other on the prairie. With them was an Indian boy riding a broomtail pony, a packhorse trailing behind.

Yet another disturbance was nearing the valley. Hidden from view by a dip in the prairie trudged a little dun mule. Her nose was to the ground following the scent of an auburn-haired girl, Lynn Duval, who was riding her pinto mare Boots. The young cowboy riding along side the girl was Will Bonner, sitting tall in the saddle of a fine looking horse he knew as ol' Red.

An occasional garble of mule talk could be heard by the small song birds of this lonesome place, flying up in terror as the mule's shuffling hooves neared their nests in the grass.

A tumbleweed, then there were two, came bouncing along with a prairie breeze, spooking their tired horses into a wild west stampede. The well-broke horses were buck-jumping and crow-hopping, showing their displeasure at being exposed to these scary weeds of the prairie.

The breeze continued to blow, the weeds continued their wild dance leaving the riders far behind, only to be smashed against a sandstone cliff; a barrier that brought a finale to their playful antics

To the wanderers of the prairie, the Blackfoot and Cree, this valley was a special place, a revered spot along the river where stood the cliffs that tell stories—the talking cliffs—a sacred place where visions might be found.

Where spirits dwell; *masinasin,* known to the white man as Writing On Stone.

The small caravan crossed over the river, dismounted on high ground and began preparing a night camp, gazing in awe at the wonder of the cliffs as they did so; a sight they would never be able to forget.

Here, within a stone's throw of the mysterious cliffs, the cowboy and his young, vibrant fiancé were happy as larks in the springtime, chattering and laughing as they prepared their camp beside the river. The saddle stock was tethered close by, eagerly munching the nutritious short grass, a native plant of this wind-blown region.

While preparing their supper the girl's chattering never ceased. She was so happy she could hardly contain herself, giggling with joy every time their eyes met. The cowboy was equally happy, and reckoned he was the luckiest hombre on the whole wide prairie

Not only were they heading to the Judith Basin country in the southern territories, to purchase a herd of cattle of their own. Their plans included stopping at Fort Benton, the only settlement between the Milk River and the Judith. To become man and wife was in their plans!

Will Bonner had been to the Fort settlement once before and found it to be a right lively place, a center of commerce he had been told. Surely there must be a preacher there. It was their fervent desire that this be so.

"This here stream is known to the white man as the Milk River," Bonner told her. "Our Blood neighbors call it the *kenushsisuht*, translated into our talk the phrase means—little river."

Lynn was all ears, learning as much as she could about this vast prairie.

Though worn to a frazzle from the long ride in the dust and the heat, Lynn was happy she had finally caught up to the cowboy. It had been a hard, grueling ride from her St Mary's river ranch, two days and part of another before she finally found him.

And then Will's suggestion they lay over another day at their Milk River camp. She sure didn't mind. She knew he was eager to head south, she also knew he was thinking of her tired self and loved him for it.

Lynn Duval could sure use the break from riding the heat-baked prairie, and was looking forward to a day of rest. Besides, they would have some leisure time to relax and unwind, they might even hike across the river and explore the talking cliffs; as Little Crow, her self-appointed protector, so aptly described them.

The sun had vanished into the west before they finally settled down to eat their supper. This was a new experience for Lynn to be sitting cross-legged on the prairie, as for some unknown reason, very few trees could be found along the river they knew as the Milk. It was a tasty supper, even though their food-filled plates were balanced in an insecure manner on their crossed legs.

"This is what life on the prairie is like, Lynn, eating like this. No stumps or logs to sit on. No wood to burn—just sage brush and buffalo chips. It is more like a desert environment, not enough moisture to nourish many trees. And the soil is plumb saturated with alkali in most places."

They were sitting on the far side of the camp fire which was blazing merrily, offering a welcome light to the now fading day. Will Bonner grew silent, appeared deep in thought. He was worried about the cattle deal at Judith Gap, and the 300 head of Hereford cattle he had made an offer on; out of sight and nothing more than the word of a stranger!

Had he been wrong to deal this way? He sure hoped not, besides the cattle dealer he knew as Logan appeared honest, which had inspired Bonner to leave a down payment of ten Yankee double-eagles.

Pushing that aside, he reckoned Lynn's well being was more important at this time. She was an excellent rider, he had seen her in action back at Lariat Cross. But it was the long, grueling ride in the heat and the dust that had worn her down.

She was worth it, dog-gone it all, she was more than worth it. He was one lucky hombre all right, she would be a blessing to him for the rest of his life.

* * *

Two Blood Indian braves, not yet out of their teens, lay flat on the prairie, hiding in the seasoned plant growth of the prairie floor. Buffalo grass, sage brush, and prickly pear cactus that was so abundant, they all grew here. Not to forget bunchgrass, it was here as well. Hunkered in with the prairie plants, their buckskin clad bodies blended in with the shadows of the approaching night.

They were wanderers of Milk River country, having left the reservation on a vision quest, and to count *coup* as many times as possible. Many vision seekers preferred traveling to the high mountains seeking their destiny—Old Chief being the favored and most revered of them all. Others like themselves, for reasons known only to themselves, preferred to stay on the prairie and seek out the sacred place known as Writing On Stone, the cliffs that tell stories! It was an isolated region along the Milk River, rife with cliff writings of the ancient ones.

It was with much interest they watched the camp of the cowboy and the girl, so near the talking cliffs, the sacred cliffs of which they had been seeking. A revered spot on the prairie where they could communicate with the spirits, and surely receive the visions they had been searching for.

They knew this was a white-eyes camp—their interest building as they listened to the strange talk and the happy laughter of the cowboy and the young white squaw. And Little Crow, they knew he was one of their own, though not of the same tribe; they could tell the difference by the strange scent that wafted in the evening breeze.

They appeared upset over strangers being here in this sacred place, especially so the two white eyes of whom they had vowed to drive away; or worse yet if needed.

Later, far into the evening, they watched the brilliance of the camp fire waning, still listening to the chatter of the cowboy and the girl as they left for their blankets in the shadows; and the silent figure of Little Crow slipping away into the night. The prairie grew quiet except for the occasional hoot of an owl over near the talking cliffs, the chirp of a night bird, and the scurry of tiny feet in the short grass of Writing On Stone country.

Much later still, the night grew as silent as a tomb. No sound could be heard, the field mice who had been scampering all about, even they had retired to their nest. "It is time now," Crazy Dog told his companion, "to go to this camp of the white eyes.

"It is there we will make our medicine—and take the white-eyed squaw with us—it is this one who will help us find our sacred vision!

"This will be a great *coup* for each of us—if we succeed!"

"Do you feel it is safe to do this thing," replied Spotted Pony. "What if we wake them from their sleep?"

"Do not worry Spotted Pony," Crazy Dog reassured him. "You will bring our horses," he whispered. "I will lead the way," and began to crawl through the grass towards the sleeping camp.

All was still on the prairie, the intense blackness before dawn lay heavy across the land. Silent as specters, two shadows with feathers in their hair stood over the sleeping cowboy and the girl. The girl stirred in her sleep, was turning over in her blankets when a grimy, fetid smelling hand clamped tight around her mouth and nostrils. Attempting to scream was of no use, she was unable to utter a sound.

Roughly she was snatched from her bed and put on the bareback of her pinto mare that had been tethered nearby. Quickly a gag was shoved in her mouth, and a leather string pulled tight to keep it there. Her hands were tied together at the wrists, her feet were lashed with a woven piece of buffalo leather, starting at one ankle passing under the horse's belly to the other; and cinched up tight.

Off into the night they rode, Lynn Duval and her two captors. They were good at what they were doing, very good, had had lots of practice it seemed! Not a sound had they made, not a sound was she able to utter. The broom-tail ponies they rode were equipped with buffalo hide socks pulled over their hooves, and lashed tight.

Tracking them would be an almost impossible task to do.

She was helpless and could do nothing but hang on to her beloved pinto's mane. Though her hands and fingers were swelling from the tightness of the wilderness handcuffs, she was still able to hang on and keep her balance.

Will Bonner who had been sleeping soundly in his own blankets on the far side of Lynn's Jenni mule, was awakened by the raucous clatter of the mule braying into the darkness. She had witnessed the whole affair, the kidnapping of Lynn and all, and was not at all pleased with seeing her being roughed up; and taken away into the night.

The cowboy reared from his blankets, groping for his six gun in the darkness—reckoned a full scale war had erupted. With his hand finally on the weapon, he was standing when a savage blow to the head drove him back to the ground. Not knowing the results, Spotted Pony was smiling as he fled camp—knowing that he had counted coup on a white eyes— the first time for the young Blood Indian boy.

Brannon collapsed in a heap, out cold, experiencing the tumultuous visions of the unconscious for some time to come.

The Jenni mule bounced to her feet, stumbling over Bonner's body as she did so. Once free from the entanglement of the two bedrolls, Lynn Duval's pet mule took off into the darkness to find her beloved friend. A garble of sound echoed back through the shadows, it was the garbled talk of a mule, whose nose was to the ground following the scent of Lynn Duval.

The eastern sky was softening, welcoming the arrival of a new day on the sage brush prairie. High in the cliffs on the far side of the river, an owl was serenading his mate nestled in a well-hidden nest, who was watching with interest her greedy nestlings devour the breakfast their father had brought them.

Nearby, close to camp, a prairie lark was trilling an overture of a new day ready to burst forth across this lonely land.

Though still shrouded with the shadows of night, a lone Indian boy sat cross-legged by a sage brush fire. He was staring at the motionless body of Lynn's cowboy, attempting to discover what had happened here while he had been gone. Where was his beloved mistress, Miss Lynn? Where was her Jenni mule? Why was Bonner laying so still on his crumpled bed?

As was his way he had been wandering in the night, thrilled with the secrets he had discovered, proud of the evil spirits he had damned into purgatory, and other unspeakable things. In reality he had spent most of the night at the talking cliffs—Writing On Stone—*masinasin* as the Cree preferred to call them—absorbing the soul stirring essence that was there. On his return to continue his vigil here at Lynn's camp, this is what he found.

Thinking Bonner dead, he arose and walked over to the cowboy. Squatting, as was his way, he stared intently at the motionless figure. He leaned over close to the cowboy's face and realized he was breathing, that he was not dead after all. He also noticed blood in his hair, blood that had trickled down his forehead and on to his face.

Little Crow was ashamed, ashamed that he had not been here when he was needed. After all, he was the self-proclaimed guardian of Lynn's camp wherever it might be, and had failed to protect her when she needed him.

The Indian lad returned to the fire, stirred up the embers and laid on fresh twigs. Soon the coffee pot was bubbling, as well as a small pan of water, which he took to Bonners blankets and gently cleansed the cowboy's nasty wound. Then from deep in his medicine bag he found a small container of salve. A secret concoction of old Lame Deer's, made by heating the fragrant buds of balsam poplar in bear grease, and then straining and saving the fat to be used as a healing salve. His Nez Perce mother had insisted he carry it with him at all times.

After covering the deep gash with a generous layer of his wilderness salve, he applied a tree-moss poultice over the wound. Returning to the fire, a steaming cup of coffee in hand, he sat back to wait; his eyes never leaving Will Bonner.

* * *

Boots, Lynn Duval's pinto mare was puzzled. Not at all pleased with the lead rope of her halter being tied to Crazy Dog's saddle. She knew Lynn was sitting on her bare back, the scent of the girl was special to the pinto, this she could never forget. But somehow things were different. There was no saddle for her to sit on!

The little horse could not hear the chatter of her voice, or her happy giggles, and feel Lynn's hands caressing and touching her as was her way. Stubbornly, she reared back attempting to turn her head to see what was wrong, but was roughly pulled back into line; her nose no where to go but facing the rump of the reservation horse ahead of her.

Boots was not happy, on edge and ready to explode. Not hearing the voice of Lynn was the reason.

Lynn Duval, soon to be Bonner, was fuming mad, as was her mare. Yet she was frightened, not knowing who had taken her from her blankets—or why! Their talk was foreign to her, yet she reckoned they were Indians.

And her darling Will—her husband to be—in just a few more days, what has happened to him? Have they killed him? They must have or he would not have allowed them to take her away.

Her head was hanging low, her eyes full of unshed tears. Her sobbing must stay bottled up inside, else the filthy rag that had been shoved far back in her throat would surely cause her to strangle. She was struggling to resist the urging of her stomach to heave up its contents, knowing that if this happened she would choke to death.

Fear gripped her like a deathly plague, her body was shaking uncontrollably from the coldness of the night and fear of what might be her fate. She was grateful she had gone to her blankets fully dressed, not in her night gown as was her way.

Grandpa Brannon was responsible for this, she remembered, "Lynn darlin'," he would say. "When out on the trail never take off your duds when you sleep—never know when you might have to leave in a hurry— could be varmits around; bears, Injuns and what not!"

She had taken off her boots though, and now finding herself in this confounded mess, could feel the cold attacking her helpless feet. "Where are you Will?" her inner self was pleading. "Come and save me…please come!"

* * *

Daylight had arrived in Writing On Stone country. At the Bonner camp Little Crow was dozing by the fire ring, having spent the night awake and on the prowl. Nothing was left of the fire but a lazy spiral of smoke drifting skyward.

Standing over him was Will Bonner, as shaky as an aspen in a wind storm. He had revived from the long sleep, and though his head was pounding something fierce from the blow he had received, he knew that his darling Lynn was not here. He reckoned whoever was the one that had downed him in the dark must have used a war club, more likely the blunt end of a tomahawk. He knew Indians had been in camp, he could tell by the scent that was still heavy in the air

Aware that someone was there, Little Crow aroused and grabbed for his weapon, all the time gazing Bonner in his eyes. Struggling to voice any words, caused by the throbbing pain from his head wound, Bonner managed to speak, "What has been going on here? Where is Lynn—tell me amigo, 'fore my head splits wide open!"

The Nez Perce boy was speechless to start with, then greeted him with a weak "*Oki*!"

"Crow does not know boss—her pinto pony is gone too! They were both gone from this camp when I came back from…magic rocks!

"*Oki*!" he continued his talk. "This is so! It was this Nez Perce cowboy who put magic medicine on your head—it will soon be better, then we go find Miss Lynn and her pinto pony."

After drinking another cup of coffee, then it was two, Will Bonner was beginning to recover. "Saddle our broncs Crow," he said. "This here coffee has got my head feelin' much better, not poundin' like before— sure tastes strange though—not near as tasty as Lynn's!"

Crow turned away from Bonner, hiding a smile on his face. Unknown to the cowboy, Crow had administered a generous dose of his secret herbs in the coffee, including among other things crushed, dried willow bark. A remedy used for centuries by the tribes to combat pain.

* * * Chapter Two * * *

Two Blood Indian vision seekers and their prisoner, Lynn Duval, rode an evasive circle on the prairie before crossing over the river. Here, not that far from where they had kidnapped the girl, they made camp in a secluded niche in the talking cliffs; gazing in awe at the pictograph symbols that were all around them. Crazy Dog secured the horses then wandered off to study this amazing sight.

After making sure Crazy Dog was absorbed in his quest, Spotted Pony untied the leather thongs that had imprisoned the girl with such cruelty, and removed the gag that had come so close to choking her to death. He helped her from her horse and watched her crumple to the ground, unable to stand. Somewhere from deep inside him he felt sorry for what they had done to her. Gently he began to massage her feet and ankles which had turned a nasty looking color from the tightness of the leather thongs that had bound her.

Then, with a buffalo-gut bag in hand, walked to the river for water, and returned to give her a drink. She was unable to speak or swallow, yet he was able to pour small amounts into her mouth which seemed to help some.

He knew that Crazy Dog had a mean streak in him, and vowed that he would not allow him to harm her again. Spotted Pony had a sister about the same age as Lynn, and knew how he would feel if this were to happen to her.

Lynn's reasoning powers were slowly returning, and after watching Spotted Pony massage her wrists and ankles; knew that this one was different. She was moaning with pain as the circulation began returning to her tortured limbs, and was thankful for the water this Indian was helping her to drink. This one is kind, she reasoned, and compassionate too. I will remember what he has done for me, and beg my Will not to do bad things to him when he comes to save me.

Several hours passed and Lynn was still not able to stand on her feet, but she was able to sit with her back propped against a sandstone buttress. Her voice was slowly returning to normal, the swelling in her wrists and ankles was doing the same. But still she was unable to stand.

The young brave had kindled a small twig fire and offered her a piece of jerky. She was hungry and broke off a piece of the iron-hard meat and put it in her mouth, finding that she was unable to chew through the toughness of it—but in time it softened, the juices trickling down her throat.

"Thank you," she spoke for the first time. "for helping me."

The Blood boy appeared as if he could not understand her talk but offered her a smile, sensing she was indeed grateful. Though it was hard for her to do, Lynn offered a weak smile in return.

Suddenly, as if from out of no where, Lynn's Jenni mule sauntered into view and spotting the girl in the hidden niche, walked over and lay down beside her; offering a garbled greeting as she did so. Close behind her came Will Bonner with drawn six-gun. Backing him up was Little Crow standing beside him—bow string drawn tight, a flint-tipped arrow ready to fly.

On seeing her Jenni mule move in beside her, Lynn shrieked with joy and wrapped her arms around Jenni's neck, hugging her as tight as she could.

Sensing something was wrong with Spotted Pony, who was staring at the new arrivals, she turned to see. A scream of joy escaped her chapped lips, she attempted to stand and was unable to do so. Tears that had been kept back for so long were now streaming down her cheeks. Her arms were out-raised as she waited for her cowboy to come to her. In a blink of an eye he was kneeling beside her, their arms wrapped around each other.

When her weeping had subsided, she was able to tell her story. And listen to Bonner tell her why he hadn't been able to protect her. He cursed like a mule skinner on seeing the condition his girl was in, and the extent of her injured ankles and wrists.

In the excitement of their happy reunion, Bonner's hat was dislodged and fell to the ground. She could see Crow's wilderness poultice still stuck in his hair and the ugly gash in his scalp. Lynn moaned with outrage, knowing that her cowboy had had a mighty close call as well.

With a growl Bonner arose and turned to Spotted Pony. "Reckon I know what to do with the likes o' this here redskin," he said, blue flame shooting out of his eyes as he walked toward him.

"No!" the terrified girl screamed. "No Will, do not harm him! He has been kind to me, took the filthy gag out of my mouth and gave me water. He also cut the leather strings that were binding me so tight.

"It was the other one Will, who was so mean to me. He treated me like I was an animal being led to the slaughter.

"This one, who told me his name is Spotted Pony, saved my life—I couldn't have lasted much longer!"

"Keep the Injun under control Crow, I'm taking Lynn back across the river to camp."

Little Crow's mind was elsewhere, his attention was drawn up into the sky and cautioned Bonner to wait. "Look boss, look with your eyes up there," and signed upwards. Bonner stopped and looked up.

There, outlined against the sky was Crazy Dog, sitting cross-legged on a sandstone buttress. His arms were raised to the sun, one hand gripping the tail of an outraged rattle snake. He was looking upward at the sun as if in a trance; deeply engrossed in a vision ritual.

"Go to him Crow—bring him down here to face his maker—if he as much as twitches his nose, shoot 'im!

"The son-of-a-gun must pay for the cowardly way he treated my Lynn!" Bonner roared. He was from the old school—the code of the west—which showed no mercy for those who mistreated women or children. Those who did so must be brought to justice from the smoking barrel of a six-gun, or a knotted rope and a branch of a tree.

Little Crow needed no urging. "*Oki!* boss." he said, and vanished in the talking cliffs.

Bonner returned and sat by Lynn, holding her close, both watching skyward at the drama set to unfold. It wasn't that long before the one known as Crazy Dog was standing, screeching a jargon of Blackfoot—facing the intruder of his attempt at receiving a vision.

Long knife in hand, he sprang at Little Crow, slashing at the boy, attempting to kill him. Little Crow's knife was out as well, and though he had received a wicked slash to the breast, was facing the crazed one with much bravery.

Those below could hear the Blackfoot's shrieks of rage, and could see blood streaming from the wound in Little Crow's breast. "Reckon I better get up there, and help him," Bonner said, "'fore that heathen kills our cowboy.

"I reckon he's sure enough got a bobcat by the tail!"

Seething with fury at this one who had interfered with his vision quest, Crazy Dog stepped back as Little Crow moved in close. He was still screeching in anger when a moccasin-clad foot slipped on the time-smoothed sandstone and upended him off into space.

A long scream of terror followed him to the valley floor, where Crazy Dog's lifeless body lay crumpled in a heap—horror-stricken eyes still staring at the sun.

"Take him home Spotted Pony," Bonner ordered. "He had it a coming—we didn't have to kill him after all—the spirits of this place took care of that.

"And Spotted Pony, I thank you for your kindness to Lynn. I reckon it's like she said, without you she would have surely died."

With that said the big cowboy known as Will Bonner stepped forward and shook the young brave's hand, the same hand that had wielded the tomahawk that come close to ending his own life just a few hours ago.

Lynn's Jenni mule, a legacy from her Grandpa Brannon, was getting on in years—white hairs showing through her thick dun-hued coat like salt and pepper. It was she Bonner and Little Crow spotted, staring at the niche where her mistress was waiting for someone to come and rescue her.

And though it was an unusual sight to see, Will Bonner turned to Jenni, and while rubbing his big hand across her body, spoke these words, "Thank you Jenni, for showing us where Lynn was at—how you do it I will never know!"

"I reckon you're welcome in my camp any old time!"

Turning to Lynn, he said, "I'm climbing up and bring down Little Crow, from what we could see from here, this Crazy Dog must o' cut him pretty serious like."

"Hurry Will!" Lynn pleaded. "Crow's hurt real bad—I just know it."

Bonner was already starting up through the cliffs, and shouted back, "Hang on to your six-gun I brought you—keep an eye on that redskin, and be careful!"

What the big cowboy found was not pretty to see. He had been right. Little Crow's body hung bloodied and torn, dangling from a large crack in a splintered cliff; one of his buckskin-clad legs securely trapped. His body was drenched in blood, a terrible sight to see. Bonner reckoned the boy, weak from the loss of blood, must have slipped on his way down, his leg became caught and that was it. There were several knife wounds on his arms and chest, but the one that killed him was a deep wound near his heart.

Bonner stood by the body. He was saddened by what he found, and knew that this would be a tough one for Lynn to handle. Even though he was an Indian boy, she had accepted his strange ways and customs, and respected his desire to protect her from the evil ones.

"Dog-gone it all," he muttered. "Her heart will be broken!"

Before leaving for the descent back down, Bonner secured Crow's body in a secluded niche of the sandstone cliffs. He placed the body as if it were asleep, his bow and guns placed beside him, his medicine bag in easy reach of his crossed hands. He never closed Crow's eyes, but left them open so the young brave could find his way to the happy hunting ground, and there be with his Grandpa—the great Nez Perce—Chief Joseph.

* * *

Bonner's head wound would take time to heal, and after spending a restless night, he left his blankets and prepared himself for the coming day. With much care he positioned his big hat over the tenderness that was there, then shook out his boots and pulled them on—he must be sure no uninvited guests—the biting kind had slept over in them.

After stomping his feet snug into the boots, confident there were no crawly varmints inside, he strapped on his six-gun and positioned it on his hip. He now reckoned he was fully dressed—he felt plumb naked without his trusty weapon a hanging where it should be.

To have this morning ritual attended to gave him peace of mind, a sure enough omen of a good day ahead. Looking long at the precious blanket-clad girl who was still asleep, and who would soon be his wife; he knew that from now on every day would be an answer to his fondest dreams.

He was smiling as he listened to the birds offering their own rendition of a new day on the prairie, of new adventures, of new challenges they must face to survive.

His smile lessened as he remembered the hullabaloo of the night before, when the girl's Jenni mule, who had bedded down between the bedrolls of the cowboy and the girl, had awakened while it was still dark as hades; stumbling over his lanky frame and wandered off into the night. Well that will change, he reasoned, just as soon as he and his darlin' Lynn could locate a preacher. No more sharing his best gal with a mule!

His frown deepened as he remembered the details, and they weren't pretty. Lynn, who had been spirited away and treated so savagely, and even himself who had failed to protect her—driven to the ground like an immature school boy from Spotted Pony's tomahawk. And Crow, killed while fighting the vision seeker, attempting to avenge the savage treatment of his mentor and revered friend Missy Lynn

Suddenly, for the umpteenth time he was fuming mad, his fury once again bringing on a pounding head ache; a stark reminder of the nearness to death both he and Lynn had experienced. Reckoned they should lay over a few days until they were both fit to ride.

The coffee pot was now issuing a delicious aroma, bacon was frying and he had even stirred up a batch of sourdough biscuits. He reckoned after the tasty supper Lynn had prepared the night before, that it was now his turn to show off his trail savvy with a skillet and a sagebrush fire.

Bonner's only concern was that he never had any hen's eggs to fry with the bacon. He was sure fond of bacon and eggs for breakfast, he surely was, and would indulge himself of the same every chance he got. He recalled while batching it at his burnt-out shack over yonder by the river, of gathering wild duck eggs to fry with his bacon; he sure enjoyed those too.

The girl from Lariat Cross was awake now, enjoying the peace and quiet of this lonely prairie. She knew her Jenni mule and the cowboy who had won her heart, were both up and about, and was relishing this private moment by herself. She reckoned Will Bonner was attending to his morning chores, might even be preparing breakfast here at their trail camp on this big sagebrush prairie.

Bonner's smile returned when he noticed Lynn was stirring in her blankets. "It's time to be up and about," he told her. "It's a breakin' daylight—soon be light enough to see."

Knowing how tender and sore her body must be, and the trials she had been through, he spoke again, "Do you need any help Lynn? Give me a shout if you do and I'll come a runnin'"

The smell of breakfast cooking and the sound of Will's voice aroused the girl. Flinging her blankets aside, she sat up, nursing her sore, mistreated body; stretching her aching muscles and then realized how tired she really was after the terrible experience with the vision seekers. It was no matter though, she had found Will Bonner, and discovered that he really cared. That he loved her and had asked her to be his wife, an offer that she had eagerly accepted.

Her mood changed, her thoughts turned to Little Crow, and the bravery he had shown while facing the dreadful Crazy Dog. And of the knife fight on the talking cliffs which resulted in the death of her Nez Perce cowboy. Lynn knew they no longer would be exposed to Crow's wilderness savvy, his quaint native ways, they surely would miss.

Brushing the sad tears from her eyes, she looked forward to the days that lay ahead, and the first settlement they came to that might have a man of the cloth in their midst. One who could repeat the sacred oath for them, an oath that would bond them together as husband and wife. Then her happiness would be fulfilled, for the rest of her life she reckoned.

Lynn was smiling when she turned towards the fire. "Good morning my husband to be, sure do love you, even if you have made me sleep on the hard ground—and with my clothes on!"

Will's smile turned into a chuckle. "Why Lynn, like I told you last night—when on the trail a ridin' hard and fast and nighttime comes—you roll up in your blankets—and sleep on the ground.

"All you take off are your hat, boots and six-gun, and leave them within easy reach…never know when you might have trouble of some kind…and have to leave your blankets right pronto."

She knew Will was giving her a lesson in survival, and loved him for it, even though she did have a kink in her back this morning. Bonner spoke again, "It is a law of the trail darlin', a law of survival!"

"Oh pooh on survival!" she replied with a smile. "All I hope is that we survive long enough to become man and wife."

Lynn thanked him for his first lesson on the trail, even though her grandpa had lectured her on the same thing many years before. "I must go now Will, to the river and attend to my morning ritual, bathe, wash my hair and such.

"If you're a wanting to be a married man," she was giggling as she talked. "This is something you will have to get used to."

With a satchel of her private things in hand, she turned towards the river. "I won't be long darlin' Will, can hardly wait to eat that breakfast you're a cookin' that smells so darn good.

"And Will Bonner, you stay away from the river! You hear?"

Will Bonner watched her leave and was mighty proud of her, proud that she had survived the savagery of Crazy Dog, proud that she was here with him, roughing it on the trail.

* * * Chapter Three * * *

Two days and another they stayed at the Milk River camp, allowing their bodies a chance to recuperate from the nearness to death they both had experienced. Though Lynn's legs and ankles were still giving her trouble, and Will's head wound, which surely must have been a fractured skull; was still not back to normal, they knew it was time to go a hunting some cows for their ranch.

Looking forward to the adventures that lay ahead, the girl from Lariat Cross and her cowboy left the Milk River camp riding south for the American border; crossed over and continued on past the eastern flank of Gold Butte.

The butte was one of a group of three, made up of giant mounds of earth and rock that reared skyward out of the wide-open prairie. The white man called them the Sweetgrass Hills, to the Blackfoot they were referred to as *greasy grass*, sacred to all that roamed the plains.

They continued on, deep into the butte country they rode only stopping for a mid-day break, nothing more than a short respite to see them through till the darkness of night forced them to stop once again.

The only thing that troubled Lynn was the absence of Little Crow, something that would be tough for her to handle

The cowboy and the girl had retired to their blankets early one night, the Jenni mule was bedded down between them as usual and Lynn was fast asleep. Bonner was troubled, couldn't seem to settle down—was tossing and turning in his blankets. It was a strangeness that had him on edge, almost as if someone, or something was out there in the darkness.

Several times he sat up, six-gun in hand, his senses straining to see, to hear, or even smell an intruder to their modest camp in the sage. But always there was nothing he could detect. Will Bonner, a straight shooting, hard riding cowboy, feared nothing that walked on two legs, or four; yet this was different.

This time his inner self would not let him be. He was pulling on his boots, reckoned he should get up and check things out. Then it happened!

One of his boots was on, the other in his hands, his foot sliding inside when he stopped—a shadow, he swore he saw movement on the far side of camp. The hair rippled on the back of his neck, his hand dropped to his Colt .44. "Who's there?" he spoke, a subdued caution in his voice. He sure didn't want to awaken Lynn, get her all worked up over nothing.

"Speak up, you hear?" his voice rising some, "'fore I start a shootin'"

Silence was heavy in the little night camp in the sage, no sound had been heard except that of Will Bonner. Once more he detected movement in the darkness, the only light was from the stars in the sky. This time he was sure that he hadn't been seeing something that wasn't there.

The next morning as he was preparing the saddle stock for the trail, Lynn called to him, "Come see Will—what I have found!" There lying on the ground beside her blankets she had been rolling up, was the tail feather from an eagle. "It wasn't here when I went to bed—I am sure Will, I checked the ground real good, making sure there were no scorpions and such!"

"Well I'll be—!" Will told her, scratching his head as he did so. "Sure beats all; sure enough a mystery all right!"

"This reminds me of old Raven Wings," she said, a smile spreading across her face. Grandpa Brannon called him an old pot-licker, who would come to our Jenni Mine under Old Chief Mountain and steal our coffee; sometimes pot and all.

"He was like a pack rat, leaving something in return. Usually it was a piece of gold ore—sometimes a bird feather!"

Bonner wasn't paying attention to her talk, gazing off across the prairie—deep in thought.

Little Lynn, as her grandpa used to call her, spoke again, "You listen to me Will Bonner! I believe Grandpa Brannon and Raven Wings are friends up in heaven, still teasing each other. Grandpa still cursing and raving over the disappearance of his coffee, old Raven Wings still stealing it every chance he gets!"

The big cowboy had a strange look on his face, was scratching his head once again when he said, "This is a mystery only the sage brush knows the answer to—it sure enough is!"

Bonner didn't believe in ghosts, or spooks, or haunts. Yet this hair-raising experience had him doubtful.

* * *

Two more days had passed before the cowboy and the girl reined in their broncs and gazed in wonder at the panorama that spread out below them. Here, high on the bluffs above the river settlement of Fort Benton, they looked down upon the mighty Missouri River and the awesome channel it had carved across the land.

"It is so beautiful Will!" Lynn exclaimed. "The big river, the boats coming and going…and all the people scurrying around like tiny ants in the sand."

"Reckon so darlin'," he answered. "Sure hope we can find us a preacher down yonder…then be on our way for that Judith Basin country!"

Will Bonner was a loner, always had been. The farther away from people he could be, the happier he was.

"I must buy some things for Lynn!" she told him, a mischievous look spreading across her face. "After all, this just might be her wedding day."

Once in the settlement that surrounded the Fort, they secured their horses and purchased what supplies they were in need of, including Lynn's. After several hours of searching they were assured that not even one of the several hundred people that were coming and going here…were legally or spiritually fit to perform a marriage ceremony.

They were sure feeling down hearted, and returned to the livery stable to pick up their horses and ride on. A whiskered old timer who was in charge of the stables heard of their quest, appeared as if he wanted to palaver some.

"Couldn't help a hearin' you two youngsters a talkin'. If it's a preacher you're a wantin', reckon I can help out."

"Oh! Please do," Lynn exclaimed, excitement spreading across her face.

"Look over yonder," he told her. "See that circle o' wagons by the river? Was told they be a wagon train headin' north to the territories of the British Queen. Them covered wagons bin sittin' there about a week now, circled round a sizable camp. The folks there are sure a praying bunch, and sing songs several times a day. Right purty songs too!

"I sure can't figure out why they're a stayin' so long!"

Lynn and Will stood hand in hand, waiting patiently for the old timer to fire up his pipe before he continued his talk.

"There's talk around the leader of this bunch is a Mormon bishop, a sure enough marryin' man if there ever was one. I reckon he can tie the knot for you two, 'bout the only one in these parts that can!"

Lynn Duval squealed with joy on hearing the wonderful news, and looked up at her cowboy, tears of happiness pooling in her pretty eyes.

Will thanked him and gave him a silver dollar for his kindness. Then hand-in-hand they walked over to the Mormon camp.

They were greeted warmly, and on inquiring about someone to say the good words for them, were ushered into a tent where sat a white-whiskered old gentleman. After introductions all around, Will Bonner told him why they were here, and if he would be so kind as to perform the ceremony for them.

"I'll be honored to do this for you," he told them, a friendly smile was upon his face.

"Well then, the sooner the better!" Bonner replied. "Lynn and I have been waiting for this day for a long time."

They were ushered outside the tent to face the old Mormon preacher, and it was here, a cowboy and his beautiful bride, both dressed in the manner of the open range, were married on the banks of the Missouri River. A sizable crowd had gathered to give their support, to both the Bishop and the happy couple.

As if planned in advance, a large wood-burning paddle wheeler, loaded with people and supplies, eased gently into the loading docks of Fort Benton. The deck was swarming with passengers eager to leave the boat, others standing in line on the dock below, just as eager to board her, all excited over the adventures that might lay ahead.

As the Bishop was concluding the ceremony, telling the cowboy and the girl they were now legally man and wife, a powerful blast from the paddle wheeler's whistle announced to one and all—a new life together for the happy Bonners.

The ear-shattering whistle could be heard up and down the Missouri, a happy coincident perhaps—as if planned in advance.

"Do you have a ring for your beautiful bride?" the Bishop asked, winking at the cowboy. Lynn's new husband was somewhat embarrassed, and looked it too. "...'fraid I plumb forgot about one...in the excitement and all. Reckon I'll head over to the trading post yonder, could be they'll have rings for sale"

"Don't leave me," Lynn spoke shyly, and stopped him as he turned to go. She had a gold ring in her hand and offered it to her cowboy. "I would like you to put this one on my finger, darling Will." Her eyes were full of tears.

"It is a family treasure and belonged to my Grandma Brannon...God rest her soul. She never had the opportunity to wear it...I will be happy to do this for her!"

And so the union was now complete, a happy Lynn with a ring on her finger, and an equally happy Bonner proudly holding a brand new marriage license all signed and sealed. A knot was now tied good and tight, the girl from Lariat Cross and her cowboy were now together until death do they part.

As a finale for the ceremony, four teen-aged girls stepped forward and sang a beautiful rendition of an old Mormon hymn, 'Love At Home'. Come time for the chorus all members of the caravan joined in, which brought tears to Lynn's eyes. Will Bonner's eyes were damp as well.

After handshakes for Will and hugs for Lynn, Will offered the Bishop a gold coin for his services. "I cannot accept payment for performing the Lord's work," he told the cowboy.

"However, you may help us another way—if you will? You see Brother Bonner, we are running low on provisions—food for our children and grain for our stock—the reason we are still here. When the traders found out we were of the Mormon faith…they have refused to sell us what we so desperately need.

"You see Brother Bonner, our younger men were sent ahead to secure land for our people to settle on. This has left the caravan vulnerable to vultures such as the traders here."

Bible still in hand, the Bishop looked the cowboy in the eye, and asked, "Brother Bonner, would you be so kind as to purchase the provisions we need—so that we may continue our journey to the northern territories."

With his free hand he offered Will Bonner a pouch of gold coins. "Our food supply is almost depleted…the traders now refuse to let us leave…say we'll probably shoot wild game that is rightfully their own!"

"I've heard a bunch about you Mormon people," Will answered. "In my wanderin's around the southwest, and all. Was told you are a people that believe in God, and are mighty fine neighbors too.

"We were told by an old timer from over at the livery stable that you have the authority to marry people, which you have done for us; all legal and above-board too. The least Lynn and I can do is see that you get what provisions you need, and a safe journey out of this hell hole!"

The big cowboy was fuming mad. "You can rest assured we'll help you Bishop. I reckon there is some traders over yonder about to get a good tunin' up."

With the gold in hand, and the list of supplies needed, Will turned to go, "Send one of your wagons over, you'll have your supplies in no time at all.

"Come Lynn—we've got us some shoppin' to do!"

The main drag of Fort Benton, nothing more than a rut-worn trail, was quiet. The passengers from the unloading paddle wheeler were now settled and preparing to go their separate ways.

From the inside of the livery stable, the old timer watched the young couple pass by. He was smoking his pipe in the shadows, a look of concern on his whiskered face. He knew of the Mormons when he was a child, his mother was a member, and had taught him and his siblings about the Golden Rule from a dog-eared bible. She counseled them to always remember it, and to refrain from cussing and swearing and carousing around.

The passing of time had dulled his memory, yet a faint thought remained of that long ago time. It was of another book that she had cherished, a new book that she would clutch to her bosom when sitting in her old rocking chair. All he had seen of it was the front cover. One word stood out from the rest of the title—Mormon.

However as a teen-ager he had drifted away from home and never joined the Church, as she wanted him to.

He reckoned he knew there was going to be trouble and, shrugging away the memories, moved an old chair closer to the open door, so he could watch. Sure wasn't about to miss what might happen next.

The Bonners entered the trading post and looked around. It was stocked to the ceiling with goods of every sort. A whiskered, sharp-eyed trader met them at the counter and asked them what they were doing here. His manner was not friendly, scowling and very uncouth, reeking of suspicion and disrespect.

He had watched them come from the Mormon camp, had seen them go there as well. Far in the back of the cavernous room sat four armed men playing cards, and sipping from a jug of river whiskey.

* * * Chapter Four * * *

Will Bonner dropped the Mormon's gold and list on the plank counter. "Reckon you can fill out this here order for us—a wagon will be here right quick for you to load it in—you hear?"

"I'm going to look around Will," Lynn told her new husband and winked. "We could use a few more cans of peaches that you like so well, and some of them new-fangled sulfur matches."

Looking at the list, the trader tossed it back on the counter. "You two must have come from the Mormon camp, we don't do business with the likes o' that bunch.

"Take your gold and leave cowboy, 'fore you get into more trouble than you can handle!" He was sneering as he spoke, a beefy hand hovering near a holstered six-gun.

With a draw that left the trader utterly shell-shocked, Bonner's big .44 was staring him in the face. "Do as you're told *hombre*...you're the one that's in trouble...a treatin' decent people like dogs, pistol-whippin' unarmed boys and all the rest.

"Get a move on!" Bonner roared. "You hear me?"

The trader was more than willing to do as the cowboy had asked, the swiftness in which the big gun appeared in the cowboy's hand sure enough spooked him—had given him a bad case of the chills. He began to gather the goods and stack them out on the covered walkway as he was told. Though the sound was faint, Bonner could detect movement from the back of the room, and reckoned he knew what was going to happen next. He looked around and could see no sign of Lynn.

The Mormon wagon had now pulled up and several teamsters were assisting the trader in loading the supplies. Three of them were teen-aged boys, their faces still battered and bruised, showing the effect of the beatings they had received from previous stops here; looking to purchase supplies. Pistol-whipped and severely beaten, the lads had been dumped in their tarp-covered wagon and ordered back to the Mormon camps

Will was closely watching, insisting the trader do all the heavy lifting when the four card players moved in behind him, six-guns in hand, and demanded that he drop his gun.

Uttering a silent curse, the cowboy knew he was in a tight spot, mentally preparing himself to spin on his heels and start pulling the trigger. It was then he detected the sound of Lynn cranking a shell into the chamber of her little rifle. "It is you back-shooters who must drop your guns" she said, her voice was a bit shaky, yet determined. "I've got you covered—all four of you,"

That they were cronies of the trader, there was no doubt, a proverbial shoe was now on the other foot!

"Kill him," roared the trader. "Do it, while you've got the drop on the cowboy.

"The girl's a bluffin'…pay her no mind, you hear?"

Two of them wheeled to gun down the girl, the other two pulled leather on Will Bonner. With no time left for palaver, the cowboy's lightning-fast reflexes took over. In a move known to the gunfighter crowd as the—waltz of death—the cowboy was able to execute three things at once; spinning on his boot heels, diving to the boardwalk, and fanning two shots that brought down the back-shooters. Lynn sensed the motive of those that swung to face off with her, the little carbine at her hip never let her down.

A crowd had now gathered, including a Federal Marshal in charge of the Territory of Montana. They had all watched in awe at the reflexes of the cowboy and the girl, the downing of four men, and the howling trader who had taken a bullet meant for the sharp-shooting cowboy.

Will and Lynn were standing together now, Lynn wrapped in her husband's arms, sobbing as if her heart would break. "I warned them Will, I surely did…I didn't want to shoot them…they just wouldn't listen to me!"

All that were present, including the Marshal, who was eyeing-up the big cowboy, listened to Lynn's talk.

The lawman walked over to stand beside them. "Reckon they had it a comin'," he said. "Bin causin' trouble here for quite a spell…a couple of killings as well…appears like they were all set to add you two—to their list."

Will then told the Marshal about the troubles of the Mormon wagon train. The trader's refusal to sell them supplies, and whose hired ruffians were ordered to make sure the train never left Fort Benton.

"I was curious as to why they stayed on, now I know…wished they had let me know what was a goin' on."

"Reckon if it's all right with you Marshal, we'll be ridin' on now, the Mormon caravan is leaving as well."

"Tell me your names, for the records and all—-so I'll know who to thank for bustin' up this gang of owl-hoots. The citizens of Fort Benton are grateful you know!"

"Bonner, Will Bonner. This is my wife Lynn—whom I'm mighty proud of today—we've only bin married a couple o' hours, and already she's saved her husband's life."

The old Marshal scratched his whiskered chin some, never spoke for a spell; appeared deep in thought. "Bonner! Will Bonner, you say. I've heard tell of you before. It was you put the run on that bunch of outlaws over in the Chief Mountain country, east o' the Rockies…wasn't it?

"I was told you tuned 'em up real good—read 'em from the good book!"

"I wasn't alone Marshal, we did it together! Lynn here, this fine lady who is now my wife, helped me out…saved my life from that bunch as well."

The lawman was now smiling as he shook both their hands, and winked at Lynn. "If you two ever need a job, look me up…could sure use a couple o' good deputies."

"Thank you for the offer," Lynn replied, a happy smile was on her face. "We're heading over yonder to the Judith Basin country, planning on buying us some cows for our ranch up in the northern territories.

"Our spread is along the St. Mary's river, not far from the Montana border."

"Tell you what I'm going to do," the Marshal responded. "In appreciation of what you've done here today for the citizens of Fort Benton and the Territory of Montana—I've got something for you both." He felt in his vest pocket and brought out a pair of tin stars.

"These here badges are genuine, the real thing. I want you to take them with you, might come in handy in your travels. I am officially making you deputy marshals of the territory of Montana.

"I must insist that you use them honorably and wisely in the upholding of the laws of our great northwest?"

Though they were both smiling, they sensed the old lawman was plumb serious in his offer and the authority it would give them. "Don't rightly know how I can refuse an offer like this," the cowboy replied.

"Me too," Lynn was giggling when she spoke. "I never dreamed the girl from Lariat Cross would become a Deputy Marshal."

The Marshal perked right up. "Lariat Cross, you say! Ain't that the stompin' grounds of Matt Brannon, the old Canadian gun fighter?

"Met him several times, saw him in action too…had one o' the fastest draws I ever did see."

"Matt Brannon was my Grandpa," Lynn said, and became a little teary-eyed. "Taught me everything I know!"

"That explains it then, your shootin' from the hip and all. You were fast Deputy Bonner, mighty fast. Reckon ol' Grandpa Brannon would be mighty proud."

"Grandpa died five years ago." she said, struggling to hold back the tears. "I sure miss him, I surely do!"

"As far as I'm concerned we've got ourselves a deal! I do realize that you are ranching north of the border, and it might seem odd that I have insisted you become members of the U.S. Marshal service. Let's face it, yours is still a wild and wooly country, as is ours. No tellin' how many border hell-raisers you might be able to apprehend, for the benefit of both countries; 'sides, I will be calling on you both to ride down and help an ol' Marshal out now and then."

You both are good, the best two gunfighters I ever laid eyes on, excepting ol' Matt Brannon and his wife Lynn. And he was your teacher I understand."

"My grandma died giving birth to my mother," Lynn said. "I wasn't fortunate enough to know her—but I love her just the same."

"I'll get the paper work done pronto, and sent into headquarters. From this moment on, you both have the same authority as I do—and good luck to you both—it will be an honor to have you with us.

"You two will be a real asset—to both sides of the border!" the old lawman said. "By the way my name is Custis.

"U.S.Marshal Custis Dunne."

With that said the Marshal turned to go, the wounded trader in tow, and headed for the local crowbar hotel.

"Make way you folks!" the Marshal ordered, his voice rising by the minute. He was amazed at the crowd that had shown up, many of them fresh off the paddle wheeler which was now safely docked, lazy spirals of smoke and steam rising from a weather-faded stack.

Having just witnessed a real live episode in the taming of the old west, a cry arose from those that were there, "Three cheers for the new deputies—for a bustin' up this gang of killers. Come on everybody, join in!" A chill rippled down the spines of the cowboy and his new wife as they listened. "Hip-hip hooray! Hip-hip-hooray!" Hats and other items were hurled into the air as they listened to the ending.

"Hip-hip-hoo-rrray!"

* * *

High on the bluffs above the Missouri River, the Mormon wagon train came to a stop, their teams enjoying a brief rest from the tough climb up from the river settlement below. The Bonners were close by and rode over to the Bishop's wagon to bid them a last farewell.

The Bishop was sitting in the driver's seat, the reins of a four-horse hitch held in his sun-bronzed hands. Behind him, sunbonnets and all, sat his four daughters. Smiles as broad as the prairie were on their young rosy-cheeked faces. These were the same girls who had sung the beautiful hymn at the Bonner's wedding.

"We wish to thank you Brother and Sister Bonner for your assistance to us," the Bishop said. "and rescuing us from the evil crowd down at the river."

He was looking Will in the eye when next he spoke. "We were in dire need, boxed-in and surrounded by those pawns of the devil. We prayed for deliverance, and were doing so when you two rode in and saved us.

"May the good Lord in the heavens watch over and protect you both!"

Lynn offered him a warm smile and leaned from her saddle and gave him a hug. "You did us a great favor too, you know, marryin' us and all.

"We'll always remember this day…and what you did for us!"

With that said, one of the Bishop's daughters offered them a bag filled with fresh-baked cookies. "A gift for your wedding day…and what you did for us," she said.

"And thank you, thank you so very much."

The four beaming girls were standing beside the big tarp-covered wagon and once again began to sing. They were sure enough singing girls, and loved to do it. The song they sang was another old Mormon hymn; 'God Be with You Till We Meet Again'.

* * *

After escorting the Mormons out of the river town, and safely on their way for the northern territories, Lynn and her husband located Jenni who had been patiently waiting on the nearby prairie.

Reckon we'll cover some country before stoppin' to rest the hosses," Will said. "Should make another twenty miles 'fore dark!"

Giggling and so happy, Lynn said, "Just can't wait to sample these cookies…they smell so good." She was eating one, and then it was another. Passing the bag to Will, she spoke again, "They are so good Will, let us eat them right now. And that beautiful song, it has made me weepy—it sure enough has!

Brushing tears from her eyes she spoke again, "Sure wish Little Crow was here, he sure liked cookies, he sure enough did!"

In no time at all the Mormon cookies were no more. The two riders, Lynn and Will Bonner, had sure enjoyed this treat on the vast Montana prairie. They had even gave the Jenni mule some, who was chomping them down with much vigor

"Let's hit the trail darlin'." Lynn was giggling when she continued her talk. "Our wedding night will soon be here, remember?

"Reckon your new wife can hardly wait!"

Though they were both in their saddles, she leaned over and pulled his head close to hers. After a long passionate kiss she remarked, "Now we can ride after those cattle, Will Bonner. Mrs. Bonner is a rarin' to go."

Later that night, the stars were twinkling down on the cowboy and his girl. They no longer were apart, their blankets were now together as one.

Lynn was giggling and so happy. "Poor Jenni," she said, and stroked the mane of the little dun mule who was resting in the grass beside her. "She's all mixed up, can't figure out why there is just one bed now, instead of two."

Disturbing the solitude of the dark night a coyote sang a lonesome tune. Crunching on a handful of oats that Lynn had given her, Jenni settled in for a good nights rest. From the blankets beside her though, the mule's sharp ears could detect giggles, laughter and could even sense there were tears. She was happy to be here with Lynn and her cowboy, a cowboy whom she had finally accepted as the girl's permanent companion.

Then a peaceful quiet returned, all was well on the darkened prairie.

The girl from Lariat Cross was content, and so very happy. She had the makings of a fine cattle ranch, and soon would have the cattle to eat the grass that grew there. She had a new husband that she loved dearly, and who was smothering her with kisses at this very minute. Oh yes, she remembered…I almost forgot; I am now a U.S. Deputy Marshal too.

"I wonder what will happen next!"

* * *

Riding side by side, Will and Lynn Bonner were in high spirits, happy and healthy and reeking with the confidence of the young at heart. That they could face up to unforeseen peril had been proven many times in the past. Always they had faced whatever it might be, head on. Always they had respected and enforced the old ways—the Code of the West.

Their ride was taking them farther into the south, a region known as the Judith country, an unknown windswept prairie neither had ridden before. They would remember this ride as part of their quest after a herd of cows, and a cattle dealer Bonner knew as Harvey Logan. Somewhere ahead on the Montana prairie they would surely find him!

Their honeymoon, although they had not been exposed to the term before, was a happy time for them both. Enjoying life to the fullest, grateful for the old Mormon Bishop who had married them, and grateful they had been able to assist the Bishop's wagon train escape the gang who had them boxed in at the Fort settlement.

And the gunfight at the trading post in Fort Benton. They could have ridden on, never got themselves involved, but it was not their way. The Bonner's way was the 'Code of the West', to help the downtrodden, those who were helpless and unable to face the bad guys on their own.

That four hell raisers had been killed, two of them by her little carbine, was tough on Lynn—even though they had been forced into the fight. 'Shoot the bad men dead—before they do the same to you!' Grandpa Brannon's advice still rang in her ears. And it had been doing the same back on the doorsteps of the trading post by the river.

Both Bonner and Lynn knew the gunfight was sure to happen. It was face the bad guys head on, or watch the wagon train folks continue to suffer the humiliation and utter tyranny at the hands of the river front gang. To sit back and watch the Mormon youngsters go hungry, deprived of the staples of life they were so desperately in need of—was not their way.

The Bonner's way was embedded deeply in their souls. Generations of hardy ancestors were responsible for this, pushing with much vigor into the West, facing the uncertainty of a wild, new land sparsely populated by white men. There to greet them were the Indian, savage never-before-seen animals, and an often savage climate.

But they were winning, spreading far and wide across the land as they continued settling the West.

The blood of fighting warriors was in the veins of the cowboy and the girl, blood of a people struggling to survive in a wilderness country. Blood of a people that were pushing farther into the West, come hell or high water!

The days were hot and dusty, the trail continuing uphill and down following the contour of the land. It was an old-as-the-hills route much traveled by the buffalo, and the prairie tribes that hunted them for the survival of their people. Now used by the white man, the fur trapper, the seeker of gold and the cowboys who were new to this northern prairie.

After a long, dusty ride of fifty miles, the tall cowboy and his girl from Lariat Cross arrived in cattle country. Judith Basin was a broad, rolling plateau—plumb between two mountain ranges, the Little Belt and Big Snowy.

Stopping at Judith Gap, nothing more than a crossroads of several trails, they rode up to a large weather-bleached structure that reared out of the bleakness of the prairie. Surrounded by several log shacks and a scattering of corrals, the old two-story trading post was complete with a false front, and a hitching rail out front. A sign near the front door advertised 'EATS AND BOOZE'.

"Reckon we'll stop here," Will said. "Hire us a room and bed down for the night. Logan, the cattle buyer who put me wise to the cattle, is supposed to meet us here.

"Sure hope he hasn't given up on us and found another buyer!"

Located on the upper floor of the old rangeland inn, the room was clean and provided a welcome bed for Lynn. After sleeping on the ground these past weeks Will reckoned she had sure earned it. Besides she would be able to enjoy the luxury of hot water to soak in, and clean the trail dust from her beautiful hair.

Later, after they had both finished cleaning up they went downstairs to find some grub. They were sure enough hungry, and looked forward to eating stove-cooked food for a change.

Lynn was sparkling like a silver dollar, her hair casting a golden glow from the kerosene lamps that provided light for the old watering hole of

Judith country. Finding a table at the back of the room, the cowboy and the girl ordered their meal and sat back to wait for it to arrive.

"Sure not many *hombres* around tonight," Will drawled. "Must not be Saturday night yet—reckon the walls are sure a bouncin' when the cowboys come a whoopin' and a hollerin' into town!"

With her happy giggle, Lynn replied, "I'm so mixed up anymore I don't know what day it is, could be Saturday though."

The meal arrived and it sure tasted good. It was the specialty of the house, antelope steak, fried potatoes and even a big slab of apple pie. They were finishing up the tasty dessert when a stranger approached the table, a stranger to Lynn anyway.

Will looked up and flashed a smile. "Well hello Mr. Logan, reckoned you must o' got tired of waiting for us...we just rode in—bin a long ride.

"My riding partner here is my new wife.

"Lynn, I would like you to meet Mr. Logan, the *hombre* who is going to sell us those white-faced Hereford cows—that is if he still has them?"

"Pleased to meet you Mr. Logan," Lynn smiled. "Sure hope we can make a deal."

Logan was dressed much like a man of means, sporting a short-brimmed hat, a full black moustache, a vest with a gold chain leading to a slight bulge in one of the pockets, and a well-worn suit to match—leading down to his dusty boots.

"My pleasure Mrs. Bonner." the cattle buyer replied, with a tip of his hat.

Bonner's attention was drawn to a well-worn holster buckled around Logan's waist. It was a quick-draw outfit holding a fresh-oiled Colt .45 with plenty of cartridges to match. Bonner was some puzzled, he had heard of riggings like this, but up until now this was the first time he had ever witnessed one up close.

The quick-fire rigs were attached by a stud to a slotted plate on the wearer's belt, and could be fired by swiveling it from the hip, a deadly weapon to the unwary.

Reckon our cattle dealing friend is a gunfighter, he mused. Reckon Will Bonner best be a keeping his eyes open and his own gun loose in the holster. Never know what a *hombre* like this might be up to!

Pulling out a chair, Logan sat down and began to talk. "Yes, I've still got the longhorns, bin a holdin' 'em for you. We moved 'em north 'bout a week ago.

"I run outta grass here to hold 'em on, so trailed the herd up on the Wagon Box, a ranch on the far side of the Missouri...not far from the mining town of Landusky."

He fired up a cigar and offered one to the cowboy, who politely refused. "The herd, all 304 head of them, are branded for the trail and ready to move out. Reckon we can be there in two or three days ride—ninety miles as the crow flies."

The cowboy and the girl were somewhat disappointed in discovering the cattle were so far away, yet elated the old buyer was still willing to deal.

"Reckon we'll head north in the morning then," Will told him. "We'll pick up a few supplies here and then hit the trail."

Logan was chuckling when he replied, "Run on to your outfit in a corral out back, the Indian boy that was there said his name was Spotted Pony, and didn't act any too friendly like.

"Reckon the redskin's sure enough ridin' for the brand, didn't much want me a snoopin' around"

The cowboy and his wife looked at each other in disbelief, they were unable to believe his story about an Indian boy guarding their outfit. Yet, how did he know about the young Blood Indian boy who called himself Spotted Pony? The one who had treated Lynn with respect back at Writing On Stone, and saved her life from the choking gag that had been stuffed in her mouth.

The last they had seen of him, he was riding back to the reservation, Crazy Dog's body lashed securely across the bare back of a little mustang pony. They never spoke, reckoned there was time for that later, after this business with Logan was over. They sure didn't need him a prying into their personal affairs.

Logan had noticed Bonner eyeing up his fast-draw outfit, had covered it with his jacket, he appeared deep in thought. He was nursing a beer when he spoke. "Reckon I've changed my mind. Instead of riding hoss-back all the way to the Wagon Box, think I'll ride north and catch the stage, up yonder aways—have the herd ready to move out by the time you folks ride in.

"I'll leave right now, be there in time to catch the northbound stage." He downed his beer, arose and left the trading post.

Appearing deep in thought, Will never spoke for a spell, "Things sure don't appear as they should Lynn, reckon Logan is up to something—something he isn't willing to share. Did you hear him mention longhorns?

"Our deal was for Hereford cattle—a new breed being introduced from England. The big ranchers are buying up all they can lay their hands on. Their claim is the white faces are beef animals that produce more roasts and steaks than a longhorn, mighty fine eating too.

"I reckon he's trying to pull a fast one on us!

"And his story about finding Spotted Pony with our hosses, seems a little far-fetched to me, reckon I'll go check things out."

"My feelings exactly," Lynn said. I'm sure tired Will, take me to our room first, that bed up those stairs is sure begging me to come."

* * *

Out back of the rangeland inn near a tumble-down corral, the cowboy approached his *remuda* with caution. The horses were quiet and appeared settled in for the night, the only light was the brilliance of the stars casting a faint glow from high in the sky.

Greeting him with a welcome jargon of horse talk was his saddle horse, sensing the approach of the cowboy, and was eagerly waiting by the weathered structure for Bonner to arrive and scratch his ears. To run his fingers through his tangled mane; and talk to him, as was his way. The horse and the cowboy were good friends, they had traveled many trails together, had endured many hardships and both respected each other to no end.

"How ya doin' old *compadre*," Brannon drawled, breaking the silence of the dark night. "Seen any boogers around—them big yaller cats—maybe even a bear?"

Brannon had been scratching the big red horse's ears, when he felt a change, Red's head raised to look beyond the cowboy, his ears now on the alert, pointing straight up toward the stars.

A chill rolled through the cowboy's lanky frame. He sensed something was behind him, and so did Red. Six-gun in hand, Brannon turned and spoke, "Who's there—speak up before I start a shootin'"

He wasn't sure, sensed it more than anything. But was certain he could see movement, a shadow and it was moving. The chill returned to play an eerie game up and down Bonner's spine, he spoke again, his voice rising, "Not a going to tell you again—speak up you hear?"

The shadow moved in close, Bonner's finger was all set to pull the trigger when he suddenly lowered the big .44 and waited. This one is human, his mind told him, not a ghost or a haunt on the prowl as he and the red horse might have thought.

Bonner suddenly recognized the scent and knew this one was an Indian. This cannot be Little Crow, he reasoned, knowing that he had laid the Nez Perce lad to rest high in the talking cliffs. "It has to be his ghost then, a wandering around in the night as was Crow's way!

"Sure wish my Lynn was here—she would know for sure—reckon she was the only one who could handle the lad, and he minded her too."

Will Bonner was not superstitious, but it was times like this that made him wonder! Was it a spirit of the night, or was it human?

And then the cattle buyer's words flashed through his mind '…an Indian lad is there—said his name was Spotted Pony…"

Bonner was getting riled up, couldn't help it he reckoned. "Is that you Spotted Pony? Step up close so's I can see you—don't much like a talkin' to a shadow!

"I come mighty close to gunnin' you down!"

"*Oki*," a voice sounded from the shadows. Sure sounds like Lynn's cowboy to me, Bonner reasoned, I must be a dealin' with a ghost after all. The thought no sooner flashed across his mind, when an Indian lad closely built like Little Crow walked in to stand beside the cowboy. He was a little taller and a few pounds heavier than Crow, but there in the shadows it was hard to tell the difference.

A cold chill again came to pester the cowboy's spine. "I reckon I'm a loosin' it sure, he thought, must be Crow's spirit a standing here—or else I am seeing a ghost!

Once again a guttural reply, *"Oki,"* a Blackfoot phrase that Little Crow was so fond of using.

All an amazed Bonner could do was stand there and listen to a tirade of jargon bursting forth from the young Indian brave—a mixture of Blood Indian words and phrases, broken English and a smattering of other things.

Struggling to interpret, Bonner was doing his best to understand what the lad was telling him. And he was the same Spotted Pony, who had taken Crazy Dog's body back to the reservation.

While making the long ride, he had had a dream, he told the cowboy. It was a vision from those up in the sky. Little Crow was there and told him to find the girl and the cowboy, to stay with them and help them bring the cows with long horns back to their St Mary's river ranch.

He also pledged Spotted Pony to a promise, to guard the girl known as Lynn Bonner, keep her safe and give his life for her if necessary.

All of these things he told Lynn's husband, who knew it would take him the rest of the night to unravel it all.

Knowing Spotted Pony, much like Little Crow would have done—cat-nap under the stars guarding the horses. Bonner returned to the old inn and found a wide awake Lynn, up and dressed, buckling on her six-gun, getting ready to go and find her husband.

"Oh, Will!" she exclaimed, a smile quickly erasing the frown that had been there. "I thought something bad must have happened to you, staying away so long!

"I was coming to find you, reckoned you must have had trouble with that mean looking cattle buyer and, and needed me to help out."

"Thanks a bunch for your concern Lynn, I'm a sure a needin' some shuteye, let's go to bed—I'll tell you all about it in the morning.

* * * Chapter Five * * *

They arose early, and one more time Lynn was able to enjoy a warm bath, wash her hair and attend to the morning rituals that are a must for those of the gentler sex; she never knew when she would be able to enjoy such a luxury again.

After a hearty breakfast, the two deputy marshals left the inn and walked out back where their horses were waiting. It was there they discovered the young Indian brave sitting cross-legged on the ground, a time-worn blanket wrapped around his bare shoulders.

"*Oki!*" he greeted and offered Lynn a smile, still not quite certain how to greet the big cowboy, knowing that it was he, Spotted Pony who had attempted to bash his brains out in the not so distant past. Lynn returned his greeting with a trace of a smile, not yet accepting the fact that he was here to take the place of Little Crow, whom was practically one of her family back at Lariat Cross.

And as Will had told her, take over Crow's self-appointed duties as her guardian, more so at night when the evil ones were on the prowl. How did Spotted Pony know these things?

Spotted Pony arose, and as Bonner was preparing the horses for the trail, began to talk to Lynn. Being too bashful back at the talking cliffs, he had not told her that he could speak a smattering of the English words, and knew enough of the strange talk that she could understand what he was saying.

The Bonners were not familiar with these border Indians, but they did know that the Blackfoot and Bloods were cousins. The Bloods being a clan of the mighty Blackfoot nation, and that they all spoke the same language. The Blackfoot were living south of the border in the United States, the Bloods were living north of the border in Canada—the two reservations less than twenty miles apart.

"Don't reckon it matters much what country they live in, they all talk the same lingo," Bonner told his wife.

"To me they are Blackfoot, a rowdy bunch when riled!"

They would now be able to converse with one another. She could tell by his talk, which included many Blood words and phrases, and an abundance of sign language, that he would be easier to talk to than Crow had been.

He expressed his sympathy that Crow had been killed by Crazy Dog, and also added one more time, that he would be happy to be her guardian as Crow had been. One of Lynn's smiles would be his reward, although he never told her that.

Once again a hint of a smile was on her lips. She would never forgive him for his attempt at killing her husband, but respected the lad for his wilderness apology, and his attempt at atoning for what had happened back at the talking cliffs,

Yet, how did he know that Crow had been her self-appointed guardian? Lynn would have to wait and see.

After three days of tough, dusk-to-dawn riding, the Bonner outfit rode into Landusky, a wild and wooly mining town nestled on the southern tip of the Little Rockies. Lynn's cowboy took one look and sensed the place was trouble waiting to happen.

Reining in at a livery stable, he reckoned they should look around for a place to spend the night, and hunt-up a good supper.

Spotted Pony was content to sleep with the horses and gnaw on jerky. As long as he had plenty of this hardy staple in his medicine bag, he was a happy Indian. Besides, he would spend most of the night prowling in the shadows anyway. Whenever these young lads found time to sleep—no one would ever know.

The main thoroughfare of the town was nothing more than a winding trail through the pines, a scattering of hastily erected log structures on either side. Saddlebags slung over their shoulders, and rifles in hand, the newlyweds walked up the trail hunting supper and a night's lodging.

"Reckon these here mining folks are sure a whiskey drinkin' bunch," Will said. Nine out of ten businesses they passed were frontier waterholes of the crudest kind.

One enterprising pair had a tarp-covered wagon backed in next to the trail, ladling rot-gut from out of a filth-encrusted barrel; shooing away a horde of yellow jackets as they did so. Attracted to the backwoods-brewed concoction by the smell, this venomous member of the wasp family was there in force, as well as all his friends and neighbors.

The illicit pair was offering it for sale by the coffee cup full. "Only five silver dollars will buy you a shot o' this here barleycorn." one of them chanted, waving an old tin cup high in the air. "Best buy in the little Rockies—guaranteed to put a bounce in your step, it will!" Unseen by the tarp, the wagon was bulging at the seams with barrels filled to the brim with the poisonous brew.

Landusky was humming like a beehive, all sorts of humanity on the move—more than a few were none too friendly looking—towards Lynn and her cowboy husband. Bonner came close to losing his temper over the way several of the woman-hungry jaspers leered at Lynn. He reckoned there wasn't a real gentleman left in the Little Rockies.

But most backed off when spotting the rifle she had tucked under her arm and the cowboy who was escorting her; equally armed and looking plenty salty. Mumbling words of unknown origin, the female-starved wretches pushed into the crowd and continued on their way.

"This place gives me the creeps," Lynn said, holding his hand as tight as she could. "Let's get outta here!"

"Reckon it's a wide-open boom town," Bonner replied. "No tellin' what will happen 'fore the sun rises again."

On up the trail they walked until spotting a sign tacked to a tree, *Widow Jones—Home Cooked Grub*. "Reckon we'll go over yonder and try out the widow's food," the cowboy suggested. A well used trail indicated the widow's diner must be a popular place to eat.

"Sounds good to me," the girl giggled. "Your wife is hungry enough to eat a buffalo all by herself."

After a delicious home cooked supper, the Widow Jones asked them if they had a place to sleep. "Reckon we were plannin' on rolling our blankets under the pines," Bonner responded, "back at the corrals where our hosses are staying."

"Tell you what!" she said. "I'll get no sleep tonight—with the mining crowd coming off shift at midnight and all—this hard rock bunch will be hungry as bears. Sure keeps me a hustling most of the night to feed them all.

"It's sure hard work though, but they're a good paying bunch—gives me a decent living since my husband died in a cave-in at the Lone Star mine."

Offering them a smile as broad as the great outdoors, she added, "You two can use my bed tonight, out back is a small log cabin I call my home."

"Thank you," Lynn said, and gave her a warm hug.

With a mischievous twinkle in her eyes, the widow said, "You two take them six guns off, 'fore you crawl in my bed…you hear?"

Settled in the widow's bed, complete with a feather tick, Lynn was giggling, "Sure beats sleeping on the hard prairie."

"Feels real fine Lynn, first time I've ever tried one out." But circumstances were such that the cowboy and the girl would get very little sleep.

When the miners came off shift it was like a Fourth of July celebration. Hoots and hollers, the constant hum of talking men, the odd outburst of profane language and gunfire echoing into the night.

Tossing and turning in the widow's bed, Lynn and Will were awake when a knock sounded at the door. It was well on toward sunrise Will figured, when the widow stepped in and asked him to come out and help her. Will tossed back the blankets and, sitting on the edge of the bed donned his stetson, and pulled on his pants and spurred-boots, in that order. "What's wrong Ma-am—what's with all the hullabaloo a going on out there?"

The good widow was sobbing. "Three of the wild bunch, Mr. Bonner—all liquored up—the cowardly bullies have pistol-whipped three of the miners, for no reason at all.

"One of them just a boy, he's hurt real bad…don't reckon he's going to make it."

"Guess it's time to put this on," he said, reaching in his shirt pocket and bringing out the tin star. "Any law around these parts?" he asked, pinning the deputy badge on his shirt for all to see.

"No! Very little that is. There's talk among the miners of a vigilante group being organized, so far it has been just talk though."

"You stay here Mrs. Jones, with Lynn. I'll feel a whole bunch better if you're both out of the way."

"Don't you go without me Will Bonner, you hear?" Lynn exploded, and had more to say. "I'm a coming to back your play!" She was dressed now, and buckling on her six-gun preparing for battle. With her saddle carbine in hand, sparks were still dancing in her eyes when she spoke, "I'm wearing a tin star too—remember!"

Knowing that time was of the essence, Deputy Will Bonner reluctantly agreed. "Stay behind me, darlin'Lynn. "No tellin' what we'll be a runnin' in to."

Most folks had been scared out of the diner before Bonner walked in the back door. He spotted the hell-raisers right off seated at the far end of the room, heads together drinking from a jug of liquor—ignoring the widow's sign—*No Liquor Allowed*—. They were all smiling as if the killing of a young boy was an everyday occurrence, they appeared to be bragging about it too. Stepping inside he knew Lynn was close behind, the widow as well who vanished into her kitchen.

A young lad, sixteen at most was down; blood staining the plank floor where he had fallen. Two men huddled over the boy, bloodied themselves, and immediately stood up, tears streaming down their whiskered cheeks. They spotted the tin stars and never spoke, waiting to watch the drama unfold. One of them nodded towards the hell-raisers.

"What's goin' on here!" Bonner roared, and moved farther into the room, his eyes never wavered from the table where they sat. "Push away from that table, hands in the air—you hear?"

Lynn scurried over to the boy, knelt beside him and gently felt his face and pulse. Her face was as white as the linen on the widow's tables. She looked up at Bonner. "There's no pulse…the boy is dead.

"He never had a chance—his skull is busted wide open!" Once again a miner nodded in the direction of the hell-raisers.

Lynn was standing now, slightly behind her husband. Both walked towards the far table. A hush settled across the widow's diner, a hush as quiet as death.

"You are three cowardly killers!" Bonner roared, his voice was terrible to hear. "I'm not telling you again…move!" Lynn was even startled, she had never heard her husband speak this way before.

"Stand up! Be mighty careful how you handle them shootin' irons!"

"I'm arresting you for the murder o' this boy you miserable sidewinders pistol-whipped to death."

They all three turned to face Will Bonner, one had a sneer spreading across his whiskered face, the other two were waiting to see. "Well I'll be dam-ned, if it ain't a kid lawman…a wearin' a tin star…too.

"Sure didn't reckon there was a lawman north of Alder Gulch."

The hard-cases remained where they sat, Deputy Bonner moved closer to the table, another Deputy Bonner was by his side.

Realizing there were now two deputies instead of one, and still ignoring Will Bonner's orders, the whiskered spokesman said, "I see you got a pard with you deputy, a right purty gal too, sure never seen the likes 'fore tonight. With that said he tipped the jug, and took several giant swallows.

Uttering a curse, that Lynn tried not to hear, the cowboy drew his big .44 and pulled the trigger. The moonshine jug exploded like a bomb, showering the arrogant one with whiskey and shattered pottery.

Off balance, he tipped over backwards and clawing at his six-gun lunged to his feet roaring mad. "Don't reckon we're going to let a pair o'—kid deputies—tell us what to do!" Then all three went for their guns. They hadn't planned on following Bonner's orders to start with.

Gunfire erupted in the old log diner. The loud bark of gunfire, the acrid smell of fresh-ignited gunpowder and the death scream of a cowardly killer, all three combined to bring to a close this drama in the widow's diner.

The mouthy one was down, howling in horror over a bullet hole through the wrist of his shooting hand, his six-gun still spinning across the floor. The second one was dead, a 30-30 slug buried deep in his chest. The third one—repentant now, was standing, arms reaching for the stars; his ashen face full of horror. He had just looked old Nick himself in the face, and didn't care for what he saw.

Keeping his eyes pealed ahead, Bonner said, "You all right Lynn? Reckon we've read this bunch from the good book...an eye-for-an-eye, like my Mom used to read us kids from her beloved bible."

"I'm fine Will, though I think I've killed another man. Don't reckon I'll ever make it into heaven—they sure won't want me up there!"

One of the pistol-whipped miners had moved in, removed the killer's guns and tied up the two who were still alive.

"Lynn darling, I want you to know I'm sure proud of you. We were only enforcing the Territorial law of Montana as we've sworn to do. Marshal Custus Dunne will be mighty pleased, he sure enough will. As far as St. Peter is concerned, I'm sure he must have heaved a sigh of relief that you were not gunned down.

"Reckon there'll be a medal waiting for you...when it's your turn to cross over the Great Divide."

Wiping away a tear, Lynn took her husband's hand. "Thank you Will, I sure do love you."

A crowd was now gathering at the diner. Along with steaming pots of coffee, Mrs. Jones was cooking bacon and eggs, and serving the food as fast as she could. The two bodies were carried outdoors and laid under the pines, the innocent young boy and the bully who had beat him to death. The two remaining outlaws were marched outside as well.

"Hang 'em...hang the scurvy-ridden devils," the cry swept throughout the crowd, that was now swarming into the clearing to watch the big show. "This bunch o' outlaws has got to be taught a lesson—bin a ridin' roughshod over us long enough!"

"Lynch 'em! Lynch the gol-darn killers!"

Ropes were now showing up, ropes with a hangman's noose already in place. Deputy Bonner reckoned his part in this drama was not yet over. "Hold it, you folks!" he shouted, drawing his Colt and firing several rounds into the air.

"Just hold on a blasted minute! I can't allow you folks a goin' off half-cocked. The law must be in control here—we will hold a trial—legal like."

An uneasy quiet settled over the little glade in the pines. All were interested in what the young deputy had to say, reckoned the least they could do is listen.

"That's better!" Bonner said, relaxing a bit. Lynn was backing him up. Her carbine was held with unwavering hands, all set to assist her husband in this touchy business. "Is there a judge here?" he asked.

A buzz swept through the crowd, neighbor looking at neighbor, not really knowing for sure if there was such a person in the camp. Then an elderly, whiskered gentleman stepped forward and spoke, "Deputy—Deputy Bonner, could I have a word with you." Neither Deputy was certain of which of them he was referring to.

"I was once a territorial judge in Nebraska—'fore we came up here a hunting gold. I'll be glad to help out."

"Best news I've heard all day. Lynn, will you take the judge here and pick us out a jury. Reckon it will save Marshal Dunne the trouble of ridin' up here and workin' it out.

"We're a going to have a trial right here, 'bout an hour from now!"

While Lynn was busy with the Judge, Bonner walked into the diner and ordered breakfast—bacon and eggs and all the trimmings. He ordered the same for Lynn, as soon as she was finished with the jury business. The two pistol-whipped miners, one of them the father of the dead boy, followed him in and sat at his table.

"Don't know how we'll ever be able to show our thanks to you two deputies," one of them said, watching Bonner eat his meal.

He began to talk, and mentioned the three troublemakers were thought to be members of a splinter group of the Hole in the Wall gang under the leadership of Kid Curry. Curry, he said, is one rough, tough outlaw, fast as greased lightning with his six-gun too. He felt concerned that trouble was still in the offing, that Curry would be seeking revenge against the miners, and the law—namely the two deputies.

"Where does this Curry *hombre* hang out at?" Bonner asked.

"When he's not at his hideout over in the Missouri Breaks he spends a lot of time at a ranch west of here, the Wagon Box spread. Some folks think he probably owns it.

"He is known around the mining camps as Logan…Harvey Logan, a livestock dealer—supplying the gold camps here in the Little Rockies with beef. Logan's pretty much on the move, buying and selling cattle all the time."

"Well I'll be a gol-darn maverick!" Deputy Bonner muttered, reckon that's the last straw. His mind was in a turmoil, sure never figured he and Lynn had been dealing with a known outlaw and cattle rustler.

What to do now?

Lynn arrived back at the diner bubbling over with excitement. She was pleased there were other aspects of wearing a tin star besides gun-fighting and shooting people. The widow Jones brought her a heaping plate of breakfast. It looked mighty good to the girl who was plumb starving by now, this deputy business sure used up a lot of energy, she reckoned.

Talking while she ate her meal, Lynn told her husband what she and the Judge had accomplished. "We found nine men who consented to act as a jury, good ones too.

"Also, the Judge suggested that before we leave Landusky a lawman should be appointed to keep law and order here in the gold camps."

"Sounds real good Lynn, was thinkin' the same thing myself. Any idea of who might handle the job?"

"The judge suggested the father of the slain boy—he appears to be willing—and honest too.

"We might have to give him a few pointers in handling a gun," she giggled. "In fact he didn't even own one. I gave him one of the outlaw's shooting rigs, and an old Henry rifle too."

Lynn wasn't finished her talking yet. "Will, before I forget to tell you, I sent two letters out on the stage this morning. One of them is to Marshal Dunne at Fort Benton letting him know what has been happening here. The other is to my mother back at Lariat Cross."

She was dead serious when she looked at Will. "I reckoned she should know her only daughter is now happily married to you, Will Bonner—and is also a deputy marshal—who along with her new husband, are both packing tin stars under the jurisdiction of Marshal Custus Dunne."

Smiling, the cowboy leaned over and kissed his charming wife. "Thanks a bunch Lynn, should have thought of it myself. Reckon ol' Custus and your Mom will be mighty grateful to find out what we've been doing!"

Fortified by the presence of the two deputies, the trial went off without a hitch all legal-like and above board. The outlaws were found guilty of murder and mayhem, and sentenced to be hung from the branch of a lightning-slashed pine, right there in the widow's back yard.

At the conclusion of this macabre dance of death, the bodies were pronounced dead and lowered to the ground. Then all four of the corpses, including the young boy, were taken farther up the mountain and interred in the camp's boothill.

It was only then the Judge called a meeting, and with the unanimous backing of all present, a new deputy marshal of the gold camps was sworn in by Will and Lynn Bonner. He was a miner known to all as Pike Landusky

With the Judge and new deputy paying close attention, the cowboy and the girl gave them last minute instructions on keeping the peace, and advised them to dispatch by stage a report to Fort Benton—in care of U.S. Marshal Custis Dunne. He should know of the gunfight, the hangings, and the newly appointed law officials that Deputies Lynn and Will Bonner are responsible for—a welcome presence of security to the citizens of the mining camps.

* * *

A prairie breeze blew gently across the land, bringing with it a pleasant scent of bunchgrass, wild flowers and sun-ripened sage. A curlew hovered high above the trail crying a shrill, lonely tune, assuring his nesting mate the passing riders offered no danger to their hidden home in the sage.

From far behind, where the tall pines grow and the miners toil for gold, echoed a forlorn call of a whippoorwill. A plaintive cry…to the Spirits perhaps…of spilt blood in the widow's diner, of fresh graves in the pines!

Lynn Bonner shuddered at the sound! "Them blasted whip-per's sure give me the creeps," she told her husband. "more so at night, when all is dark—and one is alone. Seems like they're a warning us of dangers that lie ahead…of the mysteries of the unknown!"

"Didn't reckon you was superstitious darlin'. Why, them little critters won't harm you none, they keep me company sometimes when I'm ridin' alone."

"Just the same Will Bonner, one of them cried half the night—it was the night before Grandpa Brannon died!"

Confident that a tough job had been accomplished, the Bonner outfit was on the move, riding away from the Little Rockies and the challenges they had been forced to face.

Spotted Pony was back with them now, riding drag behind the packhorse—both were happy to be back on the trail once again.

Pointing into the west, the Bonner outfit was heading to a watershed that was shaped eons ago on the southern perimeter of the Bears Paw Mountains. It was here on Cow Creek, they had been told they would find the Wagon Box spread; and the elusive white faced cattle they had been searching for.

As they rode, the sun high overhead, Will related to his attractive partner what he had discovered about the man they knew as Logan. "Sure don't know what to do Lynn—reckon we've bin dealing with a pretty salty *hombre*—Kid Curry, they tell me!

"Chances are the English cows we've been dealing for aren't his to sell. Sounds as if they could be rustled stock he has moved up here from that Judith country.

"He's a slick cuss all right, rustling and selling cattle…and making a fortune from doing it."

Lynn remained silent, she appeared deep in thought. Several minutes passed before she spoke. Finally she gave a sigh, and looked across at her husband. "Will darling, I don't really know how to tell you this, I really don't. I want to go home, back to my little cabin by the river.

"I'm sure tired of all this riding…and gun fighting and riding some more—from can see to can't see—for days on end! Why don't we forget about the cattle and go back to our ranch."

Will never answered, attempting to digest what she had just told him.

"We'll find more cows somewhere Will, cows that haven't been rustled from some hard-up nesters struggling to feed their families!"

Unable to voice a reply, silence was heavy as they rode. After a bit he spoke. "This will be a tough decision for me Lynn—reckon I know how you feel. Give me some time to mull it over.

"Besides that thievin' devil still has my two hundred dollar down payment—I reckon it's a lost cause now—this cowboy was a gullible sucker sure!"

Later, several miles down the old buffalo trail, he told her his feelings were the same as hers. He thought they should stop at the Wagon Box though, and tell Logan they were no longer interested; besides it was on the way back to the St. Mary's River and Lynn's ranch.

She fired up right quick. "Listen to me Will Bonner…I am not going to tell you again, you hear?

"It is not my ranch anymore! Since our marriage—our union for life—it is our ranch! What is mine is yours, what is yours is mine! Share and share alike!

Will's head was hanging low, reckoned he deserved the tongue-lashing from his beautiful wife. "Sorry Lynn, I plumb didn't realize what I was a sayin'. Sure goin' to take some getting' used to, sharing a wonderful ranch with a wonderful girl!"

Lynn forgave him and reached over and took his hand, gave it a squeeze and watched him look up and smile. She smiled along with him, they both knew their little spat was over and done with.

Reining to a halt on a bluff overlooking Cow Creek, they looked down on the Wagon Box buildings and corrals. It was a bitter disappointment to see a corral full of Texas longhorns, not the white faced cattle they had been expecting. About a dozen riders were hard at work wrangling and sorting the cattle, hazing them from one pen into another.

Their broncs were standing beside each other, the two young ranchers holding hands, as was their way. Lynn looked at her husband, tears flooding her eyes, knowing he must be bitterly upset over the absence of the English cows

"Well darlin', our suspicions were right," he said. "Our white faced cows are nothing more than a fairy tale—told to us by a lying, thieving skunk.

"Reckon you and Spotted Pony should stay here Lynn, crawl off Boots, relax and have a rest. I won't be long, should be back in no time at all."

Lynn was too trail-weary to protest being left behind, besides she could watch the corrals from her position on the bluff. "Hurry back Will darlin', the coffee will be hot by the time you get back."

Plunging off the bluff, then skidding to the valley floor in a shower of dust, rocks and debris, the big red horse and the cowboy were showing-off their range-savvy, a difficult maneuver at best. "I knew you could do it Red," the cowboy said, praising his horse, and the feat they had just accomplished.

Riding on toward the corrals, Will noticed there were now more riders than he first thought, one of them sure looked familiar. Reining in at the cattle pens he was plumb stunned. There, mounted on a sweat-stained bronc sat a smiling Custis Dunne.

"Sure good to see you Deputy Bonner," he said, riding over to shake his hand. "Was a hopin' we would find you here."

Marshal Dunne began to talk and couldn't be stopped. All Will Bonner could do was sit in the saddle and listen.

"While you folks were away after your longhorns here, I had the telegraph wires a hummin'—found out about this man Logan—his cattle rustling activities, and more important yet; that he is Kid Curry, once a top gun in the Hole In The Wall gang.

"The son-of-a-gun got to big fer his britches, interfering with the boss's orders and all. Why, 'twas ol' Butch Cassidy himself who put the run on him good and proper like!

"A mighty salty *hombre*, Curry is, quicker than a scalded cat with a six-gun.

"Word drifted down to Fort Benton of big trouble at the gold camps," Dunne continued his talk. "It appeared some of Curry's bunch had taken over the camp, a running wild; beatings, killings and all the rest. And of two young deputy marshals, a pair of straight-shooting newly-weds, who between the two of them—were putting the run on this nest of thieves and confidence men."

Will Bonner sat his saddle in the noonday sun, both hands on the buckskin-wrapped horn, listening to what the old lawman had to say. Reckoned he should be polite and hear him out. He already knew most of what was being told him, yet it pleased him to hear the words spoken by his new friend, Marshal Custis Dunne.

"As I was saying before, a dispatch rider arrived at the Fort with the news. With no singing wires strung-up this way yet, I was getting mighty edgy, so rounded up a posse and we put spurs to our broncs.

"I stopped the stage about forty-miles south o' hear, was told the news and given Lynn Bonner's letter—she laid everything out real plain, explained all that had happened, including the gun fight, the court of law and the hangings. Best report I've ever received from one of my Deputies."

The old Marshal was looking Will Bonner in the eyes, and he was as proud as a mother hen with a brood of new chicks. "My new Deputies," he added, "even organized the law in Landusky, a real honest-to-goodness court of law, complete with a judge and jury. And the most important thing of all, appointed a new U.S. Deputy Marshal. I'm mighty proud of you and Lynn. Reckon it has saved Montana Territory a whole bunch of time and money!"

When Dunne and his posse arrived at the Wagon Box, a gunfight ensued, three outlaws were killed and several wounded; the rest took off for parts unknown, including Kid Curry!

The Wagon Box was a perfect front for his rustling ventures, the three hundred head of longhorns were indeed stolen from different owners in the Judith Basin country. Dunne assured the cowboy, that after contacting the owners, the longhorns were still for sale. They were his to buy if he still wanted them. Payment would be sent to the respective owners.

"Marshal Dunne, I must tell you about these longhorns, it is a sad story I reckon. My deal with Harvey Logan was for them new-fangled white-faced cows from England, not these rustled longhorns you see here.

He took me for a greenhorn sucker, insisted he had spent considerable time and money a gathering them up in small bunches wherever he could find them. I never saw the Herefords as he called them, said he had 'em tucked away in a safe place—so's rustlers wouldn't get their hands on them!

I reckoned I had hit the jackpot, could make a fortune breeding them; selling good blooded bulls and such. The slick talking son-of-a-gun took me for a sucker all right, a gullible, lone riding cowboy.

And my two hundred dollar down payment, ten double eagles it was, I've lost it as well!"

The two friends sat on their horses in silence, Custis Dunne knew how his deputy must feel and respected his feelings. Finally, offering a smile as broad as the prairie, Will began to talk. "We'll take 'em off your hands, the only reason we rode down here in the first place is to buy us some cattle.

"We'll keep a lookin' and find us some white-faced bulls, should cross real good with these here longhorns—sure can't wait to let Lynn know!"

"By the way Deputy Bonner, where's my other sharp-shooting deputy?"

"Up yonder, on top of that high bluff a waitin' for us. Come and join us, the coffee should be hot by now—reckon Lynn and I have a lot to tell you!"

Custis Dunne, an old lawman long past the age of retirement, crawled down from his horse and began stretching his aching muscles. "I hate to tell you this, Will," he said, and walked around some. "I'm a gettin' old—give me a few minutes to work the kinks outta my joints.

"Must be pride that keeps me a doin' this job, bin thirty years since I pinned on the badge back in Wyoming—I was a young whippersnapper then, and full of get up and go—reckoned I could take on anything that came along.

"I was good with a gun too, still am except for my dimming eyes."

Bonner knew the old timer was stalling for time, his old body pleading for a sit down. "Tell you what Custis, ride with me up to Lynn's fire, reckon her coffee will sure hit the spot—make you feel a whole bunch better!"

Custis agreed, and after crawling back into the saddle, followed Bonner up the steep escarpment. "Must be pride," he mumbled, both hands hanging on to the saddle horn.

"Pride! All an ol' lawman has left of his past, a stubborn, ingrained trait that Custis Dunne has no control over!"

* * * Chapter Six * * *

High on a wooded bluff overlooking Cow Creek, the enticing scent of fresh-brewed coffee was strong in the air of Lynn's makeshift camp. Sitting Indian style by a small twig fire, Lynn Bonner and her new native cowhand were patiently waiting for the return of Lynn's cowboy husband. A breeze swooped down from the high places, scattering sparks from the fire, and nudging the coffee scent onward into the surrounding pine forest.

It was quiet here, and peaceful too. Lynn liked it this way. She was in no mood for talk, hadn't felt her old self lately. I'm just tired she reckoned and sure looking forward to going home. The St. Mary's River valley is God's country to me, it sure enough is.

She had rested her tired body some, only to start fretting over the absence of her husband. He should be back, she reasoned, unless he has run into trouble with the cattle buyer they knew as Logan. She was hoping he would return soon. She was sure anxious to head back to the territories and her cabin home by their beautiful river.

Unknown to Lynn who was deep in her thoughts, Spotted Pony became uneasy. He slid closer to Lynn, large obsidian-hued eyes peering intently into the pines "Bad cowboys...are here!" he said, a serious concern was evident in his subdued talk.

"Evil spirits bring them to your fire—they wish for someone to kill.

"Bad medicine! Bad medicine, for Missy Lynn!"

It was then Lynn realized the Indian boy was warning her of something. She shook off the reverie that had taken over her mind, and was more than ready to listen.

"What did you say Spotted Pony? Reckon my mind was wandering around some." A chill of caution was now stumbling back into her mind.

"They are hiding in the pines—Tin Stars are hunting them for stealing the long horned ones." He then signed down off the bluff to the cattle pens located but a stone-throw from Cow Creek.

A cold chill rippled down the girl's spine, a sensation of terror that would not go away. Suddenly, as if on cue from Pony's warning, a voice sounded from beyond camp. An arrogant voice that reeked with authority, one she had been exposed to in the not so distant past.

"Keep your hands away from that shootin' iron Deputy Bonner!

"I'm a comin' in for a cup of coffee, and to palaver with a beautiful lady." Gun in hand, none other than Kid Curry walked into the small clearing. He advanced to the fire.

"Pour me a cup!" he roared. "No tricks, you hear?"

Lynn was terrified at first, at his sudden appearance, by the rude manner in which he was talking to her; and then a seething anger entered her mind. Why is he acting this way? What has he done to my husband who should be here with me by now?

"You and ol' Kid Curry, Deputy Bonner, are going to take us a ride," he continued to intimidate her with his bravado ways.

"I'm plumb fed up with you and that deputy husband of yours meddling in my affairs. Seems like the law has taken over the Little Rockies...ain't a fittin' or proper place to make a livin' in anymore!"

He was sneering when he spoke again. "Maybe that new husband o' yours will be willing to listen—willing to bargain for his wife—who I'm a taking with me"

Lynn was sure scared and plumb ashamed. She had let her guard down, been caught unawares sitting by her own cooking fire! She now realized she had foolishly ignored an important part of old Grandpa Brannon's school of survival. All of his dedicated instructions, all of those precious hours of love and concern for his only grand daughter, and now this!

Her soul was in torment! What could she do now? Why did this happen? Shrugging away a surging panic, Lynn knew that she must not sit here meek as a lamb being led to slaughter! It wasn't her way—it wasn't Grandpa Brannon's way—to give up her guns without a struggle.

The time was long past to wish she had been more alert, to wish she had been her old cautious self. It was the present she must think of. Lynn Bonner must dig deep into her grandpa's lode of knowledge, of which she had been given, and figure out how to get out of this mess she now found herself in.

By now several men had joined Logan, all to a man eager to drink a cup of the girl's coffee. "Sure smelled good out there in the pines," one of them said. "I'm gonna pour me a cup 'fore we go."

"No time for drinkin' coffee," Curry roared.

"Time we was moving out, 'fore that fool posse shows up!"

Spotted Pony had not spoken, like a shadow he arose from the ground and clawed for his six-gun, only to be struck down from behind by the butt-end of a rifle.

The outlaws hadn't spotted Lynn's .30-30, which was tucked snuggly beside her. Horrified at the way Spotted Pony was beaten down, and he was trying to help her, she gripped the rifle in both hands and sprang to her feet. Lynn was screaming as the little gun appeared at her hip.

She was immediately grabbed from behind, a filth-stained hand clamped across her mouth—but was able to get off two shots before having the rifle jerked from her hands. Struggling to break free, once again nausea overcame her, a sickening nausea—reminiscent of unwashed hands and other unspeakable things.

Above all the violence, mere seconds is all, Lynn was able to see Curry's startled face, blood seeping down his shirt. One of her bullets had struck him shoulder-high, smashing him to the ground. The other, a well-directed shot, had killed one of Curry's henchmen—leaving only three left.

Her hands were securely bound with a scrap of green rawhide, a dirty rag was shoved into her mouth, held in place by her red polka-dot bandana. The same ruffian flung her into the saddle on her pinto mare. Her hands and feet were lashed to the rigging.

Spotted Pony moaned in pain, struggling to open his eyes. It was a wasted moment as yet another blow smashed into his skull. The agonizing pain of the brutal attack eased off some, made so by a merciful drift into unconsciousness.

"Leave the Injun here," Curry roared, who was now on his feet "Let's ride, the shots fired by that fool girl will have the posse breathing down our necks!"

Though a bit unsteady, Curry walked over to the pinto horse and glared up at Lynn. Favoring his injured shoulder, the outlaw feared across the Little Rockies as a killer reached up with his uninjured arm and brutally backhanded her across the face. "I'll take care o' you later deputy…good and proper like!"

A terrified scream was hindered from escaping Lynn's mouth, stopped by the filth-stained rag that was stuffed down her throat.

"Why again?" she moaned. I don't think I will be able to go through another ordeal like this, she reasoned. Lynn Bonner had received this same treatment from the vision seekers, and now she must endure it again from Kid Curry's bunch.

"Where are you Will? Come and save me my husband—please hurry!" she moaned through the gag.

Before mounting his horse Curry placed a note on the unmoving body of the Blackfoot cowboy. With three of his gang to back him, one of them leading Lynn's packhorse, Kid Curry led the way back up the old Indian trail into the country where the tall pines grow.

Close behind him scrambled the pinto mare. Boots sensed her mistress was in trouble, yet was unable to do anything about it. The lead rope attached to the horn of Curry's saddle left her no other choice but to follow.

Lynn was fuming mad. She wished they hadn't gagged her, so she could tell them what a cowardly bunch of killers they were—brutally beating a boy, maybe killing him; she didn't know for sure.

And treating her like she was dirt! Binding her hand and foot like a maverick steer. The filthy gag in her mouth, and the cowardly blow to her face, it was all too much. She wasn't sure if she could handle any more of this treatment or not.

She was enraged, sobbing silently, but could do nothing less with the obscene rag stuffed in her mouth. The thing had even worked its way into her throat, causing her to gag more than once.

They covered a mile, and then several more before reason returned to Lynn's troubled mind.

With her head hanging low a wisp of a voice whispered to her, a familiar voice from out of the past that reminded her of Grandpa Brannon. *"Best bide your time darlin' Lynn! Do as he asks you…else Curry might beat you again…perhaps gun you down!"*

Giving a great shudder, she felt better now, her mind was clearing and she offered a silent prayer of thanks for her old grandpa's advice. Besides, she reasoned, I must not fight the filthy gag again. Wouldn't take much for me to vomit!

Lynn Bonner would die for sure, choke plumb to death.

* * *

Two territorial Marshals, one young and riding easy—the elder of the two long past his prime, was gripping the saddle horn attempting to ease his screaming muscles. They were just starting the brisk climb up to Lynn's camp. The woods were silent as a tomb, not even the tune of a songbird could be heard.

With no prior warning the quiet was shattered by two rifle shots. Two shots so close together that Bonner knew they had been fired from Lynn's rifle. The long hair rippled on the back of his neck, an instant panic surged through his very soul.

Something has happened to Lynn!" he roared. "Let's ride!" Together they charged up the steep escarpment.

Pulling in their wheezing broncs, they looked in vain for the lady deputy. No horses! No Lynn! Nothing but the Indian boy lying close to the ashes of Lynn's cooking fire. And the corpse of the outlaw who had beaten him, sprawled on the ground beside him still clutching his rifle; bloodied-butt and all. "Lynn!" Bonner roared, a chilling panic was playing a scary tune up-and-down the cowboy's spine.

"Lynn darlin'….where are you?"

Silence, deathly silence as impenetrable as an early morning fog on the Missouri, invaded the small clearing. Not a sound could be heard except the subdued moan of a passing breeze, pausing but a moment to pester the remains of the small twig fire.

Stepping down from the saddle, Will walked over to Spotted Pony, checked him out and found him alive—just barely. "Reckon the lad is in bad shape," Dunne said.

"Thar's a buckboard down at the ranch. I'll signal a couple of the boys to come on up, reckon they can pack him down to the wagon—could be he's got a fractured skull.

"They can take him on into Landusky—heard tell of a fair to middlin' Doc over that way. Kept busy as all get out from what I've been told."

It was then Will spotted a scrap of paper tucked under a leather string on the Indian boy's medicine bag. With unsteady hands he began to read. A cold chill ripped through his heart as the words unfolded. Handing the note to Dunne, the cowboy stepped back, a terrible rage tore through his soul, an agonizing guilt of leaving his darlin' Lynn alone.

This was his fault he reckoned, for riding away and leaving her—after all they had been through together, after the times she had saved his bacon; after she had consented to be his wife. He loved her more than words can say, with all his heart and soul he loved her!

An anguished sob escaped his sun-chapped lips, followed by a terrible curse. "Da-mn the miserable cowards!" he roared.

"Da-mn them all to blazin' he-ll!"

Leaping into the saddle, Will Bonner reined the big red horse away from the clearing and took off after the retreating outlaws. The trail was easy to follow.

* * * Chapter Seven * * *

"Now hold on a blasted minute Will!" the old Marshal shouted. "Don't go a ridin' off half-cocked!

"Give me a minute to read this hear note." But his words were lost on the wind. Deputy Will Bonner had vanished in the pines. Grumbling his displeasure, Custis Dunne fumbled in his vest pocket for his spectacles, unfolded the note and began to read:

> *depity bonner*
> *a swap—yer purty wife—fer the gold you owe me on longhorn deal ride*
> *to big bend on the missoury leave gold at old sod cabin be thar in 3 days*
> *will leave instructions*
> *kid curry*

Still mumbling to himself, he tucked the note in his pocket. He remained quiet for a moment, struggling to fathom the violent drama that had taken place here. Amazed is the word, amazed at the audacious grit and courage of his two young deputies.

* * *

The remainder of the outlaw gang rode fast and furious, uphill and down with no thought for the lady deputy. Lynn knew she was in bad

70

trouble, tied as she was, and the filthy gag in her mouth. Her mouth was dry, her whole being parched and in trouble.

The gag was slowly choking her to death, she was struggling to control the dry-heaves, to vomit would be to die. She silently wept, praying too. Praying that Will would come and save his darlin' Lynn

The day wore on, hot and dusty. Four hours later the Curry gang reined in their sweat-caked horses at a small opening in the forest. "Water the hosses here," he ordered, relieved to see a modest stream of water. "Fill the canteens too—no telling when we'll get another chance!"

Shifting his attention to the girl on the pinto mare, Curry could see she was in bad shape, and realized for his plan to work he must keep her alive. He untied the leather thongs that kept her in the saddle, and helped her to the ground. Lynn collapsed at his feet, her cramping leg muscles no longer able to support herself.

She was not fully aware—semi-conscious—unable to fully understand. Cursing a blue streak, he released the tight knot that held the red bandana between her teeth—traces of bloody saliva was evident on her swollen lips. He pulled the gag from her mouth and could see the color of her face was a sickly gray.

Lynn was mighty close to death. A series of convulsive shudders raced through her body, only to stop when she was able to vomit.

Still cursing his accomplice in crime, who had bound her so cruelly, Curry released the strips of leather that bound her blooded-wrists, the flesh was raw and broken. Concern showed on the whiskered face of the outlaw. Whether it was a trace of compassion, or concern over the gold— was not difficult to tell.

Uncapping a canteen, he held it to her swollen lips and allowed the water to drip into her mouth. She could not swallow, yet the life-saving liquid trickled down her tortured throat. "Reckon we've treated you a bit rough, deputy," he spoke, and stepped back watching her closely.

""Reckon it's payback time...for shootin' my pard...and fer pluggin' me in my shoulder." Curry winced as he attempted to move his arm. He returned to the spring, and with the assistance of one of his gang, removed his shirt and began to clean the ugly-looking wound.

"It don't look so good," he said, a fierce frown on his face, glaring hard at the fallen Lynn—who had not stirred. "If that fool wife o' Bonner's hadn't a shot me, we would be home free!"

Turning to old Slim who was closely watching his boss from the far side of the clearing, Curry roared, "Fetch me that bottle o' whiskey Slim...in my saddlebags yonder," nodding towards his horse.

"Don't want any of you jaspers a drinkin' any, you hear?"

Slim brought him the unsealed bottle, and watched in amazement as his boss uncorked and swigged down half of it without lowering the bottle.

Smoothing his mustache and glaring at all that was left of his remaining gang, Curry roared again, "Ol' Kid Curry's a gonna need every drop o' this here whiskey to get me to the Doc at that minin' camp!"

The whiskey was fast taking a grip on the old outlaw's mind. With the uncorked bottle in hand, Kid Curry the terror of the Little Rockies became completely out of control, pacing back and forth like a wounded bear; stopping now and then to take another swig from the bottle and glare at Lynn Bonner.

One-by-one his gang of outlaws was being whittled down by this lady deputy and her husband; even the mining camps were now organized against him. He became plumb upset, lashing out at anybody standing in his way, including the remaining members of his gang.

He turned once again to Marshal Bonner, who had gained some semblance of her old self and was sitting in the grass by her pinto mare. The mare's velvet nose was close to Lynn's cheek, she had not moved a muscle since her mistress was pulled from the saddle.

Boots sensed that Lynn was in bad shape. That she was hurt real bad and could not speak, the little mare was sure of this. Her ears were laid back, her eyes watching Curry, a warning for him to keep his distance. Unknown to the old outlaw, Boots' agile body was poised, all set to lash-out with her hind feet at any who might harm her mistress again.

Favoring his wound, Curry walked closer to Lynn and her horse, the whiskey bottle still clutched in his hand. An arrogant sneer was spread across his whiskered face. One more time he tipped his elbow, this time draining it dry; flinging the empty bottle back in the pines. He was standing beside her now, appeared as if he was all set to give her yet another backhand across her battered face; figured this time he would use his fist!

"You're the ones who stirred things up!" he roared, his rage was completely out of control. "You and that husband of yourn…a pair o' young kids a packin' tin stars!"

An old cowhand named Slim was fuming mad. He was watching the way Curry was treating the girl and knew what he would eventually do. Tears mingled with his beard as he remembered his own daughter, Mary.

This bunch had taken her, the same as Lynn Bonner. They had mistreated her like they were doing to Lynn. Then ravaged her, again and again this happened until she was dead.

"Leave her alone Curry!" He was standing close to the outlaw, his voice was shaking, yet his hand was resting on the butt of his six-gun.

"You touch her again and I'll kill you sure, just like you killed my defenseless Mary." Those that were left of the outlaw gang were listening with interest to what old Slim had to say. "I reckon you're a gunfighter, a fast *hombre* too…but think about this!

"I'm standin' close enough, that even if you get a shot into me with that fast-draw riggin' you're a wearin', I'll get you as well!" Slim's gun was now in his hand aimed at Curry's big frame.

The outlaw was if in a trance, plumb shell-shocked, couldn't fathom what was happening. He struggled to find words, but his drunken state wouldn't allow it to be. That Slim was standing close, with a gun in his hand, he was sure of this.

Old Slim spoke one more time, "I'll take care of the girl from now on, you hear? The rest o' you scurvy-riddin' lot stay away, leave her plumb alone!"

Curry's arm had been raised, an iron-hard fist ready to strike a defenseless Lynn Bonner. Out of the blue a pair of iron-shod hooves smashed him high in the chest, one of them struck his festering gunshot wound.

Boots had been ready and waiting. She had warned him with her ears, he would not heed her warning. Like a flash of lightning she had reacted.

Curry was driven to the ground. He lay still attempting to regain his breath, gasping desperately to suck air back into his lungs.

"I reckon you'll give me your word?" old Slim said, who had silently moved up beside Lynn and offered her another drink of water. "If you don't try to escape…I'll see that you're left untied…and forget about a stuffin' that rag back in your mouth.

"If you get to actin' up, they'll shoot that husband of yourn—who I reckon is hot on our trail as I speak. Old Kid Curry will gun him down—like a dog—the minute he shows up!

"And something else! Don't talk to anyone, you hear? One peep outta that pretty little mouth o' yours and they'll plug you sure!"

Lynn still couldn't force any words from her swollen throat. I must do as he says, her inner self reminded her, no doubt they will kill me just as he said. She nodded her head in the affirmative.

Worse yet, kill her husband, whom she knew was on his way to save her.

Curry had now recovered enough to start breathing. He began rolling on the ground roaring and cursing everything in sight, including Lynn Bonner and her horse. After heaving up the contents of his stomach, he staggered to his feet and was assisted to his saddle.

There he sat, hands gripping the saddle horn, moaning a mournful tune. The 26 ounces of rotgut whiskey, plus the timely interference of Lynn's pony had tuned-up old Kid Curry, tuned him up real good!

* * * Chapter Eight * * *

Darkness had settled across the Little Rockies before Curry's bunch arrived at the gold camp. Curry, assisted by two of his gang, was taken inside the Doc's office situated on the main drag of the camp. Guarded by the one known as Slim, Lynn was kept back in the pines out of sight.

The Doc took one look at his visitors and knew this would be trouble waiting to happen. Not much he could do but clean the gunshot wound with whisky, bandage it and send him on his way.

Knowing who he was dealing with, the doctor dowsed the festering wound with a generous dose of the strong, wilderness-brewed concoction; and then another for good measure. A howl of rage and pain erupted from the wounded outlaw. "What are ya a tryin' to do?" he shrieked, sweat was pouring down his face, saliva dripping from his mouth. "This pain is the worst I've ever had to take!

"That fool girl and her bone-headed horse, and now you Doc—it's sure enough torture—far worse than ol' Kid Curry can handle!"

Curry grabbed the bottle from the doc and took a gluttonous swig. With a smack of his lips, and after an intense shudder, he sat the bottle down and turned to the Doc. "Reckon I owe you though," he said. "I feel some better already,"

Once again he picked up the bottle and drained it dry, tossing a gold coin on the table as he did so.

Deputy Pike Landusky was making his nightly rounds when he neared the Doc's cabin in the pines. Curious as to the activity that was taking place here at this late hour, the new Deputy known to all as Pike, walked into the small infirmary to see what was going on. He was the same miner sworn into office by the two young deputy marshals.

The deputy knew he was in trouble the minute he realized this was the notorious Kid Curry. He recognized the outlaw right off, his hand moving close to his six-gun. Curry tensed when he spotted the tin star, his own good hand ready to draw.

"Well look who we have here!" he sneered. "If it ain't the brand-new deputy o' the goldfields—reckon he figures he can put ol' Kid Curry behind bars. And makin' a big name for himself by doing it.

"It's Pike ain't it, Pike Landusky. Figured I recognized you—what'll it be Pike? Figure yuh can outgun ol' Kid Curry!"

The miner became plumb upset, sure never expected anything like this to happen on this peaceful night. Though he wasn't a gunslinger like Curry, he had the courage and determination to not back down. He had it to do, he reckoned, for the sake of the two deputy marshals. The Bonner duo who had restored law and order to the goldfields. For them he must do this!

Though his voice was a bit unsteady, he voiced a reply, "Drop them guns Curry…'fore I kill you. I'm a takin' you boys up the trail to our brand-new calaboose, reckon you three outlaws will be the first ones to try it out."

The room was small, plumb crowded with the doc, the three outlaws and the deputy all there at the same time. Snarling like a cornered lobo, Curry's big .45 appeared as if from nowhere, blasting two shots—point-blank at the novice deputy, who only managed one pull of the trigger as he fell.

Deputy Pike Landusky never had a chance, was downed by one of the fastest guns in the territories—shot to pieces. The lone shot fired from his own gun happened by reflex as he died; leaving a bullet hole in the floor of the Doc's cabin.

Once again the sound of gunfire echoed along the main drag of Landusky, a choking smell of gunpowder hung heavy in the small infirmary in the pines.

* * *

The two were bone-tired, the cowboy and the horse. Will Bonner and Red, two old friends who were on the hunt for the infamous Kid Curry— a cattle rustler, killer of men and a kidnapper of Bonner's wife Lynn.

Cow Creek was far behind them now, the outlaw's trail lost in the encroaching night. The lone rider reined in his horse, kindled a small fire and prepared to wait out the uncertainty of the darkened trail.

It took some time for his emotions to cool down, his temper now under control. Fueled by the loss of the girl from Lariat Cross, a deadly rage still burned deep inside his tortured soul. His darlin' wife Lynn! She was his soul mate, a loving partner in all things.

Guilt was heavy upon him, guilt over his neglect of his wife of such a short time. Not giving her a chance to rest, to have a break from the constant and tedious days in the saddle. From first light—until no can see, they had ridden. Always pushing, always pursuing the elusive longhorns they so wanted.

He knew she was wearing down, knew that she needed a rest, yet he could think of nothing but the gol-darn longhorns. And then today she had told him she was ready to go home, that she was bone-tired and that was it.

Guilt was swirling around him more powerful than before, guilt of leaving her alone on the secluded bluff above Cow Creek.

* * *

Driven by a nester from Dunne's posse, the buckboard was rolling on its way to the gold camps. Laid out flat in the wagon box, cushioned by blankets was Spotted Pony, his spotted horse tied on behind.

The wagon route skirted the pines, able to cover more miles than the old Indian trail the Marshal was using, who was hot on the trail of Bonner and the outlaws. Better time could be made this way, and besides, the nester was sure getting homesick for his little spread along the Missouri.

Nearing the gold fields, dawn was breaking across the Little Rockies when the teamster pulled in the team for a much needed breather. He had traveled all night and reckoned it was time he checked on the Indian boy.

Crawling from the rig, he walked to the rear and discovered an empty wagon box, the spotted horse was missing as well.

He walked around some, working the kinks out of his aging joints, stopped and stoked his pipe. Striking a match on the wagon box, he fired up an old corncob pipe and inhaled deeply.

"I wonder how Ma's a doin'?" he muttered. "Back at the homestead, all alone—without me there to take care of her and the kids.

"And this Injun kid, I wonder where he could have gone?"

Scratching his head in amazement, the teamster was attempting to figure out why, and how, when an eerie noise sounded in the nearby woods—a strange sound that almost had him spooked.

A work-calloused hand hovered near the butt of his shooting iron, he turned to see what could be causing the ruckus. His superstitious self was in disarray as once again he heard the fearsome sound. It was a medley of grunts and groans and high-pitched squalls—rippling up and down the scale.

Then from out a clump of willows, her nose close to the ground, sauntered Lynn Bonner's little Jenni mule. She took her time, but eventually reached the buckboard where she gave it a thorough going over with her keen sense of smell. She appeared to be searching for a scent that wasn't there.

The old nester who had been conscripted into Dunne's posse, was still a bit edgy and watched with awe as the mule with her nose still to the ground disappeared into the southeast landscape.

"Reckon that little mule is sure upset," he said, talking to himself. "a carryin' on like a mountain cat with a burr on its tail.

"Sure had my ha-air a standin' on end, the confounded noises it was makin' and all. Reckon it must be a trackin' down that fool Injun kid…I never seen the likes o' this before."

Crawling back in the rig, the nester was mumbling and still talking to himself. "Reckon I best head on into Landusky—meet the Marshal there as we planned 'fore I get myself in a bunch of trouble.

"Sure hope he don't come down too hard on me…fer a losin' that young Injun kid they call Spotted Pony!"

* * * Chapter Nine * * *

The outlaw camp was a perfect hideout in the barren land known as the Missouri Breaks. That it was a stopover on the old outlaw trail, there can be little doubt, made so by ancient fire rings, time-worn signatures scratched in the rocks, and scattered here and there; rusted tin cans dating back over the decades.

It was here, well hidden in the broken ledges of an ancient upheaval of limestone and debris, a lonely girl from the St. Mary's River looked out across the land.

A natural structure of fractured rock was used as a shelter. A roof had been improvised from salvaged driftwood taken from the nearby Missouri River. Over this was a layer of scanty prairie brush. It sure didn't appear to be rain proof, nor was it varmit proof either.

It had proved to be a perfect lookout for those who rode the owl-hoot trail, except for one thing—rattle snakes! Deputy Lynn Bonner could not stand to be around snakes, and after being exposed to several while being here, begged old Slim not to stray far; and to keep his shooting irons handy.

"Reckon there must be a den close by," he told her. "I've shot several of these big snakes while being here, and more just keep on a showin' up."

From where she sat, perched on a weathered slab of rock—high out of reach of any rattlers—Lynn could barely make out the sod-roofed cabin tucked into the rolling terrain below, of which was responsible for the big bend on the Missouri. It was here at the cabin, her husband was to come this very day with their gold—to exchange for herself.

She had been stolen away and brought into this wilderness against her will, to be used as a pawn against her cattle-seeking husband—kidnapping it is called—a downright, dirty rotten maneuver in this ongoing feud between the deputy marshals and Kid Curry.

Guilt ran amok through Lynn's tortured mind, guilt that she had been trapped in the tall pines above Cow Creek; and stolen away! True, she had let her guard down, ignored her keen senses that had always been her savior. She had even ignored Spotted Pony's warning of danger moving in close to her modest noonday fire.

This was her fault, she reckoned. Her fault for becoming bone-weary, and not heeding the dangers of this wild, desolate land!

She was silently weeping as she had often been doing since her capture, and somehow it made her feel better. It was a women's way she reckoned, a trait she had no control over.

Curry and the three outlaws had treated her badly to start with. She knew she was lucky to be alive and silently thanked old whiskered Slim for that. An old-timer who sat across the camp from her now, and who was left here to guard her while Curry and the other two rode down to wait for the arrival of Will Bonner.

Slim had been kind to her, brought her food and water when the others couldn't care less. And stood guard while she attempted to bathe herself and clean up as best she could. He insisted she have privacy to attend to those things that are a must for the gentler sex; and she respected him for this as well.

She was healing physically, her voice had returned, yet she hesitated to use it around Curry and the rest. The girl would only answer yes or no to the outlaw leader, whom she despised with all her heart. An ugly purple-hued bruise still showed on her face from the brutal blow he had given her, she knew Will Bonner would kill him for that!

Her throat and lips were returning to normal though it was still painful to swallow the food that was given her.

Old Slim had been kind to her, insisted she be allowed the freedom of the camp and to walk some, which eased the tension from the long, brutal ride that brought her here. When all of this was over, she mused, and Will has rescued me, we will take Slim home with us. He will make a trusted cowhand on our St. Mary's River ranch.

I owe him this, I surely do. If it weren't for this caring old man they would have starved me plumb to death, worse yet I would have fallen victim to their lustful ways.

"Reckon you should stretch your legs a mite," Slim broke her reverie. "Ol' Slim saw how they had you tied in the saddle, them ropes cuttin' into your wrists and ankles…the walkin' around might take away some o' the pain…must still hurt like the dickens!"

"Thanks Slim, reckon you're right…I will do this for the sake of a caring old gentleman—and this girl you have treated with respect."

She was smiling when she spoke again, "When all of this is over Slim…I'm taking you home with us…back to the northern territories. I want you to be a cowboy on our ranch beside a beautiful river."

Slim looked up at her, hope in his eyes, and a tear as well. "I'd be mighty proud to do this, but reckon Curry won't let me out of his clutches!"

"Your boss has a few surprises in store," she replied. "He sure enough has!"

To be able to walk sure felt good, and lifted her spirits too. She was excited, hoping to be back with her husband before the day had passed. She chattered as she walked, telling Slim many things—their marriage by the Mormon bishop, Marshal Custis Dunne convincing them to become deputies, and on and on.

Her words flowed like the wind. It seemed like such a long time since she was able to speak to anyone, and old Slim was sure content to listen.

Hesitating in mid-stride, Lynn was puzzled over a strange feeling that entered her mind, almost caused her to become light-headed. Whatever it was kept nagging at her until she just had to stop and listen, her keen senses straining in the brisk morning air.

Yes, she admitted to herself. She had heard the sound before, a vaguely familiar sound that appeared so out of place in this far-away wilderness. Somehow the sound was reminiscent of the ruckus her Jenni mule was guilty of, when she was upset and on the prowl. Who, if she is still alive, must still be wandering around back in that Cow Creek country looking for me!

Something else had caught her attention. It was the call of a raven, faint at first, increasing in volume as the minutes ticked by. It was only now she recognized it as the cry of a crow, other than that of a raven.

"This just cannot be," she gasped! Far as she knew Little Crow had been killed fighting the vision seeker back at the talking cliffs in Milk River country.

Could it be that her two old friends were still alive? And followed her here to offer there support, possibly be a means of her escaping Curry and his henchmen? A thrill surged through her weary soul! Lynn Bonner would not give up without a fight. She hadn't been forgotten after all.

"Reckon that bird is plumb upset," Slim said, listening with interest as the incessant cawing drew near. "Na-ah, it can't be a bird, could it? Might be a varmint close by—could be one o' them long-tailed cats that's got that crow on the warpath!

"Puma, is what they call 'em down New Mexico way."

Scratching his whiskers, he glanced long across the shattered rocks. "And that other noise…a gol-darn genuine caterwaulin' if I ever heard one. Reckon it's the ruttin' cry of one o' them big cats I was telling you about.

Lynn still had not spoken. She remained quiet as a mouse, watching and waiting. Then a shift in the wind brought her the proof she needed. It was the unmistakable scent of an Indian, of which would bring tears to the unwary!

To have been caught down wind from Little Crow was risky business. He claimed soap and water destroyed his spiritual powers. "Crow must smell this way," he boasted. "so evil spirits will not play with this one…who talks like a crow."

And keep them away it did. No respectable evil spirit could exist around a stench such as Crow's, she reckoned. Yet she loved the boy, stink or not. He had helped her out of many a tight spot, saved her life too.

Slim was not afraid of any man, yet this confounded racket had him on edge. His eyes darted to a movement beyond the girl, and there stood a challenging redskin; a birch-willow bow strung, and armed with a flint-tipped arrow—aimed at Lynn's friend.

The old cowboy's hand dropped to his shooting iron.

Turning to see, Lynn gasped. "Pony!" she screamed, fearing for the old one's life. "Spotted Pony! Do not shoot this man!"

"His name is Slim, he has been good to me...he has saved Lynn's life from the outlaws who took me!"

"*Oki!*" the boy grunted and lowered his bow, still keeping a close watch on the old-timer.

"Pony, it is you! I could a swore it was Little Crow coming, sure sounded like him with all the crow talk we were hearing!"

"Little Crow died at talking cliffs," the boy said. "It was I, Spotted Pony, who you could hear making this talk—I have listened to his talk in the night—many times, while following him on the trail.

"This Nez Perce boy who is dead now—did not know the Pony was doing this thing!"

Slim gave a sigh and lowered his own weapon, knowing he couldn't have shot the Indian anyway, as the girl was standing in the line of fire. After accepting him as Lynn's friend, the Blackfoot boy came out into the clearing and squatted by the fire.

"That cowboy job you were tellin' me about." Slim commented, and walked out where the horses were saddled and waiting. "is lookin' mighty tempting, reckon we're together now Ma-am—reckon I'll be happy to ride for your brand till hell itself freezes over."

He returned with Lynn's saddlebag in hand, and found her deputy badge inside which he pinned on her jacket. "This here tin-star is back where it should be—don't amount to much shoved in these here bags," and handed her the holstered .44. Her .30-30 carbine was back in the leathers on her saddle.

"This sure feels better," Lynn said, buckling the rig around her waist. Almost feel like my old self again if...if only my husband were here with me...I would feel complete!"

"Reckon the three of us can handle those jaspers down yonder," Slim told her. "Kid Curry worries me some though, he's as tricky as a blasted rattle snake...never know when he's goin' to strike next."

The Blackfoot boy was standing now, and began flashing signs that only Lynn could understand. "Stop it Pony! Stop it right now!" Lynn scolded. "Make white-eyes talk so Slim can understand too."

"*Oki!* Spotted Pony will make white man's talk.

"Only this many outlaws left now," he said and held up two fingers. "Pony find one waiting by trail," and gestured back in the direction he had came from. "This one was hiding in the big rocks—he wished to kill Lynn's husband—when he comes with the gold!

"This same one beat Spotted Pony with his rifle, back where Lynn was stolen—he wished to kill Pony, but this one's medicine is stronger—much stronger than the one who wishes to hide like a yellow dog.

"He is not able to kill us now…part of him is here!" the boy said, as he reached into his parfleche and withdrew a gory fresh-taken scalp. He desired the girl and old Slim to see his great coup.

Lynn gasped and Slim turned a shade of green. Spotted Pony was smiling with pride. "This outlaw's hair—good medicine!

"It will make us brave warriors…in fight down by big muddy."

Old Slim was having a hard time digesting it all, especially so when a shaggy half-starved mule showed up. Jenni uttered a garbled greeting, then settled to the ground with exhaustion, her long ears pointing straight at Lynn.

The girl could not contain herself, and gave her Jenni mule a warm hug, whose velvet nose was brushing her cheek. "I'm so happy you're here…my little one. You are a true and faithful friend, traveling all this way to find me.

"But look at you…you are starving!" Turning to Slim, she asked, "Is it all right if I give her a feed of oats?

"Reckon so," he replied. "We're a plannin' on them two hombres down yonder never seein' this camp again. You're in control now Deputy Bonner—I'll back you all the way."

In no time at all Jenni was ravenously crunching a generous helping of oats, her ears still pointing at Lynn Bonner.

Lynn was chattering, pleased that Pony and Jenni had found her. Slim was pouring a cup of campfire coffee, Spotted Pony was puttering with the scalp—a great coup for the Blackfoot lad!

"Tell me lad?" Slim asked, "why do your people set such store in taking scalps, like the one you're a workin' on there."

Spotted Pony was smiling when he answered, "It is a custom of the old ones—to take an enemy's hair—and cut other parts that are missing.

"We have been told by the spirits, that if we do this thing, the enemy's spirit will then be crippled in the after life, with no hair, and other parts."

"Thanks for telling me this lad, reckon I can now understand your ways somewhat better."

Slim had no sooner spoken when Jenni bounced to her feet, and erupted with a half-hearted bray. She alone was the first to see the cowboy ride into camp.

"Lynn turned to see what the fuss all was about, and there sat her grinning husband. "Will!" she screamed. "Will darling is it really you?" She dropped what she was doing and ran towards him, laughing and crying at the same time. He stepped to the ground and met her in the center of the clearing.

She flew into his arms, sobbing as if her heart would break, stopping long enough to shower him with kisses.

It took some doing to settle her down. Bonner sensed Lynn had been through hell though...hell with the lid off, and stepped back to look in her eyes. And then he knew!

"Your face darlin' Lynn!" he gasped in shock, the swelling and purple-hued bruise were only too plain.

"What has happened to your face?

"Was it that devil Curry treated you like this?" A deeply entrenched frown of concern was spreading across his whiskered face.

"Did they, you know what I mean?"

"No Will—thanks to old Slim here—they were unable to do this, heaven knows they tried!"

"So much has happened Will, I must sit you down and start my talk back at the Wagon Box, at our camp above Cow Creek, remember? Over two steaming cups of old Slim's coffee, Lynn Bonner told her husband the story. Not leaving out anything, including Slim's kindness to her, protecting her night and day, and facing down Kid Curry to do so.

"Slim I'll be forever beholden to you—how can I ever repay you?" Bonner said. "Reckon you're a true gentleman, without you Lynn would have been killed sure! Worse yet, fell victim to this hell-raisin' bunch."

"I had a daughter once," Slim replied. "'bout the same age as Lynn here. She was taken by a bunch o' hell-raisers like these.

"They mistreated her something fierce—ravaged her—all six of them, left her for dead. I found her that way, she died in my arms."

Tears were flowing down Slim's whiskered cheeks, yet he wanted them to hear him out. "It was Curry's bunch that did it, she told me before she died. I joined the gang for revenge—to avenge my poor Mary!

"Now, with the help o' you folks, reckon we'll get the job done!"

High in the jumbled rock above the Missouri River, silence enveloped the small hideout used on occasion by the Curry gang; a silence that was broken by the weeping of a heart-broken girl from Lariat Cross. She walked over to Slim and gave him a warm hug, a kiss on his whiskered cheek too.

Bonner was deeply moved, couldn't speak for a spell. "I'm sure sorry old-timer…about your daughter and all.

"You are a true hero—reckon you've saved my Lynn from the same fate that happened to your Mary. When we're done with this business here, you're a comin' back with us to the territories—we'll welcome you as a part of our St. Mary's River ranch."

Will placed his hand on Slim's shoulder, whose head was hanging low—hiding the tears that were streaming down his cheeks. "You have proved yourself by saving the life of a U.S. Deputy Marshal. As well, stopping Curry's bunch from treating Lynn in the dastardly way they abused your daughter.

"As far as the law is concerned, I'm absolving you of any involvement with Curry's bunch; wiping the slate clean!"

Bonner was smiling when he spoke again. "By the way Slim, you are now a free man, no need to worry 'bout the law swinging you from the end of a rope—or locking you up in the crowbar hotel for the rest of your life."

Old Slim was listening with much interest, and was watching Bonner bring something from his vest pocket. "I've got something here for you Slim," and pinned a tin star on the old timer's time-worn vest.

"You are now one of us—I am appointing you a deputy marshal under the jurisdiction of U.S. Marshal Custis Dunne.

Lynn and her husband were beaming from ear to ear, old Slim too was smiling, as he was sworn in as a lawman by Deputy Will Bonner. The former outlaw appeared stunned, and though he was still smiling, managed to speak. "Never in my wildest dreams did I reckon anything like this would happen!"

"He was shining the deputy badge as he spoke. "Reckon all I can do, is my best—and offer an old cowboy's thanks."

"I'm so happy for you Slim, this tin star will give you the recognition and respect that you deserve." With that said, Lynn stepped forward and gave him another warm hug.

* * * Chapter Ten * * *

To the wildlife of this isolated wilderness came a startling medley, that of a happy girl's singing from a hidden hideout in the Breaks. A mule deer buck stopped browsing, listening with interest, one front hoof not yet settled to the ground. A tiny rock thrush flitting from one boulder to the next, ceased its incessant feeding of freshly hatched larva, a wee feathered head jerking this way and that; as if in tune with Lynn's happy song.

Far across the rubble a lone vision seeker, keen ears listening to the singing, stood at attention on a large boulder leaning on his war spear. He stood with awed respect, certain it was a spirit singing a welcome to a new day.

Lynn Bonner was happy and singing, as she prepared a much deserved meal for the Deputies here at the hideout in the Missouri Breaks. This was the day the three deputies would wage war against the infamous Kid Currie. They were all in need of a hearty meal, even Spotted Pony who had brought in a brace of sage hens.

A steady diet of beans and jerky, jerky and beans, became unbearable after a time; especially so without sufficient coffee to drink.

The men were busy cleaning and oiling their guns, and planning the oncoming battle with the remnants of the Curry gang. Spotted Pony was roasting the sage hens on a makeshift spit over a glowing bed of embers.

All three were entranced with the lady deputy's singing, they too beside the wild ones were listening to her beautiful song.

* * *

High along the Missouri breaks, the sun was swinging into the west before Deputy Marshal Will Bonner left camp in the bluffs and rode down to the sod-roofed cabin by the Missouri River. A carefully laid out plan was now in motion, war had been declared on the notorious Kid Curry. As planned in advance, the brilliance of the afternoon sun was behind Bonner, giving him an edge over the gun-slingin' Curry.

Allowing them an hour head start, he had sent old Slim on a wide circle to the left, who would eventually ride up behind a sizable hunk of rock—a hundred yards from the cabin door. Lynn and Spotted Pony were assigned to the right flank, and should now be hidden in a thicket of chokecherry brush about the same distance away.

Reckon they're all three ready for battle, Bonner decided, as he closed in on the weathered structure. Smoke was drifting skyward from a trapper's invention, makeshift coffee-cans laced together with baling wire to form a chimney. Two horses were tied to a box elder tree on the lee side of the cabin.

A young Indian boy known as Spotted Pony watched Bonner nearing the cabin, eagerly waiting for him to rein his red horse to a stop; the cue for the lad to show off his prowess as an Indian. Bonner watched and waited, a work-hardened hand hovering near his .44. The boy moved out from the brush as planned, creeping towards the back side of the cabin.

The Deputy Marshal was smiling, proud too, as he watched the Blackfoot boy in action. The manner in which he Injuned up to the cabin, and like a shadow was soon on the roof. Bonner now realized how easy it had been for the two Blood Indian boys to sneak into their Milk River camp, and spirit away his wife into the night.

Clutching an old scrap of buffalo-hide in his hand, the Pony silently approached the chimney and placed it over the outlet, then retraced his trail back to the chokecherry patch.

The plan was working! In no time at all, a sun-wrinkled buffalo hide that served as the cabin door was flung aside, Curry and the last remaining member of his gang stumbled out of the shack—sneezing and coughing their heads off.

"Who's out here?" shrieked Curry, frantically rubbing his eyes. "Is that you Bonner? I'll kill you for this…you'll never see that purty wife o' yourn alive!"

"Drop your weapons!" Bonner roared back. "I'm a U.S. Deputy Marshal…you're both under arrest for murder, and the kidnapping of Deputy Bonner."

"The he-ell you say! No Marshal is about to take Kid Curry without a fight, you wouldn't stand a chance against me Bonner—way too slow on the draw!"

Will knew Curry was stalling for time, waiting for his smoke-irritated eyes to clear so he could see. "I'm only a tellin' you one more time, throw down them weapons 'fore we start a shootin'"

Curry stalled as long as he dared, then screeching like a banshee drew his shooting irons, one in each hand. Old Slim, a terrible look on his face, could wait no longer and fired the first shot of the war, downing Curry's second in command. This one was the same sadistic coward who had been responsible for the death of his poor Mary. Then all hell broke loose.

Spotted Pony had snuck up to the cabin, his bow armed and ready for the kill. Lynn and her husband were shooting now—Curry was riddled with red-hot lead. To add to the carnage, two of Pony's flint-tipped arrows were firmly embedded in Curry's torso.

The old outlaw was dancing a Spanish fandango, firing both pistols every which way, flinching and howling as the bullets smacked into his body. Still howling with rage he would not go down—spun on his heels and dove over the riverbank. Unknown to the deputies, an old dory was tethered to the snag of a long-dead tree, washed ashore by a flood no doubt; been there for years by the looks of it. Curry managed to shove the craft out into the swiftness of the current, somehow he was able to crawl in.

There he lay, sprawled on the rotted-out bottom of the old derelict, which was leaking like a sieve, the outlaw's blood mixing with the water in the sinking craft.

The three deputies and Spotted Pony were standing by the water's edge watching the drama unfold. The dory filled with water and quickly sank. The body of Kid Curry bobbed along with the swiftness of the current, for fifty yards or so; before it too disappeared into the depths of the Missouri River.

Until his rifle ran out of cartridges, old Slim sat on the riverbank pot-shooting at the bobbing head of Kid Curry, until it too vanished in the depths of the river. The old-timer's head lowered some, convulsive sobs tore through his body; for a long time this happened. Those that were there stepped back and waited, showing respect for the old timer's feelings.

Heaving a great sigh Slim finally spoke, "Reckon I feel better now—reckon my poor Mary has at last been avenged!"

The three deputies sat around a cheery fire eating a modest trail meal, and indulging themselves of the remainder of their precious coffee. They were silent now, enjoying the peace and quiet—deep in thought—reliving in their minds the successful war that had been waged against the famous Kid Curry. With a slab of jerky in hand, Spotted Pony had left the camp on his nightly ritual, not to be seen again until the sun returned to this wilderness land.

Other creatures of the night began to prowl as darkness moved in along the Missouri Breaks. The eerie hoot of an owl sounded loud and clear, the howl of hunting coyotes on the prowl for food to sustain their hungry families, and from far away among the splintered limestone debris; came the plaintive cry of a whippoorwill.

Only three of the multitude of species of this wilderness land had voiced their presence. A signal to both man and beast that nighttime had once again returned to the western prairie.

Spotted Pony had listened with interest, knowing this was good medicine to hear the wild ones talk. Then with a shrug of his shoulders, continued his quest after the evil ones of the night

* * *

The news of the incoming deputies reached the mining camp several hours ahead of their arrival. A nester driving a fresh team of horses, had passed by the trail-weary outfit, and had spread the news up and down the main drag of Landusky.

The fading rays of an afternoon sun reflected off a trio of tin stars, strewing an essence of security and hope throughout those who were hunting for gold. Riding point, Deputies Will and Lynn Bonner led the small trail outfit into the mining town. Trailing behind, rode Spotted Pony and old Slim, who was leading a pack horse.

Following slim were two horses, a scalped corpse lashed across each of the saddles, another with an empty saddle and a little dun mule were bringing up the rear.

Crowds of people had gathered to watch them pass by, including a mustached U.S. Marshal known to all as Custis Dunne. Knowing the deputies had been at war with the infamous Kid Currie and his band of outlaws, a rousing cheer erupted from the miners and their families.

The Marshal stepped out to greet them, his face resplendent with a broad grin. "Meet you at the jail," he shouted, and was once again swallowed up by the crowd. Lynn was thrilled with the welcome they received, and smiling shyly waved her gloved hand in return—her modest way of thanking them for their kindness.

On arrival at the jail, the saddle-weary riders stepped to the ground. It had been a long and grueling ride to get here, all four of them were mighty pleased that it was over. Lynn was exhausted, clammy with sweat and plumb covered with trail dust, as they all were.

Her only interest at the moment was to get herself cleaned-up. She walked over to the nearby diner knowing the widow Jones would take care of her. The luxury of a hot bath and clean clothes—Lynn could hardly wait.

When the marshal arrived, he insisted they have supper at the widow's diner—his treat he told them, courtesy of the U.S. Marshal's service. Scrubbed and spruced-up, the men were sitting at the table waiting for Lynn to show up.

Dunne insisted he be told the complete story of Lynn's rescue, and Curry's final defeat. And after listening to Bonner's talk, praised him highly for the efficient manner in which they had eradicated this scourge from the Little Rockies.

"Sure I wanted to be with you," he said and fired up a cigar. "Would a done it too, but my posse up and quit me…said it was time they were headin' home…had to take care o' their own affairs.

"Don't blame 'em much either, them hombres all have a wife and family to look out for."

Custus Dunne was sure pleased to know the notorious Kid Curry had finally met his comeuppance, and mentioned there was a price on his head, a bounty he would collect for his two deputies.

After a whispered conference between Will and Lynn, who was now sitting at the table, all cleaned-up and shining like a new dollar, she smiled and spoke, "Reckon we haven't been wearin' these tin stars for bounty money. To know the rape and killings are stopped…is payment enough for us.

"Will and I would like Pike Landusky's wife and children to have it, after all it was Curry who gunned him down—destroyed his life—when he was standing up for what is right!"

Marshal Dunne turned and looked Will Bonner in the eye, waiting for him to speak "We feel responsible Marshal, "Bonner said, "It was the two of us who insisted he be sworn in as one o' your deputies. It would please us if you would do this!

"You still goin' to sell us them longhorns? Reckon come first light…we're a headin' back to the northern territories," and he laid a pouch of gold on the table.

"Six dollars a head—wasn't it, reckon this should cover it."

Hefting the pouch in his hand, the marshal was smiling when he spoke, "Them Judith Basin cattle are still on the Wagon Box ranch a grazin' that Cow Creek range. Bin a holdin' 'em for you—all 304 head of 'em."

And so once again a deal was struck, between an old western marshal and a pair of young newlywed ranchers—all three wearing tin stars. Dunne was smiling when next he spoke. "I found this cash in Currie's saddle bags," and handed the coins to Bonner.

"Reckon it must be your original down payment you gave him to start with!"

Bonner took what the old marshal offered. There in the palm of his hand lay the ten double eagles. He handed the gold to Lynn and said, "Reckon our luck has changed darling'—it sure enough has!"

"I've booked us a bed in the widow's cabin," Lynn said. "I'm sure tired—take me to the cabin Will—I can barely keep my eyes open,"

"What about old Slim? Lynn asked. "We must find him a place to sleep!"

The old timer was now standing and had heard Lynn's talk. "Don't worry about me. I'm going back down by the horses, roll out my bedroll under them big pines, something I've bin meaning to do for a long time."

"Thanks a whole bunch Slim, sure bin our pleasure having you with us. I'll never be able to repay you for your kindness to Lynn, and helping her out of the tight spot she was in."

"You already have," Slim replied. "You gave me the opportunity to even the score—avenge the murder of my only daughter!"

* * * Chapter Eleven * * *

The Judith Basin longhorns were gathered and waiting to move up the trail to the northern territories. Will Bonner, trail boss of the outfit, was relieved when Spotted Pony showed up. He hadn't been seen for several days and was sure needed to help out.

Accompanying the Blood cowboy were two young Indian lads. While engaged in his nightly feud with the evil ones, Spotted Pony had discovered them huddled together in the pine forest; frightened, hungry and cold; at least this is what he told his two bosses.

Instead of scalping them, he told Lynn, he had brought them here to be her cowboys, to help out with the long ride that lay ahead. After stuffing the starving boys with food, the camp gear was stowed and the trail drive was underway. The five riders were kept extremely busy thwarting the feisty and well-rested cattle from scattering to the far winds. At the reins of a canvas-topped supply wagon, old Slim brought up the rear, his saddle horse tied on behind.

The first few hours were wild and wooly until an old one-horned roan cow, fed-up with the unruly bunch, pointed her nose into the west as if she knew where she was going. She was a natural born leader, and with no fuss or bother took control of the point, the herd content to follow her meek as a nester's milk herd.

This pleased Will Bonner immensely, knowing the stress and worry would now be lessened. Another day and the longhorns will be trail broke, he reckoned.

Moving steadily onward, the cattle were driven past the west flank of Gold Butte, situated in the middle of the Sweet Grass Hills. It was here Bonner swung the herd into the northwest to avoid crossing over Blackfoot country. He sure didn't want to tangle with this warlike bunch, reckoned it would be trouble waiting to happen.

And it was here the Cree boys rode away from the herd, a severe case of home-sickness had suddenly invaded their souls. Unknown to the Bonners, the boys were Cree—whose fellow tribesmen were mortal enemies of the savage Blackfoot—and were sure a wanting to keep their top-knots in place.

Besides, Lynn had given them two silver dollars in advance for wages earned.

Bonner smiled and reckoned the coins must have been burning a hole in their medicine bags.

The herd continued on, slow but steady, covering the dusty miles just the same. Unknown to the cattle, they had now crossed an unmarked border into the northwest territories of Canada

A rough, broken hill country was behind them, opening up into a vast short-grass prairie, a dusty, arid region that was home to antelope and prairie wolves, sagebrush and prickly pear cactus.

A mischievous breeze whispered on the cheeks of the riders, followed by another, and another. As if inviting them to come—come into the west and play with us—the superstitious Blackfoot boy interpreted it as such. He promptly informed the trail boss of the wishes of these playful spirits.

Will Bonner listened to his talk, and with tongue-in-cheek answered the boy. "Reckon that west wind is a talkin' to us Pony, was thinkin' the same thing myself."

The herd was then swung into the west, facing the constant breeze, and continued on for the adventures that might be waiting ahead.

Spotted Pony returned to his position on drag, pleased the trail boss had listened to his spirit talk.

"Thank you my husband," Lynn said, and she was smiling too. "for being considerate of Pony...and his way of explaining the unknown. He truly believes he is right you know!"

"Don't tell Pony this, but I had been plannin' on swingin' the cattle west anyhow. Should put us in line with the big mountain where you first saved my life, a time I'll never forget."

* * *

A piercing shout echoed across the dusty backs of the plodding longhorns. The girl from Lariat Cross was on the far side of the herd from her husband and was riding with a big smile on her sweat-smeared face. Once again she called, "Yaa-hoo-oo!" Will Bonner heard her shout, and waved his Stetson through the swirling dust, in recognition of her signal.

With a touch of her spurs, she spun the pinto, the little mare's nose now where her tail had been, and rode back to be with her husband; the two riding side by side. She appeared happy to be heading back to their home by the river, happy they had found the small herd strung out in front of them, and she was happy to have found Will Bonner, who was now her husband.

Though few in numbers, three hundred and four head by the last count, the small herd of longhorns was just as important to the Bonners as if there had been ten times that many. And as Lynn had said—this was a start. A good one too!

The herd was now moving away from the rugged butte country of Montana.

As the long dusty miles rolled by, the herd became uneasy, their noses reared high in the dust-laden air. The homesick cows seemed reluctant to enter this foreign land. It appeared as if they wanted to stay in Montana, and became downright cranky to handle.

A hot, humid day was closing in on night when the three riders could no longer hold them together. A thunder storm was rolling in from the west, bringing with it scary lightning bolts, hurricane force winds and a driving rain. A streak of fire fell from the sky, striking ground close to the longhorns; spooking the herd, and that was it. Off they bolted in terror and scattered into the uncertainty of the shadowed prairie.

It turned into a wild and gut-wrenching time for the B-B riders, who were attempting to swing the herd. Then, accepting defeat, the Bonners and old Slim rode back to the chuck wagon, their horses staggering with fatigue. "We'll kill our broncs for sure," Bonner said, if we keep fighting these fool longhorns, the three of us just can't keep them back.

"We sure could use more riders, and more horses too—our only *remuda* is what we're a ridin'—and they are plumb tuckered out!"

Lynn had collapsed on the ground next to the chuckwagon, her head resting in her saddle, her beloved Boots standing beside her; the pony's head was hanging low, her body covered with sweat-caked dust. Both the pony and the girl were ignoring the rain that was falling.

She was silently weeping when she spoke, "I'm so sorry Will, this stampede was just too much for Boots—she did the best she could though—I'm mighty proud of her just the same."

"Don't you be a frettin' none Lynn." He was squatting on his bootheels beside her. "Boots done just fine. Considering her size, she was doing the work of three horses, and a darn good job it was too!

"And you! You done some fine riding today little lady, the best I ever did see! I'm mighty proud of my cowgirl wife—couldn't a done any better myself."

"I love you too Will Bonner, thank you for your kind words"

Before he left to secure the horses, Will picked her up in his arms and carried her inside the tarp-covered wagon. There he prepared her a snug bed, safely away from the rain and howling wind.

Darkness had now settled across the prairie, far in the distance could be heard the lowing of lost cattle. Then off in another direction, could be heard more of the same. The wild stampede had scattered them real good. Still farther yet, the rumble of the departing storm was still making its presence known.

Slim crawled in the wagon and was standing beside her when he spoke, "The rain has slacked off Lynn, nothing more than a summer thunder storm.

"I've kindled a cooking fire, there's water a heatin' so's you can freshen up. I'll take Boots and give her a good rub down, then give her a feed o' oats—should make her feel some better."

Lynn never answered, she was sound asleep, a worn-out body rejuvenating itself for what might lay ahead.

* * *

Listening to the raindrops dripping off the nearby canvas top, Bonner and Slim sat long into the night, drinking coffee and discussing the events of the now past day. Old Slim was smoking his pipe, thick clouds of rich tobacco smoke encircling his shaggy locks. Care to join me?" he asked Bonner, offering him a pouch of the enticing weed.

"Don't use the weed much," Bonner replied. "Found when I'm on the trail for weeks on end—and run out—then I'm in one hell of a fix, with nothing to smoke but dried sage brush leaves and such."

Old Slim smiled and said, "I know what you're a talkin' about! Ain't much fun to be caught in a fix like what you bin a tellin' me."

Slim continued to talk, was enjoying his pipe too. "Wonder what happened to that Indian lad of Lynn's? he asked. "We could a sure used him to help out at our gol-darned stampede."

"Come to think of it, I haven't seen him since early this morning," Bonner replied. "I reckoned he was back on drag, hidden from view by all that confounded dust."

Old Slim eventually rolled his blankets under the wagon and called it a day. Bonner never found much sleep that night, but eventually entered the wagon and crawled in beside Lynn.

He was awake at his usual time, five o'clock in the morning, kindled a fire and soon had a rosy-red batch of coals ready for the coffee pot. With the pot a perking, he found a side of bacon and began slicing off thick slabs to be fried in the skillet.

Suddenly, and he never would know why, he stopped his carving and looked long into the darkness. His long unshorn locks were quivering on the back of his neck, a ripple racing up and down his spine. "Something is out there," he muttered. "Sure can't reckon what it might be."

And the horses, he mused, sure ain't a raisin' a fuss. Must not be a critter out their. Must be something else!

Returning to his breakfast chore, once again this strange feeling came over him that he was being watched. He turned once more and pulled his six-gun, facing into the dark. "Come on into the fire," he roared, "before I start a shootin'!

He could see the movement of shadows approaching out of the darkness, and then they were within the circle of light cast from his cooking fire—all eight of them, led by Spotted Pony who moved in close., "Oki-ii!" he greeted.

It was a guttural greeting, used by the Blackfoot talkers when saying hello, or goodby, or whatever.

"...about time you was showin' up Pony, reckoned you had pulled out and left us, the longhorns bustin' loose like they did...!"

Bonner was struggling to control his temper and lowered his voice some. "That rip-snortin' storm last night spooked the herd real bad, they busted loose in a crazy stampede, we were unable to keep them together."

"Oki!" the one known as Spotted Pony replied, having been unable to break into Bonner's wild talk. "We have help now—Spotted Pony has brought his cousins from the reservation to help you—find cows with long horns—who became frightened by the bad spirits that fall from the sky.

"Big noise!" he said. "Scary light," and signed from the clearing heavens to the rain-soaked grass at their feet.

"These bad spirits will soon be here no more. Spotted Pony and his cousins will go find the long horned ones—and bring them back to your sagebrush camp."

"Oh, that is you Pony!" Lynn squealed. "Is that really you, come back to be our cowboy once again?"

She had been awakened by the sound of strange voices, and had been watching from the entranceway of the wagon, hearing most of what had been said. Though still showing the wear and tear of the wild night, she appeared somewhat refreshed from the few hours of sleep.

Lynn crawled down from the wagon and walked over to the fire. "We thought something bad had happened to you Pony, with the stampede and all."

"These are my cousins," he said, introducing them to those that were there, including old Slim who was now up and about. "We will find your cows who have been scared away by the bad spirits—but first you must feed us—to give us strength to do this thing." Unknown to those that were there, he signed to a cousin, who left the fire and returned with a fresh-killed antelope.

The cousins, all Blackfoot braves in their teens, unlike spotted Pony who was proud to be known as a Blood, went to work skinning the small prairie animal and preparing it for the fire. Two of them brought in armfuls of fuel, including buffalo chips and sagebrush.

Lynn found a spare coffee pot in the wagon, and soon the aroma of fresh brewed coffee was drifting strong in the crisp morning air. "Reckon two pots will be enough?" Lynn asked, looking at her husband.

"Don't think so," he replied. "We'll most likely have to refill them a couple more times—heard tell these here plains Indians are a coffee drinking bunch.

The Blackfoot boys insisted on cooking the meat, all they asked in return was plenty of coffee to drink. The skinned and gutted antelope carcass was hanging on a makeshift spit rigged up by the boys, and soon a delicious aroma of roast antelope meat was mingling with that of the perking coffee.

In about an hour's time, the meal was ready to eat, the cousins eyeing it with a wilderness-honed appetite. Lynn had prepared a pan of sourdough biscuits, and gasped in wonder as the boys began to eat the same. How they did it she would never know, forcing a whole biscuit in their mouth and devouring it down.

It kept her mighty busy preparing more coffee, she was thankful they had two pots in camp instead of one.

It was an eye-opener to watch the cousins in action, who devoured the food with much vigor, eating everything in sight. Nothing remained but the leavings. Lynn prepared much more coffee than she had figured on, leaving barely enough in their supplies to make it back to their river ranch.

But Spotted Pony saved the day, explaining they would go now and bring back the lost longhorns. "We will split up," he said, signing with two bronze-hued fingers, his sign language becoming more difficult to decipher. "…two go this way, two more go that way…!

"Each team of Spotted Pony's cousins will find cows and bring them back here—for you to guard—then we go to find more; until we have them all." With that said the eight coffee-sated cousins rode away as four teams, heading off into the four corners of the compass.

"Good thing I hid the bacon," Bonner remarked, "else we wouldn't have any breakfast ourselves!"

If they had stayed much longer," Lynn added, "they would have finished off our coffee supply."

Old Slim was chuckling when he spoke. "We shouldn't have salted the meat, reckon that bunch is sure a craving salt—the worst salt craving bunch I ever did see! I've heard tell of friendly tribes fighting and killing each other over—salt!"

"And my biscuits," Lynn spoke again, "Did you see how they wolfed down my biscuits? I had to bake four pans full before they were finished.

"Not often do them boys get to eat a feast like we showed 'em," Will explained. The red skinned people never know when they might have food to eat again—the reason they eat like they do.

"Reckon I'll pick over these here antelope bones, might find enough meat to tide me over!"

* * * Chapter Twelve * * *

"Think them Injun kids will find many o' them loco cows?" The feast of the cousins was long past, and old Slim was sitting on the ground, his back propped against a wagon wheel enjoying his pipe.

"Sure hope so," Bonner was quick to answer. He had his red horse saddled and ready to ride in case this should happen. He was standing slouched against the saddle, one elbow hooked around the saddle horn. Looking over at Lynn, who was perched on the wagon tongue, he spoke again, "I reckon you might have to cook our Indian cowboys another meal."

He was smiling now, and began to chuckle as he watched her reaction. She must have been daydreaming about their little ranch back at the river, perhaps it was centered around her old home at Lariat Cross. Nevertheless her reverie had been interrupted by her husband's talk. She looked up in horror at what Bonner had told her. "Surely not again!" and she wasn't looking any too happy at what he had told her.

"You mean they will be hungry this soon—after all the food they gorged this morning: eating a whole antelope, and drinking gallons of coffee!"

"Reckon so darlin', it's part of our deal that we feed them."

With a shrug of her shoulders, she turned to enter the wagon. "I better check out our supplies—I don't know what I can feed them?

"Reckon there's enough flour left to bake some sourdoughs though!"

Old Slim sat in the background listening to their talk. He was smiling as was his way, and reckoned he was one lucky *hombre* to have become involved with the Bonners. They saved his bacon sure from Kid Curry, and helped him to avenge his poor Mary. Reckon he would have been killed by now, and unable to seek vengeance for what they had done to his daughter.

"I'll help you Lynn! When I'm not needed at the roundup, I'll be here to help you feed this hungry bunch."

He wandered over to the fire, stoked it with fresh fuel, and smiling at Lynn said, "Bring out your fixin's—ole Slim is a goin' to start bakin' them sourdoughs!"

Will Bonner was getting downright fidgety and upset. The sun was several hours above the horizon and still no sign of the Blackfoot cousins. Stepping into the saddle, he informed Lynn that he was riding out on a scout, looking for the longhorns, and Spotted Pony's cousins.

With a touch of his spurs and a gentle command from the rein, the red horse took off across the prairie, it wasn't long until Bonner noticed a faint dust cloud rising above the southern horizon. "Them Blackfoot cousins are a comin'," he shouted. "See the dust cloud over yonder—reckon they have a good sized bunch too!

"I'm ridin' over to lend a hand."

Slim and Lynn could only stand there and watch. Slim was eyeing with interest the big cowboy riding away, big Red running full out, giving all that he had. He spoke with a chuckle, "I'm surprised Will stayed in camp this long—it's not in his nature to sit around and wait!"

"I agree with you Slim," Lynn said. "Reckon the rest this morning will do him good—most likely he will be riding hard for the rest of the day."

The two camp cooks walked out from camp so they could better observe the action, and were amazed at how much ground had been covered. The herd was much closer now with Bonner riding point, the exhausted longhorns staggering close behind. The big trail boss started them into a swing; the fatigued herd only too willing to follow.

Two cousins, who had been riding their own version of the maneuver, whooping and hollering and showing off their prowess to the big boss, rode in close and forced the longhorns to follow Will Bonner into a milling cloud of dust and half-crazed cattle. Soon more cousins showed up.

Bonner rode out from the circling hullabaloo, then turned and watched in amazement. He had experienced several cattle stampedes in his short life, but never had he witnessed anything like this. The Indian boys were circling the worn-out longhorns a yip-pin' and a ki-yi-in', as if the exhausted animals had been a caravan of prairie schooners, harboring a group of frightened settlers and their families.

A grinning Spotted Pony rode up, accompanied by one of his cousins. "*Ho!*" he greeted. Followed by the now familiar, "*Ki!*"

"We have brought you the long horned ones—who were frightened by the storm spirits!

"They will be fine now, and are sorry they ran away—it was the bad spirits who made them run away from your camp."

Bonner was still speechless, as he watched more of the cousins ride in close, one of them with a fresh-killed antelope draped across his bare-backed pony. The cousin's ponies were ready to drop from exhaustion, heads hanging low, bone-dry and dust-caked noses struggling to inhale enough air to continue on with the living.

Once again Spotted Pony spoke, "*Oki! Oki, boss!*"

The Pony was smiling now, rubbing his paint smeared belly, a dirty finger pointing at his mouth; as were the others. "My cousins say they are hungry—have worked real hard finding the long-horned ones—Lone Hawk will take this meat to your camp.

"There we will prepare another feast—make plenty of coffee Bonner, it was in our deal—much *wampum!*"

Spotted Pony rode over to the wagon to be with the cousins, there would be time for more talk later.

Bonner rode slowly through the herd, careful not to spook them. Near as he could tell the herd was all here, could be a few more still missing; it was hard to tell. The dust was settling, the majority of the herd dropping to the ground with exhaustion. The old trail-maker, the one horned roan was nowhere to be found, could be she never made it he reasoned.

Bonner had become attached to the longhorn, the one who faithfully followed him through hell and high water, enticing the herd to follow.

Could be she had stumbled in the darkness, went down and was trampled by the stampeding herd. Bonner had resigned himself to some losses, he had never been around a stampede yet that didn't lose a bunch.

Spotted Pony showed up once more, he told Bonner it was now time to go eat. "A feast!" he said. "Much coffee for your cowboy's to drink, much meat for hungry bellies!"

Riding leisurely back to the wagon, the two discussed the wild stampede. "Near as I can tell Pony, the herd is all here, could be there's still a few unaccounted for."

"This many," Spotted Pony replied, and held up nine fingers.

"They are that way," and pointed into the west. "They are hiding in a secret place, the buffalo have shown us where these low places are. They make this place when the rains come—they roll in the mud—in the wet time."

"Was that old roan cow there? Bonner asked Lynn's new protector, and bane to the evil ones of the night, as was Little Crow. "She is the only one in the herd with one horn missing!"

"*Oki!*" came the reply.

"A new one has been given to this one-horned cow…fresh from her womb. This ones friend's stay with her, they wish to save this cow—and the little one—from the wolves that wish to eat her!"

Spotted Pony's sign language was in fine fettle, assisting the big cowboy to better understand the information that was given him.

"Oki! Okii-ii!" The Pony expounded once again. "The wolves are afraid of these long horns—they do not wish to be gored in their soft bellies!"

Bonner appeared deep in thought, then spoke to the Pony once again, "I reckon we should go and bring them back to the herd, after you and your cousins have finished eating your antelope."

Spotted Pony advised his boss to leave them be. "We must not take them from where they are hidden—this herd will find them—one more sun, close to trail that goes to your tepee by the river."

Riding into the small prairie camp, the two were greeted by a delicious aroma of roasting antelope meat, and even coffee. It appeared that Lynn had discovered enough of the elixir of the plains to once again sate their voracious appetites of the same.

The Pony joined in with his cousins. A prairie feast was spread out before them, a feast they would not soon forget. All the Bonners and old Slim could do, was stand back and watch, smiles on their faces as they watched the antelope slowly disappear, and frowning over the amount of their precious coffee that was being consumed.

"Beats all I ever did see!" Slim said. "Old Kid Currie's gang was a coffee drinkin' bunch, but wouldn't stand a chance against these cousins of the Pony."

Lynn, who was exhausted, and sitting on the wagon tongue of the old canvas-top, spoke up, "We're cleaned out of flour and coffee, from here on out this bunch will have to eat plain old antelope meat.

"How much farther to our ranch?" she asked, looking at her big husband. "I don't think I can handle preparing another feast like this one."

The exhausted longhorns were allowed to rejuvenate themselves from the wild stampede, and at five a.m. the next morning, were aroused from their bedding ground and one more time the drive started into the west.

Bonner and Lynn rode point, the now docile herd following, even though the one-horned cow was not there to do so. The sun was high in the sky of the next day, when the Pony, and two of his cousins, brought the nine missing animals to the herd.

The new-born calf was put in the wagon with old Slim. And the blue cow, who had reluctantly watched this happen, was trotting along side the wagon casting hate-filled eyes at the human who was handling the reins.

The herd settled in real good, Bonner reckoned they were trail broke once again, shouldn't be any trouble ahead.

A contagious giggle erupted from a happy Lynn. "We're nearly home now," she said. She was the first to spot Old Chief Mountain, a mere dot on the western prairie. The St. Mary's river and her home range were much closer now, the long, dusty prairie fading away behind them.

"One more night of sleeping on the hard prairie," she said, looking at her husband. "And best of all, we're bringing home with us the longhorns that are finally ours.

Two cow ponies knew the drive would soon be over, keen, inquisitive noses pointing into the west. Already they recognized the scent of cool running water, cottonwood leaves and other pleasant things.

More important yet were the two humans who rode them. Will Bonner in the saddle of Red, his new wife Lynn astride her Boots mare. The horses walked side-by-side, the cowboy's chap-enclosed leg brushing that of his happy companion.

Big Red and Boots listened with interest to the sound of the humans talk, the strange music of their laughter. They could sense the humans were happy, reason enough for the horses to be happy as well.

"Sure been a different sort of honeymoon," Lynn said, reaching over and squeezing his hand as tight as she could.

"Oh, Will!" a tear was showing in her eyes. "It has been nothing but fighting and shooting, and tangling with Indians and outlaws all the time; and shooting them dead too!

"Since the first day I met you—this has happened!"

Bonner's words were quick to reply. "I'm sure proud of my sharp-shooting wife. We've been quite a team together, mighty fortunate too—just as easy both been killed—a fate worse than death for you though!"

Lynn wasn't finished yet and continued with her train of thought. "Ever since I met you on the Chief Mountain trail, your darling Lynn has been shooting people, sending them to the dark place I reckon.

"I hope it's soon over. My desire is to never take the life of another person."

* * *

The girl's tears were flowing before she was finished. "Reckon I'm destined for the dark place some folks call hell. Don't reckon they will want me in heaven!"

Will was busting at the seams to speak, but out of courtesy to this beautiful lady who had become his wife, he waited.

"Reckon it was Grandpa Brannon who trained me this way—to shoot straight and standup for truth and right," she reminisced. "to champion the down trodden and timid folk—the ones who are unable to defend themselves!"

"It's a harsh law sure, the Code of the old West," Will said after a long pause. "Old Matt Brannon was right, had it to do he reckoned—and was respected for doing it.

"You and I have only carried on the tradition—the old law—the Code of the West!"

The girl was pleased with the attention her husband was showing her, and most of all his concern for her feelings, yet was dead serious when next she spoke. "Reckon my Mom will be plumb upset when I tell her about all our adventures. And that she now has two U.S. deputy marshals in her family. Wow!

"Reckon I don't know how she'll react to that!"

"We'll see," Will said. "Your Mom's a fine lady…a chip off the old block from what you've told me.

"She'll understand, and be proud of her only daughter…just you wait and see."

Lynn accepted her husband's words and was pleased. Later, after a long silence, she looked at her husband and her happy smile had returned. She was her old self again and that pleased Will Bonner immensely.

"Thank you. Seems like you're always thinking of my feelings and all, reckon you're the best medicine a girl could ever have.

"Reckon it's now time we had us a cattle brand of our own," the girl said, her thoughts no longer kept to herself.

"A brand we can both be proud of. I reckon the Double B sounds real good, out of respect for our family names, Brannon and Bonner. The B—B ranch on the west bank of the St. Mary's river, a heritage not only for me and you, but our posterity as well!"

A cloud of dust hung over the B—B trail-herd, revealing the route to the antelope, prairie wolf and a vulture that hovered overhead. The wranglers and the longhorns continued on into the uncertainty of a heat-baked prairie, resigned to a fate of dust, fatigue and a terrible thirst.

As the day wore on the mood of the cattle changed, dust-caked horns lifting, sensitive nostrils inhaling the scent of cool running water, cottonwood leaves and sun-ripened grass. Closing in on the crossing of the St. Mary's, there would be no holding them back, a swinging trot changing into a wild stampede.

Sundown was engulfing the prairie before the longhorns arrived at the mountain-bred stream. Staggering with exhaustion and tongues hanging low, the thirst-crazed herd exploded over a steep bank into the cool fast-flowing water.

After slaking a raging thirst, the herd splashed across to dry ground where many dropped in their tracks from exhaustion, others began grazing the virgin grass that grew there in such abundance.

Spotted Pony and his cousins were left there with the herd. His orders were to keep the cattle safely on the west bank. Then, as they settled down, allow them to drift up into the breaks of the Deerhorn hills. Old Slim headed upriver with the wagon and provisions.

Hand in hand, Will and Lynn Bonner rode onward for their little ranch house by the river. Reeling from fatigue, the trail-worn girl from Lariat Cross was lifted from the saddle by her big cowboy husband, and carried across the threshold of their cabin home.

She was staggering with fatigue, yet thankful to be back in her home under the cottonwoods, her new husband holding her so close. This had been a long grueling journey for her, nerve-wracking too. Bonner knew she had been through hell and back again, and after firing-up the little stove, heated water for her to enjoy a warm bath.

After she had cleaned up, including her dust-tousled hair, she found her night gown and tumbled into her soft bed; in no time at all she was out of it. A welcome sleep overcame her, a tranquil rejuvenation of the weary.

Making sure that Lynn was settled and asleep, Brannon then rode out to find Spotted Pony. He informed him that his cousins weren't needed any more, and that they could return to the reservation.

In a small buckskin poke was a silver dollar, one for each of the cousins, which he handed to the Pony. He also gave them the one-horned cow and her calf, told the Pony this was a gift for helping with the drive, the stampede and all the rest.

Spotted Pony looked long at the bag of coins, removed one from the bag and inspected it with much interest. Finally he spoke, "Oki!" "I will give my cousins your gifts.

"They were happy to help big boss with the long horned ones—and happy to drink his coffee—and will be very pleased to have silver eagle coins that he has given them. These eagle coins will be magic *wampum* to Spotted Pony and his cousins—good medicine for Blackfoot braves.

"And boss, these cousins wish to come again—when you need them—and be your cowboys!"

Spotted Pony had finally ceased his long oration, giving Bonner a chance to fathom his talk, most of which had been given by sign language. But it appeared he wasn't finished yet.

"They say, if you need cousins to come again—Bonner make big smoke—up there,"

The one who rides a spotted horse, then signed to the high wind-blown hill above the ranch, an ancient landmark of the smoke-talkers of past generations.

* * * Chapter Thirteen * * *

Deputy Lynn Bonner was her old happy self once again, enjoying each and every day of her marriage to Will Bonner, the big cowboy who had won her heart back at the big rock camp on the Chief Mountain trail.

A week had passed, going on two, since their return with the longhorns from the Cow Creek range. Lynn had now recovered from the outlaw war with the Curry bunch, and the long tedious journey of bringing the herd home to the St. Mary's river.

Time waits for no one, she reminisced. It passes as swiftly as the river that flows past her cabin home. Lately she had became restless, reckoned it was high time they saddled their broncs and rode up the trail to Lariat Cross and see her Mom, whom she hadn't seen for several long months.

She sure missed her Mom, and just couldn't wait to see her again. To tell her of her marriage to Will, to tell her of the many adventures in the wild country of Montana, and to tell her of the twin stars.

When Will returned at sundown she would tell him of her plans. Bustling around her small kitchen preparing supper, she was singing when Will walked in the door and gave her a warm hug.

"Sure smells good," he said. "I'm as hungry as a bear—old Slim is too, he'll be here right pronto."

"Do you think Spotted Pony will eat with us tonight?" she asked.

"I reckon I can't say for sure, he went off wandering by himself—said it was night time now—time for him to guard the ranch from the evil ones he's always a talkin' about.

"We'll leave him a pot of coffee out by the big cottonwood—like always—the coffee and his jerky will make him a happy Indian."

Lynn loved to cook, and she was a good one too, having been trained by her Mom, both of who carried the genes of old Lynn Brannon in their veins. Her Grandma Brannon, whom was noted as the top doughnut maker in the West. She was sure proud of her rifle-packing Grandma, proud of the gold wedding band that was now worn on the finger of little Lynn, who was herself.

"It's high time we ride up to Lariat Cross and see my Mom," she said, watching closely the reaction of Bonner. She knew he was settling into being a rancher with much vigor, and was glued in his saddle from daybreak till night time brought him back to her again, here by her beloved river.

They had finished their evening meal, and had wandered outdoors to sit by the big cottonwood that Lynn loved so well. "We have been home for a week now, Will, it's high time we go and see my Mom, and let her know that we have returned—safe and sound—and in one piece!"

Much to her surprise, Will agreed. "Reckon I can spare a few days off," he told her. "Why don't we leave at first light."

The ride into the country of tall pines and clear mountain streams was a pleasant one for Lynn and her husband. The chatter of the happy girl and the chuckles of her big cowboy could be heard echoing far back into the silent woods.

After a ride of twenty miles, they arrived at a clearing in the tall pines, and a creek she new as Lariat Cross. Here sat a fine two-story log house, built by old Paddy and his crew. And the little ramshackle cabin in the quacking trees, the one where she was born, was nothing now but a modest pile of rubble.

Lame Deer's tepee was still here, and the Brannon graveyard where rested her Grandma and Grandpa Brannon. Not stopping their weary mounts, they rode up to the graveyard and dismounted, ground-tied the horses who began to hungrily devour the tasty plants that grew there.

Lynn promptly walked into the aspens and picked two bouquets of flowers. It is in this region the plant species of the prairie merge with that of the high country, and much to her delight she was able to find an abundance of both.

She was giggling as she plucked the tender plants, happy to have found a smattering of sun flowers, the delicate bloom of the prairie rose, and even several Indian paintbrush plants. She knelt by the graves, and placed a bouquet on each of the mounds of earth. After a moment of revered silence, Lynn uttered a short prayer.

Rising from where she had been kneeling, she looked at her husband and said, "It is time now, let us go find my Mom!" With the reins of their saddle horses in hand, they walked down to the big house.

Nearing the house, they stopped and with heads close together, whispered their plans. Raising the collars of the two long duster coats they wore, the cowboy and the girl positioned their big hats to shadow their eyes; the shiny tin stars were displayed with no uncertainty of their meaning.

Will knocked at the door and waited for a reply, a slight smile showing below his mustache. Lynn stood in the background struggling to suppress a mirthful giggle. The door opened and there stood Paddy O'Niel, her Mom's Irish husband.

"What is it ye be a needin'?" he asked, squinting into the brilliance of the afternoon sun. "If it's a meal ye be after—you'll have to wait till supper time—me darlin' wife is not up to feedin' any—!"

As if struck by lightning, Paddy appeared as if in a daze, a state of shock surrounded him as he gazed long at the tin stars. "Faith and beggo-rrie!" he stammered. "—'tis me bad manners ye must pardon me of—cum on in!

"Me darlin' Lynn will have a steak—a sizzlin' in the skillet—in no time at all, she will."

The two deputies advanced into the house following a flustered Paddy. "We bin told there's a bootlegger workin' in these parts," Will said, a stern look upon his face. "The reservation police notified us of drunkenness occurring along the border and Lariat Cross—a problem that's a getting out-of-hand!

"The Chief himself contacted us, asked us to ride over and check things out."

The sun-bronzed face of the Irishman was losing its color, paling fast as he listened to the lawman's words.

Lynn's Mom had now entered the room to see what was bothering her husband so. On noticing the lawmen, she quietly stood in the background wondering what kind of trouble her husband was in this time.

"We are United States Deputy Marshals," Will Bonner continued his talk, staring Paddy in his shifty eyes. "We were wondering if you might help us out—possibly give us a clue—as to where this shady business might be located."

Lynn O'Niel happened to glance out the window and noticed the two strange horses standing hip-shot at Paddy's hitch rail. One of them was a striking pinto mare that sure looked familiar. She walked to the window and moved back a curtain to better see. "Boots!" she shrieked. "It is Lynn's horse—I just know it is!"

As the excited matron of Lariat Cross headed for the door, Deputy Bonner took off her big hat, fluffed her shoulder length hair, and stepped in front of her Mom's way. "Don't you remember your only daughter? This is me, Lynn!"

Both were giggling, and weeping and hugging each other, as a dumbfounded Paddy looked on, still attempting to figure out the whole affair. He heaved a sigh of relief, reckoned he was off the hook for the devious mention of bootlegging that had made him a nervous wreck; and looked once more at the big Deputy Marshal.

Bonner was smiling and asked, "You must not remember me Paddy?

"I'm Lynn's husband, whose life she saved up at the trail camp under the big Chief Mountain—we stayed here for a few days, remember"

"Jumpin' Jehosophats!" he exclaimed, his mind clearing some after his scare by the lawman's talk of tracking down bootleggers and such, and he did have a guilty conscience!

Paddy was still eyeing the shiny tin star on both Lynn and Will. "—'tis a shock it is, to ole' Paddy's Irish heart; to open me door—and there be greeted by two Yankee law men—a huntin' the makers of this forbidden brew of the big for-rest!"

He now realized the other lawman was none other than his wife's only daughter Lynn, and quickly changed his tune.

Paddy was a forgiving sort, even though he now realized he had been on the brunt end of a prank by his wife's daughter. Muttering to himself as he took their guest's horses to the corrals, he realized his nerves were in a shattered condition, and would remain so for some time to come.

Before returning to the big house, Paddy walked over to a small shed, and after checking to be sure he was alone, entered the structure and pulled out a jug hidden under a pile of gunny sacks. He uncorked the home-grown brew and indulged in a hearty swig.

With a sigh of pleasure, he wiped the leavings from his mustache and muttered, "Me blasted nerves are shot—they be! 'tis a bad day, it is—when the Yankee marshals cum a snoopin' about ol' Paddy's ranch!"

Checking again to make sure no one was watching, he hoisted the jug in the crook of his arm, partook of another hearty swig—and then another. Tucking his beloved jug back under the feed sacks, he arose and turned to go.

"Ole Paddy's cough medicine is what me shattered nerves have bin a needin," he mumbled, and staggered back to the house.

* * *

Lynn's Mom prepared a sumptuous feast that night. It was a delicious roast beef supper complete with all the trimmings, including fresh-baked doughnuts and a gallon of coffee.

Later they all went into the parlor, where Lynn was asked to relate all that had happened since their last visit here. Several times throughout Lynn's travelogue, old Paddy fell asleep, his raucous snores interrupted by a sharp poke from Lynn O'Neil's elbow in his ribs.

"Paddy!" Lynn chided. "You haven't heard a thing that I've said."

"Aye, lassie I have," he was quick to reply. Ole Paddy now knows that you're a married lady—to this Marshal here!

"The thing that upsets me ol' bones—is that the pair o' ye—are a packin' them Yankee tin stars!" With that said, his head dropped once again, his outrageous snoring echoing throughout Lynn O'Neil's fancy parlor.

Finally, in disgust, she roused him from the chair and took him to his bed.

"I don't know what is wrong with him today?" she said, on her return. "He's been acting funny ever since you folks arrived—crazy like, and nervous as a cornered weasel in a hen house!"

* * *

Lynn was thrilled that Bonner was in no rush to head back down country to their river ranch. He told her, considering what they both had been through these past months, was reason enough to take it easy for awhile. "The ranch is in good hands,

"Old Slim and Spotted Pony will handle things—as good a pair o' hands as I ever ran across.

"When you're ready to go home, just let me know."

The deputy badges were now tucked in their pockets, which made Paddy feel a whole lot more comfortable.

One morning Paddy, who was feeling his old chipper self once again, invited Bonner to ride with him back into the deep woods to check on some cattle he had stashed away there. "It is good grazing up that way—and needs to be eaten off, before winter sets in.

"I must warn you Bonner, 'tis a secret ol' Paddy wishes you to see—you and I will be the only ones to know where it is—my friend!"

"Why not?" Bonner replied. "I will be happy to share your secret, 'sides old Red is getting fat and sassy—a eating this lush mountain grass, with nothing to do.

"A good day's ride will do him good."

With enough food tucked in their saddle bags to feed four or five men, the two border ranchers rode up the trail into the high country, winding through the aspens and pines to nowhere but up.

After several hours of tough climbing, they pulled in their broncs near a modest stream that crossed the trail. It was quiet here in the pine forest, a peaceful spot disturbed only by the sound of the drinking horses, and the chatter of a bone-dry Irishmen.

"It is ol' Paddy's bottom end that needs a rest," he said and stepped down from the saddle, "a few short minutes here will do us all good, Bonner me boy." The horses were eagerly satisfying their thirst when Paddy uncorked his canteen, and partook of several hearty swigs.

Bonner could only watch the crafty Irishman in action, and by the way he was smacking his lips after each swig, knew the old Civil War canteen was filled with something a lot stronger than water. It was hair-of-the-dog Paddy was guzzling from the old battered relic, he was sure of this.

He was certain now that Lynn's Mom was married to a backwoods alcoholic, addicted to an intoxicating brew of his own making. And Lynn's tongue-in-cheek story of a wanted bootlegger, of which had spooked the Irishman so; was more truth than the intended fiction.

The horses were refreshed now, and so was Paddy. "You take the lead Bonner, 'tis not far now—just a hundred yards or so up yonder—we will find a big grass meadow.

"It is here ol' Paddy has his secret, guarded by the leprechauns they be—the little green devils are pleased with Paddy's new cows—these red cows have ho-orns on their white-faced heads, they do."

The big cowboy could not believe what he was hearing. He appeared stunned and pulled in his red horse. "What did you say Paddy? Did I hear you talk about white-faced cattle?"

"Aye! 'tis the white-faced ones—fresh over from the auld soil too— they cost me a bag o' me gold, they did!"

They continued on, Brannon shaking his head over Paddy's secret. To think that after all the fighting and heartache he and Lynn had endured, traveling into the southern lands after Hereford cattle, that it would be here they would find them. Twenty miles is all, just a half days ride from their B—B spread; Lynn's eccentric father-in-law had some hidden away.

* * * Chapter Fourteen * * *

Lynn and her Mom were like a pair of happy school girls catching up on their day to day lives, never one straying far from the other. Giggling and talking, always talking about those events the other was unaware of.

"Mom." Lynn asked, after a long pause from their chattering. "Where is little Mathew? I haven't seen my half-brother yet, reckoned he must be off somewhere, staying with friends?"

Her Mom was slow with a reply, her countenance appeared forlorn and sad. "I might as well tell you now as later Lynn.

"He's staying with friends, down on the Blackfoot trail. They are good folks, have children of their own the same age as Mathew. The lady was once a school teacher, she has been teaching her own children how to read and write and consented to keep your brother for a few weeks; teach him to read and write; and cipher some."

"Why Mom, that is wonderful, a splendid idea!"

"We miss him so, at least I do. Paddy says it is a waste of time and money, and that the boy can pick up these high-falutin' ways on his own, the same as he did back in Ireland. Why, my Irish husband can hardly write his own name, he can read very few words and his ciphering is done on his fingers.

"But I have another problem though, and it is about Paddy, who has no patience with his son. He never takes him with him—never shows him how to handle horses, or to use a rope, or to shoot a gun. He claims he doesn't have the time or the patience to spend with our only son."

The good matron of Lariat Cross paused, wiped a tear from her eyes before she continued her talk, "I'm worried about Paddy—he's taken to the jug, more so as each day passes us by.

"Oh! He tries to hide his weakness, but I know!

"I know my husband is making and using whiskey—trading it to others, too!"

Lynn gasped at what she was hearing, followed by a long silence between mother and daughter. She appeared deep in thought before she spoke, "I'll talk to Will, maybe we should take my brother home with us for awhile—he can live at our B-B spread!

"This would make me happy, and Will too. It would be an honor to have my half-brother stay with us. Will and old Slim will make him into a cowboy, a rip-snortin' cowboy old Grandpa Brannon would have been mighty proud of!"

"Lynn's Mom dried her tears, and gave her daughter another hug. "Thank you," she said. "I will be forever grateful to you and your good husband Will."

"It is now my turn," Lynn was smiling when she spoke, "to tell you of our adventures since last I was here." True, she had skimmed over them before, but now she described them in detail.

Her Mom listened with interest as Lynn told her of their marriage at Fort Benton, of the Mormon bishop who married them, and of the gunfight with the Mormon-hating traders. The tin stars she did not forget, nor Marshal Custis Dunne who insisted they wear the shiny badges as United States Deputy Marshals. And then the long ride to the Judith country and meeting up with Harvey Logan, alias Kid Curry.

Lynn Bonner told it all. The episode at Landusky and her eventual kidnapping and the long painful ride into the Missouri breaks. Old Slim she did not forget, and the drive that eventually brought the longhorns home to the St. Mary's river.

With tears in her eyes she spoke of the death of Little Crow, and his brave stand against the one known as Crazy Dog, at the talking cliffs. "How is Lame Deer?" she asked. "I must go now, and tell Lame Deer what has happened to her brave son!"

They were both weeping now, hugging each other too. "I don't really know how to tell you this Lynn," her Mom said. "But Lame Deer already knows about Little Crow—she insists her son came to her in a vision—and told her the whole story!

"He said that even though he was now in the Spirit World, he would continue to guard Missy Lynn—from the evil one's of the night!"

Lynn Bonner was visibly shaken from what her Mom was telling her, her tears and sobbing continued for a long time. "I loved Little Crow, even though he was a dirty heathen, never bathing and forever cutting the hair from the heads of those that had been killed.

"I must go now, and talk to Lame Deer—and tell her how much I loved her son."

"Lame Deer is still in mourning," her Mom added. "It is the custom of her people to be alone while in mourning, and not to have contact with anyone for several moons.

"You are special to her, Lynn. She just might break the rules and allow you to visit with her."

"It is the custom of these people, for those who are mourning the loss of a loved one, to have gifts brought to them, as a token of respect and friendship."

The two began hustling around the house, gathering up various items that might please old Lame Deer. A large basket was stuffed to the brim, including lots of food, a bolt of bright red cloth, and even a new Hudson Bay blanket found in Paddy's store house.

With the basket in hand, a pair of saddened Lynns walked over to the big tepee in the aspens.

* * *

Will Bonner had taken the lead, the Irishman following behind, his mental condition waning, as was the contents of his Civil War canteens; and he had brought two. Paddy was weaving in the saddle, singing old Irish ballads of questionable content. His saddle horse was a large-hoofed Percheron cross, acquainted with Paddy's ways, and was plodding up the trail at a plow-horse pace.

In spite of the Irishman's drunken state, Bonner was disturbed over what might lay in store, his trail-honed savvy sensing an unknown danger ahead. Old Red was equally on edge, head raised high and alert ears pointing up the trail, relaying a message back to the big rider.

Bonner could now hear a ruckus amongst the cattle, they too were disturbed, lowing a frightening tune, a confused medley of sound that told Bonner there must be big trouble in Paddy's white faced cows.

The steepness of the trail lessened some, topping over into a well-grassed mountain meadow. He inhaled deeply, a ripple of danger traveling up and down his spine. The Herefords were here all right, the red cows with white-faces and each with two sharp horns, just as Paddy had told him. But, they were bunched in the center of the clearing, surrounding a bear which had killed one of Paddy's cows and was attempting to drag it away into the pines.

A circle of outraged cattle, tails in the air, tongues hanging low, and bellowing a fearsome tune, had surrounded the bear, and it was a grizzly. The big carnivore would drop his kill and charge at the cows, woofing a threatening sound, which forced them to give ground. After which the bear returned to his illicit kill, determined to drag the carcass back into his forest lair.

All hell had broken loose in the meadow before a drunken Paddy rode in off the trail, still weaving back and forth in the saddle, still singing his old Irish ballads of an undetermined origin.

Brannon had ridden a circle of his own, rifle in hand, the other gripping the reins of a high-stepping red horse. "What be ye a doin'?" Paddy shouted. "What is it that has me Herefords in such a dither?

"Where are ya at, Brannon me boy? Ol' Paddy be a comin'—to lend ya his hand—he will"

Brannon heard his shouts and turning to see, cursed a blue streak. All he could do was watch Paddy charging towards the cattle and the bear, rifle in hand and still bellowing his Irish jargon.

"The fool will get himself killed!" Brannon muttered, reining his horse and riding hard to intercept the Irishman. But Paddy had a head start and beat him to the circle, scattering cows in all directions of the compass.

The rank stink of grizzly was heavy in the air. Paddy's horse, on getting a whiff of the eye-watering scent, skidded to a halt which upended the husband of Lynn's Mom, tumbling him to the ground—then turned tail and headed for home.

There lay a dazed and still intoxicated Irishman facing the wrath of a grizzly bear. There were just the two of them now facing the dead cow, old Paddy and the bear.

* * *

Lame Deer was found in a small canvas shelter out back of the tepee. The old Nez Perce matriarch was in bad shape, her lips were chapped and bloody. Blood was evident on her hands and arms where she had slashed herself with a small knife. By all appearances she had been without food and water for far too long.

Lynn Bonner took one look and gasped in shock. "I am so sorry Lame Deer," she said, and dropped to her knees embracing her old friend in a warm hug. Then she whispered in her ear. "We loved Little Crow too!"

Lame Deer recognized Lynn's voice, and ceased her silent chanting— her lips had been moving but no sound could she voice. She did however look up at the young women, whom she had assisted her Mom in bringing from the place of spirits, a slight smile of recognition was on her wrinkled face.

Lynn's Mom was shocked as well, and turned to Lynn and said, "Lame Deer's mourning is now over! We must take her to her tepee and clean this filth and blood from her, and give her water and prepare her a warm meal.

"And her slashed arms are still bleeding, this we must stop!"

Lame Deer knew the two Lynns were helping her, a faint glimmer of hope returned to her sunken eyes. She loved them both as if they had been her own daughters, and was grateful they were with her now in her time of need. A faint smile returned to her lips as she remembered of bringing them both from the spirit world. A young Nez Perce maiden, whom by chance, had used the lore of her ancestors in becoming a revered mid-wife of the Brannon clan.

Lame Deer was cleaned up now and wrapped in the Hudson Bay blanket. Her arms had been bandaged, and a kettle of broth sat simmering over an open fire. Lynn's Mom had returned to the big house to prepare supper for the men, who should be returning soon from their venture up at Paddy's secret in the high country.

Lynn Bonner sat close to Lame Deer's pallet, a cup of warm broth in her hand, the other arm wrapped around the old one's frail body. "I have some warm broth for you Lame Deer! This will make you feel much better—but you must open your mouth—so I can help you drink some."

The old one's eyes fluttered, a trace of a smile appeared on her lips, she had listened to Lynn's words; but her mouth would not open.

Lynn laid her gently back in the blanket, tucked her in, and noticed the peaceful look on Lame Deer's face. Returning to the fire, she placed several willow twigs on the embers, and sat back to wait. "Perhaps she will drink some broth later," she murmured.

A serene quiet was evident in the tepee, causing Lynn to nod off herself. She just couldn't keep her eyes open. Later she roused, placed more twigs on the fire and moved over to check on Lame Deer. Maybe she will be able to drink her broth now, Lynn reasoned, and removed the blanket that was tucked around her face.

For a long time the tearful girl looked at Lame Deer's face, she knew that it was too late for the broth now. Lame Deer, the daughter of the mighty Chief Joseph had returned to the spirit world from whence she came.

With much respect Lynn placed the blanket over the peaceful face of her old friend. She was sobbing as if her heart would break, and returned to the big house to tell her Mom.

On hearing the sad news her Mom began to weep as well. They both sat in the darkening shadows of an approaching night, their tears a token of the loss of a dear friend.

Presently, they ceased their mourning. From the darkened ranch yard they could hear the sound of an approaching horse. "The men must be back," Lynn Duval said. "You light the lamps dear, while I put the supper on the table."

The two Lynn's arose from their chairs, and hustled about attending to the chores of an approaching supper at Lariat Cross.

From out in the darkness came a shout, and Lynn knew that it was her husband's voice, "Ho! The house, I could use some help out here!

"Lynn!

"Come give me a hand!"

* * * Chapter Fifteen * * *

The fall from his horse had been unexpected to the Irishman, he received a good shaking up too. He was moaning a painful tune, on his hands and knees fumbling in the tall grass; attempting to find his shotgun that went flying when he was bucked off the old plow horse. Finally, he staggered up out of the grass, shotgun in hand, ready to take on all comers.

A bear's eyesight is somewhat cloudy, relying on his sense of smell in situations such as this, On realizing Paddy had never left with the terror-stricken horse, the bear let go of the cow carcass it had been dragging and charged towards the Irishman with murder on its mind. Paddy was sobering up fast, and on realizing the bear was closing in on him, swung the old gun waist high and pulled the trigger; there was no time for an accurate aim. The kick from the weapon sent him tumbling back to the ground.

A feral blood-curdling roar blotted out the screams of a terrified Paddy, and then the bear was on top of him ripping and tearing. Blood was pouring from the beast in a wide pattern, old Paddy's scatter gun had found its mark. The bear was still able to pick him up though, and with a grip of mighty fangs, shook him as he would have a cottontail rabbit.

It was an accurate, well-placed shot that downed the bear. The cowboy's heart was in his mouth as he watched the enraged beast wilt to the ground, the loud noise of the rifle ringing in his ears. The bear died as it fell, the giant beast's body had fallen on top of Paddy,

Bonner was soon their, and with his lariat tied to one of the bear's hind legs and a dally wrapped around the saddle-horn, old Red was able to move the bear's carcass off of his father-in-law. Bonner leaped to the ground and knelt beside the old Irishman. What he saw shocked him clean down to his boot tops. "Never have I seen anything like this!" he muttered.

Paddy was lying flat on his back, unconscious and drenched with blood from one end of him to the other. Discovering that he was still breathing, Bonner set to work stopping the bleeding as best he could, and knew that somehow he must get him down off the mountain. "I wonder where Paddy's horse went?" he muttered. "I could sure use him about now."

From a nearby stand of lodgepole pine he found a pair of slender windfall poles. From his saddlebags he found leather strings, and along with his long duster coat, rigged up a makeshift travois. "If the Indians can make one of these here drags," he muttered. "Reckon I can do the same."

But getting Red to co-operate was a different story. It took a bit of tuning up before the big horse resigned himself to the status of an Indian mustang. Lashing the body of Paddy into the travois wasn't an easy task either, but he finally succeeded.

Then he headed down off the mountain, a five-mile ride, but fortunately it was all down hill. Soon he would be at the ranch, the folks from Lariat Cross could then take over.

Over by the corrals, with the saddle still in place and his head hanging low, stood old Paddy's large-hoofed Percheron cross saddle horse. The five mile terror-stricken run had about done him in.

* * *

Lynn and her Mom ran from the house, with terror in their hearts they knew that something must have happened to Paddy. Much to the red horse's relief, Will had unhooked the travois.

The woman arrived as Bonner was lifting the Irishman into his arms. "Make way you two," he spoke to the distraught women, "I'm a takin' the Irishmen inside—he's bin mauled by a grizzly bear.

"He's in one he-ell of a shape!"

"Oh, no-oo—!" Lynn's Mom cried, and burst into tears. She then uttered a terrified scream, her sobbing then took over. Lynn had thus far controlled her own emotions, and held the door open wide for Bonner to enter packing a hapless Paddy. Her Mom had scurried down the hall to Paddy's bedroom; swinging wide the door, waiting for the arrival of her husband.

Lynn O'Niel screamed once again as she looked at Paddy, whom Bonner had just settled onto the bed. He was a terrible sight to see, his clothes in tatters, blood from head to toe. "Reckon you should clean him up," he spoke with compassion to his mother-in-law. "He has lost a bunch o' blood. I had it stopped back on the mountain—the travois ride on that mountain trail—started the bleeding again."

Turning to Lynn who had been hanging on to his hand, he asked, "Why don't you go bring Lame Deer, reckon she's the best doctor in the West, from what you've told me."

Lynn burst into tears and couldn't be stopped. Bonner looked at her with amazement. "What's wrong Lynn?" What did I say that has upset you so?"

Lynn O'Niel, who was now suppressing her own tears, looked up from where she had been cleaning the blood from her husband, and spoke, "Sara Lame Deer left us today, she must be in the world of spirits by now—with her father Chief Joseph; and all her kinfolk.

Bonner never spoke for a spell, then said, "I'm sure sorry—I didn't know!

"Reckon I sure put a foot in my mouth this time."

Lynn was now hugging her husband, her sobbing easing off. "It wasn't your fault darlin' Will—you didn't know

"It was just that I loved her so-oo—!" and again her weeping returned.

Will was in deep thought before he spoke, "Remember that willow tea you prepared for me—up at our big rock camp on the Chief Mountain trail? Come with me, we'll go over to the creek and find some willow bark. That tea of Lame Deer's will either kill him or cure him!"

Lighting one of Paddy's barn lanterns, the two left for the mountain stream to find some willow bark. On their return with an armful of delicate branches, Bonner shaved off the bark and placed it in a pot of boiling water.

Several of Paddy's wounds, including one on his face, were long and deep. The grizzly's fangs and huge claws had performed with a deadly intent. "We must stitch the skin back together," Lynn's Mom said, looking up at her daughter, and left to find a needle.

On this very day the Jenni mule had came wandering into Lariat Cross, her keen sense of smell leading her on to Lariat Cross and Lynn Bonner. At the urging of Lynn, her husband left the room and returned with a long hair from the mule's tail.

"I can do this," Lynn said, "I've watched Lame Deer work her magic ever since I was a small girl.

"Why, there was seldom a scar showing—remember when Grandpa Brannon tangled with that grizzly—Lame Deer used one of Jenni's tail hairs then too?"

After the doctoring was finished, and Paddy peacefully resting, Lynn and her husband returned to the big kitchen and sat near the table.

Glancing at the untouched meal the women had prepared, hunger pangs attacked Lynn's big cowboy. "I'm starvin' plumb to death Lynn, while that tea's a brewing lets eat some of this supper.

"And I see the coffee pot is boilin' too."

"I reckon you're right," she replied. "I'm hungry too. I'll eat with you Will, and we can drink my Mom's coffee."

Later, as they sat in silence enjoying their coffee, Bonner looked at her and smiled, "This here coffee your Mom makes, must be Matt Brannon coffee you bin a tellin' me about—sure tastes good!"

Lynn turned her head and suppressed a giggle. It was she who had made the coffee, not her Mom, who had been busy carving the roast beef. "I like this coffee too," she said with a straight face. Grandpa Brannon showed me his secret recipe when I was just five years old."

* * *

Lynn's father-in-law had been used hard and put away wet. But he was tough as an old rooster and was slowly recovering. Lame Deer's willow bark tea, the only medicine available in this isolated country, surely saved his life.

The morning he aroused from the deep sleep he had been in, he was welcomed by the two Lynn's and the cowboy. Bonner had been sitting by his bed the morning Paddy opened his eyes, Lynn and her Mom were catching up on much needed sleep; having spent the nights at his bedside, taking turns watching over the old Irishman.

Paddy O'Neil was staring at Bonner and uttered a groan. He attempted to sit up and found that it was an impossible task to do, more agonizing groans escaped his fever-cracked lips. The first words he spoke brought a grin to the cowboy's face.

"Jumpin' Jehosophats, ol' Paddy has bin thru the fires of he—ell he has, and back agin'—!"

Bonner moved his chair closer to the bed so he could make out the Irishman's mumbling jargon. "Who be ye?" he asked, realizing that he wasn't alone. "Where is me darlin' Lynn?"

"You better lie still," Bonner told him. "You've been mauled by a grizzly bear, come mighty close to getting' yourself killed!

"I'm your son-in-law, Will Bonner. I brung you home from your secret cache of white-faced cows—remember?"

Paddy's mind was still in limbo, cloudy as a rainy day in the spring time. He attempted to move, even to sit up again, and each time a pain-wracked scream escaped his tortured lips. Bonner had his hands full to keep the old one quiet, knowing his fussing like this would start the bleeding all over again.

The women had been awakened by Paddy's screams of agony, and quickly were standing beside Bonner admiring the way he was handling the tortured Irishman. They were certain that they alone couldn't have done this, and were sure thankful that Bonner was here in this time of need.

"Better bring some of that willow tea," Bonner said, "and some scaldin'-hot coffee—blacker than sin—'tween the two of 'em, might settle him down!"

* * *

A week passed and Paddy was slowly improving. It appeared the wilderness medicine, cowboy coffee and willow tea, was doing the job.

Will Bonner was becoming edgy though, reckoned it was time he headed back home to their ranch, check on old Slim and Spotted Pony, and find out if everything was all right down by the big river.

But first he and the Irishman must have a medicine talk. "Paddy!" he said, looking the old one in the eyes, who was now able to sit up in his bed; a pillow propped at his back. "What will you take for some of your white-faced cows?

"Lynn and I are looking to start a herd of our own—the reason we rode all over eastern Montana—and wound up with only a bunch of longhorns!"

Paddy listened with interest, but failed to answer the cowboy's question. Bonner decided he better plunge in with both feet, strike while the iron was hot. "A bull or two, is all, and about a dozen cows. Looked to me like you must have around seventy head or so—up on that mountain grazing—shouldn't harm your herd none to part with a few."

Paddy still hadn't answered the cowboy's request, he groaned some as he attempted to move his bandaged body, but there was a hint of a smile showing on his old scarred face.

"Bonner me boy—and you are old Paddy's family you know. I'll make a deal with ye, I will!

"But first ye must find me jug, I have one tucked away—under me bed, it is! Ol' Paddy be dryer than a po-oor wanderin' devil—with nary a swallow to drink—lost and sufferin' on the lonesome prairie!"

Despite Paddy's picturesque portrayal of woe, a strong surge of elation rippled through the cowboy's lanky frame. Here it was, laid out before him, an offer for a deal if Bonner would return the favor. A favor asked, for a favor given.

He knew he would be in big trouble with the women if he gave Paddy his jug. He also reckoned that if he refused, there might never be a chance of obtaining any of Paddy's cows. What was he to do?

"Give me your answer, me boy," the Irishman said. "Ol' Paddy be a stranglin' with the terrible thirst o' me Irish ancestors, he be!"

He sensed hesitation on the cowboy's face, and with much experience at this sort of thing, spoke again. "You see, I must have a swig or two outta me jug—strictly for medicinal purposes—it be!"

With much effort he attempted to move, a convincing groan escaped his lips, and it was real. "Tis a terr-rrible tastin' brew, it be. Used by the leprechauns to ease their sufferin' ways—it will surely ease ol' Paddy's achin' bones, it will—from the awful pain he's bin a sufferin'."

Elation once again took hold of the cowboy. This just might work, a way out of trouble with Lynn and her mom," he reasoned. Medicinal purposes, was the answer!

Paddy received the jug with much delight, "Thank ye Bonner," he said, "Tis good it is to have an ol' friend in me arms again. With his beloved jug in hand, he took several hearty swigs, smacked his lips and handed the moonshine back to Bonner.

"Hide it again for me," he said. "Paddy be fine now!

"Me mind seems to be a workin' as it should, me tortured nerves are a settlin' down and me eyes are no longer seein' the frolickin' of the little green devils—surely the Leprechauns followed ol' Paddy from Ireland, they did!

"Old Paddy be now ready to start his dickerin', with me favorite son-in-law!"

Will Bonner was prone to laughter, but this time with tongue in cheek, he reckoned—the hair of the dog—was just what the old Irishman had been in need of. And as for being a favorite son-in-law, Will was the only one he had!

Lynn now had entered the sick room of her mom's husband, and stood beside her darlin' Will. Standing together, they listened to Paddy's history of the white-faced cows. It was a long rambling tale of mystery and intrigue, laced with blarney and Irish adjectives that left them both in a quandary of unanswered questions.

Paddy had left Lariat Cross on one of his secret journeys into the southern lands. His wagon was loaded with trade goods, he told them, Lariat Cross cough medicine, though he didn't explain it as such.

The Bonners knew his hidden meaning, and could do nothing but listen. On his journey he traveled a long ways south, he told them. It was at a stop over at an Indian encampment he met a cattle dealer with Hereford cattle for sale. Paddy had taken one look and was smitten, he just had to have these cattle that had been born and bred from across the big ocean.

The Irishman began his dealing and haggling, and in no time at all had bought the herd, and paid with gold from his poke, that was kept hidden under the floor boards of his wagon.

"—'twas a tuff time it was—a dealin' with this Logan fella—but ol' Paddy won out!

Lynn gasped when she heard him mention the name, Logan. Bonner was equally uneasy, and told Paddy to finish his story, who had become silent now, catching his breath.

The Irishman sensed that something was wrong, and proceeded with caution. "You see, this fella assured me the cows were his own—that he was in trouble with some money lenders—and needed me gold, he did!

"I pulled out me poke—and paid him on the spot, helped the poor beggar out of the tight spot he was in. The cows cost me a fortune, they did—thirty Yankee dollars apiece—the cost of the seven bulls was two hundred dollars for each one!"

Bonner could only groan as he listened, once again it seemed, even if old Kid Curry had been taken to his maker, the old cattle-rustling outlaw was still mixed up in the Bonner's cattle business. He was amazed at the dexterity of Curry, and the pains he had taken to move the cattle far from where they had been stolen.

He reckoned he should let Marshal Dunne know about Paddy's herd! Paddy was in the clear, even though he had purchased stolen goods, and was harboring the same. And now he, Deputy Bonner, had dealt for two bulls and a dozen cows from this same rustled herd.

The Irishman was true to his word and did deal the white-faced cattle to his son-in-law. It cost Bonner dearly though—a thousand dollars for the twelve cows and one bull, the second bull was given to Bonner for saving Paddy's life.

There was one more condition to the deal, Bonner must roundup the remains of Paddy's herd and drive them down to Lariat Cross. A recovering Paddy could then keep an eye on them.

* * * Chapter Sixteen * * *

After fording the creek they knew as Lariat Cross, the trail up through the pass became steep and winding, breaking a sweat on the two saddle horses Lynn Bonner and her husband were riding. They were heading for Paddy's secret cache in the high country to bring his white-faced cows down to Lariat Cross. On arrival at the secluded glade in the lodgepoles, they began gathering the highly sought after animals, bunching them close by the trail that led down to the home ranch.

While riding through the meadow, Bonner took Lynn to the remains of the bear carcass that had mauled her step-father. A flock of greedy carrion eaters flew up in alarm at the sight of the two riders, squawking their displeasure at being spooked from their morning meal.

"Not much left to look at Lynn, pretty much hide, head and bones. The coyotes, wolves and what not, as well as them ravens and magpies we scared away, have sure worked it over."

Lynn gave a great shiver and turned away. "Sure am glad that old Paddy wasn't killed here, and you Will! You might have been too!

"You saved his life you know.

"These here cows are sure different than our longhorns," Lynn's chatter rang clear in the high mountain air. Her husband was riding beside her, the two riders wrangling the last of the cows to the trailhead. "Not near as wild as them old mossy horns, they can be driven much easier too.

"I know I am going to like them—they are not skittish to handle. Our longhorns are always acting plumb crazy like, as if they have a cockle-burr under their tails!"

Bonner grinned as he listened to his wife's chatter. It was a joy to have her ride with him, each of the happy pair would have it no other way.

Sure eased the monotony of a long, hot day a riding alone!

The herd was easy to gather, it appeared as if the cows were more than ready to leave this lonely mountain meadow. Another bear kill had been discovered, reason enough, Bonner reckoned, for their willingness to travel without raising a fuss.

Let's do it," Lynn shouted. Let's take 'em home to Lariat Cross!" Bonner signaled his approval with a wave of his hat, and smiled as he watched her take the lead, reining her Boots mare down through the rock-strewn winding trail. the cattle following her with much caution. Bonner brought up the rear, riding drag for his beautiful trail boss.

After wrangling longhorns for the past months, Lynn was amazed at how these white-faces trailed behind her, as if they had been doing it forever.

Several long hours later, with night time closing in, the little trail drive arrived on the valley floor, the buildings of Lariat Cross a welcome sight to both the riders and the cattle.

How the Irishman ever got them up there, they would never know. His close-mouthed ways were well known by both Lynn and her husband. It was a secret herd, hidden in a secret place, not even Lynn's Mom knew they were there.

After confining the cows in a small fenced pasture, the riders cared for Boots and big Red, then hand-in-hand, left for the big house to clean up and partake of the hot supper they knew would be waiting.

Old Paddy O'Niel, a displaced mercenary from the land of the Shamrock, was overjoyed when the Bonner's arrived back at the ranch with his secret cows. "—'tis a great favor ye have done for ol' Paddy, it is.

"Me ol' bones are a healin' enough for me to do me chores now—and look after these white-faces ye have brung down to me!"

On hearing of another bear kill, the Irishman began to rave and rant with much vigor. "—'tis the curse of the evil ones, it be—and the little green devils who be in cahoots with them murderin' grizzly ba-ars!"

After his initial outburst, his face reddened and he began to cough. He arose from the table, still coughing and spoke, "It is me cough medicine—I be a needin'—in the worst way, I do."

All that were present knew that Paddy's cough medicine was indeed manufactured in his hidden wilderness brewery, another of his secrets that only he believed was secret. They all were smiling as they watched him go to his room, even Lynn's Mom who was shaking her head.

Lynn and her Mom talked long after the men had gone to their beds, talking about such things as only Moms and their daughters discuss with each other. It was then Lynn divulged her own secret.

"I am not really sure how to tell you this," she said, "but here goes.

"Your only daughter is expecting—Will and I are going to have us a baby!"

She silenced her talk and looked long at her mother, expecting the worse, she didn't know why. The older Lynn, the mother of this young vibrant girl, never spoke, to start with that is. "This is as I expected," she finally said. "Bound to happen you know!"

Then a happy smile erased her maternal ways, and with an ear-to-ear grin, stood up from her chair and embraced her daughter. Tears of happiness were streaming down both their cheeks, a token of love and great joy.

"I love you Mom," Lynn sobbed. "Just imagine—I'm going to be a mother—and you will be a grandma!

"Please don't say anything to Will, I will tell him soon."

* * *

It was breaking daylight of the next morning when the Bonners left Lariat Cross with their start of English cattle. They had cut out their fourteen head, twelve cows and two bulls, while the ranch was still in deep shadows. Their intentions were to arrive at their river ranch before night time over took them again.

Spotted Pony met them a few short miles west of the river. He told them he could hear the lowing of the red cows from down by the ranch, the ruckus swept down the long hills by the wind. Thinking rustlers must be helping themselves to the B—B longhorns, he reined his pony's nose into the west and took off expecting to do battle.

"You stay behind and ride drag Pony, I'll ride up with Lynn for awhile—then head down to the ranch."

* * *

Bonner and old Slim had the corral gates open wide when a triumphant Lynn and Spotted Pony rode into the ranch yards with the cattle. She then scurried to the cabin to clean up and prepare supper. She knew the B—B cowboys would be starving.

After serving a hearty meal, Lynn appeared deep in thought as she and her husband walked out to the big cottonwood by the river. This was a favorite spot for the young couple to come in the evenings, a place where they could sit on the river bank, relax and unwind.

The stars hung heavy in a moonless sky, the soothing sound of running water a comfort to their very souls. "What's wrong Lynn?" reckon you seem to be troubled tonight—anything I can help you with!"

She moved closer to him and gripped his hand. "I've been thinking about what I want to tell you for quite a spell, I reckon now is the time!" Silence followed, she must be collecting her thoughts Bonner reckoned.

Finally, she raised her head and could see the reflection of the stars in his eyes. Oh Will! What have you done to me?" Tears were flowing as she spoke.

"Reckon the reason I've been so tired and downright cross this past while, a fighting outlaws and wrangling them longhorns all over northern Montana, and all is, is...you and me Will Bonner...are going to have us a baby!"

The cowboy was stunned, at a loss for words, struggling to digest what she had just told him. Lynn looked in his eyes again, waiting for a reply. "You don't approve, I can tell," she said, struggling to rein in her tears.

"We're in this together, Will Bonner, and don't you forget it; the making of babies is as much your doing, as mine!"

Another silence followed, although a short one, to be shattered by a cowboy's shout of joy that startled Lynn Bonner. Picked up by an evening breeze, the unexpected outburst drifted on past the girl from Lariat Cross, beyond the river and out onto the wide open prairie.

From far out in the darkness, a coyote skulking through the night stopped his hunting and listened with interest to the faint sound. Could be a hungry relative, the hunter of the night might have reasoned; and yip-yipped a friendly reply.

"Sorry I took so long to answer darlin', I just could not believe what you just told me."

He was grinning from ear-to-ear as he lifted her into his lap, and showered kiss, after kiss upon her beautiful lips.

"Sure Lynn, I'm the happiest cowboy on the prairie to hear this wonderful news. This means you're going to become a Mom, and this husband of yours a Dad. Reckon we've got us a family started.

"You and I, darlin' Lynn, will be a continuance of a dynasty, one that will continue on through the test of time.

"A ranch stocked with cattle, a beautiful wife whom I love dearly, and the start of a family of our own. This is the answer to my fondest dreams!"

"Thank you, Will. I love you too.

"Thank you for being my big, handsome husband," Lynn replied. "You have told me what I needed to hear.

"You have made me so happy, so very, very happy!"

* * *

As the weeks passed so swiftly, the B—B began to flourish, a bunk house was built with a kitchen set up at one end. The improvements were many, even a large barn had been built with corrals and a barb-wire fence around the home place. The crew now consisted of six riders, which consisted of Spotted Pony and four of his cousins, who had ridden away from the confines of the reservation to live the life of a cowboy.

The Bonners assigned old Slim to be foreman of the ranch. Though getting on in years, he handled the young riders with kindness, and often rode with them across the Deerhorn hills, and up and down the big river.

And even a cook had been hired, an elderly widow lady who was thrilled to be given the job. She had been found by Lynn while exploring the valley, living alone in an ancient log structure that was her only home. The cabin was in deplorable condition, falling apart at the ever widening cracks between the logs. Lynn was shocked to see the widow living like a pauper, and just a few miles up river she and her husband had so much.

Lynn dismounted from Boots and from the saddlebags took out her trail lunch, which she shared with the widow. She discovered the woman's trapper husband had died from a severe case of the ague this past winter, leaving her destitute and alone with nothing but her memories.

On her return to the home place, Lynn sent old Slim down river with a team and wagon to fetch her back to the ranch. Slim was equally shocked on seeing the conditions the widow had been living in, and treated her with much kindness.

But she was proud and held her head high, her only worldly possessions tucked in a time-worn satchel. The clothes she wore were tattered and soiled, her body wasted away from the lack of nourishing food.

A comfortable bed was prepared for her in the bunkhouse kitchen, there was plenty of room there, and it was a room she would be proud of for the rest of her life. She proved to be an excellent cook, and in new clothes given to her by Lynn, fed the crew three fine meals a day, and was happy to do so.

Each and every cowboy rallied around her, and though her given name was Susannah, they preferred to call her Aunt Sue.

* * *

One of the Hereford bulls was put out with the longhorn bunch. The other stayed with the twelve white faced cows in a special pasture by the river. Old Slim referred to Bonner's prize bull as ol' Vic, in recognition of the famous British Queen. Victoria, the supreme ruler of uncountable possessions scattered around the world; including Canada.

The calves from this match up would be purebreds, Bonner reckoned. It was purebred bull calves he was hoping for. As mature herd sires they would be worth their weight in Yankee double eagles.

* * * Chapter Seventeen * * *

Packing an armful of freshly split fire wood, Will Bonner headed for the cabin and the breakfast he knew would be waiting. Lynn met him at the door, smiling as he walked in and deposited the fuel close by her cook stove. "Thank you," she greeted with a happy giggle. "I was just on my way to the wood pile—breakfast will be ready soon."

Brannon took off his hat and hung it on a wooden peg by the door. He sat down by the table watching Lynn put fresh fuel in her cook stove. The coffee was hot and ready to drink, and with two cups in one hand, the other holding the steaming pot, she brought them to the table.

They both enjoyed this morning ritual, a time when they could relax and talk over their plans for the long day that lay ahead. After a silence they both enjoyed, wondering what the other might be thinking, Bonner spoke "It is time we wus taking us a ride, Lynn," He was watching her fill his cup with the satisfying drink they both were so fond of.

He had been up and about taking care of the morning chores, been over to the purebred pasture admiring the small bunch of white-faced cows, and was now ready for his coffee and breakfast. "It will be you and me a riding together—like we used to do!

"I reckon we should check our south range over along the border. Old Slim was telling me the longhorns have drifted up that way. I'm anxious to see our other white-faced bull, too—and see how he is faring amongst the longhorns."

Lynn was thrilled over his invitation, excited too. "Sounds good to me, I haven't ridden Boots much since our adventure of bringing home the white-faced cattle from Lariat Cross.

"Sure will do her good to be on the move again—instead of eating all the time, and getting fat and sassy.

"I won't be long Will, give me a half-hour or so to get ready."

"Better pack us some grub Lynn, we might camp out a few nights. This will be just like old times, remember?

"And be sure and pin on your tin star Deputy Bonner, never know when we might have to use them!"

Later that afternoon, they arrived at the longhorn bunch and found them grazing the fresh range as if it was the last grass left on the prairie. In reality, this high country had not been grazed since the days of the buffalo, some twenty years back.

The herd had moved to within a half-mile of Canada's southern neighbor, eating their way towards the boundary line of the Blackfoot reservation. "There he is!" Lynn shouted, excitement bubbling over when she spotted the Hereford bull. The big white face appeared to be in fine fettle, with nothing but wilderness romance on his mind.

After finding all was well with the herd, the two riders reined their broncs into the west, riding up the 49th parallel, known to the Blackfoot and Sioux as the—*Medicine Line*—a division between *old Grandmother's Land* and that of the *Great White Father.*

It proved to be an easy ride up the border slash into a region where the treeless prairie met up with the wooded breaks of the high country. The sun was sinking into the west before they reached a small creek lined with diamond willow clumps.

"Old Slim has given this here crik the name of Boundary Creek. He reckoned it was a fitting name, as the stream winds along the border of both countries. He is a corker at naming things, enjoys it too!

"Remember how he named ol' Vic! A right fittin' name—fits right in with our B—B spread."

Continuing on, Bonner led the way until nearing a thick tangle of this hardy willow of the high country, and discovered an opening leading inside. Ducking his head to save his hat from being swept to the ground, he urged Red to continue on into the brush, and discovered a modest clearing surrounded by diamond willow clumps.

"Follow me Lynn," he shouted back to his wife. "I've found us a real fine campsite.

"It has shelter from the wind, scads of firewood, and even a seep of water from that hidden spring over yonder!"

Lynn was giggling as she rode into the clearing. "Sure is like old times, Will. Why, it has everything we might need—old Grandpa Brannon would be mighty proud of you—he surely would!"

Darkness was now strong in the border country, having followed the departing sun. The Bonner camp was in place, a coffee pot was bubbling a merry tune over a willow twig fire, and the Bonners were relaxing nearby; sitting in the grass; upper torsos resting snuggly in their up-turned saddles.

The night was silent and serene, no sound could they hear but that of the horses munching the tender plants that grew there. The stars were bright, the milky way a splendor to behold. To be here together on this beautiful night brought back memories of earlier times. Of their wedding night in Montana, and the wild times that followed. They were sleeping on the ground then as well.

A wandering coyote yip-yipped an inquisitive tune, disturbing the silence of the camp in the willows. The sly denizen of the night stopped and listened, wilderness-honed senses probing the night-cooled air. It was a bothersome scent that disturbed the coyote, that of wood smoke, horses and—humans!

Human scent is not pleasant to the hunting carnivore, the coyote is no exception, who turned tail and fled down the border slash. It was here he met up with Bonner's longhorns.

The herd was spread out on a rise in the prairie peacefully chewing their cuds. As was the way of these semi-wild beasts, some were bedded in the knee-high grass, others were up and about continuing their incessant grazing. The coyote, who was sitting on his haunches near the outer fringe of the herd, yodeled a lonely song; ever alert for an easy meal.

Suddenly, the small animal was on the move, fleeing in terror from a big white-faced bull that was closing in on the elusive shadow of the night—bellowing a chilling tune.

The outraged herd-sire from across the big waters, had just been involved in a vicious sparring match with one of Bonner's longhorn bulls, and was in no mood for the sneaky ways of the small prairie wolf.

* * *

After one of Lynn's campfire breakfasts, the Bonners continued their scout into the west, riding parallel with the border slash. Topping over a rise in the prairie, they reined in big Red and Boots for a breather and gazed at a lake of considerable size. "Someone must live here!" Lynn said, breaking the silence of this high country. "See the smoke rising out of that bunch of quakin' trees.

"It is far across the lake, Will—in the direction of Chief Mountain."

Will Bonner could see what she was telling him, a look of concern spreading across his face. "We must ride with caution darlin'—might be an Indian camp! Could be a cattle rustling outfit hiding back here, in the seclusion of them quakin' trees.

"By the way Lynn, them quakin' trees you're talking about are aspen, quaking aspen—their leaves are always a flutterin' with the slightest breeze."

"Thanks for telling me this Will, I didn't know. You are always teaching me new things—just like old Grandpa Brannon used to do!"

Her reply pleased him immensely, he was smiling when he spoke, "Best we ride over and check things out!"

Though on the alert, the ride around the lake was a pleasant one for Lynn and her husband. A long-legged blue heron was disturbed from his morning ritual of hunting frogs and other small shore-line creatures, for his morning meal. The long billed bird arose from the water, uttering a squawk of protest, as he flapped his way to the far side of the lake.

Ducks and geese were abundant here, as were dozens of small shore-line birds, all of them busy hunting for food as well.

"I just love the birds," Lynn confided. "As a small child up at the old cabin on Lariat Cross, birds were my friends—I had no other playmates—just the wild things and a lonely little girl!"

"I too like the birds," Bonner told her. "The eagle and the raven were my favorites, each with a different story to tell if one would but listen. They were good company too, breaking the monotony of riding alone.

"When I was riding on the trail, the ravens would follow me, often warning me of hidden danger ahead. The eagle, who stayed high in the sky—soaring with the thermals, was like a beacon at times, showing me the way I wished to go."

As they neared the aspen grove, the wilderness chatter of the birds was lessened by the sound of someone chopping wood, the bark of a dog, and the muted sound of men talking.

The two deputy marshals reined in their broncs, pinned on their tin stars in recognition of the authority they were involved in, and prepared themselves to enter the clearing in the quakin' trees. "Better take the leather whang off your six-gun Lynn," Bonner spoke in a subdued voice.

"Have your rifle loose in the scabbard too."

"I'm ready to fight a war," Lynn answered. "Let's ride in and find out who is here, we might as well get it over with, now as later."

"Follow me Lynn," he said, and touched a spur to big Red.

"Lynn would have no part of trailing behind, and spurred Boots up along side her husband. as she had done many times before. "You listen to me Will Bonner," she said somewhat perturbed.

"We're in this here deputy business together—remember? I'm a riding along side you, as well I should!"

And so it was they rode into the clearing, a pair of deputies riding together, twin stars glistening in the early morning sun. The first thing to grab their attention was an impressive looking flag flying above the largest of the three log structures, of which included a horse barn. The flag was the red, white and blue bunting of the British colonies in North America, the Union Jack.

A young trooper was chopping wood near the aspens, another stepped out the door of the cabin, shading his eyes against the intense rays of the advancing sun. He was attempting to see who the visitors to their lonely outpost might be.

A third one followed him out. This one must be the boss, Bonner reckoned, noticing the handle-bar mustache, the uniform he was wearing, and the hat that was perched on the top of his head. Never had he been exposed to this kind of uniform before.

The Bonners gigged their horses closer, staying in the saddles, and stared in wonder at the uniformed personage who was walking towards them. He was impressively clad in a scarlet jacket, steel gray riding breeches and gleaming black boots. In his hands he held a pair of white buckskin gauntlets and a riding crop.

Bonner was smiling, attempting to suppress a down right outburst of laughter, as he had a closer look at the military headwear that was perched on the man's head. It reminded him of an overturned sauce pan, placed at a jaunty angle, held in place by a leather strap crossing under the man's lower lip.

Lynn was busting at the seams as well, turning her head to better control the mirth that was taking control of herself. "Howdy," Bonner greeted. "We were just passing by and saw your smoke, reckoned we should ride in and pay you gentleman a visit.

"We was hopin' your coffee pot might be a perkin', we could sure enjoy a cup 'bout now!"

The Corporal, as the two stripes indicated, remained silent. He was staring at the twin deputy badges, one on the beautiful long-haired girl, the other on the tall salty-looking cowboy who rode by her side. And the six-guns they wore, both free and easy in the holsters, both appeared to be well taken care of and ready for war.

After his rather rude scrutiny of the deputies, he cleared his throat, and smoothed out his carefully manicured handle-bar. "We have none of your Yankee coffee here!" he said, the accent of his English upbringing ringing strong in his voice.

"It is tea we drink here in the colonies, an oriental beverage you know, favored by good Queen Victoria herself—and all her subjects!"

"Never touch the stuff myself," Bonner said, and looked at Lynn who was still struggling to suppress one of her giggles.

"What outfit you boys belong to?" the big deputy asked. "I reckon this must be a military outpost—judging by the looks of things—the flag and all."

"This is a police outpost of the North West Mounted," the Canadian lawman replied, "Stationed here along the border to catch border riff-raff, and other illegal visitors to Her Majesty's colony.

"We are known as the Police Lake Outpost! I am the Corporal in charge—Corporal Winston Williscroft.

"Who might you be?" Williscroft asked. "I presume a Yankee, by your show of tin badges."

"Tell me your business here. This is British territory, you know!"

Bonner was starting to get his dander up, the Mountie's arrogance was almost more than he could handle. "You see, Mountie, we are United States deputy marshals. When we're not hunting outlaws and such, we have us a ranch down on the prairie, along the St. Mary's river.

I reckon it is about a twenty mile ride as the crow flies."

"I know where it is Deputy, we have a detachment down there as well. It appears you Yanks must be running short of lawmen, allowing the ladies to do your dirty work for you!

"By the way old chap," he added, looking at Lynn. Does the pretty one have her knitting with her!"

His remarks were like a slap in the face to Bonner, and to Lynn as well. He vaulted from the saddle and stood face to face with the Englishman, blue flame pouring from his eyes. "Watch your mouth Corporal—you've just insulted my wife—and the U.S. marshal's service.

"Put up your dukes, you've got a lessen to learn you miserable sidewinder. Out here in the West, no matter which side of the border it might be on—we treat our women with respect!

The Englishman's face had turned a sickly white, he now knew he had spoken out of turn. "By jove!" he uttered, and he was now squirming. "It must be a duel you are asking me for.

"I prefer the sword you know, give me a moment and I'll dash in and fetch my weapon."

"Hold your hosses, Mountie—I have no sword—I prefer to fight with pistols." Bonner said.

"Oh jolly well then," he turned and faced Bonner. "Back to back, and a ten pace walk if I remember correctly," and returned to stand beside the big cowboy. Lynn leaned from her saddle and whispered in her husband's ear.

He looked up at her and spoke, "Are you sure Lynn?"

"I am sure, after all it was me he insulted"

Bonner turned to Williscroft. "My lady deputy you insulted, prefers to face off with you herself. She reckons it is her duty as a U.S. deputy marshal to handle her own affairs.

"She wishes to duel with you as if she were a man."

Williscroft acted as if he couldn't believe what he was hearing. "It is rather unorthodox old chap, don't you think?

"It will not be a fair fight a—North West Mountie—facing off with a mere woman, a pretty one at that.

"I can not do what you ask!"

"Do it!" Bonner roared, his six-gun in hand, which was all it took to put the fear of the dark place in the Englishman's soul." Lynn had now moved in behind Williscroft and positioned her back against his. "You count Will, ten paces if I am not mistaken."

Bonner started the count, one—two—three—and on it went. At the count of nine and half of another, the Englishman spun on his heels and fired. The ball from the Corporals pistol clipped the brim of Lynn's cowboy hat, sending it flying to the ground.

A split second is all and the girl from Lariat Cross returned the fire, fanning four shots that left Williscroft shuddering in terror. The first bullet sent his saucepan hat flying, the second clipped a brass button from off his tunic, the third one singed him just above the elbow, destroying his corporal stripes, and the fourth! The fourth bullet clipped an inch off one side of his handle bar mustache.

The two troopers were amazed at being in on the duel, standing with mouths agape, having a hard time digesting it all. Bonner was smiling, relieved that Lynn had not been hurt, and still plumb furious over the way the Englishman had not waited for the full count of ten.

However he calmed down, watching the Corporal cowering in shock and terror. He reckoned the sneaky rascal had paid for his breach of etiquette and lack of good manners.

Lynn was now in her husbands arms, weeping a passel of tears. Her nerves were shattered, she was upset that the Corporal had not waited until the count of ten. "He cheated Will, caught me unawares. I could have killed him easy.

"But reckoned he wasn't worth the bullet!"

"You done just fine Lynn, your shooting was a sight to behold. I don't reckon the cocky scoundrel will make fun of any more lady deputies.

"I'm proud of you, you know!"

"And my hat Will," she sobbed, showing him the bullet hole through the brim. "I was so proud of this hat, it is my favorite, the one you gave me on our wedding day."

One of the troopers assisted the Corporal into his quarters, the other approached the two deputies, still in awe over Lynn's shooting prowess. "Howdy," Bonner greeted.

"I don't reckon the Corporal is fit to talk to for awhile, so I'll tell you. If you ever need assistance up here, with trouble of any kind, let us know and we'll come and help out."

"Aye, sir," the trooper replied. "—'tis that we will do. I'll ride down to your ranch me ownself, I will.

"You say you live by the big river?" the trooper asked, a touch of old Irish brogue in his talk. "A twenty mile ride, you say?"

"Yes! the big cowboy answered. "It is a twenty mile ride, uphill and down, dodging willow clumps and badger holes—riding hell-bent for the B—B!"

"Let's go home Will," Lynn pleaded. The lady deputy from Lariat Cross had had her fill of gun fighting the English way.

* * * Chapter Eighteen * * *

The eastern sky was turning a rosy pink when Will Bonner rode away from the ranch on his way to the Mormon settlements. A pack horse was trailing behind to be used in bringing back supplies for a growing bunch of hungry cowboys. Other plans included stopping at a nester outfit on his way back to the B—B. It was here, along the Blackfoot trail some months back, his mother-in-law had brought little Matt to get some learning from a retired school teacher

She reckoned it was high time her only son learned how to read and write, and cipher some. She was right on all counts, and also desired that little Matt be brought to live with his sister and her husband at their B—B river ranch. "It is time now," she had told her daughter, "that my son be taught the ways of a cowboy.

"My Dad, God rest his soul, would want it this way—your Grandpa Brannon would not have rested until his grandson was taught how to rope and ride, become an expert with guns; and always respect the Code of the West!"

Lynn Bonner's heart was filled with joy the day Bonner brought her half-brother, Mathew O'Niel, home to live with them. The day had been a long one for her, an eager excitement growing as the shadows of an approaching night consumed the prairie. Many times she had left the cabin that day, scanning the trail leading into the ranch. And then finally, she could see them coming.

She was standing outside the cabin watching the small procession enter the ranch yards, Bonner atop big Red, leading a pack horse loaded with supplies. Trailing behind came a small, but lively pony with her eight year old brother sitting in the saddle.

Lynn walked over to meet them, a happy smile on her face. Then a squeal of delight escaped her lips, as her brother slid to the ground and ran to meet her with outstretched arms. She hugged him tight and just would not let him go. "I'm so happy you are here," she told him. "I love my only brother a whole bunch!"

"I love you too, Lynn," little Matt replied, tears were streaming down both their cheeks.

"I am happy to be here!" he told his sister. "I sure did miss you and my Mom."

"I brung us another cowhand," Brannon said, as he stepped down from the saddle, a mile-wide grin spreading across his face. "He sure don't know much—but reckons he will make us a top hand here 'fore long!"

It was a happy time at the B—B that night, the hustle and bustle of getting little Matt settled, unpacking the supplies and storing them away. Old Slim came over from the bunk house with Aunt Sue in tow. They both welcomed Lynn's brother, old Slim shaking his hand in a dignified manner, Aunt Sue's greeting was a bear hug and even a big kiss on his cheek; which the blushing boy promptly brushed away.

Lynn's cabin home now had four rooms, a kitchen, two bedrooms, and another where they could gather and sit by a river-rock fireplace, built for her by old Slim. It was a work of art that thrilled Lynn and her husband. He had even hewed several benches, and stools too, from out of cottonwood logs, which Lynn had discreetly positioned around the room.

She was thrilled with this special room, and had decorated the walls with various artifacts that had been in her room at Lariat Cross, even a brand new four-point Hudson Bay blanket given to her by her mother. And best of all, a beautiful tanned elk hide, given to her by her dear friend, old Lame Deer.

The Indian cowboys enjoyed coming over on occasion, sitting cross-legged in front of the dancing flames, watching in awe the indoor campfire.

"Much medicine here," Spotted Pony would tell Lynn, signing to the heavens, and the elk hide on the wall; and the grizzly bear pelt they were sitting on, a gift from old Paddy.

"Good spirits stay in your tepee now!" The Pony would never leave without performing a ritual, sprinkling the crushed leaves of sweet grass and tobacco amongst the flames.

After eating a hearty supper, little Matt was ready to call it a day, and was put to bed in a bunk in the spare bedroom. His mind was unable to rest though, busy conjuring up all sorts of small boy's dreams. Grizzly bears and Indians, wild cowboys; and a small pony too, that had been given the name of Brownie!"

Over and above the hullabaloo of his boisterous dream, appeared a vision of a beautiful lady with long auburn hair. Her red rosy lips were smiling, showing pearly white teeth. And just off to the side stood another who looked the same as the first. Hovering in the background was yet another, an exact replica of the first two.

Somehow he knew, he could never say why, that the first one was his sister Lynn Bonner, the second was his mother Lynn O'Niel, and the third one was his grandma Lynn Brannon; the matriarch of the gun fighting family.

Each of them was holding a small carbine rifle, one hand on the barrel, the other on the lever-action, all cocked and ready to fire!

It was a disturbing phenomenon that left young Matt trembling and upset. It took awhile, but eventually the lad was able to slip off into a comforting sleep.

* * *

Life on a cattle ranch is full of long days filled with hard work. It meant rising with the sun, working from can see to can't see, the tasks often carrying on long after dark.

The Bonners were no exception. It was their way of life, a deep-ingrained custom of cattle country.

The next morning Lynn was up and about, and after taking care of her morning rituals, she went to see how her brother was faring. She peeped through the tanned deer skin that served as a doorway into the room, and gasped in shock on discovering that little Matt's bunk was empty

Turning to her husband, who had just entered the cabin with an armful of wood for her cook-stove, she asked, "Will, have you seen my brother? He is not in his bed."

Will was grinning. "Look out yonder Lynn—by the corrals."

Lynn hurried out the door and spotted the boy right off. He was sitting on the top rail of the corral, several members of Bonner's horse *remuda* were crowded in close to the boy, inspecting this new arrival at the B—B ranch.

Off in a far corner stood her Jenni mule and the little brown pony, bosom buddies it seemed; having been rejected by the more elite of Bonner's saddle stock.

"This Jenni mule of yours, and her new friend,—who must be a Welsh pony crossed with a mustang—by the looks o' things, they will become life long friends Lynn.

"Wherever one goes, the other will be sure to follow."

"I agree with you," she giggled. The two can baby sit each other, as well as my brother." Lynn's happy giggle was a sure enough reason for a good day ahead.

For little Matt, life on his sister's real live cattle ranch was an exciting adventure, full of learning and fun. The days passed swiftly, turning into weeks and then it was months. The happy youngster was changing for the better. He dug in his heels and was learning the ways of the West as best he could.

It helped immensely to have old Slim tuck him under his wing. Slim loved the boy as if he had been his own, and the boy thought the world of the old timer too. They were constantly together—Slim teaching—the boy listening and learning.

Among a host of other lessons, he taught the boy how to braid horsehair into usable equipment, bridle reins, quirts and even fancy studded belts. Leather work and braiding were just two of old Slims many talents, which he willingly shared.

Will Bonner was equally patient with the boy, and told him that if he was going to become a cowboy, he would have to learn how to care for horses; feed and groom them, and care for their hooves. One day little Matt never showed up for his dinner, and was found out in the corrals with a hoof pick and a farrier's rasp in hand. He was patiently cleaning Brownies hooves, then rasping off the rough outer edges. It was hard work for the boy, who was dripping wet with sweat from the noonday sun.

Though she appeared bored, the Jenni mule was standing close by watching the whole affair. Perhaps this new friend of Brownie's was wondering if she would be the next to partake of the young lad's zeal.

Lynn was reluctant to start the boy's training with guns, yet she showed him how to take them apart and clean and oil them, and the importance of doing the same. She reckoned his lessons in shooting would have to wait a spell, a year or two perhaps, when he was strong enough to handle them.

It was then a thought entered her mind—the light-weight .22 calibre, lever action, old Grandpa Brannon had given her so long ago. Why hadn't she thought of it before?

While at Lee's Creek, the same day he had brought the boy home with him, Bonner had purchased his brother-in-law a cowboy hat, boots and jeans, and all the rest that included a pair of red polka dot bandanas. The boy was sure proud of his new duds, and wore them with dignity and respect. Strutting around the ranch yards as if he was the top hand of the spread.

Having closely watched Bonner, he had even picked up a quaint way of walking. It is known in the ranching fraternity as the 'cowboy swagger'!

The B—B ranch was now the setting for a big celebration, little Matt was having a birthday party, nine candles would be on his birthday cake. His mother had come down from Lariat Cross for the special occasion, they both were overjoyed at seeing each other again.

Lynn and Aunt Sue had prepared all kinds of good things to eat, they knew the hungry cowboys would be in attendance, and made sure there would be plenty for everyone.

After the feast, and it was that—a roast beef dinner—with all the trimmings, all gathered at the big cottonwood for the slicing of the cake, and the present giving. Little Matt O'Niel was the happiest boy on the prairie when he was presented with a small rawhide-braided lariat, given to him by old Slim. Lynn brought out her little .22 rifle and presented it with a big smile, letting him know that it was just on loan until he was old enough to have a big one of his own

Bonner presented the boy with a minature shell belt complete with holster, another piece of old Slim's handiwork, who had willingly crafted it for his boss's gift to the boy. Lynn O'Niel brought her son a whole passel of gifts, including mostly clothes and blankets for his bed, and lots of love and kisses.

Ol' Paddy, who had accompanied his wife to her daughter's river ranch, was sitting out by the corrals content to be alone. "Come on over, Matt me lad," he asked, "and see what your Daddy has brung ye."

Little Matt was somewhat puzzled that his Dad would bring him a present, but bowed to Paddy's wishes just the same. "See, there in the corrals, standing by the Jenni mule—"—'tis a wee bo-ourn calf—a white-faced one too.

"The wee one's momma would not claim her poor baby—so ol' Paddy had to care for this hungry calf. 'tis yourn now Matt me boy—a start of your own herd it be—and it be the makin's of a herd sire too!"

The boy was thrilled as could be over his Dad's gift, and gave the old timer a warm hug and a kiss. "I love you Daddy!" little Matt told him."

Though he never spoke, Paddy was moved as well. His scarred face a rosy red, he brushed a tear from his eyes and spoke again, "You shouldn't be a wastin' your kisses on an old Irishman lad—save 'em for the lassies you'll soon be a courtin'"

Lastly, Aunt Sue arrived at the cottonwood with her present, a birthday cake lavishly covered with a mouth-watering coat of chocolate. She sliced it with much aplomb, and after the boy was honored with the first piece, all hands were standing close by to receive a slice of their own.

Before returning to Lariat Cross, Lynn's Mom and old Paddy stayed another week, the two Lynn's spending many happy hours together enjoying Mom and daughter talk. A goodly share of their chatter was about the new baby that would soon be arriving.

Before his Mom left for home, little Matt who never talked much anyway, asked his Mom about the size of his sister's stomach. He never knew her as being so plump, and in his childish way, was concerned about her welfare.

Suppressing a giggle, she never answered for a spell, figuring out how to tactfully answer the boy's innocent question. Then, looking him in the eyes, she began her talk.

"Her plumpness will be a surprise Matt—Lynn has a surprise hidden inside her—soon she will show us her surprise.

"Then her stomach will return back to its normal size."

"Oh!" he replied. "I can hardly wait to see—I like surprises!"

Her young cowboy appeared satisfied with her answer, and returned to the corrals to go for another ride on his little Welsh pony he had named Brownie.

* * * Chapter Nineteen * * *

Time passed as swiftly as the river that flowed past their cabin home. Lynn had recovered from the outlaw wars in the southern territories, and the long, tedious journey of bringing the longhorns home to their ranch along the river. Having had two good visits with her Mom, and bringing little Matt to live with them was mighty good medicine too. Though well along with child, she was healthy and happy and feeling just fine.

That is until a young Indian lad arrived one evening with a message from Marshal Custis Dunne. The message was simple and to the point.

> *'Thar's trouble along border—south o' your ranch*
> *need help with sum hardcases got myself in one he-ell*
> *of a fix whar big river crosses border*
> *bring your tin stars—Hurry!*
> *Custis'*

Will's hands were unsteady before he finished reading the note, she remembered, and reckoned she knew what would happen next. "I've got to go and find ol' Custis," he said, after a pause while digesting this unexpected news. "Reckon he's sure enough in trouble, sendin' this here note and all.

"Here Lynn, you read it and tell me what you think."

Nothing more than a scrap of brown-paper sack, Lynn smoothed the wrinkled paper and scanned the urgent message; the print scrawled from the business end of a .44 cartridge. "Oh, Will!" she pleaded. "We must go and help Marshal Dunne...sounds as if the poor man is in big trouble, and needs us real bad!"

"Don't know how to say this Lynn, reckon you'll be plumb upset. But dog-gone it all, you're in no condition to be packin' a tin star, and a chasin' after border outlaws!

"Reckon you should stay here and manage the ranch, take care of our little baby you're a packin'...and yourself. I'll take Spotted Pony with me and leave ol' Slim here to guard you and the ranch."

Surprisingly, Lynn never raised a fuss, encouraging her husband to go and find the old Marshal as quickly as possible. He assured her the border was only a ten-mile ride, that he would be careful and send word back with Pony if need be.

Within in the hour Will, and a young Blackfoot cowboy he knew only as Spotted Pony, were in the saddle heading up river to help an old Montana lawman who was in trouble. They were prepared for war, each with a rifle, and six-guns hanging where they should be. They carried plenty of ammunition, and food in the saddlebags, thanks to the insistent nature of Lynn.

It was nearing sundown before they left the ranch, and though not as yet familiar with this border country, Will reckoned on following the river for a few hours, then make camp and continue on at first light. Several hours had passed, they were making good time, he reckoned, when Pony reined in his pony, and cautioned Will to do the same.

"Ki-ii!" he spoke, a hush in his voice. "Listen! The spirits of the night...wish to talk to us...!"

A playful breeze of the night was pestering the leaves of an aspen tree. A foraging night hawk whirred high above the silent riders, making strange noises as it dived low, skimming the restless waters of this mountain-spawned stream. Then all was quiet.

From the time of his birth, the Blackfoot boy had been gifted with an ingrained sense of survival, much like the wild ones; the coyote, the wolf, and the bear. He appeared uneasy, yet remained still. His nostrils were quivering, obsidian-hued eyes searching the shadowed woods, wilderness-honed hearing straining to detect what might be lurking in the dark night.

The boy spoke again. "Lynn's cowboy boss—make camp at this place—rest until the sun comes again to see this river.

"The sun will be good to us...scare away the evil ones!" With that said, Spotted Pony rode away, vanishing in the shadowed woods.

Stillness settled around the lone rider, broken only by the chatter of the river and the call of a departing Pony. Then, from far upriver could be heard a faint gunshot, followed by another.

Bonner's temper flared some by the hasty departure of his Indian cowhand, was all set to give him a good talking to, make him realize who was boss, but now it was too late. The rascal had simply vanished in the night.

Still muttering to himself, Will Bonner dismounted and brewed a pot of coffee over a small twig fire. He found one of Lynn's tasty sandwiches in the saddlebags, reckoned maybe a bite to eat and some rest might do him good.

Feeling refreshed and preparing himself to fight a war if need be, Bonner was on the trail, heading south to rescue his old friend. The sun was not yet up, but it was getting light enough to see.

* * *

Though still feeling left out, not able to ride away with her deputy husband and all, Lynn brushed away her disappointment and wandered out by the river and sat by her favorite cottonwood tree. Lulled by the sighing of the moving waters her mind took over, racing back and forth in time. Far back to the days of Grandpa and Grandma Brannon and the heartaches they had endured, it traveled. Then back it would come, bursting into the present, reminding her of the day of her marriage and the rough and tumble events that followed.

Lynn Bonner was silently weeping, her memories as strong as the tears she was shedding. Her heritage that she was so proud of—a heritage started by old grandpa Matt Brannon the Texas gunfighter. And her grandma, Lynn Riley Brannon., who was sure no slouch with her yellow boy rifle—given to her by great grandpa Ben Riley as a wedding present.

To be finally back at the new cabin along this peaceful river had been a great blessing to Lynn Bonner. Another blessing she would never forget was having survived their short stint as U.S. deputy marshals. How they tamed the hard cases in the Landusky gold fields, her kidnapping by the Curry gang, and of the final battle which saw old Kid Currie go down for good at the hands of the two Bonner deputies; an old cowboy named Slim and an Indian lad named Spotted Pony.

Then, finally after what seemed like an eternity of fighting and killing, the young newlyweds took possession of their longhorns and headed them back for their northern home. We brought old Slim back with us, she remembered.

He was a broken-hearted, grieving old cowboy, who has mourned for his poor ravaged daughter for so many long years. To the end of his days he would have a welcome home here at Lariat Cross, as she preferred to call their ranch.

It didn't bother her none that her Mom's spread was known as Lariat Cross, why not hers as well. After all they were one and the same—her Mom and herself. Both of them with Brannon blood strong in their veins—old Matt Brannon's genes—and they were mighty proud of it.

From the Nez Perce tepees her mother had came, a young girl frightened and alone. But she was strong and determined, just had to discover what was in this northern country—a powerful influence was here, one that was urging her to come seek out her roots.

The girl had been distraught, and upset. A mature sixteen-year old and with no means of support, how could she manage such a journey into the unknown of the northern territories?

Finally, no longer able to resist this constant tugging at her heart strings, she relented and gave herself to a dashing, young Frenchman from the eastern lands, who was traveling to the northern territories. A pawn perhaps! It was though, the only means in which she could satisfy the powerful influence of her mother of whom she had never known.

Lynn Brannon was a young beautiful lady who had fell from a Nez Perce war club, and struggled to stay alive long enough for her baby to be born.

Lynn just had to find Matt Brannon, her father. That he was still alive, she did not know—it was just something she had to find out. From the only home she had ever known, the Nez Perce tepees, her mother had came, a young girl married before her time; her intent to follow the powerful influence of her dead mother. Lynn Brannon was her name, whose name they all three wore so proudly.

Great grandma Lynn(Riley)Bonner, who died shortly after giving birth to Lynn Brannon, Duval, O'Niel, her only child; and Lynn(Duval)Bonner, known lovingly as little Lynn; of whom is myself.

Her memories were as strong as the tears she was shedding. A heritage dating back to Matt Brannon—an ol' Texas gunfighter of whom she was darn proud of. Drying her tears once again, Lynn's thoughts returned to the present and the baby that she knew would soon be a continuance of the Brannon heritage. Her pregnancy had been frightening at first, yet the thrill of becoming a mother far exceeded the haunts and fears of the other.

She sure missed Will Bonner, she surely did. She knew that she should be with him, wearing her tin star and backing his play. No matter, she must remain strong. Lynn knew that if he had been with her now, he would have put a strong arm around her and held her close—saying something like this, "Reckon you look plumb upset darlin' Lynn— anything I can do to help out—sure hope I haven't done anything wrong!"

And she would have replied, hugging him as tight as she could, "I'm fine now Will Bonner, now that the love of my life is holding me so close!"

* * * Chapter Twenty * * *

Saddle sore and sure in need of some hot coffee, an old law man knew he was getting close to the Blackfoot encampment. Off in the distance he could hear dogs barking, the laughter of children at play and smell the smoke from their cooking fires. His big dun gelding knew it too, ears on the alert, and walking with caution as if he were crossing over thin ice.

Bone weary from the long ride, U.S. Marshal Custis Dunne entered the Indian encampment, urging his high-stepping horse onward to a large impressive tepee that surely must house the sub-chief of this splinter clan of the Blackfoot nation.

Half-naked children and vicious looking camp dogs stared with suspicion as he crossed the clearing, stepped down from the saddle and loosened the cinch from around the belly of his sweat-caked gelding.

A young dusky-faced brave, just a teen-ager, approached the Marshal, his eyes wide with wonder as he spotted the shiny tin-star pinned on the stranger's shirt. Taking the reins from the lawman's gloved hand, the lad signed towards a small stream nearby, and led the horse over to slake a raging thirst.

By now a crowd had gathered around the marshal. Along with the dirty-faced urchins and their dogs, were buckskin-dressed women, some with babes in arms and several swarthy looking braves—complete with bows and arrows and brightly painted war spears, reminding everyone there of nothing less than blood. That they were showing their age—*long in the tooth*—mattered not, they were treated with respect just the same.

The old warriors closed in on the marshal, scowling like devils, doing their best to intimidate him and let him know they had fought with many enemies, including white eyes—and bravely had counted *coup* on many of the same, taking their scalps too.

Keeping a stern look on his face, Custis stared them in the eye and signed towards the large tepee and then to himself. The old warriors came closer, aware of the marshal's six-gun and what it could do. Hand hovering near the butt end of his weapon, Custis knew he was in a tight spot—what was he to do?

He was no coward, had resigned himself to go down fighting, knowing he might be able to down one, possibly two. Also knowing his fate would be sealed if he started shooting. There were just too many of them, too many blood-chilling war spears staring him in the face—any one of which could down him for good.

The old lawman sighed with relief when the tent flap of the tepee was flung aside and out stepped an impressive looking figure, adorned with a feathered head dress complete with bison horns, and even a grizzly bear claw-necklace hung around his neck.

This one barked an order at the old ones, who backed away from the lawman, still glaring wickedly—still smirking at a nerve-wracked Custis Dunne. Perhaps there was a chance of his survival after all, perhaps the chief would listen to why he was here in their camp.

Heaving a sigh of relief, Custis knew this must be the chief and greeted him with the peace sign of the plains. By now the young brave had returned and was standing by the lawman, watching with interest the reaction of the old one.

Speaking in the only language he knew—Blackfoot, the Chief signed to the young brave and invited them both inside the tepee. "Come with me—follow the great Chief," the young brave interpreted.

"He wishes to talk medicine, with the white eyes who wears a shiny star." And though surprised at the brave's knowledge of the English talk, Custis Dunne walked over to the chief and followed him into the tepee.

They were invited to sit cross-legged around a small twig fire, only then was a long-stemmed pipe, freshly packed with tobacco, passed to all that were there including several of the militants who had came in unannounced. All in the circle were expected to take a puff or two, inhale deeply and pass it on around the circle, it was a custom of the People. After a lengthy interval of listening to the Chief and the young brave interpret his jargon, the medicine talk with the lawman was finished.

The lawman walked over to his dun horse, preparing to leave, when the young one rode up on a pinto pony. "My name is Spirit Talker," he said. "The only one here who can make talk with white eyes.

"My mother was a white-eye woman, taken as a slave by Blackfoot warriors. This happened at her ranch in the Dakotas, where her husband was slaughtered in front of her eyes. She taught me to speak the white eye's talk before she died from a beating…given to her by the People…I am her mixed-blood son, the Chief is my father.

"The Chief wishes me to ride with you—help you catch the evil ones—who have been stealing his horses and ravaging his women!

"*Oki*! My father is a great chief—and is honored with many wives— some of them slaves, as was my mother."

"Reckon you can come," Custis replied. "I can use all the help I can get, sure beats a ridin' alone!"

* * *

Reining in his saddle horse at the 49th parallel, U.S. Marshal Custis Dunne glanced across a small clearing to a field stone cairn that marked the boundary line between Montana and the northern territories known as Canada. There were no fences here, nothing more than an imaginary line stretching across the prairie. The division of the two countries was dependant on the odd survey station and field stone cairn, of which were systematically placed for hundreds of miles across the land.

A stone's throw from the border marker, Marshal Dunne stepped from the saddle to stretch the kinks out of his body and give his suffering backside a reprieve from the long ride he had endured. "I'm a getting too damn old for this marshalin' business," he muttered. "Sure hope my deputies from the territories over yonder," gesturing north of the boundary, "get here soon to help an ol' lawman out!"

He was not only sore in body, but sore in mind, in fact plumb humiliated over the actions of a would-be posse he had conscripted from the Indian agency at Rattlesnake Butte, who had left him cold, seeking a vision of the evening star, they told him. In reality they left the marshal to chase after the pair of renegades who had mistreated several of their women.

"Don't know how I ever got myself in such a mess as this," the marshal muttered.

With an effort that left him wheezing, he crawled back in the saddle and rode back through the aspens to an old trapper cabin, where he would wait for the Bonners to get here. "Lucky thing I run on to that young brave back yonder," he spoke once again. He had given the boy a silver dollar and a note, to deliver to the Bonner ranch if and when he found it. From what Deputy Lynn Bonner had told him previously, the ranch was not far, about an hours ride down river from the border.

The two hell-raisers he was after, though he wasn't sure of their names, were Porcupine Eater and Sore Backed Horse. Their law breaking had been reported to him, both by the white settlers and the reservation authorities as well, leaving little choice but to track them down and bring them in to face just retribution for their evil ways.

Charges would be filed against them for attempted murder, savage rapine, as well as various other charges, including boot-legging and molesting young Blackfoot girls. Unbeknown to old Custis Dunne, he and the turncoat posse were after the same two renegades and weren't aware of the fact.

* * *

Safely above high-water line along a mountain stream known as St Mary's, an old weather-ravaged cabin sat in a grove of aspens, The exact location was known to few, among them Porcupine Eater and his son Sore Backed Horse, who claimed it as their own. Their only reason for doing so was it was near the reservation line and the border between Montana and the northern territories, and came in right handy as a hideout when the reservation police were hunting them for whooping it up at the settled encampments of their People.

These rowdy escapades never happened often, twice a month as a rule, taxing the very dexterity of the police in trying to catch them for disturbing the peace, and other unmentionable infractions of tribal law. Always Porcupine Eater and Sore Backed Horse eluded them, proud as could be of their native skill in covering their tracks and fading away into the darkness of the surrounding woods.

But this time was different. This time the posse was hot on their trail, following closely as Porcupine Eater and Sore Backed Horse headed for the mountain stream known to all as St. Mary's; and their hidden cabin in the aspens. Still under the influence of the highly sought after firewater they had bartered from a white man, the two headed deep in the aspens and hid themselves in ground litter and dried leaves of the forest floor.

Proud as could be of their knowledge of the stalk and hunt, the two watched the tribal posse ride on by, where they discovered the secluded cabin on the river. The posse stopped and waited, watching the dawn of a new day chasing away the eerie shadows of the night.

Their interest was now centered on the cabin, watching intently at a sun-withered buffalo hide covering the entrance into the cabin. It was shoved aside and out came a white man with a canteen in his hand, who sauntered down to the river. Shoots First, the youngest of the Blackfoot posse was overjoyed. This would be his day to count coup. He promptly raised his rust-pocked weapon and fired at the white man, watching the body fall into the water. A joyous whoop erupted from deep in his throat, only to be stopped by an older, more sedate member of the posse.

He was cursed right soundly for his stupidity, a cursing he would never forget. After searching the cabin, the posse turned their horses and headed back down the trail to the encampment. "We'll now be known as white eye killers," the old one said, still upset over the ways of Shoots First.

"We must now go and hide as cowardly coyotes—in the safety of the big ones that are white on top—Rising Wolf Mountain might be a good place to hide, perhaps Curly Bear or even Almost A Dog.

"White Eyes, who wear shiny stars, will come and hang us from the branch of a tree. Twisted rope that chokes—a bad way to die—our spirits will then be sad and lonely.

"They will wander forever with no friends to play with, like the raven who is this way. Only this bird returns to his nest, long enough to mate, then he leaves never to return for another year.

"The raven is lucky—we will never be able to mate again."

* * * Chapter Twenty-One * * *

Back at the Bonner's Lariat Cross ranch, Lynn just could not settle down. Back and forth she paced between her cabin home and the river. Old Slim sat on a cottonwood stump near the cabin door watching with interest her actions.

He loved this beautiful lady as he would have his long dead Mary, whose life he was unable to save from Kid Curry's bunch of ravaging wolves. The two deputies, Lynn and Will Bonner, had rescued him from the gang—allowed him to get a just revenge for the killing of his daughter—and in his own quiet, stubborn way had saved Lynn from the same fate as had been his Mary's.

Lynn was now sitting on the doorstep of her cabin, still panting from the exertion of her incessant pacing to the river and back. He was smiling as he stoked his pipe, he reckoned he knew why she was this way. Upset as all get out, her high-strung nerves on edge, and just not satisfied with the way things had worked out.

A slight smile remained on his whiskered face. He chose his words with care when he spoke. "Reckon you're a feelin' bad Lynn—not being with Will and that Injun kid.

"Sure wish you wouldn't get so all-fired het-up...might bring on that little cowboy you're a packin' before his time! Reckon ol' Slim wouldn't be of much help to you if this were to happen, in the birthin' and all. I'm a pretty fair hand at birthin' calves and colts, but babies!

"Old Slim would sure get the shakes helpin' out a birthin' mother!"

Lynn listened to her good friend's words, and then smiled some herself. "I didn't reckon it showed Slim—can't help it though.

"I should be with my husband. A deputy marshal badge pinned on my blouse, a .45 strapped on my hip and my little rifle in hand—ready for war. I would surely feel better if this were to happen Slim, I surely would."

She then arose from the doorstep, entered the cabin and returned with two steaming cups of coffee. Offering one to Slim, she returned to the doorstep and carefully eased herself down.

"Will needs me Slim, I just know he does, reckon it's a woman's thing—intuition my mother calls it—something that stirs a woman's heart, an itching in her soul that cannot be scratched!"

"Them sure are mighty pretty words Lynn, makes good sense too— words I've got to palaver over in my mind some though...!"

"Thank you for listening to my talk.

"Why, we're a team Slim, Will and I, we work together as deputy marshals and we are good ones too. Old Marshal Dunne told us so!"

Old Slim was silent, enjoying his pipe and coffee. He was troubled too, sure couldn't figure out any way to change her mind, knowing the baby could be on its way any day now.

The silence was welcomed by both Lynn and her good friend Slim. Two minds struggling on a decision of what is the right thing to do. Slim was sure wanting her to stay put at the ranch. Lynn was all for saddling her horse and high-tailing it up river to find deputy marshal Will Bonner.

In the background the river was singing a mind soothing tune. Not to be outdone, the quaking aspen had partnered up with the fast-flowing water in a wilderness serenade of the wild places.

* * *

The sun was showing itself above the eastern hills when Will Bonner heard a lone rifle shot. Though not that far away, the sound was confusing to pinpoint, echoing back and forth through the wooded breaks of this aspen country.

He reined in his bronc, wilderness-honed senses straining to detect what might lay ahead. It was quiet now, no sound could he hear but the rustling of leaves from a nearby stand of aspens.

Bonner's mind was in turmoil though, just would not let him be. His Lynn, who he had to leave back at the ranch? It had grieved him to do this, yet in her delicate condition—what else could he have done? Never in his life would he be able to forget, the look on her face when he told her she could not be with him. It was if he had slapped her in the face!

And then Spotted Pony! The red-skinned rascal, who had ignored Bonner's instructions and ridden off alone.

And then there was old Custis Dunne, who was somewhere ahead, all by himself and facing who knows what all; and then the rifle shot!

With a cue from his spurs, the big red horse carried the B—B rancher farther into the south, his destination the international boundary; and crossing trails with old Custis Dunne.

No one was in sight as he neared the field-stone cairn. He stepped to the ground, and cautiously approached the unseen boundary line of two great countries.

Ground tying his horse, he searched the small clearing in the aspens, stopping often to listen. The silence was a clue, he reckoned. Not even a bird was chirping, not a squirrel was chattering, the quaking trees were not even sighing their lonesome ways.

Widening the circle, he found another clue, fresh horse droppings and the track of a lone horse wearing shoes, both appeared to be five or six hours old. Retrieving his horse, he followed the tracks back into the woods. The trail took him towards the river where he discovered an old cabin set in a grove of aspen, the St. Mary's river but a stone's throw away.

Dismounting once again, he wrapped the bridal reins on the branch of an aspen tree. No smoke came from the chimney, no horse could he see. Yet the track ended here in a melee of horse tracks, made so by more than a few horses milling about—none of them wore shoes!

"Indians!" he muttered. "a riding unshod ponies."

"With six-gun drawn, Will Bonner approached the old structure with caution, he swung the weathered-hide aside and slipped inside the open doorway. No one was there, but he did find two unrolled blankets and open saddlebags lying beside it; and the blankets had been slept in.

This was the Marshal's trail gear all right, the saddle bags carried the insignia of the U.S. Marshal's Service.

He left the cabin and stood quiet, ears straining to hear any strange sound, eyes sweeping the nearby woods for any movement. It was then he noticed a faint trail leading to the river, someone has walked here, he reasoned, not that long ago by the looks of the dew-soaked grass.

Reckon I should walk over and check it out. Once again he drew his trusty Colt, once again he walked with great care—a trait ingrained in him by his father when just a young boy.

* * * Chapter Twenty-Two * * *

A faint trace through the dew-soaked grass led Will Bonner to the river where he discovered old Custis in a heap of trouble. The marshal was sprawled near the fast flowing stream. His body was curled up on the rocky shore, his legs were dangling in the river. "Custis!" he shouted, as he bounded down the bank "You all right?"

What he found was not pleasant to see. The old timer had been shot while at the river for water, the wire handle of a small pail still clutched in his hand. He was in rough shape, losing blood, but still breathing.

At the sound of the cowboy's voice, Custis stirred some, his voice weak when he asked, "—is that you Deputy Bonner—?

"Wus sure hopin' you would show up!"

"Don't talk or move Custis—I'm a goin' to get you out o' this mess, and pack you up to the cabin."

Bonner stooped low, knees bent, preparing to pick up the marshal in his arms, when a voice, with a trace of an accent, spoke from behind him. "I will help you, boss!" This startled him so, that he spun on his boot heels, a drawn six-gun ready for action.

There stood Spotted Pony, his red face turned to a sickly pale, realizing how close he had come to being gunned down. "...'bout time you showed up," Bonner snapped, his own nerves ready to explode.

Together, they packed the marshal back to the cabin, and settled him into an old dusty bunk.

Brannon had sent the Pony to the river for a pail of water, then kindled a fire in a small rusty stove. With a lighted match in hand, he was once again interrupted by a voice, one that meant more to him than anything in the whole wide world.

Will Bonner dropped the match and turned to see, astonishment written all over his face

There stood his darling Lynn. Her face was drawn and haggard looking, streaked with dust, sweat and tears. A faint smile was on her face. "Sure is good to see you Will," she spoke, almost a whisper. The smile was still on her face when she collapsed on the old dirt floor; and she was wearing her tin star.

Bonner hurried over and sat beside her, her head cradled in his lap. He smoothed her wind-blown hair, and still he hadn't spoke, struggling to control his emotions. He just could not believe she was here, and how she got here. Then he did know, as he could see her Boots mare standing outside the door.

He finally spoke, "Why Lynn? Why did you come in your condition, and all?"

She stirred in his arms, and was looking into his eyes when she responded. "The baby's coming today Will—it will be here any minute now.

"I wanted us to be together when our little child is born!"

Tears were streaming down both their cheeks. Then a wild hullabaloo could be heard outside the cabin. Quickly, the cowboy removed his coat and placed it between the earthen floor and her tangled hair, then rose and turned to see what in the dickens was happening.

"I wonder what will happen next?" he muttered, as he walked out the door—his hand hovering near his six-gun. He was greeted by one of his teams hitched on a wagon, entering the clearing in a cloud of dust. At the reins of the lather-soaked horses was old Slim pulling them to a sliding stop.

Sitting beside him was Aunt Sue, a frazzled looking lady, made so by the roughness of the trail and the wild, bone-jarring ride in the wagon. A bundle of blankets was snugged tight in her arms. She was helped from the wagon by Slim, only to brush past Bonner as she entered the cabin.

Bonner still had had no time to speak, he could hear the ranch cook utter a shocked gasp,

"The baby is on it's way," she told him, while she was preparing a clean bed for Lynn to lay on. "You men stay outside!" she ordered. "Go on—sho-oo—begone with you!" Bonner was still speechless, meekly obeying her orders.

Turning to Slim, he finally found his voice. "What in the world are you folks a doin' here?" he asked his top hand, who had unhooked the team and ordered the Pony to take them to the river for a much needed drink.

"Well you see Will, it's a long story. Come and sit—I'll try to explain. There is nothing we can do inside, we just as well sit for a spell, I'll do the talking."

He told of Lynn's restless ways after Bonner had ridden away from the ranch. She wanted nothing more Will, than to be with you when the baby came.

"The baby?" Bonner asked.

"Yes! The young one is on it's way. She made that clear before she left this morning, and if I hadn't a saddled her Boots mare, she would have come a riding hell-bent-for-leather on a bareback horse.

"No tellin' what might have happened to her!"

"Well, I'll be a gol-darned bonehead," Bonner said, tears showing in his eyes. I never reckoned she felt that way!"

Old Slim continued his story, and told when she left the ranch, he and Aunt Sue followed, hoping to reach her in time. "You must have been close behind Lynn, she arrived about fifteen minutes before you folks rolled in."

A lull prevailed, as the two sat in silence, in awe at the events that brought them here. Then Bonner told him of finding old Custis down by the river, that he had been shot, and then of the appearance of Spotted Pony, who had assisted him in packing the old marshal to the cabin.

Old Slim was smoking his pipe, Bonner was fidgeting and on edge, his eyes never leaving the cabin door. Then, a new sound could be heard, one which brought them both to attention. It was a muffled scream closely followed by the cry of a new-born babe.

Old Slim was grinning and heaved a sigh of relief, happy that Lynn had her baby, and all was well. Bonner galloped inside the cabin. There to greet him was a jaded, exhausted Lynn Bonner, a trace of a smile on her face; offering him his new baby girl to hold.

"Reckon Bonner owes me a cigar," old Slim said, and arose from the log he was sitting on.

"This is a first for an old Marshal," Custus finally spoke, who had been forgotten after Spotted Pony had treated his gun shot wound the Indian way; tree moss, willow tea and sacred salves. "to be on hand when one of my favorite Deputies has a baby. He had missed most of the birthing, but roused enough from the effects of the willow tea to witness the finale.

"We're taking you back to the ranch," Brannon told him. "You need some rest and a bit of Aunt Sue's nursing. In about ten days time, you and me Marshal Dunne, will declare us a war on some outlaws."

* * * Chapter Twenty-Three * * *

It was long after dark before the Bonner outfit arrived back at the ranch. Old Slim had been driving the team with Aunt Sue sitting beside him. Behind the seat were the wounded marshal and Lynn who was snuggling her precious bundle; all three wrapped in warm blankets. Bonner had ridden ahead picking out the least bumpy ground to travel on.

Tied on behind was the marshal's bronc, and trotting along side was Lynn's Boots mare, her nose was within reach of Lynn and the baby. She sensed there was a new addition to the ranch family, and appeared proud as could be; as if it had been her own.

With a teamster's bravado, old Slim reined the wagon in close to the cabin, where Lynn and the baby were hustled inside. There to greet them was little Matt, who was overjoyed to see them. He had bravely stayed alone that day, although the ranch hands were never far away.

He noticed the small bundle Lynn had snugged in her arms. His face lit up with joy, noticing the bulge in her stomach was no longer there. 'That must be the—surprise—my Mom was telling me about Lynn!" eagerly watching her unwrapping the little bundle.

"Come and see Matt, it is a surprise—one I will cherish the rest of my days!"

"The boy took one look, his eyes wide as saucers, he never spoke, a broad grin spreading across his face. "It is a baby!" he finally shrieked. "a surprise baby, right!

"I sure do like surprises."

All that were there were smiling at the boy, and the excitement that was flowing from his small frame. "This is your new niece Matt, a baby girl that will grow up to be another little Lynn!"

"I reckon we should name our daughter Mary Lynn," Bonner said, having just returned from the corrals.

"Mary, out of respect for old Slim's daughter, and of course you darling Lynn—after the little one's mother," He was grinning with pride as he spoke. "The name will be the continuation of a dynasty, given to four remarkable women of the old West.

"The Brannon women! A gun-fightin' bunch—right salty when riled!"

Lynn was thrilled as could be, on hearing her husband's talk, and agreed whole-heartedly with his wisdom.

For several days Slim was seldom seen around the ranch yards, no one could guess what he might be up to. Then on the third day, he walked into the cabin holding a hand-hewn cradle. "This is for little Mary Lynn," he said, presenting it to Lynn. "She will now have a bed of her own—a safe place to sleep I reckon." Tears were flowing down his whiskered cheeks when he walked out the door. Those that were there could here him mutter, "My Mary would have made a good Mom too, if she had been given the chance!"

Lynn ran to catch him, and gave him a big hug. "I just love the cradle Slim, it will be in our family forever.

"We all love you Slim, and thank you for this wonderful gift!"

Though bashful to talk of such things, Slim told her that he loved her too, and sure appreciated the name of his Mary being given to little Mary Lynn Bonner.

Lynn returned to the cabin to admire the gift that old Slim had made for the baby. She gasped when she had a closer look. It was a carefully crafted piece of art, carved from a seasoned piece of a box elder tree. Carved near the top of the head board were the two names, *Mary Lynn* .

Happiness reigned supreme at the Bonner's river ranch, the arrival of Lynn's baby was welcomed by one and all. She was a beautiful addition to the Brannon clan, an exact replica of the three Lynns before her.

On hearing of the happy news, Lynn's Mom came down from Lariat Cross to see the baby. She planned on staying awhile, to assist her daughter adjust to being a Mom, and would have it no other way. This was a Mom's God given right, a custom dating back to old mother Eve.

Two weeks had turned into three before Custis Dunne recovered from the gunshot wound. It was still painful to the touch, otherwise okay. He was sure becoming impatient and was ready to ride after the Blackfoot renegades.

* * *

A pair of territorial marshals arrived at the Blackfoot encampment in time to witness the tribal punishment of Shoots First, who had ambushed Custis Dunne at the river. Spirit Talker watched them ride in, and stopped them at the edge of a large tepee-infested opening in the aspen trees.

"*Ho!*" he greeted, followed by the now familiar "*Oki!*" He was admiring the two tin stars glistening in the morning sun, and advised them to wait here by the shaking trees while the Chief administered justice to Shoots First. Bonner and the Marshal reckoned they would be wise to do just that, and sat relaxed in their saddles watching this wilderness drama unfold.

The young brave known as Spirit Talker stayed with them, making sure the Tin Stars did not interfere with his father's wilderness court of law. Shoots First was brought to the center of the encampment by two heavily armed guards, who threw him to the ground, and spread-eagled his arms and legs; which were tied to four wooden stakes with rawhide strings cut from a buffalo hide. The eyes of the unfortunate Shoots First were facing the rapidly rising sun.

A group of rowdy women and children, all with supple willow branches in hand, were ordered to surround the prisoner and told to wait for the Chief's command. Much spitting and foul language was showered on the helpless prisoner, who was uttering silent words to the now blazing sun.

Suddenly, the hullabaloo of the camp settled down some, even the stick dancing women and their mimicking kids ceased their rehearsal of the torture ritual. All were watching an impressive clad figure leave his tepee and approach the circle. It was the Chief, Spirit Talker's father. With arms upraised, he gestured towards the sun, doing the same to the four directions of mother earth.

He gazed long at the helpless prisoner, then after once again praising the sun, tipped his war spear and touched Shoots First on the shoulder. "*Oki!*" the word rolled from his mouth. "The punishment will now begin."

The squaws and their eager children began shrieking and wailing a fearsome tune. The circle began to dance, a strange variation of the one-step, only with much more vigor. The one-step continued on in a hip-hop shuffling manner. Around and around they danced, shrieking and wailing, at the same time lashing the prisoner's naked body with their willow branches.

From Shoot's First ears to the tip of his grimy feet, they methodically lashed him with the fresh-cut willows. Blood was streaming from his lacerated body, his screams of anguish were overpowered by the frenzy of the ceremony.

Marshal Dunne tapped Will Bonner on the shoulder, who turned to see what his boss wanted. "I reckon this miserable hombre is one of my original posse—who up and quit me cold.

"One never knows about these People—sure a tough one to figure out."

Spirit Talker was watching the reaction of the two marshals. "He is the one who shot you Tin Star."

"He left you for dead—the People thought you had been taken to the world of Spirits!"

Bonner and his old boss listened closely as the boy continued his talk. "His punishment will be harsh, he has killed others before you were left for dead—white eyes too!

Spirit Talker eyes never left the two marshals before he spoke again, "This is why this one was given the name of Shoots First.

"Our great chief, who is my father, has much wisdom of such things, and has spent many hours deciding how to punish him. After the women and small ones have finishing playing with him—he will be sent to the world of Spirits by my father's war spear."

"Don't seem right to slaughter him like he was an animal," Bonner muttered.

Spirit Talker, who had the keen hearing of the wild ones, frowned as he listened to what the young marshal had to say. "You, Tin Star, will be the one to use my father's war spear!" He was looking at Will Bonner when he spoke.

Disbelief was strong on Bonner's face, he just couldn't believe what had just been piled on his shoulders. It was the execution of a helpless man, even though he was guilty as sin. Girding himself to refuse Spirit Talker's request, old Custis moved in close and spoke to Bonner so no one could hear.

"Reckon you should do as he says, else we will lose our top-knots sure!"

A silence grew heavy in the Blackfoot encampment. All eyes were on Spirit Talker who had now received the war spear from his beaming father. He carried it to Bonner, who had just witnessed a small brown-skinned urchin slip silently from the crowd, a tomahawk clutched in his hand.

The little one moved in close and with a mighty swing smashed it into the head of his disgraced relative. He then turned and scurried away, once again losing himself in the restless crowd.

Few besides Brannon were aware of what had happened, those who had seen the boy swing the old war club, remained silent. Bonner was stunned himself. Then an idea brought about by the actions of the little one, enabled him to return to his normal self.

He wasn't pleased to have been given this grisly chore, but reckoned he had best do as Custis had advised, else they would fall prey to the same fate as Shoots First. After watching the urchin administer the *coupe de grace* to the unfortunate prisoner, Bonner knew that this one known as Shoots First was now one dead Indian.

Accepting the war spear, Bonner gripped it with both hands, raising it high and driving it toward the corpse. Faster than a bolt of lightning, the cowboy's right hand released the hold on the spear and came up with his .44 spouting hot lead. One pull of the trigger is all that was required to still the restless crowd.

Shoot's First head had been a bloody mess from the lad's tomahawk attack. The war spear wielded by Bonner was driven into the ground, the quivering shaft snugged along side what had been the Indian's cheek. The other cheek showed a bloody gash, the .44 cartridge too had been shot into the ground.

All in the crowd were silent, awed by what they had just witnessed. None of the clan had ever witnessed a fast draw before. Bonner's .44 was still smoking when a lively cheer rippled through the crowd.

A jargon of Blackfoot talk blended with whoops and raucous laughter, the clan members knowing that Shoot's First spirit was with them no more. Many of them began to dance, a macabre dance of death, still circling the dead body of Shoots First.

Leading the dance were the howling squaws and their dirty-faced urchins, their blood-soaked torture sticks now trampled underfoot.

"I reckon we should get outta this place," Custis said. "'fore them dancers decide they don't like us a lookin' on!"

"My feelings exactly," Bonner replied, both riders reined their horses to leave the camp.

Spirit Talker, who was keeping a close watch over the two Marshals, stopped them and began to talk. "The Chief, my father, wishes you to know that Shoots First will not harm you now.

"He also wishes you to know, that the old Tin Star has been avenged from the cowardly way Shoots First tried to kill you.

"He wants you to know that his interests are the same as yours, keeping peace among the People. He is pleased that you are the law now, not the Blue Coats—who slaughtered so many of the People."

Both old Custis and Bonner told Spirit Talker to thank the Chief for his wise words, and if they ever needed them, they would come again.

"*Adios*, Spirit Talker," Bonner said, and doffed his hat. "Tell the Chief he is welcome at my B——B ranch down the river. It is in *old grandmother's land*, north of the *medicine line*.

"Tell him we will drink coffee together, and feast on the meat of the longhorn cows.

"Ride in peace Tin Stars, you may come to this camp again—and talk with the Chief," Spirit Talker said, his talk and sign language making the message clear.

"We will welcome you as friends!"

* * * Chapter Twenty-Four * * *

Excitement and concern rippled through the residents at the river ranch when old Slim and his riders rode in with the news. "Thar's a fire up yonder," he told them. "Up by the big Chief, a smoke is putting on quite a show!"

All ears were tuned into Slim's talk, they wouldn't miss a story like this for anything in the world. News of any kind was a scarce commodity out hear along the lonely river. Most times the foothill grapevine was the only link to the outside world.

From the home ranch along the river valley the famous landmark known to all as Old Chief could not be seen. To view Lynn Bonner's mountain one had to ride to the top of a high hill above the buildings, known to the Bonner's and their crew as Ol' Lookout. It was here could be found several tepee rings, fire pits and various other relics and baubles of the ancient ones.

Bonner and Lynn were the first to react, riding to the top of Ol' Lookout for a view of the western horizon. "Oh, Will!" Lynn was the first to speak. "The smoke is coming from where our Jenni Mine is at—I wonder what is happening up their?"

The gold diggings had been given the name by her Grandpa Brannon, out of respect for his Jenni mule, who in her own stubborn, eccentric way had shown him where to dig. Before he died he had bequeathed the diggings to his granddaughter, little Lynn, who even now was riding beside her husband Will Bonner.

"I reckon come morning we should ride up and check things out," he said. "Could be some claim jumpers have moved in on the mine!"

Lynn felt somewhat ashamed over her neglect of the old mine, in fact she hadn't been there since before her marriage in the southern territories, and the hair-raising adventures that followed. And now, smoke coming from the site of the Jenni Mine sure got her to fretting and plumb upset. Nothing to do but Lynn and her husband must ride up and see what was going on.

With a packhorse trailing behind, carrying food and camp gear for a long stay if needed, Deputies Will and Lynn Bonner headed into the southwest.

Lynn was chattering as they rode, both she and her husband enjoyed to ride together and enjoy each other's talk. "I'm sure thankful Will, for old Slim and Aunt Sue—knowing that the two of them will be there to look after my brother and our Mary Lynn."

"You are right Lynn, without them you would not have been able to come on this ride—would've sure bin lonesome a ridin' alone—and you at home a tendin' the kids."

"I know Deputy Bonner," she groaned, "it would have been terrible. But knowing old Slim worships both Matt and our daughter—Aunt Sue the same, takes a great load off of my shoulders.

From the Bonner ranch along the St. Mary's River to the Jenni Mine located in the shadows of Old Chief Mountain was a tough thirty mile ride. It was a long day's journey, riding through high wind-blown hills, onward into thick brush country, there to flounder through bog-induced terrain made so by the seepage from numerous beaver dams. Once free from the uncertainty of the treacherous terrain, was the coolness of a pine forest—a welcome break from the bogs and the brush. Closing in on the mountain the route left the lodgepoles behind, encountering a steep rock-littered game trail leading no where but up; a challenge to the best of cow ponies.

Riding single file, the Bonner deputies were nearing the Chief, following a faint trace through a lodgepole forest. It was a seldom used route, used on occasion by elk and sheep. The Bonners had not taken the old route from Lariat Cross that Lynn knew so well, she knew it as the

Chief Mountain trail. For lack of time, they had pointed the noses of their horses into the southwest, charting a course as the raven would fly.

Breaking free from the small forest of lodgepoles, the scent of wood smoke was wafting strong in the air. It was here they reined in their weary mounts for a breather. Facing them was a steep rock-strewn climb, not far, perhaps fifty yards or so.

Lynn was chattering as they sat their trail-weary mounts, Bonner was taking a pull from his canteen. Suddenly he cautioned Lynn into silence, a sun-bronzed finger on his pursed lips, a sign that meant—hush!"

The cowboy and his wife sat their horses in silence, senses straining to unravel a mystery of the unknown. Silence was noted in the forest, no birds chirping, no squirrels chattering as was their way. Not even a mountain breeze was pestering the lodgepoles.

"I swear it was a gunshot Lynn," Bonner's voice was barely above a whisper. "I reckon my talking muffled the sound so's we will never know for sure."

"Oh, pooh," she replied, her own voice much more subdued than normal. "The horses hooves on this rocky trail, and my chattering are the reason—don't take all the blame Will—I'm as much at fault as you are!"

The two riders remained silent, the only sound they could hear was an occasional movement of the horses—long tail hairs lashing out at horse flies, the shifting of hooves and such.

With fifty yards of a tough climb still facing them, they decided to continue on for the trailhead, which appeared to be just out of sight. The smell of smoke was now strong in their nostrils, the fire the reason they were here under the big mountain, a mystery they had came to solve. Besides, this was Lynn's claim, a gold mine under the shadows of the Chief.

* * *

"Best we ride easy Lynn," Bonner cautioned, as the old game trail faded away into a small clearing of succulent mountain grass. Surrounded by massive boulders on two sides, the clearing was no more than an acre, maybe two in size. On the far side was a modest stream of water trickling a pathway down through a maze of rocks and debris. And rearing high above the stream was a massive shale slide, an alluvial fan on the lee side of the mighty Chief.

And then something else! Within a stones throw of the stream was a pile of smoldering ashes—the same shape as that of a square-built cabin.

It was ironic to the girl, that from where she sat she had spotted the fire ring. Her Grandpa Brannon's old camp site, and though it was grassed over, she could detect the ring of rocks just the same. Tears filled her eyes as she remembered of the many times she had camped here with her grandpa, of old Raven Wings, her Jenni mule and the adventures that had thrilled a small girl.

There they sat in their saddles, absorbing all that lay before them. Will had removed his sweat-stained Stetson, the flat brim caked with trail dust. Lynn was bare-headed, her long auburn hair fluttering at the whim of a mountain breeze. But she had not forgotten her cowboy hat with a bullet hole in the brim, it hung from her shoulders by a leather string—within easy reach.

Her attention now shifted to the little stream, the best tasting water in the world as far as she was concerned. Then onward to the scattered boulders and debris that led up to the hidden entrance to her Jenni Mine. Somehow things were different, it sure never looked the same as before. Studying the area closely, she could tell a recent rock slide had buried the mine site under tons of fractured shale and scree.

Tears rolled down her cheeks, she now knew that Grandpa Brannon's old gold mine was gone forever. Bonner remained silent, he knew that his wife was reliving memories of her childhood, and respected her silence.

His keen eyes were active though, his attention was drawn to wisps of smoke rising from what must have been a cabin. Without a blink of an eye, his head kept moving, scanning every nook and cranny of the small oasis for signs of human presence.

Lynn was now through with her reverie, and asked, "Will! The smoke! Do you reckon it was a cabin?

"The last time I was here there wasn't a cabin, just a camp site here by Grandpa Brannon's fire ring. Whoever it was must have been planning on a long stay."

"I figure them as prospectors Lynn, quite likely claim jumpers have been living here; looking for your Jenni Mine no doubt.

"They most likely found a trace of color here along the crik, reason enough for them to throw together a shelter. Prospectors, when discovering a trace of gold, rather it be from a pan or clawed loose with a rock pick, will set up camp and stay awhile—often erecting a shelter to protect them from the elements."

Lynn Bonner appeared satisfied with her husband's talk, and after securing their horses close by, they walked across the clearing to inspect the smoldering ruins. An intense heat was still evident on all sides of the ashes, along with an eye-watering, stomach-turning stench, that forced them to move up wind in a hurry.

It was a strange nauseating odor that had Lynn gasping for breath. Her eyes were watering, her nose was running, and her stomach was ready to heave up its contents. "What in the world is that awful smell Will? Never in my life have I smelled anything like this before!"

"I'm not sure Lynn, but reckon I've got an idea of what it might be. You stay here by this small crik, I sure don't want you getting any sicker than you look!

"I'm a goin' over for another look."

With his bandana covering his nose, the big cowboy walked back to the still glowing embers. He looked long at the ruins, shifting here and there to better satisfy his curiosity. "It's just as I thought!" he muttered, and walked back to the small stream.

"I don't rightly know how to tell you this Lynn, but reckon I better try." She was kneeling beside the stream washing her face and hands, and even her hair, attempting to rid herself of the terrible stench. "What were you saying Will, reckon I couldn't make out your talk from the babbling of this little stream."

"The smell that has sickened us both is burnt flesh, two bodies are mixed up in that mess over yonder—could be they were caught unawares and died in the fire.

"On the other hand, they could have both been murdered and the cabin set on fire to hide the evidence!"

"Deputy Bonner, you're thinking like a lawman would think—old Marshal Dunne would be mighty proud of you, if he were here to listen to your talk."

Suppressing a smile, Bonner spoke again, "Another possibility is they were pards, they could have got into a fight over gold. In the hullabaloo that followed, they up and shot each other, knocking over a lantern as they did so.

"Could be the cause of the fire that burnt down the cabin, I spotted the remains of a lantern over yonder in the ashes."

"Well done Deputy Bonner! I reckon you could be right though, any one of your three theories just might be what happened."

Darkness was now moving into the high country. Leaving the fire sight, the two deputies picked up their horses and walked on down the creek to set up camp. To be away from the awful stench would be a blessing to Lynn.

Much later, while laying in their blankets, they were admiring the star studded sky, and listening to the eerie music coming from high up in the crags of the mountain. "Sure a strange sound," Bonner said. "Reckon I've never heard the likes before."

"I have," Lynn replied. "The first night I ever slept here I was terrified at the sound, even though my bed was beside Grandpa Brannon's. He knew I was awake, and he knew why. "There's nothing to be afraid of Lynn," he told me.

"Why it is nothing but the mountain breezes a playin' hide-and-seek up in them thar crags. It's not spirits a moanin' up thar, although some folks think so!

"The last thing I remembered that night was the comforting voice of Grandpa consoling me."

* * *

Sleep was hard to find for Bonner that night, his mind in a frenzied turmoil. To have his darling Lynn here, sleeping peacefully beside him was a great comfort. The thing that puzzled him so was the rifle shot! He was sure he had heard one, even though the deputies were both chattering at the time.

He also knew the acoustics in these high mountains could play tricks on one's sense of reasoning, the source of the sound appearing much closer than it really is. Many times he had experienced this phenomenon while riding the lonely trails. It was the ravens who had put him wise to this strangeness. Their harsh croaks sounding loud and clear, only to have the wandering scavengers show up some time later.

Come morning, he reckoned, he would make a thorough search of the clearing, and the immediate surroundings.

An eerie mist had enveloped the mighty Chief, and was even now sifting through the lodgepoles by the Brannon's camp. Deputy Lynn Bonner stirred in her blankets, turning to her husband, and discovering that he was not there beside her. She sat up, her blankets snugged close around her, eyes straining through the eerie mist. She could smell smoke and a hint of coffee, and noticed a figure hunched over their small cooking fire.

"Darlin' Will has done it again," she muttered. "He is preparing breakfast for me, when it should be his wife doing the same for him." Bonner loved to cook while out on the trail, and he was a good one too.

With a blanket snugged tight around her slim body, Lynn headed for the creek to prepare herself for the coming day. "I'll be back soon Will," she called out, as she passed the fog-shrouded figure. "Don't drink all of the coffee you hear!"

On her return, she approached the fire. The early morning mist was now lifting, allowing her to see an Indian boy sitting by the fire, not her husband as she had reckoned. "Oh, it's you Spotted Pony—you startled me so.

"I thought it was my Will sitting here! "Have you seen him this morning?"

As was his way, the Indian boy took his time in answering the lady he had sworn to protect from the evil ones, an oath he had once made to Little Crow in a spirit dream. "I have come to be with you," he said.

"It is the wishes of your old friend, Little Crow—who is now up in the sky—that Spotted Pony protect Missy Lynn from the evil ones."

"Have you seen my Will?" she asked again, knowing that he would not answer until he was good and ready.

"Spotted Pony was hiding over there," he said, pointing towards a large chunk of lime stone, that sometime in the distant past had came thundering down off the mountain. "This Indian was guarding your camp here by the big rock—that has fallen by the sacred stream.

"Two hours!" he signed with two upright fingers, which had no meaning to Lynn in her agitated condition. "Your husband left you sleeping in your blankets."

"Spotted Pony! Tell me what happened next? And stop that fiddling around with your sign language."

"*Oki*, Spotted Pony will do what you ask.

"Bonner go that way," and signed back up the creek, paying no heed to the order she had just given him. "He is looking for someone who killed the two hunters of gold—in the fire. He has heard strange voices in the darkness—he is now by a blanket camp, where bad Indians who rape Blackfoot girls and drink white eye firewater are hiding from the people.

"He has sent Spotted Pony to bring him his lady deputy, who wears a tin star—he wishes you to be with him when he fights these evil Indians."

Lynn was somewhat shocked at what the boy was telling her, yet elated that Will wished her to be with him. "We must go and help him Pony— I will go and prepare myself to fight with my husband—I must pull on my boots, strap on my six-gun and pin on my tin star. Then with my little carbine in hand, the same one Grandpa Brannon gave me so many long years ago, I will be ready to fight a war."

"*Oki!* Spotted Pony take you there! He will wait for Missy Lynn by the sacred water," and signed to the small stream that chuckled past the camp.

"The great Chief is pleased when we drink this water, he knows that it will make us strong and brave.

"This sacred mountain," and once again he used his sign language, gesturing to the massive mountain rearing high above them, "allows this water to escape from deep inside his bowels, to bless those who use it and their ponies who drink it."

* * *

Daylight was closing in on the eastern front of the Rockies, chasing away the shadows of the now past night when Lynn Bonner, who was following Spotted Pony, skirted the clearing of the old Jenni Mine. The stench here had abated somewhat since the night before, though Lynn wore her bandana over her nose as a precaution. She reckoned this was no time for her to be getting sick again.

She was panting as she attempted to keep up to the boy, who was flitting here and there through the lodgepoles as silent as a lobo wolf on the hunt. Several times he would stop and sign to her which direction he was going, then faster than a blink of an eye he would be out of sight again.

Standing alone in the forest, Lynn was turning into a nervous wreck, waiting for Spotted Pony to show himself again. An eerie silence grew heavy in the lodgepoles, a frightening sensation to the girl, who was still plumb spooked by the discovery of the two corpses in the fire-ravaged cabin

Then, the sound of a twig snapping, a slight caress on her shoulder, and old Matt Brannon's little Lynn spun on her boot heels—the little carbine on her hip ready to fight a war. "No!" "No, Lynn! Do not shoot your husband!" It was Bonner talking in a hushed voice, who knew her dainty finger had come mighty close to pulling the trigger. The barrel of her rifle lowered as Bonner covered her mouth with his hand, knowing that within a heart beat a shock-induced scream would gush forth.

With his free arm holding her close, he whispered in her ear, "Don't speak darlin' Lynn, I am sure proud of the way you reacted—you had every reason to shoot, me and you didn't!"

With her long hair buried on Bonner's shoulder, Lynn's convulsive sobs could not be stopped. All Bonner could do was hold her close, knowing that she had just endured a very traumatic experience.

Several minutes passed before she was able to gain control of her shattered self. Knowing that she had came within a heart-beat of shooting her darling Will, the lady deputy finally spoke. "I'm so sorry Will—I didn't know it was you—I would have shot you dead if my, my finger hadn't frozen on the trigger."

"Settle down Lynn and I will explain what has been happening here. The two bodies we discovered in the ashes were victims of a murder. They were killed by two Blackfoot renegades, who then set the fire, attempting to cover up their cowardly deed.

"They are on the run from the tribal police and old Custis Dunne, who have been hot on their trail for murder, rape and molesting Blackfoot women. The two, Porcupine Eater and Sore Backed Horse, from what I could gather from their talk, are heading south of the mountain to hide from the law in the mountains along a large glacier-fed lake.

"The three of us are riding after the renegades. Spotted Pony, you will ride on ahead scouting out the trail."

"*Oki!*" the boy replied, and vanished in the forest.

* * * Chapter Twenty-Five * * *

The cowboys were out on the range that day, moving the B—B herd to fresh grazing. Old Slim had been with them all morning and was returning to the river to take care of his other chore, assisting Aunt Sue in the care of young Matt and Mary Lynn.

His desire was to have accompanied the Bonner deputies up to the big smoke under the Chief, but knew that he was needed here to assist Aunt Sue with the kids and keep track of the Blackfoot cousins—his cowboys.

The old timer was nearing the river trail that entered the ranch from the reservation, a well used trail often traveled by the cowboys. To visit their clan was the reason they gave. Smiling as he rode, Slim reckoned they must be sparking a few of those pretty little Blackfoot maidens over yonder.

He had listened to their talk around the bunkhouse—he could understand more of their Blackfoot jargon than they gave him credit for. He didn't blame them none, reckoned they were only human the same as his own kind—hot blood a boiling—on the hunt for a mate. It was an itch that just had to be scratched by all humans.

Once at the river, he dismounted and after both he and his horse had refreshed themselves with a drink of cool water, he sat in the shade of a big cottonwood tree near the singing waters. His horse, though ground-tied, began to graze on the tender plants that grew there. Slim stoked his pipe and settled back for a rest. He deserved a break, he reckoned. He had been on the go since five o'clock this morning.

Couldn't help it he reckoned, old age must be the reason. The soothing music of the river flowing into the unknown, the sighing of the leaves on the quaking trees, was just too much. His head dropped, his pipe slipped into the grass, and old Slim drifted into a sound sleep.

Much later old Slim stirred, his mind still clouded with sleep. The sound of grazing horses he could hear, and something else that sent cold chills racing down his spine. Muffled giggles and the subdued talk of at least one man, and both were close by.

"Reckon we should shoot him?" young Matt asked, watching the old timer's hand moving towards his holstered gun. The boy was armed with a .22 caliber Marlin rifle.

"No—ooo! No Matt, we must not shoot him—old Slim is my best friend." The two youngsters from the B——B were sitting cross-legged in the grass, watching him wake up from the deep sleep that had overpowered him.

Mary Lynn was shocked to hear her uncle talk this way, and reckoned she would tell her Mom and Dad when they returned from their ride up to see the big smoke.

* * *

Old Slim's mind was now conscious of where he was at, and what he was doing here, yet he hadn't opened his eyes. He recognized Mary Lynn's giggles, and was proud of the way she had stuck up for him when young Matt talked of shooting.

He knew the boy was only teasing the girl and would never have shot him. He also reckoned the boy needed to be taught a lesson. Slowly Slim's eyes opened, his six-gun had appeared in his hand, a fast draw the likes of which the boy had never been exposed to before.

"Drop your weapon boy—'fore you get yourself in more trouble than you can handle," Slim growled. The little gun fell into the grass, the boy's arms raised high, a look of astonished misbelieve spreading across his face.

Mary Lynn never moved, tears welling in her pretty eyes. "Uncle Matt never meant you no harm," she said. "Please don't shoot him—we were just playing cowboys and Indians."

Struggling to keep from breaking into laughter, Slim was able to say, "I reckon I must have been a make believe Indian."

"Yes," she replied. "You had captured me and Uncle Matt was going to save me."

Old Slim holstered his gun, no longer able to hold back his laughter. "I admire you for tellin' me this, and Matt, your bravery in facing up to an old outlaw, or an Indian as you two had me pegged for—is highly commendable."

The old baby-sitter lectured them on confronting an enemy, as their small drama had cast him as. He also told them to never draw, or aim a gun unless they were willing to use it. He told them many things, a real lesson in the use of a gun and the reasons for using it.

The lesson now over, old Slim gave an order, one that the children eagerly accepted. "Time we was heading down river, reckon Aunt Sue's dinner is waiting for us to come and eat it.

"I'm sure enough hungry!"

"Me, too!" Mary Lynn giggled, "Let's put the spurs to our broncs and go find us some grub," A phrase often used by her great grandpa Brannon, as told to her by her Mom.

Mary Lynn's uncle Matt was still shaken from the fast draw incident. He never had much to say other than, "Wait for me, I'm hungry too,"

Three mounted riders entered the ranch yards, continuing on to the bunk house where they found Aunt Sue in a real dither. "Where have you two been?" she scolded. "I've been worried sick when you never showed up for your meal!"

"We've been playing cowboys and Indians," Mary Lynn piped up. Slim was our bad Indian, Matt and I were the good cowboys."

Slim reckoned they were all three in trouble with the cook, and resisting a smile, didn't have much to say. Then after a piercing look from Aunt Sue he decided maybe he better explain, "Found 'em up river aways, reckon a half-mile or so. Reckon we plumb forgot about the time."

"Well, all three of you get yourselves washed up—then come in for your meal, I was about to throw it out for the magpies and crows,"

Aunt Sue soon calmed down, and hustled about the kitchen putting food on the table. She had reason to be concerned though. She loved all three of them as if they had been her own, and felt somewhat ashamed of her harsh remarks.

She atoned for it though, with a big slice of apple pie.

* * *

A week had passed since the Bonners had ridden away to check on the Jenni gold mine. All were becoming concerned, including old Slim, who reckoned he should ride up to the Chief and find them. "Could be they've run into a heap of trouble," he told Aunt Sue. "You take care of these here young 'uns—don't let them out of your sight!"

Old Slim's mind was in a state of frenzy as he mounted his bronc ready to ride. Aunt Sue and the two youngsters watched him ride away, a sack of Aunt Sue's grub swinging from the saddle. As he settled in for a long ride, his confounded mind just would not let him be. Try as he may he couldn't control it, it seemed to do as it darn well pleased.

Having been rescued from the clutches of the Curry gang by a compassionate lady deputy, an old outlaw headed into the west to check on the whereabouts of Lynn, and her husband Will Bonner.

The gang had all died with their boots on, and thanks to old Slim who had shown Lynn the same compassion, as she had him, he was brought home to the river ranch to live out his days.

It had been a tough ride for old Slim before he reached the site of the cabin burn, and was sure thankful he had one of the Indian cowboys with him to ride ahead and nose out sign. He shook his head in wonderment, the tracks now heading south into a hellhole of ancient downfall timber.

He marveled at the skill of the Indian lad, who much like a hound following the scent of a rabbit, unerringly stayed on the Bonner's trail. It was going on three days since leaving the ranch and he was sure tired. Reckoned he was getting too old for this deputy business, he also knew this would be the last time he would wear his Tin Star.

Slim seldom saw the Blackfoot cowboy, yet the sign he left was plain to see. It was sundown of the fourth day before he rode into the clearing. He spotted the old caved-in cabin and the light from a camp fire near a boisterous mountain stream.

He stepped to the ground and almost fell, his aching bones protesting the tough journey up from the B——B. One hand gripping the saddle horn, Slim leaned against the saddle until his head cleared, he reckoned hot coffee and his pipe is what he needed. He looked long at the fire across the clearing, there were people sitting there, at least two, maybe three.

Leaving his horse, Slim walked towards the fire, his hand hovering near his six-gun. He stopped in the shadows back from the brightness of the flames, his trail savvy honed to the finest edge.

Fury raged in his breast at what he could see. There sat Lynn and his Indian cowboy, hands securely tied, facing a pair of long-haired men of the wilderness. They wore full beards, and clothes that were so ripe they would have made a dung beetle back away in shame.

Slim's cowboy had been bloodied, and Lynn appeared as if she had put up a scrap. "You two a gonna talk?" one of them asked with a sneer.

"Whar's that gold mine located at—reckon you should know. We were told you're the one who inherited it from the old gunfighter." He was holding a burning brand from the fire, moving it steadily towards Lynn Bonner's face.

Lynn screamed as the fire stick neared her long hair. "I told you before there is no more gold," she shrieked. "The mine was buried by a rock slide. "No one can find it now!"

"You'll tell me the truth, time your hair catches on fire," A sadistic smile was spreading across his hairy face.

Slim was boiling mad, he had heard it all and was ready to act. Stepping out of the shadows he fired his .44, watching the crazy one fall across the fire. Facing the other who was clawing for his own weapon, he watched him go down, a feather-tipped arrow buried deep in his chest.

Out from the shadows strolled Spotted Pony, who promptly retrieved his arrow, then scalped the unfortunate hunter of gold. "*Oki!* he greeted to one and all, then turned and watched old Slim untie Lynn and the B——B cowboy.

"Pull that one out of the fire!" Slim roared. "The stench will make us all sick."

"*Oki!*" Spotted Pony replied, and did as he was told. He was disappointed though, the crazy one's hair had been burnt off—there was nothing left to scalp.

Without being told, Spotted Pony and his cousin drug the two corpses out into the pines, far enough away that foraging bears would have singed meat for their nightly meal. They knew the bodies would be gone by morning, and really didn't care.

Slim was aware of what the Indian boys had done, and reckoned he knew the reason.

"Save us a diggin' a hole in the ground," he said, and he was grinning as he spoke.

After composing herself some, Lynn asked Spotted Pony a pointed question. "What has happened to Deputy Bonner?

"Where is my darling Will?"

* * *

Seldom did the deputies see Spotted Pony that day, yet Bonner knew he was somewhere ahead scouting a passage through an ancient forest of pine and spruce. Giant fir trees were encountered, many having fallen victims to the hurricane-force winds that howled along the base of the Chief—stark windfall skeletons clogging the movement of man or beast.

The two deputies were forced to dismount, leading their horses this way and that, seeking a way through to the other side. Trusting the ingrained savvy of his Blackfoot scout who was seeking a way through, the cowboy and his wife were able to continue on—a fresh blaze on a tree, an overturned log, even fresh cut branches positioned in such a way that only the deputies knew their meaning.

Scattered islands of fractured rock were encountered which had tumbled down off the Chief eons ago. Dotting the landscape were the skeletal remains of fifty foot trees, a stark reminder of a long past wild fire in the forest.

Bonner stopped often to give Lynn a break from the wild scramble of horse and rider. The roughness of it all was a humbling experience, a challenge that had about done them all in. Finally, with the horses ready to drop from utter exhaustion, the deputies rode away from the chaos left behind into a modest mountain meadow

There to greet them was Spotted Pony, sprawled in the grass beside the tumbled down remains of a cabin, his horse was close by feeding on the lush mountain forage. With one foot still in the stirrup of her saddle, Lynn was dismounting when she lost her balance and fell to the grass; utter exhaustion had caught up to her.

Bonner was there in an instant, and while kneeling beside her, could tell she had been pushed to the limit, that his darlin' Lynn was in a bad way. She was silently sobbing when Bonner lifted her into his arms and held her close. "I'm so tired Will, I don't think I can go any farther—I'm hungry too!"

Remorse and anger filled his soul, anger at himself for treating her this way, ashamed at having not considered that she might be wearing down, her small body crying for a rest. "I'm sorry darlin'," he told her. "Reckon I'm a bone-headed, son-of-a-gun a pushin' you this way—we're campin' here tonight—givin' you and our hosses a much needed rest!

"Come mornin' we'll see."

"Thank you Will," she said, while still cuddled in his arms, then drifted off into a deep sleep of the weary.

Uttering an exhausted snort, the Bonner's pack horse stumbled into the clearing, having had a dickens of a time making it out of the forest entanglement. It too, much like Lynn, settled into the grass too weary to take another step. Bonner lowered his wife to the ground, then walked over to the exhausted animal and released the pack from its back.

The pack such as it was, was tattered and torn, no doubt losing some of the supplies, but the basics of survival were still there—most of the food and their bedrolls.

Spotted Pony loved to show off his wilderness upbringing, forever amazing those around him of his prowess as a disciple of the old ones. With little effort he slipped away unseen from the clearing, and vanished in the surrounding forest, and returned shortly after the arrival of the packhorse. His arms were full of supplies that he had picked up off the incoming trail, including various canned goods, a sack of sugar and a coffee pot. He never spoke, a haughty look on his face as he deposited his find by the packhorse.

Bonner gave no thought to sleeping in the cabin, discovering it was over run with vermin, the crawly kind. It was also the home to a clan of pack rats. The roof was partially caved in from the deep snow that was common to this high country, the windows were missing, and a weather-battered door was hanging from a shred of what once had been a leather hinge.

While the Indian boys were kindling a fire, Bonner prepared a modest camp not far from the noisy mountain brook. After settling Lynn in her blankets, he returned to the fire and began to fix them some trail-cooked grub.

He was sitting near the fire, legs crossed Indian style, when his attention was once again centered on the cabin. Must have been put together by a prospector, he reasoned, perhaps a fur trapper—reckon we'll never know. The small structure had been erected using hand-split logs hewed right here in this small, narrow valley.

The location was along the southern flank of Chief, a rough gut-bustin' all day ride from the location of Lynn's Jenni Mine. Another trail came in from the east, continuing on into the western forest to follow the shoreline of a glacier filled lake. Chief Mountain reared its massive bulk on the northern side of the lake, a slide-ravaged Yellow Mountain stood on the south.

In the distant past, a gigantic rock slide had thundered down off the mountain, successfully damming off a valley drainage, which in time formed Slide Lake.

An eerie silence lay heavy in the valley, broken by the hoot of an owl, the howl of a wolf and the wind sighing in the forest that surrounded the Bonner camp. Bonner and Lynn were asleep in their blankets, the boys were still sitting by the fire, there attention drawn to the massive bulk of the Chief, a faint silhouette sitting high in the sky amongst the twinkling stars.

They were gnawing on iron-hard jerky and drinking cup after cup of coffee, both the main stay of their native diet; unless they could feast on fresh meat. Except for the coffee which they had become addicted to, the ways of their ancestors suited them just fine.

Suddenly Spotted Pony stood up, his attention drawn to the silence of the surrounding forest, his eyes straining to see, his ears struggling to hear. A slim silhouette blended in with the darkness as he vanished into the forest. Spotted Pony had sensed movement in the darkness, his keen senses suggesting an animal close by; the snap of a twig had been the cue.

Bonner awoke to the savory scent of cooking meat, a sure enough pleasant smell. That it was venison he was sure of, and while pulling on his boots he could see Spotted Pony sitting by the fire, now a bed of glowing coals.

The lads had fashioned a spit over the fire, from which hung the skinned carcass of a small animal, a yearling mule deer by the looks of it. Leaving Lynn, who was still asleep, he approached the fire. "Good morning Pony—see you found us some fresh meat—sure smells good."

"*Oki!* This deer found Pony in the night. It wishes Missy Lynn, who is sick, to feast on its tender flesh.

"This will make her feel much better, and the little warrior who is living in her belly—!"

Bonner was stopped in his tracks, plumb thunder struck over what Spotted Pony was telling him. "What makes you talk this way?"

"How do you know these things?" Irritation was evident in his voice as he spoke.

"Missy Lynn does not wish to wear Tin Star anymore—she wishes to stay at her river ranch and give you many sons, like the one that is inside her now."

"Does Lynn know this?" he asked, an irritation still tickling his craw.

"Yes Will, she knows," The voice was Lynn Bonner's, who had been standing in the background quietly listening.

"I too reckon the baby will be a boy, I can tell by all the ruckus that he's been making. How Spotted Pony knew all this, we'll never know?"

Bonner poured himself a cup of coffee and settled himself by the fire, attempting to digest the news that had just been told him. Lynn moved in beside him, tears in her eyes as she spoke, "You don't approve Will, I can tell!

"I am getting too old for this gun fighting business—all I want is to stay at our ranch—and give you more children to enjoy, as you have enjoyed our Mary Lynn."

Bonner poured her a cup after which he settled down beside her. Still he hadn't spoke, until he looked in her eyes. He knew what would happen and he didn't much care, one look is all it took and he was smitten; knowing that she was telling it like it was.

"I reckon you're right darlin'. I've been thinking the same as you—it's sure enough time we were hanging up our Tin Stars. But I'm obligated to see this one out, I told ol' Custis, if we ever find him, that we would meet him here.

"I am taking a ride up the lakeshore, heard tell there's a waterfall up that way—could be that's where them renegade Injuns are a hanging out. I wish you would stay here at our camp, the Pony will be close by to keep you company."

"I will stay Will, but remember one thing—you come back to me, you hear?"

* * *

Several hours had passed since the departure of Deputy Will Bonner into the deep forest. He had this last assignment to finish before hanging up his badge, then he and Lynn were heading back to the B—B.

Though it had been a shock to find out that once again he would be a father, he was happy the baby would be a son. How Lynn and Spotted Pony knew this he would never know.

He rode with caution as he neared the waterfall, the ominous roar of the gushing cataract a sound that just would not go away. The forest trail opened up into a barren rock-cluttered clearing, the vastness of the lake changing into several beaver dam ponds surrounded by willow brush— the waterfall in the background.

It was then he discovered what he had been looking for, a spiral of smoke rising above a cluster of shattered boulders.

The deputy's eyes swept the cluttered mess below the falls, the incessant roar of the plunging water wiping out any sound that might have been. Slowly, and with great care, his eyes scanned the scene before him, searching for a movement that might be there.

Several long minutes passed before his patience was rewarded. A movement caught his attention, a silent figure sitting on a cabin-size boulder watching the smoke below him. Sure looks like Spotted Pony, he reckoned, but what in the blue blazes was he doing here, the boy had been told to stay and guard Lynn

Securing his horse in a nearby patch of willow brush, Bonner began working his way towards Spotted Pony. It was a scramble through the debris of a long ago upheaval, but he was determined to continue on and find the Indian boy.

Sweat was pouring down his face, the mid-day sun a force to be reckoned with. His legs were cramping something fierce, he was sure fearing a twisted ankle. Riding boots were made for the saddle, not scrambling through this rock-strewn environment, yet he had a job to do.

Continuing his scramble, the big cowboy cursed as one of the high heels became wedged in the shattered rock. It took some effort to remove his foot from the boot, he was sure fearful he had sprained his ankle.

From where he sat perched on a boulder, he could see Spotted Pony. He staggered to his feet and waved his Stetson, attempting to catch the boy's attention. Then settled back and waited, knowing that Spotted Pony had seen him, and would soon be here.

* * * Chapter Twenty-Six * * *

The sound of the waterfall could be heard far into the forest, glacier-chilled water tumbling from the heights of a mysterious valley. The boom of the angry waters was constant, never wavering from one day to the next, chewing a pathway down a hundred-foot cliff.

Hidden behind the raging waters was a small cavern, dark and dank and chilled by this phenomenon of the Rocky Mountains. Inside sat an old lawman, Marshal Custis Dunne, who was fuming mad, rising on occasion to pace back and forth, praying for a miracle to happen.

He would curse the turncoat posse, then tiring of doing so, turn his attention to the roar of the falling water. The constant roar was telling on his mind, day after day, night after night it boomed, as if mocking the lonely prisoner in the cavern. If ever he was freed from this confounded mess, he was heading to Helena and hand in his badge and resign from his chosen profession as a lawman.

To help retain what little sanity he had left, his mind would travel into the past, conjuring up the reason he had traveled to the mountains, the reason he was now in this blasted prison behind the fearsome waters.

He recalled of the kindness shown him at the Bonner ranch along the big river. Of Aunt Sue's nursing him night and day, and Spotted Pony administering his strange medicine, these kind acts he never could forget. And then his recovery from the gun shot wound, and the continuing, stubborn vendetta of an old lawman against the Blackfoot renegades.

He now knew that he had been foolish to come into these mountains, a lone stubborn Marshal who was getting long in the tooth. He couldn't blame his Bonner deputies none, he reckoned they had a growing family and an equally flourishing ranch to think about. The Bonner deputies who had helped him out of many a tight spot—and had saved his life more than once.

He missed them, dad-burned it all, he surely did. He was proud of them, especially Deputy Lynn, who was the best lady gunfighter he had ever seen, including Annie Oakley herself. She had courage, and would face the hard cases without hesitation, never flinching, never backing away.

Custis Dunne was cold and wet, hungry too. He would have given all he owned for a hot cup of coffee. Once again he crawled to the small entrance of the cavern, a mere space between the shattered boulders, and pushed with all his might against the slab of rock the turncoat savages had placed there to imprison him. Had he been in the prime of his life he might have moved it, but now it was of no use to even try.

* * *

He lay in the debris, panting and exhausted. He reckoned a few minutes of rest is what he needed, in reality it had been several hours. The old Marshal was ready to give up, he reckoned it must be time to cash in his chips and silently slip away. He relaxed some, the boom of the water shoved far back in his mind.

Much later he was aroused by a familiar sound. Someone was calling his name, he was sure of this. With great effort he moved to the prison gate, a faint glimmer of light could be seen through a small space in the boulders. He reckoned there might be room for his arm to reach through to the outside, sure worth a try.

His hunch panned out, his arm passed through, and in his open hand lay a shiny tin star!

* * * Chapter Twenty-Seven * * *

The lad had seen Bonner's signal, arose and started back through the maze of boulders. Satisfied, Bonner sat down again and waited. He had been in a tight spot, and knew that he was lucky to have spotted the Indian boy.

The boy was closing in on Bonner's perch before he realized that it wasn't Spotted Pony as he had assumed. He looked familiar though, and then he knew. It was Spirit Talker, the son of the Blackfoot chief from the encampment. This was the same one who insisted that Bonner end the life of Shoots First. Luckily the small urchin had already done so, saving Bonner the humiliation of killing a helpless man.

Spirit Talker was the first to speak, with the now familiar "*Oki-ii!*" The Blackfoot boy immediately spotted Bonner's boot, and together they were able to remove it from the rock entrapment. Stomping his foot into the boot, Bonner arose and tested his twisted ankle. He moved around some and found out that it wasn't a sprain after all, with very little pain.

"Spirit Talker, have you seen the Marshal? I came to give him a hand in catching those reservation boys, that's bin runnin' wild all over this border country."

The Indian boy began talking and couldn't be stopped. He told him the bad ones he was looking for, were camped by the big waters that roared its anger sun after sun. gesturing towards the waterfall. "They are frightened of this mighty Spirit, and of what they have done to the old one who wears a tin star.

"Spirit Talker has been close to their camp," and gestured to where he had been sitting. "The old one is in a cave, behind the falling water. They think he is dead now—and are frightened of his Spirit that wants to be set free!"

Bonner was terrible to see that day by *Otatso* Falls, cursing and raving, worried sick over the fate of his old friend, Marshal Custis Dunne. "Let's go find him Talker," he told the Indian boy.

"You and me are declaring war on that bunch—then we must rescue ol' Custis!"

Spirit Talker was only too eager to agree, and together they made their way across the maze to hunker down above the camp. "We'll outflank them!" Bonner ordered.

"You stay here, I'll work my way over yonder—when you see me in position—we'll both start a shootin'."

"*Oki!*" the boy replied, and already was stringing his bow.

Two things happened that put the fear of the dark place in the renegades below. One was the sight of a lone warrior, standing straight and tall, an armed bow with a flint-tipped arrow ready to fly. The other came from the far side of their hidden camp, a blood-chilling sound, the long, lonely shout of a rebel cowboy on the attack—Will Bonner.

Pandemonium quickly spread throughout the camp. Appeared there were six or eight warriors below, along with several kidnapped Blackfoot maidens.

A rifle shot sounded, one of them went down. Another staggered in terror, Spirit Talker's war arrow buried deep in his chest. Yet another, still clutching the hand of a terrified maiden, was sent to the dark place, the echo of a rifle shot the last sound he would ever hear.

The remaining renegades were shrieking in terror, and they were cowards of the worst kind. The four young maidens were wailing in fright, huddled together on the far side of camp, watching their captors go down, one after another. The girls were a disheveled lot, dirty and unkempt, having just endured a living hell.

The mayhem continued, after which a silence swept across the camp. Nothing could be heard but the sobbing of the maidens and the booming of *Otatso* Falls.

"Cave that way, Tin Star," Spirit Talker said, and gestured up through the boulders. "Behind magic waters—that fall from the sun!"

"You stay here Talker," Bonner said. "Help the girls get themselves cleaned up—make 'em feel much better, if you do!

"I'm headin' up yonder to find ol' Custis!"

"I will do as you asked," Spirit Talker said. "One of them is my sister."

It was a steep scramble up through the debris before Bonner reached the falls. He stopped by a steep escarpment to catch his breath, the water cascade and the cliff blending into one. Turning, he could see the maidens splashing in a backwater pool below, their buckskin clothing spread out to dry in the warmth of the sun.

Spirit Talker was standing guard, his head discreetly turned, watching the progress of Deputy Will Bonner.

Bonner was smiling as he turned his attention back to the escarpment, he reckoned there was still an honorable Indian left on the reservation after all.

He was close now, his trail-honed savvy struggling to locate the entrance to this wilderness prison. His eyes were on the move, sweeping every nook and cranny for a clue to the fate of Marshal Dunne. A tear, then there were two showed on his sun-bronzed face, realizing that perhaps his good friend never survived, that he might be laying dead behind the booming water.

"Custis!" he roared, attempting to break through the incessant roar of the water. "Marshal Dunne, can you hear me? Don't give up old friend, I'm here to get you out of this mess you're in.

"Custis Dunne!" he roared again. "Help me find the entrance if you can!"

Bonner's eyes continued to sweep the area, his sense of hearing straining to detect a response to his shouting. Once again he roared at the top of his voice, "Cust—!" and was stopped before the word could escape his mouth.

It was a faint gleam that caught his attention, and then it was gone. He was certain it had not been there before. Cautiously, and with great care, he scanned the rubble, and then his roving eyes spotted it again—the rays of the sun reflecting off of an unknown object.

A thrill surged through Bonner's lanky frame. "This could be the clue I'm lookin' for," he muttered, and began to work his way towards the mysterious sparkle of light.

It wasn't far, perhaps a dozen steps through the debris, and he was there. Another thrill surged through his perspiring body as he recognized a human hand offering a Marshal's tin star to anyone who might see it.

He stepped down into a slight depression, and with ease was able roll the slab of rock to the side. And there lay a wretched looking sight, old Marshal Dunne.

His clothes were dirty and torn, his face showed the signs of a vicious beating and he lay as if he were dead. The old lawman's holster was empty, he was an unarmed man. Bonner discovered him still breathing, and heaved a sigh of relief. Must have passed out, Bonner reasoned, to lay here like this. I reckon his old body is all set to give up the ghost.

With two husky arms around him, Bonner pulled him up and out into the late afternoon sun, that he was still alive he was now sure of. With one arm around Dunne's waist, Bonner walked the old lawman back down through the rubble. He roused some, his voice barely above a whisper, "That you, Deputy Bonner? I reckoned if anyone was to find me—it would be you.

"I was able to hear gun shots, sure figured something was going on—reckoned my Marshal badge might help some!"

"That tin star saved your life old friend, I would never have found you save you a pokin' your arm through that small hole like you did."

It turned into a touchy struggle to walk him down to the Indian camp, where stood Spirit Talker who had been busy while he had been gone. A cheery fire was blazing, a pot of coffee was simmering in the embers waiting for the two lawmen to come and drink it.

In the background stood the horses all saddled and ready to ride, and close by were the maidens who looked some different after getting cleaned up. They looked refreshed after scrubbing their bodies clean, their long, black hair freshly washed and gleaming bright in the setting sun.

Bonner hunkered by the Marshal and poured him a cup of coffee. "Best medicine in the west," he said, and poured himself a cup as well.

"You better drink a cup or two—do your old bones some good!" In reality it was the only medicine they had at their disposal.

Old Marshal Dunne did as he was told, and in no time at all tipped over to the ground, sound asleep. "Leave him be," Bonner said, and wrapped a blanket around his shivering body. He now knew the Marshal had been locked in the small cavern for two days and a night.

"I reckon he hasn't had a decent sleep lately, locked up behind that waterfall like he was."

Two hours is all they gave him to sleep, then Bonner roused him and said it was time to go. Darkness over took them by the time they left the boulder-strewn rubble, and headed down the lake shore on a seldom used trail. All seven of them were in the saddle when they rode away from *Otatso* Falls—Will Bonner, Custis Dunne, the four maidens and Spirit Talker. Behind them trailed seven Indian ponies, empty saddles a reminder of what had taken place

They talked as they rode, Spirit Talker telling of rolling the dead ones into a deep crevasse, and covering them with debris. "Spirits of these cowards will not bother us again," he said, a smile spread across his bronzed face. "They must now stay beneath the rocks—unable to leave!" He was smiling as he glanced at the bag hanging from his saddle.

"What you got in that bag?" Bonner asked, noticing the interest the boy was making over the dangling bag. He reckoned it must be some kind of treasure the boy had found. "Spirit Talker must take these things to the great Chief—my father.

"When he sees these scalps, he will be proud—and no more will he mourn for his daughter. The scalps will hang from a tepee pole—proof that the bad ones are now dead.

"He will know the dishonor that was given to his daughter, my sister, and her friends has been avenged, the four maidens will be back in their tepee homes with their families—rescued from those who disgraced them."

To travel in the forest at night is a mysterious experience for both man and beast, the rider trusting the ingrained savvy of his horse to stay on the trail. This night was no exception, seven riders strung out in single file, the leader, Will Bonner allowing his big red horse a loose rein. Red felt the slackness of the reins, and proudly led the small caravan onward to the base camp at the creek known as *Otatso*.

* * *

Assisted by old Slim, Lynn had a meal prepared for the incoming Marshals, who she reckoned should arrive back here soon. Lynn was sitting by the fire, her back resting on the upturned saddle, when she nodded off to sleep. The lady marshal just couldn't keep her eyes open any longer.

Much later Lynn became downright restless, a strange sound had disturbed her sleep. It was the sound of voices and the giggling of young girls. She was awake now, though her eyes remained closed. A familiar scent, a familiar hug, and her eyes opened to find her husband holding her close, who offered her one of his happy smiles.

Squealing with delight, she managed to say, "Oh, Will—you're back! I am sure happy you came back to me safe and sound."

Over his shoulder she could see the others, still sitting in their saddles watching the big Deputy greet his darling Lynn.

"We're going home in the morning," he told her. "The war is over, and we're a going home!"

Lynn was now wide awake, and watching with interest the chattering maidens, the strange Indian boy, and the poor mistreated Marshal Dunne, who was assisted to the ground and brought over to the fire. The blanket was still wrapped around his shivering body.

She also was aware of old Slim, who was now feeding them their supper, a meal that she herself had prepared several hours before.

Spirit Talker approached the Bonners who were still sitting together by the fire. "Ho, big Chief!" he said, and he was smiling. Spirit Talker wishes to make talk with Tin Star and his woman."

He then began to speak in his broken English, relating many things that left the Bonners wondering what it all meant. When he finally slowed down, Will and Lynn had figured out what he was trying to tell them.

Spirit Talker wished to take the Indian girls back to the reservation, and Custis Dunne as well. His sister and her three friends will be good to the Tin Star, he told them, and treat him with much respect.

"We will give him sacred medicine—his old body will like this—and once again be free from evil spirits.

"He is a good Tin Star! I will take him to his home—this will make my father, the Chief, happy too!"

Bonner was impressed with Spirit Talker, and reckoned he was one fine Indian. He told him this would be just fine with the two remaining Tin Stars, Lynn and Will Bonner, and wished him a safe journey.

"*Oki-ii!*" We will leave when next the sun shines on the sacred mountain!" and gestured up in the direction of the one he knew as the Big Chief. There were two Big Chiefs in Spirit Talker's life, the first was his father.

The second was—Old Chief Mountain!

* * * Chapter Twenty-Eight * * *

A young vibrant Mary Lynn Bonner was maturing into a beautiful fourteen-year old girl, and was often mistaken of being several years older. Much like the three Lynns before her, she had long auburn hair, a glowing symbol of the genes that flowed in her veins.

She was an adventuresome girl showing no fear of man or beast, and became an excellent rider. She learned the ways of her Mom and became highly talented at shooting from the hip. She had graduated from the little .22 lever-action that had been her Mom's to a .30.30 Winchester that became her prized possession. "I reckon it's high time you had a gun—with a bite," her Dad told her, the day he had given her the gun.

"The little .22 you been using has been plenty good to learn on, this here .30.30 I'm a giving you is the real thing—use it with care!"

Mary Lynn loved her life here at the river ranch, she loved the outdoors and riding up and down the river exploring every nook and cranny. Though it was unknown to most folks back at the ranch, she even had ventured along the border, checking things out, becoming familiar with this wild and wooly region.

The folks at the ranch had told her of her birth in a deserted cabin up that way. She discovered it one day and spent several hours absorbing this special place. That it was on the reservation mattered not to her, she had told no one of her find. It would be one of her treasured memories, knowing the reason her Mom had been there—wearing her Tin Star.

It was still pitch black when Mary Lynn Bonner rode away from the river ranch. She was in the saddle on one of her Dad's old gelding saddle horses, Rocky, who was happy for the affection the girl always gave him.

Mary Lynn was sure homesick for her Mom, and was heading into the west to find her. Besides, she and Aunt Sue had been at odds over her activities as of late—the elderly cook giving her the dickens for riding Rocky from daylight till dark, sometimes even later before returning to the river.

She was angry and upset, and she did have a temper. Aunt Sue wasn't her boss, she reckoned, and after lashing a blanket roll behind the saddle and a satchel of food dangling from the saddle horn, she took off into the west.

She was comforted by the big bay horse she was riding, by the Winchester rifle in the deer-hide scabbard, and the water canteen that she always carried. The old gelding was easy to ride, and though she missed her little bay Shetland-cross, she had out grown him; her long legs now dangling in the bunch grass. Anyhow she reckoned, she knew that Brownie would be content with her Mom's Jenni mule back at the ranch.

She knew that old Slim, her dear friend, had left for Chief Mountain the day before, and reasoned that she could follow his sign as he had many times trained her to do. The day wore on, warm and windy, the young rider and her horse stopping often, Mary Lynn to stretch her legs, Rocky to nibble on the grass that grew here in such abundance.

Mary Lynn Bonner reckoned she must be about half-way to the Chief, and the old Jenni Mine, where her Mom and Dad had gone for a time to be together, a two night camp out they had told her. She knew different and realized they both needed a break from the longhorns, the cowboys and the kids.

The girl was fully aware of the position of the sun that was closing in on the mountain. She also realized it was high time she was finding a place to spend the night, and began thinking of old Slim and his kindly manner in passing on his knowledge of such important matters.

She had never camped out alone before, and her emotions were twofold. A family-induced pride of roughing it on her own was strong in her make up, lurking in the background of her mind was a hint of something else. A foreboding omen of the unexpected, danger perhaps! She reckoned she wasn't frightened though, she must be careful, she must remember her upbringing!

The girl was now in an area where the rolling grass country met up with the wooded brakes and valleys. As far as she could see were quaking aspen groves and entangled clumps of diamond willow brush. Through all of this wove a mountain stream known to her Mom's family as Lariat Cross.

She was amazed as she watched the sun disappear behind Chief Mountain, at the same time reining Rocky into a copse of willow brush. She was happy as she prepared her meager camp in the willows, even singing some. On the banks of the boisterous mountain stream she would spend the night, an abundance of firewood was here, shelter from the night-time breezes and plenty of grass for her big bay horse.

Even though her camp site was high up the creek valley from her Grandma's Lariat Cross ranch, she felt a sense of comfort here. Remembering her Mom's stories of this revered place, Lariat Cross, a place where her Mom had been born and spent her childhood. Old Great Grandpa Brannon and his Jenni mule had been her constant companions.

Darkness was settling into the high canyon. The girl had kindled a cheery fire, and was sitting beside it munching on a sandwich, entranced with the music of the water, the chirp of an inquisitive night bird and the yip-yip of a coyote. From close by she could hear Rocky munching on a supper of his own picking, a comforting sound to the young Mary Lynn Bonner.

The stars were bright in the sky, the constant drone of the creek was making her drowsy, and then it happened. Drifting down the canyon with a night time breeze, came a long, scary howl, sending cold chills racing up and down the girl's spine.

Rocky, who was tethered close by, ceased his incessant grazing, his head raised, his ears too. The scary howl had un-nerved the girl, who arose from the fireside and walked over to her horse. She could tell he was upset, the same as she, and brought him over by the fire—which would be a comfort to both the horse and the girl.

The girl snuggled the blanket tight around her, and settled into the grass beside her good friend. She had no sooner relaxed and was drifting off to sleep, when once again the frightening sound of a hunting lobo was heard above the chatter of the creek. The howl was much closer now, she could tell!

Pushing her blanket aside, the girl arose and placed more fuel on the fire, the ensuing flames lighting up the small clearing in the willows. Mary Lynn then settled back with her blanket, both her rifle and horse within easy reach. Snuggling the blanket tight, she relaxed hoping that she might find sleep.

But such would not be the case! Her mind was in utter turmoil, never had she been this way before. Back and forth her memories raced, mixed in with visions of hungry, attacking wolves. She roused once again and found Rocky had moved in close to her blankets, his ears at attention staring into the darkness. With her rifle in hand she left her blankets and checked the clearing. The light from the still smoldering fire allowed her to see what was there.

Her heart gave a leap when she spotted them, two large scary looking denizens of the forest lurking in the shadows on the far side of the fire. Never had she seen Rocky act this way before. He was more than uneasy, crowding as close to her as he could get; his attention never leaving the two wolves.

"Take it easy Rocky," she said, a soothing tone in her voice. "Those two critters try to harm us—they'll be in for a big surprise!" Levering a cartridge into position as she spoke, Mary Lynn knew that from past experience the sound of her voice was comforting to her animal friends, to herself as well.

The wolves became uneasy, noting the movement of the girl, listening to the strange sound of her voice. Their hackles were rising, vicious snarls gushing forth from their saliva-drenched lips.

Though she had every reason to be so, the girl wasn't frightened. She wasn't prone to fright, she never really knew the meaning of the word. But this time was different, this time she must make a stand. She had no other choice but to face down the wolves, as would have her Mom, her Grandma O'Neil or her Great Grandma Brannon before her.

The wolves had split up, an often used strategy of the wilderness hunters. One of them was slinking around one side of the fire, the other doing the same on the other. Mary Lynn steeled herself, watching and waiting, her trembling finger on the trigger of her rifle. She reckoned she knew what they were up to, their intent to make her their next meal.

Then, with a scream, she fired her rifle, watching the nearest wolf go down. Swinging her rifle towards the other, she was knocked to the ground by Rocky, the remaining wolf gripping one of the horse's hind legs; ham-stringing the lunging animal was on its mind.

Rocky was squealing in terror, kicking and bucking this way and that, attempting to dislodge the large timber wolf, who had one of his hind legs securely trapped in steely jaws. The girl had to roll out of the way of Rocky's flying hooves, and scrambled to find her little gun that was somewhere on the ground.

Luckily, she found it and after cranking another cartridge into the weapon, was ready to continue her war against the remaining wolf. She was terrified that Rocky would be crippled, worse yet killed and eaten by the savage beast. She dared not shoot for fear of hitting her Dad's old bay gelding.

Then a peaceful aura surrounded the girl. It was if a mist had enveloped her, and there in the center of it all, was the profile of a beautiful lady. "*You must be ready, Mary Lynn—when next the horse lashes out with his hind feet—pull the trigger. Shoot from the hip, stay calm Lynn—stay calm—!*"

A moment is all, a moment when time stood still and the vision was no more. Lynn was shaking like an aspen leaf, but had presence of mind to do what her Great Grandma had told her to do. She pulled the trigger for the second time, and watched the wolf's jaws slacken, its mouth opened as it wilted to the ground.

Rocky continued to buck and squeal until he realized the wolf was no longer chewing into his leg. Another few seconds and he would have been crippled for life, the tendon severed by the tactics of a ham-stringing wolf.

Mary Lynn slumped to the ground, her nervous system a jangled mess. Her rifle lay in the grass beside her, two brass shell casings as well, testifying to the drama that had just taken place. She was sobbing and thankful that it was over, silently thanking her great grandma for the support that was given to her granddaughter in her time of need.

Her attention was drawn to the two dead wolves and knew that Spotted Pony, if she ever found him, would come and take the pelts from the dead ones. And then tan them as was the way of his ancestor's.

The wolves were clad in prime pelts in preparation for the coming winter. It would not be right, she reckoned, to leave them lay and go to waste.

Rocky had calmed down, and was standing close by with his injured leg lifted off the ground. She arose and went to him, cooing and caressing, great concern showing on her tear-stained face. She massaged the injured leg and could tell how sore it must be. He would not allow her hand to come near the open flesh-torn wound.

With a scarf from her saddle bags she rigged up a bandage, there wasn't much else she could do until morning, she reckoned. Once again the girl curled up in her blanket, and in no time at all was sound asleep.

* * * Chapter Twenty-Nine * * *

A playful breeze was teasing the aspens when the sun returned to the high country. The girl awoke at daybreak as was her way, and felt somewhat refreshed. Mary Lynn welcomed the arrival of the sun, she always had, knowing that a new day had returned. That new adventures lay ahead, that the mysterious shadows of night had been chased away.

She knew that she must continue her journey to Chief Mountain and find her Mom. Tears filled her eyes as she removed the blood-soaked bandage from the horse's leg, a stark reminder of the night before

After building up the fire she heated some willow bark tea, and thoroughly cleansed the scary looking wound. The horse allowed the girl to do this, as if he knew she was trying to help him. And that she had saved his life from the savage wolves—as well as her own.

Remembering her Mom's stories, she packed tree moss over the wound, and once again lashed the make-shift bandage over it with leather strings. There is nothing else I can do, she reckoned, as she started walking up the valley, Rocky hobbling behind, a noticeable limp in his gait. "I cannot leave you here Rocky!" once again she was making talk with the horse. "I cannot ride you either—until your leg begins to heal."

To talk and listen to the sound of her voice was a comfort to the girl. "I'm sure sorry I got you into this mess Rocky," she said, continuing her chatter. "I reckon by nightfall we'll be at my Mom's camp."

Late that afternoon the girl and her horse arrived at an evergreen forest. It had been a tough scramble getting this far, what with the beaver dam swamp, the deadfall trees, and a noticeable litter of huge rocks and boulders now showing up. Rocky had done well making it this far, but was now showing signs of wear, even though he was packing nothing on his back but the girl's saddle.

Mary Lynn was tiring too. Hiking like this in her riding boots was not to her liking. Tears were in her eyes, knowing that she would never find her Mom before dark, and that she would have to spend another night alone. Last night with the wolf attack and all, had been an experience she prayed would never happen again.

An eerie silence was evident as the girl and her horse, both were following a faint trace, entered the land of the lodgepole pine. "Sure smells good here Rocky," Mary Lynn said, having just left the muck and grime of a beaver dam swamp. "These big trees are sure purty too—first time I've ever run across any.

"At my Grandma's ranch down at Lariat Cross, there are trees that grow needles—some different than these tall, spindly ones you see here."

Her Mom's Jenni Mine and the big mountain were close now, much closer then Mary Lynn realized. She continued on until finding a modest opening in the lodgepoles. "We'll camp here Rocky," she told her weary horse. "There's plenty of grass to give you a good supper,"

Looking long at her saddlebags, she knew there was only one sandwich left, enough for her supper she reckoned, and several strips of jerky; so hard that she could hardly chew them. It worried her to be out of food to eat, surely she would soon reach her Mom's camp at the old Jenni Mine!

"Dog-gone it all Rocky," she said. "We have just got to find her—we sure enough do!"

Both the girl and her horse were bone-tired, sleep would be a welcome break from the two hectic days that was now behind them. Rocky had stuffed himself with the juicy mountain plants, and was standing close by the blanket wrapped girl. Though he was dozing, he was aware that Mary Lynn was restless in her blanket, tossing and turning and murmuring strange words. Several times her eyes opened, a smell of wood smoke had been tickling her nostrils.

It was nearing first light, though still dark as sin. The girl awake with a start, and sat up staring long into the darkened forest. A scary chill was playing havoc with her spine, she sensed some living thing was close by, how she knew this she did not know, she just knew it was there.

With caution she picked up her rifle, knowing it was loaded and ready for war. "What good is an empty gun," her Dad had cautioned her. "Reckon you could save your life, knowing there were cartridges in your Winchester!"

Struggling to control the shakes, the girl managed to speak, "Who's out there—speak up before I start a shooting!" And she meant every word of what she spoke. The wolf episode of the previous night had her nerves riding a fine-tuned edge.

A silence followed, almost the suffocating kind. Then she sensed a movement in the shadows, followed by another. There was something standing there, she was certain as another paralyzing chill rattled through her body.

Once again she called into the darkness, and gasped as the two shadows moved towards her. She cocked the little Winchester, remembering her Dad's advise to 'be ready'. "Stay away from me!" she was screaming when she pulled the trigger.

Again a scary silence invaded her camp site, even the chirp of the night birds grew silent. Far away through the lodgepoles came the hoot of an owl.

A young fourteen year old girl was once again weeping. "I must be loco," she said, "shooting at shadows, like I'm a doing!"

She sat back on her blanket, and knew the shadows were no more. The sky was growing brighter as the long minutes passed by. Mary Lynn Bonner was up the creek without a paddle, she sure enough was! She had spent a sleepless night, she had no food but the time-hardened jerky, her horse was lame and her nerves were a frazzled wreck.

The arrival of daylight made her feel much better, she could see now and that made a big difference. No more stumbling around in the dark shooting at shadows. She was standing now, feeling much more confident, and saddled the horse. After packing her meager belongings she continued on into the unknown of the big mountain—she must find her Mom—she just had to find her Mom!

She was badly shaken, but determined to keep going. With old Rocky trailing behind, she continued through the forest. An hour had passed when she stopped at a modest mountain brook, where both the girl and the horse drank their fill. "Reckon we both were a needing a good drink," she said, and was kneeling near the water filling her canteen when she heard a familiar noise.

It was the snuffle of a horse, the blowing of air from their nostrils when at war with flying insects that collected around their moist nostrils. "Was that you made that noise?" she asked, looking at Rocky who was still savoring the water. She then knew it wasn't him, he was still drinking the one thing that all living things must have—water!

She arose, glancing around through the lodgepoles, and discovered what had made the noise. There stood a horse, complete with saddle and bridal, standing hip-shot in the shade; his tail at war with a horde of flying ants.

Mary Lynn was startled, gasping as she reached for her Winchester. A familiar voice spoke from behind her, "*Oki-ii!*

"Do not shoot at Spotted Pony—as you did when the stars were the only light—come, you must ride Pony's spotted horse. The big boss and Missy Lynn, will be happy to see you.

"*Oki-ii!* Your Mom and Dad are not far from this place!"

Her shock from meeting Spotted Pony subsided some, she squealed with relief and ran over to him and gave him a warm hug. "It's so good to see you Pony, and I am sorry that I shot at you last night—I couldn't help it none—what with the wolves and all."

Though a bit taken aback by the girl's show of emotion, he managed to show her the nasty slash on his upper arm he had received from her shot in the dark. It was only inches away from killing the night-wandering boy from the land of the Bloods.

"Follow Pony," he said. "Your family is this way." And left in a different direction from the one she would have taken.

* * *

Will Bonner's trail outfit was on the move, riding single file down the trail to the river ranch. Bonner was out in front, Lynn was right behind him, old Slim was riding drag a pack horse trailing behind. Rounding a hairpin curve in the rugged terrain, he reined in his bronc at the sight of a mounted rider ahead, facing the incoming riders.

Why, it's a young woman a riding Spotted Pony's pinto hoss!" Bonner exclaimed. "I wonder what the wandering rascal has been up to now." Then, from out of the lodgepoles stepped Spotted Pony leading Bonner's old bay gelding, who was tenderly pampering his injured leg.

Bonner continued on, Lynn was now riding beside him. Suddenly with a squeal of delight, Lynn vaulted from her saddle, and ran towards her daughter whom she had recognized. Even though the girl was tattered and torn, her lovely hair a tangled mess; her Mom knew this was her only daughter.

Mary Lynn had done the same, and both met with outstretched arms. They stood on the trail, arms wrapped around each other, weeping and hugging—and weeping some more. Eventually, Mary Lynn, who was almost as tall as her Mom, stepped back and said, "I'm so hungry Mom, have you got any food I could eat?

"Then we'll talk—I have so much to tell you!"

"Reckon we'll take a noon day break here!" Bonner said, irritation showing in his voice. "Climb off your broncs and well have a bite to eat.

"No more food from here on until we reach the B—B, and Aunt Sue's kitchen."

Bonner and Lynn sat on each side of their daughter offering their support. That she had been through hell and back, they could tell. Struggling to control her weeping and eat at the same time, the starving girl managed to relate her story. It all started with the squabble with Aunt Sue, she told them, and her decision to ride to the Jenni Mine under Old Chief Mountain.

She told of the terrifying night with the two wolves, of Rocky being maimed by one of the wild beasts, whose intent was to cripple the horse and then eat him. She did not forget to praise Spotted Pony, of his timely arrival and bringing her to safety, even though she had shot him in the darkness of the night. She had told it all, and felt relieved that she had done so.

Mary Lynn turned to her Mom and both began their weeping once again. "Bonner's arm was holding his daughter close, struggling to contain his own emotions. "We're sure proud of you Mary Lynn, I reckon your Grandpa Brannon is too.

"And your two grandmas, I reckon they knew you would win out, and right this very minute are celebrating your safe return."

Lynn was now hugging her daughter, Bonner sat back and left them to their weeping. He reckoned a Mom and her daughter should be encouraged to strengthen their bond, and those that might be watching from above were smiling with joy. They knew all right, those that had gone before, that blood was thicker than all earthly ways—and would remain so down through the generations. Yes, he reckoned, they knew!

With Lynn in the saddle of one of the spare horses, she rode beside her Mom and Dad back down to the river and their B—B ranch.

* * * Chapter Thirty * * *

An hour had passed, and then it was two when the Bonner trail outfit met up with Lynn's half-brother Matt O'Niel and young Willy Bonner, the oldest of Mary Lynn's younger brothers. In their own adventurous way they had ridden away from the ranch to find Mary Lynn.

On hearing the ruckus of the incoming riders, Matt reined in the green-broke, three-year old he was riding, little Willy did the same with Brownie, who was always willing to stop and nibble at anything he could find worth eating. Farther down was a sharp bend in the trail—coming into view was a little dun mule, her nose to the ground; on the hunt for her beloved mistress Lynn Bonner.

Lynn spotted her right off. "I just knew she would show up," she said to Bonner. "I'm surprised she hasn't found me sooner."

"I reckon old age is catching up to her Lynn—sure slows down one's body, and mental capacity as well—don't matter much if it is a human or an animal, old age shows no mercy on any of us!"

Mary Lynn was watching too, and with a squeal of delight, put the spurs to the mustang she was riding and galloped down to greet Jenni. Vaulting from the saddle, the girl wrapped her arms around the mule's neck, petting and cooing and showing her love.

The mule acknowledged the girl's affection, then answered with her garbled mule talk. With that attended to, Jenni continued on up the trail to greet the others, the scent of Mary Lynn's Mom strong in her nostrils.

It was the older Lynn the mule was looking for, the one who had treated her with such kindness over the long years.

"We'll see you later, Mom," Mary Lynn shouted back," the three young riders continued on down the trail for the river ranch. "I sure am in need of a bath," the girl's words come drifting back on a fitful western breeze. "And some clean clothes, I surely do!"

"I never seen the like," Bonner said. "These young sprouts are sure full of it—energy and get up and go."

Lynn replied with a laugh. "Remember when we were that age—we were the very same way."

The Bonner outfit continued on for the home ranch, confident the three youngsters would be there to greet them. Trailing behind them shuffled a little dun mule.

Their tin stars shining in the late afternoon sun, the deputies gave a sigh of satisfaction knowing that a long, tough journey was now over and done with.

Aunt Sue was sure pleased to see the Bonner's ride in to the ranch yards, so were the three young ones who had sure missed their Mom—but where was Mary Lynn, Matt and Willy? She told of the boys riding away early that morning, without any warning, and hadn't seen them since.

"And Mary Lynn!" she told the Bonners. "She left several days ago, angry and in a huff.

"I must apologize when next I see her, I reckon we both said some unpleasant things to each other."

"Be that as it may Aunt Sue, we've got big trouble on our hands—the three of them are not here as they should be, and I'm downright worried!

"And by the way, Mary Lynn has endured a terrible experience, both she and Rocky come within a whisper of being killed by wolves." Lynn Bonner was weeping when she left to find Will, they must do something mighty quick, Marry Lynn could once again be involved in something too much for to handle.

After all, she is only fourteen years old, and already she has been forced to use her gun in defending herself, and saving the bay gelding of being maimed for life. No way am I going to chastise her for the spat with Aunt Sue. I love my daughter, I surely do!

This was still a wild and wooly land, sparsely settled and not for the faint of heart. The dangers were real, always lurking in the background ready to pounce. Not only were there renegade Indians and those that rode the outlaw trail to worry about, there were the wild ones—the bear, the big cats and the wolf, who were always a challenge; as had been the case with Mary Lynn and the savage attack on the bay gelding that she had been riding.

Her parents were sure proud of their only daughter, who had stood up to the two wilderness killers, and downed them both with her little Winchester. Proud! You can bet your boots they were proud, knowing old Grandpa Brannon's genes were still alive and rarin' to go in Mary Lynn's veins—as they were in her Moms.

* * *

A cloud of gloom hung heavy over the Bonner's river ranch, all hands had been called in for the search, not only was Mary Lynn Bonner once again missing, her Uncle Matt and brother Willy were missing as well. No one could remember of seeing them for a day and a long fearful night, after which the hunt began.

A thorough search was organized by their boss, Will Bonner. All hands had been called in for this new assignment, every coulee and hilltop must be penetrated with much vigor, even a signal fire on the summit of ol' Lookout brought in a group of Blackfoot braves led by Spirit Talker; to help in the search.

With saddlebags bulging with food and armed to the teeth, the hands were split up into pairs and scattered across the range. The brush along the river, the deep coulees, every square foot of the grass country must not be overlooked in their search for the Bonner's beautiful daughter, and the two boys that were with her.

Spirit Talker and two of his top trackers were assigned to the southern border country, from the St. Mary's River to the brush covered hills around Police Lake, and even the reservation south of the border.

"Watch for clues," Bonner ordered. "Anything that might seem out of place, check it out!"

Mary Lynn's Mom was devastated, she could do nothing but weep and worry. Knowing she must stay near the home place with Mary Lynn's small brothers, and help Aunt Sue with preparing food for the increasing number of hungry mouths to feed.

"It's a breakin' daylight!" Bonner roared. "High time we was a movin' out!" Seven pairs of riders listened to the big boss's orders and put the spurs to their broncs, spreading out across the range of the Deerhorn Hills in all directions of the compass.

A weeping Lynn Bonner stood beside Bonner's horse. He bent over from the saddle and gave his wife a kiss. "Bring back our kids, Will!" she sobbed. "Please bring them back!"

"Calm down Lynn," he replied. "We're a ridin' through hell and high water until we find them!"

"Don't you worry none—you hear? Besides, You have an important assignment here, never know when the kids might show up and be a needin' their mother's love and care!"

She stepped back as he touched his spurs to ol' Red, leaving a cloud of corral dust swirling around his beautiful wife. Waiting at the big pole gate was old Slim, who had chosen to be Bonner's riding companion.

A shiver rippled down the spine of the girl from Lariat Cross as she listened to a wild cowboy yell. A yell originating in the great war between the States, that signaled—'the Rebs are a comin'—best have your shootin' irons handy—and your powder dry'!"

Still coughing over the corral leavings, Lynn was smiling as she remembered her Mom's stories of old Grandpa Brannon, and his famous cowboy yell. She was proud of her husband and his own cowboy yell.

Somehow it made her feel secure, and that everything would work out just fine.

* * *

Knowing the Bonner trail outfit was bringing up the rear, three youthful riders turned their horses, nose to tail, and headed back down to the ranch. Uncle Matt was leading the way in the saddle of a high-stepping three year old colt, having a dickens of a time holding him in to a reasonable pace.

The old axiom 'as fast as a horse heading home for hay' rang true, being played out right here in the wilderness country; in the shadow of old Chief Mountain.

Next come Mary Lynn. Though still pale and worn from her nerve-shattering fight with the timber wolves, she was riding an Indian *cayuse*, that must have belonged to one of the unfortunate renegades who had received his comeuppance at *Otatso* Falls. Old Slim had spotted it in the timber, and after a lucky toss of his lasso had brought it back to camp. The little horse proved to be a decent sort, responding to the gentle ways of the old outlaw.

A little bay Shetland-cross was trailing behind, doing it's best to keep up to the galloping pair in front. Up top in the saddle was Willy Bonner, the Bonner's oldest son.

The trail was steep, too steep for the rapid pace of Uncle Matt's colt, who had taken the bit in his teeth and was having his own way. Suddenly, with no prior warning, the animal skidded to a halt and began to buck and squeal, sun-fishing this way and that. Matt, who reckoned he could ride anything with hair on its back, was taken by surprise and bucked off good and proper like.

There he lay in a daze watching the colt head across the rock-littered terrain, doing its best to buck off the saddle. With a groan and a cowboy curse, the young cowboy was left where he fell—every bone in his body felt out of kilter.

Cursing again, an addiction he had picked up from the older cowboys, he stood up and plunged off the trail, hip-hopping his way through the boulders and the rough.

If nothing else he must rescue his saddle, it was only a few weeks old, purchased at the Mormon settlement with a year's worth of hard earned savings; his wages while riding the range at the B——B.

Without hesitation Mary Lynn's mustang, and even Brownie too, veered off the trail, both determined to follow the rampaging colt down through a maze of boulders and shattered debris; determined to buck off Uncle Matt's new saddle.

Little Willy was hanging on to his own saddle horn, upset over the unexpected change of a normally docile Brownie.

Down through a maze of boulders and shattered rock they went, an upheaval that had originated from a long ago disturbance on Chief Mountain, whose massive bulk dominated the western skyline.

Mary Lynn was doing her best to control the crazy mustang that she rode, knowing that she would be in big trouble if the horse was allowed to buck her off. She had presence of mind to keep Uncle Matt in sight, but the colt that had dumped him on the ground was nowhere to be seen.

The girl spotted a sea of green on the far side of the rubble, and knew that it was a pine forest. Riding through the forest would be much easier she reckoned, surely she would find her uncle there somewhere.

The horse was tiring allowing her to once again gain control. Nearing the forest the horse settled into a walk, his head hanging low and on the verge of collapse. She knew her brother must be close by, she could hear his shouts. "Mary Lynn—Mary Lyn-nn!

"Where are you?"

She could detect fear in his voice, and reckoned she should wait for him, and shouted back. "Give Brownie his head Willy, he will find me— don't be frightened!

"Be brave Willy—you can do it!

"I will wait for you."

Young Willy Bonner could hear his sister's voice, his fear lessened as he followed her instructions. Next to his Mom and Dad, he loved his big sister the best, and would follow her through hell and high water if need be.

Mary Lynn Bonner, a fourth generation of the Brannon women, stood by the exhausted Indian pony listening, waiting for the boy to show up. She never had long to wait, when an equally exhausted Brownie staggered from around a large boulder, the youngster still in the saddle.

Willy spotted his sister, that he had been crying there was no doubt. The boy half-fell from the saddle and ran to his sister, arms outstretched, his sister was doing the same. She held him close, comforting him as best she could.

Willy's weeping quickly subsided, taking comfort from the warmth of his sister's body. The scent emanating from her long hair was comforting too, reminding him of his Mom. Their scent was closely connected, that of a Mom and her daughter, no one knew it any better than the Bonner siblings.

And most of all, the advice that both of them had given him on various occasions was to remember who he was; and to be brave!

The girl and her brother sat close together, one of the girl's arms was around his shoulder, a comfort to little Willy, who was experiencing his first taste of the real world. She continued to chatter of pleasant things, knowing the sound of her voice would be a comfort to him.

Several hundred yards up though the rubble, a mountain breeze brought to her the sound of passing horses, she was certain that she could hear the happy giggle of her Mom as well. A cold chill coursed through her body, knowing that now they were alone, that there was now no one behind them.

She scrambled to the top of a boulder and began to wave her hat and scream for help. But her efforts were lost on the breeze, as she watched the last horse of the departing riders disappear around a bend in the trail. And it was her poor mistreated Rocky.

She returned to her weeping brother, struggling to hold back her own tears. I must not let him see me cry like this, she reasoned. I must be strong and brave, like I have asked him to be. After a time Willy began to chatter and ask questions, she then knew that he was feeling much better.

"I reckon it's time we should be moving on," she said. "We must find Uncle Matt and the crazy bronc that bucked him off."

"Okay Mary Lynn—I'm ready—but, I'm sure enough hungry. We started without breakfast this morning, he has our grub in his saddlebags though."

The girl thought of her own food supply, knowing that it was down to part of a sandwich and several hunks of jerky. She found the sandwich and gave it to her brother who began to eat it with much vigor.

"The bread must be dried out by now, Willy."

"Sure tastes good to me," he replied, smacking his lips. "Have you got anymore?"

Lynn was smiling when she handed him a chunk of jerky.

After weaving their way through the last of the boulders, the two rode into the silence of the pines. It was peaceful here, with several birds chirping their alarm at the passing riders. "Where is Uncle Matt?" the boy asked.

"I sure miss him, he was good to me."

Off in the distance Mary Lynn was sure she had heard a gunshot, closely followed by another. Changing course, the girl and her brother rode in the direction of the sound. She was fretting some, concern over the whereabouts of her Uncle Matt becoming more of a burden as the waning day progressed.

It was nearing sundown when they both smelled smoke. "You follow me Willy, stay close and be as quiet as a mouse.

"No telling what we might be running in to!"

"That smoke sure smells good," he answered. "Like someone cooking their supper!"

The two riders were closing in on the pleasant smell when they were startled by the whinny of a horse, and just as suddenly rode in close to a makeshift camp. There stood the 'wild thing' as Willy had named the green-broke colt of his Uncles.

A quick glance by the girl and she could tell the wild thing was lame, like her beloved Rocky who was even now limping his way back to the ranch. It was a wicked sprain by the looks of it.

Matt O'Niel, who had been sitting by his fire arose, and with rifle in hand, walked over to meet the incoming riders. "I reckoned you two had got lost," he said. "Was worried you might have run into trouble.

"What are you cooking Uncle Matt? Sure smalls good—I'm sure a hungry boy—Mary Lynn's jerky is not easy to chew."

Their eighteen year-old uncle was laughing at little Willy, and told him that he had made a lucky shot and was able to down a yearling mule deer. And that it was venison roasting over his cooking fire that smelled so darn good.

He struggled to hold back a tear, remembering the training that had been given him by his big sister. In spare moments she had tutored her brother in the way of the gun, be it a rifle or a six-gun it mattered not. For hours on end she would do this, until he became highly skilled with them both, an ingrained trait that had been inherited from his sharp-shooting Mom.

To shoot accurately from the hip was his favorite, though he was no slouch with the fast draw as well. He now packed a six-gun, as did all the B—B cowboys, and would practice faithfully the art of the fast draw. Bonner had given him a few pointers, admitting the kid was learning well, turning into a better than average gun slinger.

Most of all, young Matt adored his big sister Lynn Bonner. He respected her to no end, and was sure thankful that she had welcomed him to come and live with them, and become a cowboy at the B—B.

"Just hold your horses a little while longer," he told a starving Willy. "This here tender meat will be ready to eat soon—there will be plenty to eat for us all."

"While you two are talking about food," Mary Lynn said. "I'm a going over to that little stream and get rid of some of this trail dust.

"I'm sure enough a dusty girl!"

She scurried to the small spring-fed stream, a clean shirt in hand which she had discovered in her saddle bags. After bathing and washing her hair, she scrubbed her soiled shirt with much vigor, and felt much better for doing so. She now had a spare shirt to wear, and after donning the other, felt better knowing that once again there would be a clean one tucked in her saddlebags. One would never know when the other might come in downright handy.

Mary Lynn was standing now, and as she turned to return to camp, the mouth-watering aroma and all urging her on, she squealed with delight on spotting several wild onion plants. A closer look convinced her there was yet another species, whose delicious plump bulbs would be a tasty addition to their wilderness supper.

The soil was moist, the pull was easy, and out came a batch of wild vegetables to grace the appetites of three hungry members of the Bonner clan.

* * * Chapter Thirty-One * * *

Spotted Pony was not happy to be paired up with Bonner and told him he would rather ride alone. The Blood Indian boy would then be more in tune with the spirits, he told his big boss, and added the spirits would help him find Mary Lynn and the two boys,

Bonner wasn't at all pleased with his decision, and had planned on the boy riding with him so he could keep him from wandering off on one of his spiritual dreams. He knew the Pony's mind was made up, and that he was a stubborn sort. Nothing he could say would change the boy's mind.

"*Ok-ii!* I will leave now Bonner," he said, and gigged his pony into the west.

Spotted Pony rode at a reasonable pace. He had a keen sense of where he was going, and what he would do when he got there. He was an excellent tracker—his keen ears not missing a sound, his sharp eyes not missing an overturned pebble, his quivering nostrils not missing the vaguest of odors.

The stealth of unknown generations of wilderness trackers were embedded in the boy's genes, a gift from the sun as far as the boy was concerned.

The spotted horse he rode was tireless, heading up the trail at an easy pace, and though the mountain trail had many twists and turns to overcome, west was the way he was going; always west.

Spotted Pony's horse had a rich background, a bloodline overflowing with strength and endurance, of which was inherited from an ancient ancestor, the wild mustang; and was noted for keeping a ground-covering pace from sun up until the sun once again left the land. And now, high up the Chief Mountain trail, the boy reined in his pony and slid to the ground.

He was certain he was near where he had last seen the missing youngsters, and from hear on he would walk, his pony trailing behind him. It would be easier to pick up sign this way, and he was right, as had been Little Crow before him.

Slowly he walked, his keen eyes sweeping the trail from one side to the other. Often he would crouch low inspecting an overturned pebble, perhaps the tiny track of a grasshopper would attract his keen eyes.

And just as darkness was settling across the wilderness he found what he had been looking for. One horse, perhaps two had left the trail into the south, a death trap of gigantic boulders and debris that spread out for a half-mile. It was a small hoof print that caught his eye. That it was made by the small one the young ones knew as Brownie, he was sure of. As further proof was a scattering of horse droppings, much smaller than that of a larger horse.

His horse followed him down off the trail where he stopped on the lee side of a large boulder. Here he prepared a meager night camp. He dare not chance taking his horse through in the darkness, a sprained ankle, perhaps a pulled tendon or even a broken leg could easily happen.

Securing the horse near a small patch of mountain plants, Spotted Pony would now be free to wander through the night, as was his way.

* * *

Although eighteen year old Uncle Matt was not frightened of the darkened forest, he remained uneasy, knowing Mary Lynn and Willy were in his care. All three of them found sleep was hard to come by, tossing and turning most of the night. A cheery fire was kept blazing in the center of the clearing, a much needed comfort to all three. Close by were their blanket beds.

Willy had finally fallen asleep. Mary Lynn lay quiet, her blanket tucked under her chin. The girl's weary body appeared to have found sleep, yet her high-strung inner self would not allow this to happen. In reality, all kinds of phantom images were flitting through her mind. Savage wolves, enraged grizzly bears, and fierce Indians decked out in war paint and feathers. Always in the background floated a dim profile of a beautiful lady. The face was familiar, yet she couldn't put a name to it.

It must be one of my Grandmas, she reasoned. Perhaps it is my Mom, might even be myself! She did know that all four of the Brannon women, including herself, had the same frontier-busting blood flowing in their veins. She was rolling and tossing, uttering strange sounds, when suddenly the blanket was tossed aside and she was standing, the little carbine positioned on her hip ready to do battle.

She appeared to be wide awake, her sleepless eyes sweeping across the clearing. All she could see was someone sitting in the shadows on a windfall tree, a rifle rested across his knees, struggling to keep awake.

"Don't shoot me!" the startled boy shouted, who was now wide awake and fearing for his life.

"This is me, your Uncle Matt!' He arose from the old log and walked out of the shadows, his profile now plain to see.

"Ooh!!" she gasped, now aware of the surroundings. "I'm so sorry Uncle Matt—I reckon I must have been dreaming—please forgive me!"

Matt O'Niel was still shaking in his boots, amazed at his niece and the swiftness in which she had handled her little weapon. Remembering her story of killing the two wolves, he knew it had really happened, and was mighty grateful they were in this adventure together, not the other way around.

The girl insisted that her Uncle return to his blanket for a few hours sleep. "I will keep watch," she told him. "I couldn't go back to sleep even if I tried."

The boy agreed, knowing that she was as capable as he in guarding the camp from uninvited guests, the two-legged kind or four, he knew it wouldn't matter which.

Much later the girl was still sitting on the windfall, knowing her uncle was asleep in his blanket. It was then she noticed a change, a mysterious silence emanated from the darkened pines, the flickering light from the dimming fire fading away into a bed of smoldering embers.

An eerie chill was moving across the clearing, forcing Marry Lynn to go fetch her blanket and wrap it around her shoulders.

She was much warmer now and returned to the downed giant of the forest, a lookout that had been used by Matt, and she was doing the same. The drop in temperature was the sign, telling her that soon the sun would return and spread light and warmth across the valley. She also knew that it was always the darkest before dawn, and that a chilled, dew-dampened morning would announce a new day ready to burst forth across the land.

* * *

Back at the ranch the hustle and bustle of an organized rescue mission was in full swing, keeping the women folk busy preparing food for the incoming riders. Some were changing mounts and receiving fresh orders, others were eating a hot meal before they rode away.

They were organized though, Bonner spreading the pairs out in ever widening circles.

Old Slim was riding with Bonner the morning of the third day. He had suggested they ride to where they had last seen the lost children, could be they might be able to find a clue; a suggestion that Bonner accepted without question.

And so they headed into the west, a now familiar route leading into Chief Mountain country. It was dark before they arrived at the field of boulders, setting up camp in a stand of lodgepoles that graced the north side of the trail.

After a trail supper consisting of coffee and bacon, Bonner walked back to the trail, his eyes sweeping across the rubble left from an ancient slide. From deep inside himself he sensed a warm feeling, they were close to where they had last seen his kids, he just knew it. He hunkered down on a rock staring across the darkened rubble, and though he wasn't a praying sort like Lynn, he uttered a prayer that they might find them in time!

Brushing a tear from his eyes, Will Bonner returned to ol' Slim's fire and curled up in his blanket. The mind-soothing smoke from the oldtimer's pipe was the last thing he remembered that night.

It was raining the next morning when they began their journey across the maze. Big Red was not happy about crossing through the slippery terrain, neither was Slim's horse, who was refusing to obey the urgency of the oldtimer's spurs.

"Best we lead them through," Bonner said, who had taken the lead. "If we get the hosses all worked up—could be we'll get bucked off good and proper like!"

"I reckon you're right," Slim responded. "Could be one of them might break a leg—or worse yet break one of our own."

On they went, moving with caution, giving the horses plenty of time to sniff out the pathway through, gaining confidence by doing so. Two hours later they walked away from the slide and found themselves in a pine forest.

Ol' Slim was about all in, and so was his horse, yet all four of them made it through without any serious injury. "Reckon I've got to rest awhile," he said, a wry grin on his whiskered face. "This here old age is sure not a laughing matter."

Showing respect for his old friend, Bonner suppressed a grin of his own before he spoke, "I reckon you're right, it's been a tough one all right—what with the rain and all!

"A hot cuppa coffee would sure hit the spot," and he left to gather fuel from the underside of a big pine.

Finding sufficient dry fuel for the fire, Bonner turned back for camp and stubbed the toe of his boot on an unseen obstacle. A closer look showed him a rock, one of a ring of rocks that had encircled the leavings of a recent camp fire.

Excitement surged through the big cowboy. "Come see what I've found Slim," he shouted.

"I reckon we're plumb lucky—we are on the right track sure!" and showed old Slim the ring of rocks surrounding the charred remains of a fire.

Slim squatted beside this new clue, studying the position of the rocks, the charred remains of a recently used cooking fire, and any other clue that might be there. He knew the fire had been built by Mary Lynn or young Matt, he was sure of this.

"I Reckon it was me who showed Mary Lynn how to build a fire ring like this one, and the reason for doing so," he told Brannon.

"And young Matt too—when he first come to stay at the B—B, I found him tinkerin' around with a fire out back o' the horse corrals. He could easily have burnt down your whole outfit, lock, stock and barrel."

Bonner was all ears listening to old Slim's talk. "Them young sprouts had fresh meat to eat Will, see the remains o' that hand-fashioned spit over yonder!

"I reckon ol' Slim showed them how to do that as well!" he said, and he was smiling when he spoke.

"The fire ring Slim! How do you know that it was our kids that built it?"

Slim was a bit reluctant at first then decided to tell Bonner like it was. "You see it dates back to my outlaw days, when I rode with the Wild Bunch.

"It was old Butch Cassidy himself who came up with the idea, it was then passed on down to Kid Curry's bunch. Along the outlaw trail that stretches from old Mexico up to the Canadian border, and beyond—are fire rings positioned about a days ride apart. These here rings are all different, and each have a hidden message for those who know what to look for!

"Cassidy's outfit used the same design that I showed the kids, a ring of rocks using fist-size rocks, and larger ones the size of a man's head. They were positioned like this—a big rock next to a small one—followed by another big one and then a small one, continuing in a circle until you have a bona fide fire ring."

Bonner was amazed and could do nothing but listen to his old friend's talk. "You must tell me more Slim, I'll never be content until I hear the rest of your story!"

"The design of the ring is the secret! Cassidy's design was known and used by no one but a trusted few of the Wild Bunch," Slim recalled. "And relayed a hidden message of where they were going and where they might be found.

"The rocks used in the ring were positioned close together, except for two of the large ones which were positioned about the span of a man's hand apart, leaving a space in between. This is the code Will! This is only one of the Wild Bunch's many secrets of survival along the outlaw trail. The gap between the two larger rocks indicated the direction where old Butch was traveling, and where he might be found.

"Well I'll be a knot-headed maverick," Bonner said. "I would have never known!"

"Mary Lynn built this fire ring, I can tell by the way she has positioned the rocks," a proud look was evident on Slim's face as he continued his story.

"Can you find the gap Will? That will tell you what direction they are heading."

Will Bonner was speechless, not realizing until now the wilderness savvy of his only daughter. After several minutes of deep study, he found what he was looking for. It was not easy to find. "Once you find the unique spacing of the two larger rocks, Slim, why it jumps right out at you!"

Old Slim was beaming as he looked at his big boss. "Turn over the big one on the left side of the gap. Bonner was quick to do as Slim had asked, and was shocked at what he found.

There on the bottom of the rock was scratched the initials M L B, the initials of his missing daughter, and a small arrow pointing into the southeast, the same direction as the gap in the fire ring had indicated.

Bonner was still amazed at his daughter's knowledge of this sort of thing, and the lore of the old west that she was using. Both he and his top hand could hardly contain them selves, Bonner erupting with a cowboy yell, his partner tossing his hat high in the air.

They now knew the lost kids were in trouble and wanting to be found, and that Mary Lynn was helping out the rescuers, if any, in the only way she knew how.

Slim's eyes were damp, knowing that Mary Lynn had known he was the only one that would be able to decipher the code of the fire ring. It also made him proud to know that Mary Lynn, had faith in ol' Slim, and that he would be the first one to find her.

* * *

The two top hands of the B—B river ranch were out of their blankets at the crack of dawn, continuing on their journey into the southeast. The ride through the forest was much easier than the boulder field of the day before. On they rode, noon time came and then it passed, still they continued on, sharp eyes sweeping the ground for any sign. Suddenly Bonner signaled it was time to stop, the horses were sure in need of a rest, and so were the cowboy's who rode them.

The pine country was now behind them, quacking aspen groves and willow brush were dotting the landscape as far as the eye could see. They reined into a sheltered clearing surrounded by willows, pulled the saddles from their lathered broncs and watched them roll in the knee-high grasses that grew their.

"I reckon I've got to walk around some," Slim said, a trace of a smile on his face. "My old bones are sure a needin' a break from the saddle!"

Bonner knew it had been a hard ride on his old friend, and felt somewhat ashamed for pushing him this way. Yet, there were the kids, and his Mary Lynn to think about! No telling how they were faring?

"Go ahead Slim," Bonner said. "I'll rig us up a fire and put on the coffee pot, a good hot drink will do us both good."

Slim never answered and was moving around, working the kinks out of his tortured back side. With head lowered, searching the ground, old Slim found himself out on the trail. He was walking easier now, feeling some better too.

Not far from the clearing he stopped, a wide grin spreading across his whiskered face, there in front of him was one of Mary Lynn's fire rings. Elation spread through his old body like a prairie fire running from a west wind. He sat down on a long eroded stump and waited. He knew Bonner would come and find him.

Bonner had rigged up a simple night camp, the horses were secured nearby, the coffee was hot and just waiting to be drunk. He had moved it back from the flames to simmer some, waiting for Slim to return.

Reckon I better go bring Slim back, Bonner reasoned. He was sure looking all in when he climbed off his bronc. The big cowboy left the clearing and spotted the old timer down trail a ways, a lonesome looking old gentleman sitting alone, smoking his pipe.

"You feelin' all right?" Bonner asked, as he approached his foreman. "I feel bad a pushin' you like I did—just couldn't help it I reckon."

"I'm all right—and am sure glad you did," Slim replied. Have a look see over yonder by them willows, reckon we've hit the jackpot once again."

A thrill surged through Bonner's lanky frame as he spotted another fire ring, a closer look convinced him that it was the handiwork of Mary Lynn. He stooped low, the gathering darkness making it hard to see.

"Bring me the clue rock Will, I'll light a match so's we'll know for sure."

From the flickering light from old Slims match they could make out the initials M. L. B. "Bring the rock back to the fire, there's more scratching here that's too small to read from the light of this here match," he told Bonner.

Back at the fire, a cup of coffee in each of their hands, they discovered a hidden message. The usual arrow was their, pointing into the east, a slight change of direction from the first one. There was more, the letters almost too small to read. Moving in close to the flames, Bonner was able to read the following message:

lame horse matt walking
Willy Ok!

Once again the two were thankful for Mary Lynn's determination and presence of mind to bring the boys back to the ranch safe and sound. "I figure those kids are about a days ride ahead of us," Slim said.

"I reckon a lame horse will slow them down some—appears as if our cowgirl is turning into one fine trail boss!" He was beaming with pride when he spoke. The old outlaw couldn't help it none, knowing that it was he who had shared the secret code of the fire ring with a charming young girl."

"Young Matt must be walking," Bonner commented. "It'll be a tough one sure, walking in those high-heeled boots of his."

* * * Chapter Thirty-Two * * *

A cloud of gloom hovered over the river ranch. Lynn Bonner was having a rough time of it, her mind in constant turmoil, stewing and worrying over Mary Lynn and the boys. Added to this was the constant coming and going of the search parties, feeding them, issuing fresh instructions, and such.

I must be losing it, she reckoned, this job I have been given is much tougher than I thought. If only I could be out on the trail with my Will. Try as she may, Lynn could not settle herself down.

No matter how hard she tried, something was always there foremost in her sub-conscience. It was a constant nerve-wracking panorama that portrayed Mary Lynn, her only daughter, sitting in the saddle of the bay gelding, Rocky. She looked tired and trail-worn, her beautiful hair was a tangled mess, but she held her head high. Trailing behind come her oldest son Willy, his head hanging low, riding the Shetland-cross he knew as Brownie.

And then there was her brother Matt O'Niel. He was walking, leading his horse, both the horse and the boy were limping. That they had been injured she was sure of. Over and above all this was the face of a beautiful women hovering in the background. It was a familiar face, one that could have been any one of the Brannon women. They all four had the same famous profile—including young Mary Lynn.

The face was smiling, an aura of warmth and love floating out of her rosy lips. calming Lynn's shattered nerves as nothing else could. She was able to take control of her troubled self, sensing that it was Great Grandma Lynn Bonner who was hovering over her grandkids, influencing them to stay on the trail and make it back to the ranch safe and sound.

Perhaps it was a vision, perhaps it was not. Lynn Bonner would never know for sure, but she had faith in her great grandma, a faith that couldn't be shaken.

"Our darling kids!" she moaned, and she was praying. "Where are our kids?"

To keep her mind intact, Lynn spent most of the daylight hours at the bunk house kitchen, helping Aunt Sue with the cooking and serving of the meals. The three youngsters, Joel, Dirk and Ty weren't far away, never out of sight of the bunk house.

But night time was much different. Tucking the boys into their beds, she would leave the cabin and sit under the old cottonwood tree. It was here she could finally relax and unwind.

The night of the big storm Lynn was sitting on a well-worn stump under the cottonwood, a beloved old tree that was accepted as one of the family. It was midway between the river and the cabin, a friendly giant who treated the Bonner clan in all the same manner. The old patriarch of the valley providing a welcome shade when the day was hot and muggy, a tranquil peace and quiet at days end, and most of all; an essence of being at home.

A strange wind was moving in from the high country, an eerie sound that was even now overpowering the familiar babbling of the river, perhaps a warning of things to come. She could now hear a rip-roaring ruckus nearing the ranch, sensing a drastic change in the making. The aspens in the background were the first to issue a warning, tender leaves being viciously ripped from the branches of the trembling trees.

High in the darkened heavens sheet lightning was playing with the wind, both in a race for the river ranch and the wide-open prairie.

And then it was upon her! Hurled along by an enraged wind, came a sheet of torrential rain accompanied by the deafening boom of thunder, and the intense glow of lightning bolts striking the ground. Lynn was terrified and in mere seconds was soaked to the hide.

Quickly, she left the stump and ran to the darkened cabin. Once inside she fumbled around for a match and lit a candle, then hurried to check on her boys. She knew they would be awake, frightened and sure in need of their Mom.

With a gasp she found their beds empty, not a soul could she see, and she had tucked the kids into their beds—even read them a passage from the family bible; a gift that had been given to her Mom by the Mormon woodcutters, so long ago at the old cabin on Lariat Cross creek.

Not only was Mary Lynn and Willy missing, Joel, Dirk and Ty; her remaining boys had turned up missing as well!

"No-oo!" she screamed. "This can't be!" Her anguished voice overpowered by the sound of crashing thunder.

The storm raged outside the cabin door, inside Lynn Bonner found herself alone, her beloved children were nowhere to be found!

Her weeping was intense as she located one of Bonner's barn lanterns, and touched a match to the kerosene-soaked wick. Now, better able to see, she checked through the cabin one more time—under the beds, high in the open beam rafters, even the two-hole privy out back of the cabin. But no kids could she find.

Lynn wasted no time in buckling on her six-gun, pinning on her tin star, and donning her long duster coat, only then did she walk out to face the raging storm. She tried shouting, but to no avail, the tempest consumed the sound of her voice.

The nagging fear and trauma of the wild storm, and her missing boys, was now pushed into the background, to be replaced by much stronger emotions; anger, determination and grit. She felt her old self returning, a gun-fighting lady marshal, ready to face the demons of hell if need be.

It sure felt good too!

Her confidence was strong and unwavering, her head bowed into the storm as she headed for the bunkhouse. Perhaps the kids had gone to be with Aunt Sue, not sure as to the whereabouts of their Mom.

With her Winchester in one hand, the lantern in the other, she burst through the kitchen door to find Aunt Sue wide awake, sitting in her old rocker, a knitted shawl draped around her shoulders.

"Aunt Sue!" Lynn gasped, attempting to catch her breath. "Have you seen the kids? I can't find them.

Aunt Sue was startled by Lynn's sudden appearance, and she had been weeping, terrified of the thunder and lightning outside her door. She couldn't help it none. She had been this way since a small girl, when she had been left alone to baby sit her siblings and a storm such as this had erupted in the night.

It became a dreaded phobia, one that had dogged her all through the years. This night was no different, her inner self torn apart by thunder and lightning.

"Aunt Sue!" Lynn Bonner screamed again. "Are you listening to me? "Have you seen my boys?"

At the sound of Lynn's frantic questions, Aunt Sue shook herself some as if she had been in a trance. She shifted in her rocker, looking up at Lynn, "Oh my!" she said, her cobwebs clearing.

"I didn't know you were here." Once again Lynn asked her the same question, had she seen her kids."

The elderly lady appeared ill at ease, fluffing her hair and re-arranging the shawl around her slumping shoulders. Then Lynn knew for sure that Aunt Sue was frightened to be alone on this lonely, stormy night.

A streak of light flashed from the sky, followed by an ear-shattering boom that shook the bunkhouse. Oh-hh!" she whispered, suppressing a scream and pulled the shawl tighter around her trembling body. The light from the lantern allowed Lynn to see her reaction from the burst of heaven-sent energy that struck ground in the midst of the ranch buildings.

"Oh my goodness!! That was sure close—lightning storms frighten me so."

Knowing that Lynn was waiting for an answer, she finally replied to her question. "It was just before the thunder and lightning came."

"It was dark when they passed by the bunk house, I could hear their talk and laughter, I reckoned they must be going to the corrals to see if Mary Lynn and the boys had returned."

Lynn felt compassion for her elderly friend, whom she had rescued from starvation and certain death. She now knew the haunts and fears Aunt Sue must have endured while living at the old derelict cabin down river. Her dead husband's grave just outside the cabin door.

Lynn knelt beside her and gave her a warm hug. "I must go now," she said, "and find my kids.

"You will be fine now, the storm seems to be calming down some— soon it will be no more." She arose and lit a barn lantern that was hanging beside the door, the light would surely ease Aunt Sue's troubled mind.

With her own lantern in hand, she was standing at the door when Aunt Sue spoke once again, "Lynn, when the kids are back, and this is all over, would you take me down river to my old home?

"I would like to see my husband's grave one last time!"

* * *

Lynn Bonner continued on for the corral. The storm was not so fierce now, moving out across the open prairie. Though sheet lightning was still rippling across the sky, and thunder still booming its displeasure at being left behind, the terrible storm was leaving the river ranch.

The wind and the rain were still a worrisome thing, overpowering her vocal attempts at discovering her boys. "Joel," she shouted, the oldest of the three that should be in bed back in the cabin.

"Where are you? Answer me if you can hear me, I have come to help you—escape from this awful storm."

But no answer could she hear. The old barn lantern was still in her hand, still offering a feeble light, though having received a severe buffeting by the wind. "Joel Bonner! You answer me, right now!" Lynn screamed again, her frantic words carried away with the wind.

Satisfied there was nowhere they could take cover, she crawled through the corral rails and found her way out back to the stacks of hay. Once again she screamed, "Ty! Little Ty, can you hear me—this is Mommy come to take you back to the cabin.

A distraught Mom stood close to the hay, wilderness-honed senses straining to detect a reply. Long she listened, but to no avail. She began to move around checking every nook and cranny of the three stacks of freshly harvested prairie hay.

The wind eased off some to allow her to hear a noise, an alien sounding noise, yet one that was vaguely familiar.

At first it was a faint garble of sound, and as she moved in closer she knew that it was the greeting of her Jenni mule, who was nestled down between two of the big stacks. There she lay, nothing but her head showing, the rest of her body covered with loose hay. "Oh, Jenni, it is you! You almost scared me to death.

"Do you know where my boys are? I have lost them in the storm?"

Jenni gazed long at Lynn and the flickering lantern, finally after a long silence, a faint garble of mule talk escaped from her open mouth. Lynn gasped with joy, she was certain that her mule was trying to tell her where her boys were.

"Ty Bonner, this is your Mommy! she shouted once again, "Tell me where you are, I'll come and get you!" This time she could hear a faint reply. "Mommy, mommy I am here." followed by the sobbing of a frightened little boy.

Frantically, she dropped to her knees and began pulling armfuls of hay from around the mule, the lantern and her rifle were propped against a nearby fence post. With a groan, Jenni turned her head, her long ears pointing behind her. Now able to move some, the old mule staggered to her feet allowing Lynn to crawl in behind her.

"Ty! she screamed, "Can you hear me?"

Frantically she worked, armfuls of hay flying all around her like a badger digging a fresh hole in the ground. "Hurry Mom," she could hear the pleading of the small voice.

"Please hurry!"

The rain had now moved out on to the prairie, the storm clouds too, leaving a clear star-lit sky. Sweat was pouring from her frenzied body, forcing her to discard her ankle-length duster. Reaching far into the cavern she had created, she sensed movement and then her hand clasped that of her youngest son.

Thanking the heavens that the hay was loose, she was able to pull little Ty out into the open air, holding him close to her trembling body. His body hung limp in her arms, his breathing almost nothing. The rain-cooled air and the efforts of his Mom revived little Ty, who began silently sobbing, his tiny arms clasping her warm body as tight as he could.

"I love you Mom," he whispered. "I knew you would find me!"

After laying him out of harms way, she tucked her coat around him and said, "I love you too Ty—with all my heart!

"Can you tell me where Dirk and Joel are?"

On hearing her question, his sobbing increased into a full-fledged cry. He turned his head some, a small arm pointing into the dungeon of hay.

Back into the small cavern she crawled, flinging hay this way and that, until at last, on the verge of giving up; she found them. They were lying together, side by side, seemingly with no life left in them.

Though dark as hades inside, she was able to work one's arm free and drag the boy out into the starlit night. Lynn felt for a pulse on the boy, who she knew was Dirk, and found one; though weak it was.

Then the frenzied Mom quickly re-entered the cavern, after the much heavier Joel. With one of his hands in each of her own, she began to tug and pull, jerk and yank, inching her precious son towards the entrance from which she had came. Several times she fell, losing the grip on his hands, allowing his upper body to drop back to the ground.

It seemed like an eternity, though only short minutes, before she drug him out to lay beside his brother. Once clear of the narrow cavern, she dropped from exhaustion, losing her hold on the boy whose upper body fell with a thump to the hard ground.

Gasping with an agonizing exhaustion, Lynn Bonner heard a scary swoosh of air, as the cavern she and Jenni had been responsible for collapsed, leaving nothing but a hard mass of sun-cured hay.

Glancing at the boys, she could see that Dirk was awake, though unable to speak, she could tell that he was aware of what was going on around him. Nestled beside him was little Ty, who had wormed his way over beside his big brother.

Turning to Joel who was laying as if dead, she rolled him over and began to push on his chest, down and release, down and release, without let up she toiled until suddenly his mouth opened wide gasping for air.

Lynn collapsed utterly spent. There she lay on the hard ground, thrills coursing through her body, knowing that her three boys were still alive. Her weeping came back, much stronger than before, and she didn't much care.

Stirring some, about to get to her feet, she found little Ty snuggled beside her. A small arm was around her waist, he looked up at her and said, "Don't cry anymore Mommy, it makes me want to cry with you.

"We sure love you Mom for saving our lives," close by were Dirk and Joel, who were now able to sit up; both were nodding their heads in the affirmative.

Little Ty had one more thing to tell his beloved Mom, "You sure do smell good Mom!" his head was nestled near her shoulder length hair.

"You sure enough do!"

* * *

Lynn waited until Dirk and Joel could stand and move around some, then with little Ty in her arms she headed back for the cabin. Trailing behind came the two older boys, one packing her rifle, the other with their Dad's barn lantern in hand. Behind them came the old Jenni mule, garbling her mule talk, upset over being left behind.

Once at the cabin, she continued on and found her nightly roost under the cottonwood tree. With a huge sigh she settled to the ground, a sigh of satisfaction no doubt, that the Bonner kids were still alive and back where they should be.

It was her self appointed chore to look after the Bonners, starting with her best friend Lynn, on down to little Ty.

A mighty thankful Mom offered a silent prayer as she ushered the three boys into the cabin. After a good scrubbing and a hot drink, they tumbled into their beds, not to be heard from again until a new day again arrived along the river.

Lynn hadn't the heart to punish them, knowing that tomorrow they would be expected to explain their actions—sneaking out of bed when their Mom's back was turned, sneaking on down to the big stacks of hay to play cowboys and Indians, and coming within a heart beat of suffocating under the massive stack of hay.

No way could she punish them with a fresh-cut willow or a buggy whip. She loved them too much for that, a good dose of her sharp tongue would be punishment enough.

A tired worn-out Mom went outside once more, and gave Jenni a generous helping of oats. She knew that if it hadn't been for the mule, finding the kids and staying with them, they would have all perished.

The little dun mule, whose coffee-hued hair was turning gray, was a hero in Lynn's eyes, and was responsible for the rescue of her kids. She was sure enough a hero, one that Lynn Bonner would remember for the rest of her days.

* * * Chapter Thirty-Three * * *

Mary Lynn Bonner and the two boys had put in a rough day. Somehow they became confused, plumb lost in fact, and found themselves wandering aimlessly in an ever widening circle. After wasting several hours they finally arrived back to where they had started from. It was the grit of the young girl that brought them back, and a streak of Brannon stubbornness.

By this time the horses and their riders were about worn out, forcing Mary Lynn to call a halt. "Two hours is all!" she told the boys. "Then we'll make up some ground before nightfall." Young Willy was having a hard time, bone tired and homesick for his parents. He was weeping more often now, taxing Mary Lynn's diplomatic nature.

"We're getting closer to home," she kept telling him. "One more night of sleeping under the stars is all—then we'll make it to the ranch.

"Don't you worry yourself none, you hear?" she was hugging the boy as she spoke. "Mom and Dad will be so darn happy to see us ride in Willy, they'll forget all about scolding us—you just wait and see!"

Mary Lynn spent a restless night, tossing and turning and uttering strange things. Her mind appeared in turmoil, conjuring up all kinds of outrageous situations. Not helping matters any was the scary croak of a bird of the night. It was a loud raucous sound that sent shivers coursing up and down her spine.

Finally, in disgust, she tossed her blanket aside, arose and went to a nearby stream. Reckoned she would attend to her morning ritual while the boys were still asleep. She knew they were tired and would stay asleep for some time to come.

The eastern sky was softening before she finished washing her hair, and though the water had been freezing cold, she had enjoyed her bath in Boundary Creek. With her few valuables tucked back into a small satchel, she turned back for camp.

The sun was fast approaching, the trail ahead was beckoning her to come, and no longer was she able to resist the inquisitive nature of her feminine makeup. Curiosity is what it is called, curiosity that lured the girl down the trail to see what might lay in store for three lost kids.

The landscape was now plain to see. The girl hadn't walked far when she stopped and was amazed at what lay below. From her position on a wind-blown hill was a large, sprawled out lake on the prairie. But what was of the most interest were the few log buildings that sat nestled in the quaking trees beside the water.

A flag flew proudly above the largest of the cabins, she knew at a glance that it was the red, white and blue of the British Union Jack. A dog was looking her way and barking as if she was a hidden menace to his domain. A spiral of lazy smoke was drifting skyward from the largest of the buildings. Though she was hidden in a patch of willow brush, Mary Lynn knew the dog had sensed something amiss, and knew that she was here!

The morning sun had now arrived, and after a last look, the girl turned back for camp finding two grumpy boys building up the fire and wondering what they might find to eat.

The mysterious croak sounded again. Looking skyward, the girl spotted a long-billed bird skimming the treetops. It was a graceful bird, not only did it have a long bill, it had long legs as well. Although she was uncertain of its name, the bird was a blue heron traveling from a hidden tree-top rookery far back in the woods, to peck out breakfast in a marshy backwater of Police Outpost Lake.

The girl knew the name of the lake from hearing of her Mom's adventure there, and that the buildings below were those of a British police outpost.

* * *

The dog had watched them riding in, two horses with riders up top, a third horse with an empty saddle favoring an injured hind leg. The animal was being led by an equally lame cowboy, whose tortured feet were shoved into high-heeled riding boots; blistered raw from the long, rough walk they had endured.

An Irish Constable had over-slept that morning and was awakened by the outraged barking of the dog, who in his usual protective manner was greeting the strangers like a dog should do.

"Faith and beggorie!" he grumbled, pulling on his trousers. "'tis the spawn o' auld Nick himself, it be—a waking up an auld soldier like this mangy cur be a doin'!

"A good thing it is, the Corporal has gone a gadding off to the Fort," he said, gazing at an old alarm clock sitting beside his bunk. Pulling his suspenders into place, he stepped out the door and gasped at the three strangers who were standing beside their horses. Mary Lynn stepped forward, and with a smile introduced herself and the two boys. "We would be grateful Sir, if you could spare us some food—we have been lost up yonder," and gestured into the west.

The constable never answered, attempting to digest what he was hearing. "We can pay for the food, and a feed of oats for our horses, if you can spare some. We are heading down to the big river and our B—B ranch."

The Irishman finally recovered his speech, and after a show of importance said, "Why 'tis a look o' hunger ye do have—tie up your harrses and come on in, 'tis a good feed o' mush all three o' ya be a needin."

The constable hustled back in the cabin, put more fuel in a well-used cook stove, and began to brew up a large pot of mush. At the same time he stoked up a coffee pot, the biggest one the kids had ever laid eyes on, and found some hardtack in a wooden crate.

The young cowboy, the girl, and her younger brother were seated at a sturdy plank table, their eyes as big as saucers watching the lawman prepare their breakfast.

Closely eyeing the Constable scrape green mould from off the hardened biscuits, known to the military chefs as hardtack, little Willy leaned over to his sister and whispered in her ear, "Mary Lynn, I don't think I'm hungry any more!" His face had lost a good share of its normal ruddy glow.

The Bonner kids were each brought a steaming cup of black coffee, strong enough to float a spoon. Mary Lynn looked up with a frown and said, "Pardon me Sir, my brother is not allowed to drink coffee.

"Our Dad said that it might stunt his growth, and that he must wait until he is old enough to be a cowboy!"

"Jumpin' Jehosaphats!" the Irishman muttered. "Your Daddy is a strange one. Why me Saintly old Mom fed us kids coffee from the time we were weaned from her bosoms—she could not afford to buy a cow, you see—to feed her baby's the war-rm rich milk!"

The breakfast went off without a hitch, or so the constable thought. Hand-ground oat mush, flavored with milk from a can, and sprinkled with sugar that was brown was set before them. The hardtack was chewable after being soaked in the coffee, and that was about it.

Little Willie was not impressed. Though he was hungry enough to eat almost anything, the oat mush was more than he could handle. In desperation, Mary Lynn would soak a biscuit in her coffee and slip it to her brother, who devoured it with much vigor.

After their military meal, the children left the cabin and found the horses finishing up a generous helping of oats. Mary Lynn, who had a few dollars tucked in her jeans, brought out the wrinkled bills and offered them to the constable.

"We thank you," she told him. "For the meal you prepared for us!"

"No-oo me Lassie!" he sputtered. "It is not needed for you to pay me, the sight of your happy smiles is payment aplenty for a homesick Irishman—so far away from his native sod."

Several days after the departure of the Bonner children, Constable O'Casey found himself in the stables shoveling out horse manure; a task that he detested with all his soul. But the feisty Corporal had given the order. It was his punishment, the Corporal told him, for destroying the evidence by drinking all the coffee.

Thirty days of hard labor was the punishment given him for consuming the evidence, the remains of a five-pound satchel of confiscated coffee which had been taken from a Yankee border runner; who had insisted that he was still in the States. Along with the coffee were seized several other items, including his horse and guns, leaving the man with nothing left but the clothes on his back.

After a few days lock-up in a dugout jail, the Corporal escorted the unfortunate Yankee to the Fort, a journey of a day and part of another. On his return, and discovering the evidence had all been drank up. All three pounds of Arbuckle's best, his English temper had erupted.

Time was hard to keep track of that day, the Constable was aware of the sun's position high overhead, and left his labor in the horse barn for a noon day break. Sitting on the threshold of the outpost cabin, Constable Casey's mind was in turmoil

He was nursing a cup of tea, detesting the very smell of it. His Irish upbringing had been to drink coffee, an addiction that he would surely take to his grave. He thought of the three youngsters, they drank a share of the coffee, as did Will Bonner and old Slim, who had stopped by several hours after the departure of the children.

And of course himself, he had enjoyed three days of constant bliss, until the day the Corporal had returned from the Fort; and then all hell busted loose. He had a big smile on his face when he muttered, "It be a satchel of the devil's brew, I have tucked away—must be a pound or two. Just around the corner 'neath a loose chink in the plaster!"

He had tried to explain to the Corporal about the visitors that stopped by while he was away at the Fort. "A coffee drinking bunch," he attempted to explain. "None of them would drink the good Queen's tea.

"Will Bonner said it wasn't fit for the cowboy's to drink, reckoned it might poison them and stunt their growth!"

It was then, Constable O'Casey remembered, after hearing the name of Will Bonner the Corporal had thrown a fit! "You had him in this cabin?" he screeched. "And fed him the good Queen's food; and even allowed him to swig down our evidence?

"You must be given thirty days of hard labor Constable, twelve hours a day, and a good caning too—we'll see, you Irish blighter—we'll see!"

Out back of the kitchen was a hand-dug prison, nothing more than a dugout positioned in the side of a small hill. It had a heavy plank door, the upper half of which was outfitted with iron bars, plus a fire-forged padlock. Constable O'Casey was led to the wilderness jail and locked inside. Part of his thirty day punishment was to be locked up in the prison each night after the evening meal.

It was past midnight at Outpost Lake, all were asleep except the Constable, who was patiently digging in the hardened soil next to the doorway.

He was using a long knife which was always strapped inside his boot. "I thank me Saintly Mom for telling me to hide this weapon," he muttered. "'tis she who will help me escape from this stinking hole!"

The earth was softening, making it much easier to dig, allowing him to crawl out and escape the inhuman Corporal's clutches. The night was calm with no moon, and dark as Hades itself. A great horned owl broke the silence, hooting a mournful tune.

'tis not fair to be treated like an animal, he reasoned, and was hell-bent on getting away from the demented Corporal. While shoveling the accumulation of months of neglected horse droppings he had carefully planned his escape.

His horse was saddled and waiting, there was food in the saddlebags and an old coffee pot he had scavenged while the Corporal was indulging in his afternoon nap. He did not forget the satchel of stolen coffee.

O'Casey borrowed the Corporal's guns, which were always kept by his saddle in the tack room. Silently he led the horse into the quaking trees, crawled aboard and headed for the border. He had only been transferred to the Outpost a month back, and already he was leaving it behind. He figured on riding south into the territories, a deserter on the run.

He had heard through the grapevine of jobs aplenty down that way, and reined the nose of the police horse he rode into the southeast, Fort Benton his destination. Perhaps mining, maybe the railroads, even becoming a cowboy on a ranch, he would accept any one of the three.

A week later the deserter arrived in Fort Benton, and was immediately hired on as a fireman on a departing paddle wheeler, heading down river for parts unknown to the Irishman. "Don't matter much to me," he reasoned, "I can pitch wood with the best o' 'em—and it's a start, it is—

to be away from the overbearing Corporal who rules the roost at Police Outpost Lake."

Several days later, far down the Missouri River, a deserter from the good Queen's North West Mounted was tossing chunks of wood into the furnace of a large river boat. His shirt was cast aside, his upper torso covered with sweat and grime.

But he was happy and singing an old Irish ditty, 'My Wild Irish Rose', a favorite folk tune of his Gaelic Mom.

* * *

The Bonner kids rode out of a winding coulee, and there it was, the B—B ranch buildings just five hundred yards away. They had survived a wild and wooly adventure, and though they were a disheveled lot, battered and trail-worn, they had found their way home in one piece.

The horses were staggering as they neared the big pole gate that led into the corrals, little Willy was whimpering and could hardly contain himself. Tears were streaming down his face, his nose wrinkled up for a good cry. "Don't cry. Willy!" his sister told him.

"Be brave—and act as a cowboy should—after what we have been through you are now a cowboy,

"Cowboys don't cry!"

Willy glanced at his big sister, she was sitting tall in the saddle, her head held high and she wasn't crying.

"I'll try," he whimpered.

"You just wait and see, Willy Bonner. When our Mom sees we have come home, she'll do enough crying for all three of us kids put together."

Unknown to the kids Will Bonner and old Slim were not far behind them. They had been for several miles and were holding back, riding drag in the dust, allowing the kids to ride in on their own.

Lynn Bonner was the first to see the kids and their horses stagger in, she had been patiently waiting and watching for their safe return. She left the cabin and ran to the big corral, tears streaming down her face, uttering a shout of joy and relief. Lynn entered the corral in time to watch them ride in through the gate, and there she stood to greet them, a beautiful lady and most of all a Mom, with arms open wide and a passel of tears streaming down her rosy cheeks.

"See, I told you so Willy—our Mom is crying her head off!"

Closely trailing the kids could be heard incoming riders, and a spine-chilling shout of the open range. Two mounted riders entered the corral in a cloud of dust and slid to an abrupt stop. One of them was Will Bonner, who sprang from the saddle.

In no time at all he had little Willy in his arms, holding him close, and brushing tears from off the boy's dust-caked cheeks. Lynn Bonner and her Mary Lynn were doing the same, hugging each other, both were crying their heads off.

Mary Lynn Bonner knew she was crying and didn't much care, she reckoned there were times when a cowgirl just had to cry!

The girl was the first to push away. I sure need a hot bath and some clean clothes," she told her Mom. "And my hair must look a tangled mess." A happy Lynn Bonner smiled and agreed.

It sure enough does," she said. "You look like a wild thing!" They both began giggling, a gene-inspired trait of the Brannon women.

"I'll hustle Willy to the river for a good scrubbing while your bath water is heating," the matron of the river ranch reckoned her daughter had certainly earned one. "And your hair sure is a tangled mess!" A Mom and her daughter were still giggling when they turned to go.

The news of the return of the lost kids spread like wildfire across the range. The cowboys and their Blackfoot cousins rode back to the ranch, once again to feast on Aunt Sue's home-cooked grub. Not only was a vast amount of food consumed, vast amounts of coffee were drank as well.

Peace had returned to the river valley. Their Indian neighbors returned to the reservation each with a bag of food tied on their saddles and a shiny Yankee double eagle in each of their pockets.

The B—B cowboys were given a reward too. Some would pay a rare visit to see their families, others would ride to the nearest settlement and whoop it up.

* * * Chapter Thirty-Four * * *

Although old age was creeping into her bones, Aunt Sue was still top gun in the bunkhouse kitchen, specializing in sizzling steaks and mouth-watering apple pies. Old Slim and young Matt offered her a helping hand with the burdensome tasks, packing firewood into the kitchen and pails of water from the nearby river.

More often as of late, Lynn would come down from the big cabin to give Aunt Sue a helping hand, both having a fun time and enjoying their time together. And Mary Lynn, who several times a day would drop by for a visit, there to enjoy the delicious sugar cookies she knew would be waiting for her to eat.

Their not so distant clash of personalities was over and done with, and still remaining good friends as well they should be.

Lynn Bonner's emotions were torn to pieces when she was told the sad news about her Jenni mule. Young Matt and Mary Lynn had found her body when returning from a ride up the river valley. It lay beside one of the large stacks of hay out behind the corrals. It appeared as if she had gone to sleep and forgot how to wake up. It was in the same place where Lynn had discovered her and the buried kids

On hearing the news old Slim called in the cowboys, and together they dug a grave in the shade of the big cottonwood tree; a favorite loafing place when Jenni was alive. The mule worshipped Lynn, and knew this was as close to her as she could get without entering the house, which she knew was forbidden territory.

No funeral was held, though Aunt Sue wanted one, who for years had been slipping the mule enticing tidbits from her kitchen.

Come time for the grave to be filled in, all were gathered under the cottonwood offering their last respects to a little friend. Except for the sobbing of Lynn and her daughter, all was quiet. The cowboys crowded around the grave, hats in hand, showing their respect to a revered icon of the Brannon clan.

Though her emotions had been torn apart, Lynn felt a peaceful presence here by Jenni's grave. The two of them had been a team, Lynn saving the mule's life, Jenni returning the favor by saving Lynn's life as well. Many times this had happened.

The peaceful presence was a comfort to her, somehow she knew that it was her Grandpa Brannon, who was waiting close by to escort his Jenni mule to that big prairie up in the sky.

Will and Lynn Bonner were content and happy, their life along the river an answer to their fondest hopes and dreams. One goal was yet to be fulfilled, to live to see their children grow into respectful law abiding citizens. And to have grandchildren, which would be like icing on the cake.

* * *

"Them white-faced longhorns are looking mighty good," old Slim told his boss one day. "I never had a notion I would see the like—a white-faced cow sporting horns two feet long." The two were sitting under the cottonwood lulled by the soothing music of the river.

"The herd is looking mighty good," Bonner replied, "thanks to you and the boys. Best lookin' herd in the Deerhorn Hills."

Old Slim was fidgeting some before he spoke, appeared to be uneasy with something on his mind. "I feel kind o' guilty like a sittin' here—not able to do much but sit on this here stump, or over yonder on the porch— in my rocking chair."

"Don't fret on it so, Slim! You are still my foreman.

"Why you know every badger hole and blade of grass that grows on the B—B. The crew is still under your orders!!"

No one along the river knew him as anything but Slim, a graceful old cowboy whose shaggy hair and whiskers had turned a snowy white. He preferred it that way, and worshipped the Bonners for allowing him to live out his days here along the river.

"Tell you what," Lynn said, who had been listening in the background. "Each morning after the cowboys have eaten their breakfast, they must stay near the bunkhouse to receive their orders for the day—save Slim the worry of tracking them down."

"That's a splendid idea Lynn," her husband said, and gave her an admiring smile. "I'll give our Indian cowhands a talkin' to this very day."

* * * Chapter Thirty-Five * * *

An inevitable transition was evident along the river, the years passing by as surely as the sun coming up each morning. The now famous B—B outlasted the good years and the bad, becoming a thriving, productive cattle ranch.

Vast herds of crossbred cattle grazed the Deerhorn Hills, the Hereford influence showing strong in their blood. Purebred white-faced bulls, the genes of ol' Vic strong in their make-up, were becoming highly sought after by other ranchers, who were spreading across the prairie staking their claims to this grass-rich region.

Neighbors were not uncommon as in the past, although some were fifty miles apart they were still considered as neighbors, and treated as such. The Code of the old West still ruled this northern prairie, arriving in the territories with the early settlers; old Matt Brannon and his good wife Lynn were one of the first. It was a simple law, dating back to the Golden Rule of bible times.

* * *

The shadows of night had once again crept into the river valley. It was the end of a perfect day here at the Bonner ranch, Lynn and her husband were sitting under the old cottonwood, a mere stone throw from their cabin home. It was peaceful here, quiet too, except for the chattering of little Ty, who was crawling in the grass beside them.

Their family had grown to five children, Mary Lynn and her four brothers: Willy, Joel, Dirk and little Ty. Will was the proudest rancher in the territories to have his Lynn present him with four healthy sons, and Lynn equally so of her blossoming daughter Mary Lynn.

Mary Lynn Bonner was a vibrant happy girl, a spitten' image of the three Lynn's before her. The residents of the ranch teased her as being a tom boy, spending most of the daylight hours out of doors, exploring the woods and prairie of this wilderness valley.

Will Bonner adored his beautiful daughter, being accused of spoiling her. But as Lynn realized, her Mary Lynn never had a Grandpa to make a fuss over her as had Grandpa Brannon treated his little Lynn; which was of course herself. This made her happy that Will was filling the gap, accomplishing much more as a Dad.

Lynn's half-brother Matt O'niel, worshipped his young fourteen year-old niece, who was equally enthralled with her cowboy uncle. Together they were part of many adventures. Matt riding a high-strung, green-broke gelding, Mary Lynn riding beside him on Rocky; a ten year-old gentle bay gelding.

Young Matt was now eighteen years-old. He was a tall lad and growing like a weed. Everyone was certain they could see traces of his Irish father in his makeup, but his half-sister Lynn insisted that he reminded her of their grandpa Matt Brannon.

Thanks to the tutoring of Bonner and old Slim, he had turned into a better than average cowboy—riding the rough string with the best of the wranglers. He not only nurtured the ways of the working cowboy, he was able to reason his way through the toughest of situations that might arise.

With tongue in cheek, Bonner advised him one day to use his head for something besides a hat rack.

Bonner was taken with Lynn's half-brother though, and kept him mostly around the ranch, assigning him the chore of looking after the working *remuda*; the position of horse wrangler of which made the boy mighty happy.

* * * Chapter Thirty-Six * * *

As sure to happen as the sun setting in the west, the passing years were evolving into history. No longer a vast unsettled prairie, homesteaders were moving in by the droves, settling their meager possessions on to quarters, halves, and even sections of land; all surrounded by barb-wire fences.

No longer were neighbors fifty plus miles apart as in the distant past, their little spreads now a mere mile or so from each other. Long used buffalo trails were gradually being upgraded from well-traveled Indian trails into rut-scarred dirt roads.

A new invention owned by the more affluent was now able to run by its own power, replacing the age old custom of a wagon pulled by a team of horses. Tin Lizzies they were known as, the Model T. Ford, one of several such machines to be found chugging their way to the settlements and back.

Usually, at the crossing of two or more trails a trading post could be found. Most times nothing more than a log shack or two with a set of corrals out back, yet they would keep on hand enough of the basic supplies for the scattered ranchers to survive on. In time a settlement would evolve complete with a lonely one-room school. Thanks to the religious sects, a Church was sure to follow.

Though the rancher's kids rode many miles by saddle horse to enroll into a house of learning, they would arrive in plenty of time for their classes and the three R's they were so eager to learn; likewise eager to meet and associate with others of their own age.

Lifetime friends originated from these early schools, more than a few of the girls and their beaus paired off for life, marriage and raising families of their own was in their plans for the future.

The lawless element was now pushed into the background, the N.W.M.P. and border Marshals responsible for keeping the peace. The Blackfoot and Blood were mostly peaceful now, settled into reservation life as was their lot; more than a few with growing spreads of their own.

These hardy people took to ranching life with much vigor, still traveling to the settlements in horse-drawn wagons, though the majority still preferred riding their saddle horses. They loved their horses, a symbol of wealth and prestige; many with large bands of unbroken animals roaming free on the vastness of the prairie.

The Indian was still a colorful personage—no more war paint and feathers, although the old ones still prefer the same. The majority of the younger ones now dress as the white-eye cowboys do, who are now their neighbors.

Big hats, fancy neck scarves, denim jeans and ornate spurs jingling on their cowboy boots; they would have it no other way.

* * *

A calm autumn evening arrived in the river valley, the river was singing a wilderness tune, the evening star was offering an eternal glow. Underneath an old cottonwood tree sat Lynn Bonner and her husband listening to the golden leaves above them, rustling a protest over the antics of a playful breeze.

Old Slim was sitting nearby smoking his pipe, the glow from a harvest moon reflecting off a tin star that was pinned on his vest. A faint smile was on his face, a sign that he was content and enjoying his remaining years here at the Bonner ranch.

"I reckon we've had us a good life together," Bonner broke the silence between him and his darling wife, a sense of contentment strong in his voice.

"I reckon so," Lynn replied. "This has been an answer to our fondest dreams. A fine ranch stocked with cattle, a family of our own making—and a wonderful daughter and four handsome boys.

"What more could we ask for?"

It was then a boisterous ruckus could be heard coming from the horse corrals, interrupting the peaceful reverie of those sitting under the tree. Bonner spoke again, "By the sounds of things, I reckon a wild-west stampede has moved on to our ranch."

Amid the dust of pounding hooves, three young cowboys were sitting on the top corral rail cheering on their bronc-busting older brother, Willy Bonner. Up top of his favorite rope horse sat their Uncle Matt, keeping a close watch on the young bronc rider; lasso in hand just in case!

"One never knows what my range-born kids will be up to next" Will drawled.

Old Slim's smile was turning into a full fledged grin. "Could be the kids are following in the footsteps of their wild-and-wooly Daddy!"

"I reckon so," Lynn's answer was slow in coming, worry lines creasing her brow as she gazed long in the direction of the corrals.

Suddenly her manner changed, a startled gasp escaped from her pretty lips. "I reckon their wild-and-wooly Mom too!" she exclaimed, her attention still on the horse corrals.

Issuing another muffled scream, she was watching her Mary Lynn, long hair flying in the dust and the breeze, riding one of Will's longhorn steers. She was doing a good job of it too, her four brothers hooting and hollering their support for their sister, their youthful cheers echoing up and down the valley.

Lynn Bonner was struck with amazement, filled with fright and horror; she just couldn't believe her eyes. "I don't know what we are going to do with Mary Lynn," she said, turning and looking at her husband. "I was hoping to make her a lady"

Will was struggling to control his mirth. I reckon darlin' Lynn, our daughter Mary Lynn must be a chip off of the old block!"

If he was any prouder of his only daughter and the four boys, he would have had to buy some new shirts, the buttons would have all been popped off his old ones.

"I'm so tired Will—take me in the cabin 'fore I fall asleep right here. It is our bed I must find—and a good nights sleep."

Will Bonner was beaming with pride, knowing that his oldest son was practicing to be a bronc rider, and equally so was Mary Lynn, who he had just witnessed topping-off one of his longhorn steers.

Reluctantly, he escorted his darlin' Lynn to the cabin.

Once inside Will fired up the old lantern to better see. Lynn was still standing by the door, something was still bothering her, Bonner could tell.

"I would like you to see what makes me so darn proud, Will," she pleaded. "Come and I'll show you," and she lured him back to the door.

"See Will, on the log above the door—below my little rifle.

"That is what makes me so proud!"

There, the light from a kerosene lantern glistened off the polished surface of a pair of Tin Stars. U.S. deputy marshal badges, which had been worn by a sharp shooting Lynn Bonner and her gun fighting husband, Will.

A wild and wooly border country had undergone a change, the lawless element brought to their knees by a gun fighting pair of deputies determined to uphold the Code of the West. Those that chose to fight died where they stood, their lifeless bodies left for the raven and eagle to fight over. Those with a desire to stay alive, threw down their guns, a long term behind bars would be their fate; at least they were alive!

Along a wild border country between two great countries, a legend had been created that would stand the test of time.

Twin Stars!!

Epilogue

The Code of the West was a simple law, some old-timers say dating back to the Golden Rule of bible times.

Lend an ear to those who are down-trodden!
Never turn a hungry man away from your door!
Clothe those who are destitute and in need of a kind word!
Leave your gate open wide for those in need of nothing
more than a word of encouragement and a friendly handshake!

More important than all the rest, was to nurture and protect the women and their little children. Allow no one to mistreat them or physically abuse them, treat them kindly and with respect! To mistreat the woman folk or their children was a serious breach of the Code of the West, no matter their color or race. A sin punished many times in the past by a cowboy's lasso and a sturdy branch of a tree.

'Our father gave us many laws which they had learned from their fathers. They told us to treat all men as they treated us, that we should never be the first to break a bargain, that it was a disgrace to tell a lie, that we should speak only the truth.'

Chief Joseph—Nez Perce

Also available from PublishAmerica

SLEEP TIGHT
by Barbara Wagner

Attractive Caryl Stewart, a western artist, has inherited a fortune and fallen in love with David Eagle, the confident and sensual man of her dreams. When her flamboyant, oil-rich great-aunt, Savannah Buckman, dies, the young redhead travels from Scottsdale, Arizona, to manage her great-aunt's estate in upscale Winter Park near Oklahoma City. After a disturbing secret from Savannah's past is revealed and a manipulative friend, almost Caryl's exact twin, becomes the third victim, Caryl knows she is the target of a cunning killer, an unknown murderer who is slowly going insane. Tormented by Oklahoma wind and trapped in the eerie atmosphere of a mysterious mansion, she struggles to escape from a maze of terror, revenge and murder. When her Native American lover is accused, Caryl makes a startling discovery and a cruel psychopath prepares to combine her death with his pleasure.

Paperback, 289 pages
6" x 9"
ISBN 1-60610-096-3

About the author:

Both a writer and an artist, Barbara Wagner lives with her husband in a suburb of Kansas City close to their grown children. She grew up in Oklahoma, has a degree in fine art from the University of Oklahoma, and studied creative writing at Butler University in Indianapolis. An award-winning artist, her work was marketed in Scottsdale, Arizona, for many years. Though *Sleep Tight* is entirely a work of fiction, the artistic life of the novel's protagonist, Caryl Stewart, is drawn from Barbara's own experience and adds a strong framework to the suspenseful story.

Available to all bookstores nationwide.
www.publishamerica.com

Also available from PublishAmerica

EMILLEE KART AND THE SEVEN SAVING SIGNS
THE TALE OF BEASLEY'S BONNET

by Vanessa Wheeler

From the minute she met her eccentric missionary aunt, Emillee Kart's life would never be the same. During their first lunch at the Butterfly Café, Emillee is inducted into a secret club known as the Monarch's Army; minutes later she is running for her life. Not only is Emillee launched into an age-old battle between the Skywalkers and the Hexiums, she may very well be the key to saving the Earthtreadors. Twelve years ago, on the day Emillee was born, a prophecy spread throughout the land of a child that would turn the tide of the battle. Five children were born on that day; two have disappeared. The Hexiums will stop at nothing to eliminate any threat to their victory. Emillee needs to learn who she is in order to help uncover the clues that will bring the Skywalkers closer to their goal.

Paperback, 202 pages
5.5" x 8.5"
ISBN 1-4241-8597-1

About the author:

Love of fantasy combined with spiritual conviction guided this mother of three to spin this faith- based tale. Joanne Strobel-Cort, born in Bethlehem, Pennsylvania, now lives in Summit, New Jersey, with her husband and three children. She works on Wall Street and is a committed Sunday school teacher who relies on faith to meet the challenges of each day.

Available to all bookstores nationwide.
www.publishamerica.com

Also available from PublishAmerica

DOVIE
A TRIBUTE WRITTEN BY HER SON

by Ken Eichler

My first recollections of my life was when I had
just turned three. I was in an orphanage and my
mama was crying. I didn't know why. She was
just crying and I wanted her to feel better. As I
grew a little older in the orphanage, I realized
what it was all about. I had become three and
the rules were that a child could no longer stay
in the room with their mother after that. They
had to be transferred to a dormitory with other
children of about the same age and sex. I believe
that was when my mama firmly made up her
mind to leave the orphanage to seek a new
husband and a new home where we could all
live together again. It didn't exactly work out
that way and it was a crushing blow to Mama.
But that had become the norm for my mama
and grandparents. They all had lived their lives
from birth in dirty, dark and dangerous mining

Paperback, 142 pages
5.5" x 8.5"
ISBN 1-60672-171-2

camps, going through one mine explosion that killed 30 of their friends and
acquaintances. And shortly thereafter, losing several loved ones to a national
and worldwide devastating disease. And traumatic deaths followed my mama
and grandma throughout their lives, even my daddy, who died at the age of
40 of bee stings that left my mama with six small children, including me at
the age of three weeks. But we had a Savior that led us to the greatest
fraternal organizations in the world, and still the greatest ones in existence
today—The Masonic Fraternity and The Order of the Eastern Star. A large
part of my story deals with our lives and experiences in the Home they built
for us, as well as the lives and experiences of hundreds more who came
there to live with us. My mama and my grandma spent almost a lifetime in
abject poverty and grief when, except for fate, they would have been among
the wealthy and aristocratic families in Birmingham and Jefferson County. I
have often wondered: what, exactly, went wrong?

Available to all bookstores nationwide.
www.publishamerica.com

CAUGHT MIDSTREAM
by Uta Christensen

In *Caught Midstream*, Janos, a successful executive, reveals the untold experiences of his youth quite unexpectedly to Sparrow—a young woman he is attracted to. She is allowed to relive his epic journey and becomes drawn into an unnerving yet moving tapestry of travails and extraordinary events that take place in prisoner-of-war camps deep within Russia. Taken by force at age sixteen from the protective circle of his family in Germany, Janos is tossed into the cataclysmic, last-gasp efforts of World War II. His journey takes him to a place of darkness, where he lives through a near-death experience and goes through physical and emotional starvation, hard labor, and ostracism; yet it also carries him into unlikely places and relationships where friendship, compassion, healing, mentoring, and love can, amazingly, still flourish. As the story unfolds, Janos's journey accelerates from adolescence into manhood. Almost miraculously, Janos survives while vast numbers of his co-travelers perish.

Paperback, 271 pages
6" x 9"
ISBN 1-4241-0967-1

About the author:

Born in Germany, Uta Christensen spent years in Ireland, New Zealand, and Australia but settled permanently in California. Holding a B.A. in English and German literature, she taught English at a community college and was an administrative analyst at the University of California. Her first book, her father's memoir, was published in Germany.